S0-DFC-395

Deadly Diversions

by

Russ Graham

Bloomington, IN authorHOUSE® Milton Keynes, UK

AuthorHouse™
1663 Liberty Drive, Suite 200
Bloomington, IN 47403
www.authorhouse.com
Phone: 1-800-839-8640

AuthorHouse™ UK Ltd.
500 Avebury Boulevard
Central Milton Keynes, MK9 2BE
www.authorhouse.co.uk
Phone: 08001974150

This book is a work of fiction. People, places, events, and situations are the product of the author's imagination. Any resemblance to actual persons, living or dead, or historical events, is purely coincidental.

First published by AuthorHouse 9/23/2008

ISBN: 1-4259-5507-X (e)
ISBN: 1-4259-5506-1 (sc)

Library of Congress Control Number: 2006908104

Printed in the United States of America
Bloomington, Indiana

This book is printed on acid-free paper.

For our grandchildren, Ted and Laura, with the hope that the world will be a safer, saner place by the time they are old enough to read this novel.

1

SUNDAY, JUNE 22

Rod Weathers knew his golf plans for the afternoon were doomed as soon as he saw the headline on page three of the *Mail on Sunday*.

LONG FLIGHT DELAY AFTER CAPTAIN FOUND DEAD - FOUL PLAY SUSPECTED

A photo under the headline showed a departure lounge crammed with passengers dozing in chairs or stretched out on the floor.

'a body found yesterday morning on an embankment alongside a north London roadway has been identified as Albert R Rosen, age 48, an American citizen and captain with Atlantic Best Airlines' read the article.

An elderly resident out walking his dog had discovered the body. At press time, the police would not comment on the cause of death.

A spokesman for the airline, reached at the company's office at Stansted Airport on Saturday afternoon, told the newspaper, *'Atlantic Best is obviously shocked by this tragedy and is bringing in another captain from Brussels to operate the flight. Flight 8823 to Boston is now expected to depart at 7:30 this evening. The airline will issue a press release on Sunday once further details are known.'*

Captain Rosen's flight was originally scheduled to depart at 10 A.M.. The passengers, 375 members of a tour group from the New

England states, had been traveling around Britain for the past two weeks. Atlantic Best Airlines was described as a privately owned, medium-sized player in the competitive trans-Atlantic market. The airline operated a regular cargo schedule to cities in the UK and Europe, augmented with passenger charters during the summer months. The airline's home base was Chicago O'Hare and it was named after its founder, well-known American entrepreneur Wallace Best.

Weathers checked his watch. It was 9:55, five hours earlier in Canada. He thumbed through his address book, found the unlisted number he wanted, and then placed the overseas call. The phone rang five times before it was picked up.

"Yeah?" said the sleepy male voice. His short reply was tinged with both annoyance and bewilderment.

"Morning, Don, Rod here. Sorry to disturb you so early, mate, but you'll understand soon enough."

"Oh Rod, yeah...okay. Give me a sec to get a light on." The line was quiet for almost a minute while Don Carling shrugged off his interrupted sleep, swung his body into an upright position, opened the bottle of spring water he kept on his bedside table and took a few long swigs. He let out a long yawn before picking up the phone again.

"Alright, Rod, I'm here. What in hell can be so important for a call at this ungodly hour? Did you finally break eighty on that pitch and putt course of yours?"

"No, no, nothing that earth shattering," chuckled Rod. "Actually, I wish it were that mundane. Don, another captain has been found dead, this time right here in London. But unlike the three previous deaths, there's no bloody way this could be construed as an accident."

"Ah, Hell!" exclaimed the Canadian. "Jeez! Anyway, I'm wide awake now. So, go ahead. What happened to him?"

"It's in today's newspaper. Not much to go on yet, but here's what it says..."

Rod Weathers relayed the gist of the article and then added, "I knew you would want to know straight away, hence the early call, mate. Thought you might want to be involved before the investigation is too far along."

"You're damned right I do. This could be the break we need, if we can call this poor guy's demise a break." Carling was now on his feet and thinking fast. "And I might be able to get out of Toronto today.

If I'm not mistaken, I think Air Canada still has a morning flight to Heathrow. If there is, I'll see if there's a seat available. Call me back in an hour."

"Will do" Rod replied, "In the meantime I'll make a few calls to see if I can get further info. Derek might be able to help." Derek Houghton, a detective with the Metropolitan London Police, was Rod's brother-in-law.

"Okay. I'll get onto the airline and see how soon I can get a flight."

*

Forty-six-year-old Don Carling was the head of KayRoy Investigations. Most of his firm's work came from airlines or aviation-related businesses. After graduating from high school in Calgary, Alberta in 1971, Carling joined the RCMP. He spent five years patrolling the mostly quiet highways in the western provinces of Saskatchewan and Manitoba before applying for the force's aviation branch. His didn't find his four-year stint flying light aircraft much more appealing than ground-based patrolling, and, when an opportunity arose to join Wardair, Canada's largest charter airline, he jumped at the chance and resigned from the RCMP.

Although Don was personally happy with his career change, especially after he checked out as a first officer on 747s, his wife was not. The final straw for Donna came in 1989 when Wardair was purchased by Canadian Airlines International [CAIL]. Faced with a significant loss in seniority - as well as a pay cut - Don opted to change direction once again, left the airline and enrolled in an advanced course in Criminology at a university in California. Donna filed for divorce and moved back to her native Regina, Saskatchewan, where, a few years later, she married a university professor.

In June 1990, Don returned to Canada, obtained his private investigator's licence and set up KayRoy. For the first few years he worked out of his country home north of Toronto, making just enough to pay the bills. By 1993, though, he had gained a reputation as an effective and reliable investigator and had all the work he could handle. With a healthy bank balance and solid credit rating, Don was able to lease office space on the airport strip adjacent to Pearson International Airport [PIA] and hire a full-time secretary to look after the administrative side of the business.

Most of his early contracts were with companies operating at PIA. Baggage theft, ticket scams, and equipment sabotaging were the most common problems for the airlines. Tracking down and prosecuting the criminal elements responsible was an ongoing struggle for all levels of law enforcement.

KayRoy's first major coup came in 1995. A six-month investigation provided the key information that helped the RCMP and Toronto police crack a sophisticated drug ring. The ring had been smuggling cocaine into Canada and the US on cargo flights from Central and South America.

Don ran two undercover agents employed as baggage handlers during the investigation. Their real identities were still known only to him. Both men lived in western Canada and never set foot in the Toronto area unless they were on assignment for KayRoy.

*

Rod Weathers called again at 6:15 Toronto time.

"I'm still here, but packing as we speak. I've got a seat on an Air Canada flight leaving this morning at nine o'clock...got the flight number here somewhere...yeah, Flight 3226. Get's me into Heathrow at nine twenty-five tonight," said Carling, before the Englishman could ask. "Can you set me up with a room at that airport hotel I stayed at in February?"

"That won't be necessary, I'll put you up here. Kate and the boys are up north visiting her parents. Won't be back until Wednesday next."

"Sounds good, Rod. I'll even replace that bottle of single malt we killed the last time I was over!"

"Aha! In that case I'll throw in breakfast with your lodgings," retorted Rod.

For the next few minutes their conversation took on a more serious note. "I did get in touch with Derek. He's going to call me back once he's had a chance to speak with the officers investigating Rosen's killing," Rod said. "I'm sure I'll hear from him before you arrive."

"Okay, that'll be a big help. I'm going to stop by the office to get my files on the investigation. Gotta run! See you tonight."

"I'll be waiting...Terminal Three, nine-thirtyish."

2

Thirty minutes after take-off, Don sensed rather than felt the aircraft levelling off as the autopilot smoothly captured the programmed cruising altitude. Moments later his experienced ears discerned the slight decrease in engine noise as the throttles were retarded from climb power to cruise power.

He'd been thinking about his stalled investigation and how Rosen's death might be the catalyst needed to jumpstart it. With any luck, his presence during the early stages of the investigation might provide fresh evidence to support his theory that the deaths of three other airline captains were somehow linked. He was wondering how the London police would react to his request to liaise with them when his thoughts were interrupted by a pleasant female voice...

"Ready for breakfast, sir?" asked the smiling flight attendant.

"Uh-h, sure. In fact I'm more than ready," Don replied, straightening up his chair back. "I'll have three eggs over easy, sausage, hash browns and whole wheat toast."

The attractive, forty-something ash-blonde giggled at his humorous request. "You should have stopped at Denny's! Will you settle for a mushroom omelet and bite-sized steak? I'll even throw in some fresh buttery croissants and a coffee refill."

Don returned her smile. "That'll be just be fine, hon. Affirmative on the coffee too."

"Thank you, sir. I'll have it ready for you in about five minutes."

"Okay, five minutes or it's free, remember," he joked.

"You really *have* been spending too much time at Denny's!" She laughed, and moved down the aisle towards the couple seated in the last row of the business class cabin, two rows behind Don.

'Actually I probably have been putting away too many king-sized breakfasts lately,' he mused, as watched the flight attendant make her way back to the galley area. The lean teenager who reported to the RCMP's training depot so many years ago was now battling middle-aged spread. And his liking for British beer would make it hard for him to keep from adding a few pounds in the days ahead, he knew.

*

At 8:40 P.M. the flight's captain made his pre-arrival announcement. They would be starting their descent in approximately two minutes, he advised, just after passing over Manchester, and gave an estimated arrival time at Heathrow of 9:20, ten minutes ahead of schedule.

Dusk deepened over the English countryside as the 767 descended effortlessly, its twin engines at idle power. The sun slipped below the horizon as the pilot banked to starboard four thousand feet above the city and intercepted the final approach path for runway 27R at Heathrow. There was just enough daylight left to allow Don to pick out Big Ben, Buckingham Palace and Hyde Park as the flight passed a few miles south of Westminster Bridge.

The Boeing touched down smoothly at 9:12 P.M. and the pilot used a combination of reverse thrust and brakes to slow the jet before turning onto a taxi strip halfway down the runway. Five minutes later the captain eased the aircraft into the gate designated Mike 24 on the north side of the terminal complex. The aircraft would remain there overnight and be used the next morning for Air Canada's first flight of the day to Toronto.

Don shunned the moving sidewalk, opting instead to stride briskly to the Arrivals hall, hoping to work out the slight stiffness in his lower back. The hall was nearly empty, and his wait to present his passport and landing card to an immigration officer was less than two minutes. Satisfied with the Canadian's answers as to the purpose and length of his visit, the young man stamped the passport and handed it back, adding an emotionless 'enjoy your stay'.

The Canadian's checked bag was one of the first to appear on the rotating luggage belt, thanks to the priority tag the airline used for its business class clientele. It was a large suitcase, but the wheels made for easy handling. He set his briefcase on top of it, slung the computer case over his shoulder, and headed towards the green 'Nothing to Declare' exit. The two uniformed officers on duty observed him without comment as he passed by them.

After exiting through the automatic doors to the terminal proper, he quickly picked out the familiar figure of his tall, curly-haired friend standing behind the gaggle of expectant greeters. At six-foot two inches, the Englishman was a good four inches taller than his friend, but at least fifteen pounds lighter. Rod took charge of Don's bag and led him to the car park. By 10 P.M. they were on the motorway, heading around the west end of Heathrow's long runways, eventually turning southeast along the M25 towards the Weathers' home in Milne's Marsh.

*

Forty-seven-year-old Rodney Weathers was a captain with British Global, the United Kingdom's third largest carrier. The airline's pilots flew an average of seventy-five hours a month. Rod preferred to fly one-day trips, known in the business as 'turnarounds'. For instance, if he departed from London for Istanbul in the morning and flew back later the same day, he would log an average of nine hours flight time. After eight or nine such working days, he would have accumulated enough hours to be 'maxed out' for the month. This left Rod with plenty of time to devote to his voluntary position as Safety and Security Chairman of the International Pilots Federation [IPF].

IPF was formed in 1972 as an umbrella organization for pilots flying for small airlines, mainly charter and cargo carriers. A president and board of regional directors were elected at a convention held every three years. Committees, such as the one Rod headed, addressed specific areas of concern to the members, reporting to the board on a regular basis. IPF's permanent staff worked out of the federation's headquarters building near Staines, a few miles from Heathrow.

Rod had been involved with flight safety for most of his career, first in the RAF, then with British Global. He'd spent three years as a member of IPF's safety committee before being appointed chairman at the last convention in November, 1995. At that time the committee was renamed the Safety and Security committee to reflect the ever-increasing terrorism threats to world aviation.

He'd first met Don Carling in 1983 at an airline-sponsored ski meet held in Banff, Alberta in the Canadian Rockies. They became friendly rivals in downhill racing events and still got together every few years or so for a ski holiday.

*

'The previous deaths' Rod had referred to in his early morning call to Canada were the reason Don Carling had been retained by IPF. The deaths of three pilots in less than two years while on layovers in Europe had puzzled Weathers. Even though they had died in different cities - and local authorities had classified them as accidental - the numbers didn't fit the historical pattern. When he searched through the Federation's files, Rod discovered that only two of their members had died on layovers in the previous twenty years. He voiced his concerns to the IPF board and suggested that they take a closer look at the most recent cases.

In the end the board agreed, but not before some members expressed their reservations as to what good would come of it. Did Captain Weathers not think the local police or coroners' findings were accurate? Was the number of deaths that surprising, given the enormous increase in trans-Atlantic flying in the past ten years? Was he suggesting that these pilots died as a result of foul play, and if so, what was he basing his suspicions on?

No, he'd replied to his questioners, he had no proof that their deaths were other than indicated. Still, he thought it prudent to have someone investigate them, if only to put to rest the uncertainty that a few of the Federation's local associations had expressed over the rather baffling accident that had felled one of their own. After the board passed a resolution to hire a private investigator, his recommendation to retain KayRoy met with unanimous approval.

*

While Don was winging his way across the Atlantic, Rod had made a number of calls, trying to get more information about the killing of Captain Albert Rosen. His brother-in-law had updated him on the police investigation and Rod gave Don the latest information as they sped along the motorway.

Carling listened quietly to Rod's account, saving his questions until he'd finished.

"So, there you have it. That's all I know as of earlier this evening. Derek is going to keep some time free to meet us tomorrow afternoon. That will give you a chance to brief him on what you've learned about the other deaths."

"Yeah, definitely, that's a good idea," Don replied. "But remember, I'm here in a purely information gathering capacity. Don't want to get on the wrong side of the UK authorities."

"No, no, we won't let that happen. Derek will see to that."

"Good. So see if I've got it straight. Rosen was supposed to fly out yesterday morning - Saturday. But just before the pilots were to get picked up for their trip to Stansted Airport, the company's local manager called, told the first officer that Captain Rosen was dead, and the flight would be delayed indefinitely. And until then the other fellows weren't even aware that Rosen wasn't in his room."

"Right on," agreed Rod.

"So when was his body discovered?"

"The call to the Hampstead police station was logged at 5:45 A.M. Apparently the elderly gent who spotted the body is quite the early riser. Gets up at five, and heads out to walk his dog just after sunrise. He was about ten minutes from his house when he reached the bridge, and, alerted by the dog's barking, looked over the rail and saw what he thought was a body.

"He wasn't physically capable of climbing down the steep embankment, so he returned home and called the police. Then he hurried back to the bridge, arriving at the same time as the first police officers, who confirmed that it was a man's body and that he was surely dead. This was just on six o'clock, give or take a minute or two," said Rod. "We can have a look round there tomorrow."

"Yeah, I'm having a hard time picturing the scene. So the police found his wallet in his jacket, with his identification, and called Atlantic Best Airlines and told them one of their employees was dead."

"Exactly. And once the airline's headquarters in Chicago got the word, they contacted a crew that was just landing in Brussels. After they took their crew rest, they deadheaded to London to work the delayed flight. I believe it finally got off just before midnight."

"What about the pilots who were flying with Rosen?"

"They're still here. They're deadheading home tomorrow afternoon on a United flight. Want to speak with them?"

"Yeah, I sure would. I --"

"I've already set it up," Rod interjected. "We're meeting them at their hotel at ten o'clock. Their transport to Heathrow doesn't pick them up until midday. Then we can head on up to the crime scene."

Don reached over and tapped Rod's shoulder. "Well done, my esteemed chum! Not only are you an adequate skier, and a fairly competent pilot, but you'd make a good appointments secretary."

"Hah! You couldn't afford me," he replied, braking behind a large, slow-moving lorry to turn off onto the secondary road just ahead. Once they cleared the motorway, it was only a short trip on the narrow, winding road to the now-darkened village of Milne's Marsh. The modern, roomy cottage that was home to the Weathers family sat on a spacious, leafy cul-de-sac on the village's southern perimeter. Five other distinct dwellings encompassed the bushy central patch.

Proximity lights outlining the cottage's front exposure came on as Rod coasted to a stop in front of the garage. He used a remote control to open the door, revealing a Ford Fiesta parked inside.

Rod answered his friend's questioning look. "Kate's car. Normally she drives up north, but this time they flew and her father met them at Manchester Airport."

Rod retrieved Don's bag from the boot of his two-year-old Volvo and led him into the house. "Guest room this way," he indicated, leading the visitor to the bedroom at the rear of the cottage. "Why don't you change into something casual while I get us a beer," he suggested.

*

A few minutes later Don padded into the family room, having shucked his jacket, tie and dress loafers. He set a bottle of Glenmorangie on his host's snug bar. "Tuck this away, Rod. A beer will do me just fine tonight," he said.

"Fair enough, and thanks, mate," he said, setting the bottle of single malt on the shelf above the bar. "What's your pleasure? Boddingtons or Stella?"

"Decisions, decisions. I'll have a Stella," he answered, settling onto a bar stool. Rod emptied two cans into pewter tankards and pushed one towards Don.

"Cheers, glad you could get here so quickly."

"Cheers," said Don, returning the toast. "Let's hope Rosen's killing wasn't just a random act by a mugger. By the way, do the police have any idea why he was in that area of the city? Is it near the crew hotel?"

"No, not even close. The layover hotel is in St John's Wood, a good four or five miles away. Derek hinted that the police were of the impression that he may have been visiting a lady friend before he was killed."

Don perked up right away. "You don't say! If that's the case, it could be a possible link to one of the other victims."

"Really? Which one?"

"The first one, Len Newson."

"But he died in Germany, as I recall," Rod frowned.

"Yes he did. But when I interviewed a few of his buddies back in Toronto, I learned that Newson apparently had a girlfriend here in London at one time. If Rosen *was* seeing someone here, maybe the fellas he was flying with will be able to confirm it."

"Point taken. Let's hope they're in a cooperative mood tomorrow morning," said Rod

3

MONDAY, JUNE 23

Both men had slept soundly and were in good spirits as they drove towards the heart of London on a superb summer morning. Rod repositioned his side visor to lessen the sun's brightness as the roadway curved north along the A23.

"Man! This trip would be a real ball buster if you had to do it five days a week, wouldn't it?" said Don, as the pace slowed to 20 miles per hour. They had just passed Streatham and traffic lights ahead were coming into play.

Rod nodded. "Yes, it's incredible. The Englishman loves his car. We'd have to bring back petrol rationing before some of these blokes would even consider taking the train."

Rod's mobile phone rang as they edged their way through Shepherd's Bush.

"That's probably Derek. Why don't you take it?" he suggested, handing Don the phone.

Don pressed the talk button. "Hi Derek, Don Carling speaking."

"...Oh, Good Morning, Don, and welcome back. It would appear you've another case on your hands..."

Don had met Derek Houghton a few years ago when he spent a few days at Rod's after a ski trip to Austria. They had gotten along well but only briefly talked shop . Derek was a twenty-two-year veteran of the Metropolitan Police Force, with the rank of Detective Chief Inspector. He was presently assigned to the Paddington Green branch, and headed the criminal investigation squad. He and his wife, Sonya, lived in a modest yet comfortable townhouse in the Little Venice neighborhood. Sonya was a dietitian at a private seniors home in Ealing. The couple were childless.

When Don told him that he and Rod were heading into the city to talk to Rosen's crew members, but would be free after that, Derek suggested they meet between 12:30 and 1 P.M.

When he mentioned the name of a pub, Don said, "I'd better let you tell Rod where it is, Derek," and passed the phone back to Rod.

Rod listened to his brother-in-law's directions. "Got it. See you around 12:30. Bye."

*

By 9:30 traffic had eased slightly as they reached the Edgware Road flyover and descended onto Marylebone Road, heading east. Rod turned left onto Gloucester Place, and a few blocks later merged into Park Road north of the Baker Street Underground Station. The tree-lined thoroughfare continued past an ornate white mosque, the main place of worship for London's populous muslim community. The crew hotel they were heading for was on a side street northwest of Regent's Park.

As they passed Lord's Cricket Ground, Rod said, "Keep your eagle eye peeled for Pembury Road. It should be the third or fourth turning on the left."

Don spotted the street sign thirty seconds later and Rod eased around the corner. Like most residential streets in central London, parking spaces on Pembury Road were at a premium. Rod passed the hotel and turned onto the next cross street before finding space to park. It was 9:50 when they completed the short walk back to the hotel. The thirty-five-mile trip from the suburbs had taken them almost ninety minutes.

*

The only indication that Pembury House was different from the other buildings along the street were the pavement markings in front.

Bus or taxi parking only read the yellow lettering. The nondescript building, constructed shortly after World War II, had originally contained private one and two-bedroom flats. When the boom in trans-Atlantic air travel began in the mid-seventies, two soon-to-retire BOAC executives recognized a need for crew accommodation in London for the smaller airlines - companies that might only require two or three rooms each night. Major airlines required anywhere from fifty to more than a hundred rooms a night year round, and were able to negotiate reasonable discounts with the large hotel chains.

The two men purchased the property and, after a complete interior make-over, the Pembury House opened its doors. The hotel had forty-four rooms available at modest rates. Attracting business had not been difficult. The hotel's main function was to provide a clean, quiet room for flight crews on short layovers, usually just one or two nights. It did not have a restaurant or bar, but the hotel's proximity to the St John's Wood business section and the Swiss Cottage area afforded crews a good variety of restaurants and pubs to choose from. Pre-packaged continental breakfasts were provided every morning in the ground floor lounge though, and coffee, tea, and juices were available twenty-four hours a day.

Staff numbers were kept to a minimum. Four receptionists and a like number of telephone operators split two shifts between 7 A.M. and 10 P.M. Six chambermaids handled the cleaning duties. A night man came on duty at 10 P.M. and left at seven the next morning. He was responsible for ensuring that only registered crew members were admitted during the overnight hours.

Bob Lewis had been Rosen's co-pilot. He was sitting in the lounge when Carling and Weathers entered. After introductions, the three men seated themselves in chairs at the back of the room. They were alone. A large screen television set on a console in the corner was tuned to the Sky News channel, with the sound muted.

Lewis, a balding, rather rotund man in his late 40s, seemed apprehensive to Don. When he asked about the other crew member, Lewis said he thought he would be along soon. He didn't sound as if he would wager his last dollar on it, though.

"He tied one on last night, probably not feelin' all that great. I only drank half as much as he did and I feel like shit myself," he offered quietly. He sipped black coffee from a mug.

Rod spoke first. "Well, I'm sure it was quite a shock to hear that Captain Rosen had been killed."

"Indeed it was," he sighed, "indeed it was. Bert and me go back a long way. Started together at Braniff in '71. After they went belly up, we flew for peanuts with crappy outfits for years." His voice trailed off. He shook a cigarette from the package he had been toying with, lighted it, and took a deep drag.

Don asked, "So when did you catch on with Atlantic Best?"

"Bert got hired first. That was in '91. He put in a good word for me and I signed on in January of '92."

"So you were close friends?" he prompted.

"Yeah, I guess you could say that. I probably flew with him more than other co-pilots," said Lewis. "Didn't see as much of him on days off as I did before his divorce, though." he added.

"When was that?" Don asked.

"His divorce? Oh, three, four years ago, about. Yeah, at least that long. His wife took him for a ride - or should I say her fuckin' shyster of a lawyer did. Bert was strugglin' with payments to her for the first few years."

"And then what happened?"

"Well, things seemed to get better for him financially. He never said anything about it, and I didn't ask."

This was starting to sound familiar to the investigator. " Was it a raise in pay, maybe?" Don asked.

"Ha! No-o-o, don't think it could've been that!" Bob Lewis smiled for the first time. "Don't get me wrong. AB pays pretty good for a charter outfit, but the last raise wasn't enough to make much of a difference." Don and Rod both picked up on the short form he used for his airline.

"Did Rosen have a girlfriend in London?" Don asked.

"That's what the police wanted to know, and yeah, he did. Probably been seein' her for the past year, maybe longer. Not every trip, at least not recently. I got the impression he was tryin' to end the relationship."

"Really. Why?"

"Well, he mentioned he'd had enough of London for a while. I know he wouldn't be flying here next month, he'd bid for Frankfurt layovers."

"...Ahh, that would be one way to avoid her, wouldn't it," agreed Don. "Did you ever meet her?"

Lewis hesitated just a second too long before answering. "No."

"But what?" pressed Carling.

"I did catch a glimpse of her once. I was walkin' back to the hotel here about six or seven months ago. In fact, I was waitin' to cross back at the corner." He waved a hand in the direction of the street. "A taxi came from this direction. Bert and a woman - who I assumed was his girlfriend - were in it. All I can tell is what I told the police. She had an attractive face, and dark hair, probably wavy. I guessed she was about forty. That's all I could tell them," he shrugged.

"Well, that's important info, Bob. That's the first definite confirmation that one of the victims was involved with a woman here in London," Don told him.

The American stubbed out his cigarette and quickly lit another one.

"Yeah, what about those guys? Captain Weathers mentioned them, said you thought there might be a connection to Bert's death?"

Don ran over the similarities for Lewis's sake. When he finished, he pointed out the major difference. Rosen's was the first death that made headlines, mainly because of the flight delay as it related to the passengers. In the previous deaths, the captains were flying cargo and the subsequent flight delay didn't make the local news, he explained.

The co-pilot perked right up. "Son ova' bitch! We were supposed to be flyin' freight too!"

"What? Say that again?"

"Yeah, this was our fourth trip of the month. We've been operating cargo flights both ways up until now. Sometime last week scheduling called and changed our return trip to the passenger charter on Saturday."

"Bob," Don leaned towards him before he continued. "Do you remember exactly when you heard about the change? It could be real important."

"Shit, I'm not sure. But I..." Lewis stopped in mid-sentence and looked past them.

"Here comes Zack now. He might remember."

Don and Rod stood up and turned around as the newcomer

approached, coffee cup in hand. Zack Bryski, the crew's flight engineer, looked every day of his sixty-four years, and then some, observed Carling. A hangover from hell.

Bob Lewis introduced them. Bryski shook hands without comment and sagged into a chair beside Lewis.

"Zack, when were we notified about the change to our return flight? It was sometime last week, wasn't it?"

The older man thought for a moment or two before replying. "...Yep, it was the day before we left, Wednesday morning. That asshole Larry in scheduling called real early. Woke me up," he grumbled.

"Yeah, that's right, it was Wednesday," verified Lewis. "It was on my answering machine when we got home." Bob explained that he and his wife had been up to Milwaukee visiting their daughter on the day before their flight.

The revelation about the flight change brought more questions to Carling's mind, but he only had one more for Lewis.

"Bob, you mentioned Bert's change in, uh, financial fortunes . Anything else you can tell me about that?"

Lewis sighed heavily and rubbed his forehead with both hands. Don and Rod waited patiently for his answer.

Eventually he said, "I didn't tell the police this, but I think the poor bastard was mixed up in something a bit dodgy. I don't know what it was, you know. I just got the impression he was lookin' for a way out."

"Something illegal, you mean?"

Lewis looked at his watch, then almost jumped to his feet, startling Don and Rod. "Sorry, I've gotta go and pack. I've probably said too much about things I know nothin' about. I just hope they find the fuckin' lowlife who killed Bert."

Bryski drained his coffee and stood up too. "Amen to that," he said.

Don thanked them for their cooperation and shook hands again with the Americans. He gave both men his business card and asked them to get in touch if they thought of anything that might help his investigation.

*

Before they left the hotel, Don told Rod he wanted to have a word with the person who handled crew bookings. The receptionist directed them to the manager's office located behind the front desk area. The manager, Ruth Headley, rose to greet them. She wore rimless eyeglasses that left her looking older than her forty-two years. Her frown deepened when Carling explained why they had come to the hotel.

"Dreadful business, just dreadful," she offered. "I had to assist the people from the airline who came to pick up the poor man's effects. This, after watching the police search through his belongings. Most upsetting."

"I'm sure it has been, and we won't take but a few minutes of your time. I just have a few questions about how crew bookings are handled," said Don.

Miss Headley explained the procedures that the airlines were expected to follow. They were to forward their room requirements by fax or e-mail, preferably by the 20th of the preceding month. Last minute changes or cancellations did occur, of course, and the hotel did its best to accommodate them.

Yes, when possible, crew members' names were also included before their arrival. Some airlines were better than others at this, she added. When Don asked specifically about June bookings for Rosen and his crew, she pulled a thick binder from the shelf behind her desk and thumbed through it until she found the sheet she was looking for.

"Yes, the fax from the Atlantic Best scheduling department booked rooms for two nights every week, arriving on Friday, and departing Sunday. In this case, the crew names were included with the original booking request: Rosen, Lewis, and Bryski. Their incoming flight number was 704 and the outgoing flight was 715," she said, closing the binder.

"Good, thank you," smiled Don, who had been jotting down the information. "But their return trip this time was changed, according to Lewis, and they were only going to be here for one night last weekend. Did you get notification of the change before they arrived?"

"I should think so, but let me check." This time she reached for a smaller binder containing loose sheets of fax paper. She quickly found the information. "Yes, AB sent the change. We received it, umm...here it is. On Wednesday last, the eighteenth. Oh, and they inquired if we had rooms available for ten flight attendants, but we were unable to provide them," she added.

"So it was just Rosen and the other two pilots who arrived here on Friday," said Carling. It was more of a statement than a question.

"That's correct. The flight attendants probably would have been booked into one of the hotels near the airport."

"Who else has access to crew booking information, and changes like this one last week for Rosen's crew?" he asked.

The manager gave Don a puzzled look before replying. "My secretary, Jane Redan, who isn't in today, and the receptionists who look after the check-in desk. If a crew comes in after 10 P.M., the night man checks them in," she said.

Don had one more question for the manager. Did crews from the Canadian airline Northern Flyer stay here? What about GlobeWide Cargo and International Airways?

"Northern is a regular customer, as is International," she replied. "We have booked rooms for GlobeWide on occasion, but not on a regular basis."

Carling rose and extended his hand. "Thank you for your time Miss Headley, you've been a great help," he smiled.

*

As they were walking back to the car, Rod asked Don what was behind his questions to the manager.

"Well, going on the assumption that Rosen's killing has a tie-in with the previous ones, I've been wondering why whoever is behind them would change their tactics and risk the publicity that it attracted."

"You mean not trying to make it look like an accident?"

"Yeah, that too. But more troubling is the timing. The captain's death causes a long flight delay, which becomes a big news event because of the inconvenience to the passengers," answered Don. "The photos in the papers, etcetera."

"I still don't quite follow you," said Rod.

"The switch in flights, man! Rosen was supposed to operate a cargo flight. That's probably the information his attackers were going on. In the other cases, the victim was killed on his the third or fourth trip of the month. Cargo trips exclusively."

They had reached Rod's Volvo wagon . As he unlocked it he said,

"So you think the killers must have known the pilot's schedule well ahead of the date they made their move, and--"

"Exactly! Gave them time to maybe shadow him a few times, check on his routine, things like that." When they had seated themselves and strapped in he continued, "For instance, we know that Newson, the fellow who died in Germany, liked to take Rhine cruises on his layovers, and it was on just such a trip that he died."

"So you don't think they knew that Rosen's return flight had been changed?"

"No, not if my assumptions are right," replied Don.

Rod made two left turns to reach the main road again and headed north towards Swiss Cottage.

"Any idea how these people would get the pilots' schedules?" he asked, braking to let a double decker bus pull away from the curb ahead of him.

"There are a number of possibilities that come to mind: a tip-off from a hotel staff member, or an airline employee, for instance. But one would think an employee would have passed this information onto their contact," said Don, then added, "Or it could be the woman."

"In what way?"

"Well, we can be fairly certain Rosen was seeing someone here, and apparently Newson had been as well. If the girlfriend was part of whatever it was they were mixed up in, it's conceivable she would know their schedules, even when they weren't flying to London," explained Don.

"I see, yes. And she could pass on the information that so and so won't be in London this month, but he will be laying over in Frankfurt, or Paris."

" Right, that's one scenario," replied Don.

"Hmm. If there is a conspiracy at work here, though, you're going to need a lot of help getting to the bottom of it, aren't you?"

"Yeah, I will. But let's not lose our focus here on why you hired me," said the investigator. "My main purpose isn't to find out who killed these men. Rather I'm hoping to establish what it was that got them killed. And I think we're making progress. Both Newson and Rosen had financial problems, and someone apparently offered them a way out. Substantial sums of money in exchange for their help, is how I see it. It will be up to the police to make the cases for murder. Maybe my investigation will turn up a few leads that will help them...

4

Rod found a parking space on the street behind the Green Parrot pub. They had just sat down with their pints and the lunch menu when Derek Houghton came in. The Canadian rose to greet him and insisted on buying him a beer.

"I'm on expenses, you know. I'll charge it to your brother-in-law's overpaid pilot group!" he joked, evoking a profane response from Rod.

The threesome ordered lunch and chatted while waiting for the food to arrive. They made short work of their respective meals - fish pie for Rod, Ploughman's lunch for Derek and Don - and then ordered coffees.

The noise level increased as the tables around them filled up. No one paid any attention to them while Derek outlined what was known about Rosen's death as that morning.

"Rosen had apparently put up a struggle," he told them, "and there were probably at least two attackers. It would have been nigh on impossible for one man to lift the victim over the bridge railing. The drop was almost forty feet. There were signs of trauma to his head, indicating he had suffered multiple blows from a heavy object. No witnesses have come forward and no one living nearby heard anything. The nearest house is thirty yards away, east of the bridge. The coroner put the time of death between 11:30 P.M. and 1:30 A.M."

When Derek paused to finish his coffee, Don spoke up. "So he lay there for what, some five hours before he was found?"

"That's correct," replied Derek. "That will be evident to you once you've had a look at the scene. The body wouldn't have been visible from passing vehicles, at least not until after sunrise. And the bridge is closed to vehicular traffic while it's being resurfaced. Only pedestrian traffic is permitted on it at the moment."

"Interesting. That could account for there being no witnesses to the attack," said Don.

"Yes, the assailants wouldn't have had to be concerned with headlamps surprising them."

"And the police are looking on it as an assault and robbery, you say?"

"Yes, that's the line the investigation is taking at the moment. The victim's wallet was found in the underbrush near his body. There was no money in it, or on his person, except for a few coins," said Derek.

"Credit cards?"

"Still in his wallet, along with his airline ID card and driver's license. It would appear he was rendered unconscious, his wallet searched and then tossed over the railing, followed by his body."

"Any theories as to why he was in this part of the city?"

"Nothing definite yet on that score. He had a One Day Travelcard in his jacket pocket, as well as a business card from a restaurant in Highgate Village. He didn't eat there, though. A private party had taken over the place Friday night."

"But he might've been a customer on previous occasions," mused Don.

"Well, that's a possibility. The officer I spoke to this morning just mentioned that it wouldn't have been on the night he died because of the private party," answered Derek. "The investigating team has checked all the other restaurants and pubs in the immediate area but haven't turned up anyone who can recall seeing him Friday evening."

The detective pulled a black and white photo from his pocket and handed it to Don.

"Here's a photo of Rosen, taken three years ago. You can keep it. It came from the airline's office in America."

Albert 'Bert' Rosen had been a handsome man, in a rugged sort of way. His wide nose had a noticeable bend in it, and had probably been broken more than once. Thick dark eyebrows contrasted with the salt and pepper effect of his full head of wavy hair.

"Well, you'd think anyone who had talked to him that night would have remembered him," Don suggested.

He passed the photo over to Rod Weathers.

"Yes, he definitely looks American, if you know what I mean," said Rod, after studying it for a moment. "At least compared to the average Brit of his age."

Don brought up Bob Lewis's revelation that Rosen had a lady friend in London.

"Yes, he gave the police that information," confirmed Derek. "And they have men looking for her. No trace of her yet, but they're working on the assumption that she resides locally."

"You would think she would have contacted them by now, wouldn't you? His death certainly has received enough publicity," said Rod.

"Unless the woman doesn't want to be identified," said Don, thinking out loud again.

*

The bridge on Hornsey Lane carried traffic over Archway Road, a busy thoroughfare with two lanes in each direction. The three men approached from the west and stopped in the middle of the bridge.

"A great view, if nothing else," offered Rod, pointing off to the south. The dome of Saint Paul's Cathedral stood out, as did the modern towers at Canary Wharf. They admired the vista for a few moments before Derek continued his account of what supposedly happened.

He led them to a spot near the east end of the bridge. White chalk marks were still visible on the sidewalk. "This is where the attack took place. Blood was pooled here," he said, "and a six-inch piece of material from the left sleeve of Rosen's jacket was caught on the wire mesh just below the railing."

The bridge's original ornamental wrought iron work was enclosed on both sides by clear, heavy-duty acrylic panels and then covered by the wire mesh. In addition, a spiked bar topped the protective barrier.

"Looks like they're doing all they can to stop people from climbing onto the top of the fencing. Are these fairly recent modifications, Derek?" asked Rod.

"Been this way for sometime, I believe. The locals call it 'Suicide Bridge'," Derek answered.

"Ah, I see..." said Rod. Don just whistled his amazement.

*

Roughly half the steep bank below the bridge was covered with dark green, bushy shrubs two to three feet high. Various weeds, about the same height blanketed the rest of the surface. Numerous rocks dotted the pitch, too. Derek pointed to a grouping of three rocks just below them.

"That's where he landed. The medical examiner suggests that the body hit those rocks head first, breaking his neck. If he wasn't already dead from skull fractures, the broken neck would have finished him."

The area below was still cordoned off with yellow crime scene tape.

"Hmm. Not hard now to see why the body wouldn't be visible to passing traffic at night," observed Don. "And you're right, it would definitely take two guys to lift him over this railing."

The private detective turned his attention to the pedestrian walkway along the top of the embankment. The cement footpath sloped down to merge with the main sidewalk about fifty yards south of their vantage point. A bus stop shelter squatted another ten yards further along.

"Do you think Rosen might've been taking this route in order to catch a bus?" Don asked. "Probably why he had a travel card, right?"

"Certainly possible. Buses from here would take him towards the city center . Even if the regular buses had stopped running, this is a major route and there would be a night bus service on it, I should think," he replied.

"Good spot to flag down a taxi heading back towards central London as well," suggested Rod.

"Quite. Then again, if he'd been seeing this lady for sometime," pondered Derek, "one would have expected him to spend the night..." He turned to the Canadian, inviting his comment.

Don wondered if he should mention that Rosen's co-pilot thought Rosen was looking to end the relationship, but decided not to.

Instead he said, "Well, because his return flight had been changed, and their crew call would have been fairly early Saturday morning, he may have wanted to sleep at the hotel Friday night rather than stay over."

"How would the flight change come into it?" asked Derek.

"Because the switch meant they were only going to be in London for one night instead of two. If Rosen's crew had been on their normal schedule - arriving Friday and not leaving again until Sunday - he wouldn't be getting a crew call on a Saturday morning," explained Don. "Saturday was an extra day off, you see."

When the detective still wore a puzzled look, Rod jumped in. " The cargo flight they had been operating back to the States didn't depart until late Sunday afternoon. If he was in the habit of staying over on the previous Friday nights, he could head back to the hotel anytime the next day."

"That's right," agreed Don. "So they must have been following him, and when he left her place last Friday night, they were given an ideal opportunity to attack him under cover of darkness."

"Sounds plausible enough to me," shrugged Rod.

"Most interesting. I wouldn't think the investigating officers have considered that scenario. I'll pass it on to them," said DCI Houghton.

5

TUESDAY, JUNE 24

Over a meal and drinks at Rod's golf club last night, the two men had drafted a plan for today. Rod was scheduled for a simulator session at 10 A.M.. at the British Global training facility near Heathrow. Don wanted to return to the city and do some snooping around Highgate Village. He was working on the same assumption as the police: Bert Rosen's lady friend probably lived reasonably close to the crime scene.

Why else would he have been there at that time of night? That was the question that kept popping into his head.

At 9 A.M. Rod had dropped Don off at the rail station in Redhill, on the eastern side of Reigate, and a fifteen minute drive from his home. Don would catch a commuter train to Victoria Station and then make his way about the city using the Underground or buses. Rod had some business to take care of at IPF headquarters after his training session finished, and estimated he would be back in Reigate by five o'clock, give or take fifteen minutes. They settled on the Highwayman pub across from the station as a rendezvous point.

"Keep the blue side up, captain!" Don kidded, as they parted. 'Blue side up' referred to the artificial horizon, the main flight instrument pilots used when flying without visual reference, either at night or in cloud. The top half of the instrument was blue, for sky, and the bottom half brown, for earth.

*

Just before ten o'clock Don arrived at Victoria, purchased a multi-day travel card, and made his way up to Highgate. The High Street stretched for five short blocks and he walked up the east side, noting the restaurants and cafes along the way. There weren't that many, and he quickly spotted the Glory of Venice, halfway up on the west side of the street. A charity shop on one side and a newsagent's shop on the other framed the restaurant's narrow front. The business card found in Bert Rosen's pocket came from that restaurant. As Don watched, the front door opened and a middle-aged male came out carrying a stack of white linens. He set about readying the three small square tables out front.

It was another fine day, sunny and warm. The temperature had already reached 20C. The man bustled about and the tables were quickly set for the lunchtime trade. Don's watch read 11:40, and he decided to make his move before the first customers arrived. He crossed the street and bid the man, who was now standing in the doorway enjoying a smoke, a cheery good morning. He offered the man his business card.

Yes, he was the owner/chef of the Glory of Venice, and his name was Luigi Rossani, he admitted, albeit somewhat reluctantly. Don quickly explained why he was investigating the American's death, showed him Bert Rosen's photo, and asked if he could spare a few minutes to answer a couple of questions.

Luigi shrugged his agreement, but said he had to get back to the kitchen and his lunch preparations in a few minutes.

Did he recognize this man? If so, had he been into the restaurant recently? Was he a regular customer?

"I didn't know him," he answered, "But my wife recognized him, and told the police that he came in Friday night."

Don said he was aware the police had been around, and he knew about the private party in the restaurant on Friday night.

"Is your wife working today?" Don prodded.

Rossani stuck his head inside and yelled a name Don didn't catch. A few moments later a woman appeared beside Luigi, drying her hands on an apron.

"This is my wife, Julia. She handles bookings and seating the customers," he said. The husband handed her the photo of Rosen, and spoke rapidly in Italian. She nodded when he finished. "I explained to her why you are asking questions about this man," he told Don.

The wife, who was modestly attractive and perhaps ten years younger than her husband, spoke directly to Don. "He want to have reservation but I tell him is not possible," she said.

"Right, I understand. But do you remember if he has been a customer before? Maybe earlier this month? Or even two or three months ago?"

"Yes, he come here before," she replied.

"Do you remember when? Would his name be in your reservation book?" probed Don.

"I only keep for one month. I don't remember last time he is here."

Would she mind checking her book for this month? If he had made a previous reservation it would have been on a Friday or Saturday evening, he suggested.

Don followed them inside. The small standup desk with the 'Please Wait For Hostess' sign attached to it stood just to the left of the entrance. The chef said he had to get back to the kitchen and walked towards the swinging doors at the rear of the room. Don waved and thanked him for his help.

His wife pulled a well-worn leather book from the desk drawer. Don took in the small restaurant's interior while she thumbed through the pages Five tables for two lined one wall: three larger tables that would seat four or six patrons were opposite.

"Yes, he was here. Saturday, June seventh. Table for two, 8 o'clock," she announced.

"Thank you very much, Mrs.Rossani, that's a great help!'

"Oh please, just Julia," she said, with a hint of a smile.

"Can you describe his companion, Julia? I'm assuming it was a woman," he added.

"Yes, it was a woman, that I remember. Nice looking too."

"Hair colour? Her age? Anything you can remember will help."

"Hmm. Not sure. We have many customers on Saturdays. Dark hair, I think, not blonde for sure. And they have been here before this time. Maybe two, three months ago."

"Good memory, Julia," complimented Don. "What about her age? Was she older or younger than Mr. Rosen? He was forty-eight years old."

"She was not that old," she hesitated. "More like me."

Don waited, and smiled. "I won't tell anyone!"

Julia broke into a giggle. "Okay, I am next time forty-one."

"No kidding! I would have guessed thirty-one!"

Julia's shy smile told him she knew he was exaggerating, but appreciated the implied compliment anyway.

"Do you remember if this woman has ever come in alone? Maybe for lunch? Or with other men or women?" Don was fishing now, but wanted to plumb Julia's memory while she was still focussed.

"Ahh, I don't think so. But I don't always work for lunch business." She shook her head as if to confirm her recollections. Then she suddenly slapped her forehead. "But I see her on the street sometimes, going into Mr. Patel's shop next door!" This revelation heartened Don, and he urged her to continue. "I don't hear her speak, but she does not look British. I think she is maybe European. Not Italian or French, east from there." Julia was on a roll. "And now I believe her hair is, umm... what is English word? Yes, auburn. But maybe from bottle, not her real colour," she concluded.

"You have a very good memory, Julia," smiled Don, "but I think you are about to get busy so I won't take any more of your time." Two young ladies were studying the menu board beside the entrance door. "May I leave you my phone number? If you do remember anything else I'd sure appreciate it if you would call me."

She shrugged. "Si. Maybe I ask Antonio if he knows about her for you." Antonio was their full-time waiter, she explained, and her husband's nephew. She took Don's business card on which he he'd written Rod's mobile number.

*

Don paused outside the newsagent's shop, pondering the best way to warrant his questions to the man standing behind the counter inside. He assumed the elderly Asian was the Mr. Patel whom Julia had referred to.

He was, and after introducing himself, Don launched into his story. He was trying to trace the woman friend of the American airline pilot who had been killed on the weekend, he said, without saying why. He quickly described the few details about her appearance that Mrs Rossani had provided. Attractive dark-haired woman, average height and weight, age about forty, and probably spoke with an east European accent.

Did Mr. Patel have a customer that fitted her description? Perhaps she bought one of the foreign language newspapers advertised in his shop window?

The proprietor shook his head 'no' almost before Don had finished speaking. Either he really didn't know or he wasn't buying the private investigator's line. He acknowledged that he carried some foreign papers, though, and indicated where they were. Don thanked him and went over to the aisle where the overseas newspapers were on display.

*

Don was pleased with his morning's inquiries, and jotted his findings down in a note pad as he sat in a cafe across from the newsagent. Now he had some solid leads to help him track down Bert Rosen's companion. He was certain she must live in the village, and with her description, he felt it would just be a matter of more digging until he or the police found her.

What was bugging him, though, was why she hadn't come forward yet.

Prominently displayed on a lamp post less than twenty-five feet from the café's window was a large photograph of Rosen. It was a blown-up copy of the photo DCI Houghton had given to Don. Underneath the poster's photo was a request for anyone who had seen this man on Friday last to call the police. All information would be treated confidentially, it read.

The array of foreign newspapers in the shop had provided Don with another possible clue. Not French or Italian according to Julia Rossani, so that eliminated two Paris papers and one from Rome. The rack held two other Sunday papers. One from Berlin, the second apparently from Poland. He couldn't read it, of course, but recognized the Polish spelling of Warsaw in the title.

Either a German or Polish accent would qualify as east European, thought Don. He'd put one more question to Mr. Patel before he left the shop. Did he have regular customers for the Sunday papers from Berlin and Warsaw?

Patel seemed surprised. Not at the question, but the fact that the papers were still there.

"Yes," he'd muttered, "they're quite expensive, so I only order a few. They're usually gone by Monday evening." He didn't know the names of the customers, but thought they were both women.

Don watched the people entering and leaving the shop as he ate his tuna fish sandwich. Maybe the lady in question would come in for her paper today. He ordered a second coffee and made it last until one o'clock. The last few sips were cold, and pedestrian traffic had thinned noticeably as he paid his bill and stepped outside.

For the next hour Don checked out the residential streets leading off the High Street. He was looking for apartment buildings. He didn't find many, and most of them were relatively small, containing between six flats and twenty flats. If a list of tenants was displayed where he could see it, he checked them for a possible lead. He was looking for a foreign name, preferably with Miss or Mrs in front of it.

He came up empty, though. Most of what he took to be lone tenants just had an initial before or after their surname, leaving no clue as to their gender. *'Not all of my bright ideas pay off,'* he told himself, but he had learned a good deal today.

He decided he had time for a quick half pint before heading back to Victoria Station. No one was sitting at the tables in front of The Morning Sun pub at 2:30 P.M., but inside a few senior citizens were watching a billiards match on the telly. Don ordered a beer and took it outside.

As he was enjoying his drink and the sunshine, it struck him that the pub's location - at a T-junction just short of the top of the High Street - was an ideal spot to 'people watch' from. He was looking east along Mulberry Street. The largest concentration of apartment blocks he hadn't checked out yet lay along the north side of the street, just past Highgate School, which was kitty-corner from the pub. And it wasn't that far a walk to Hornsey Lane, the road that led east towards the bridge over the motorway where Rosen had been attacked.

If this mystery woman lived locally, and *If* she lived in a flat, it was a good bet that she might reside in one of those buildings, Don was thinking. And *if* she shopped locally - even just occasionally - she would have to pass the pub as she turned down the High Street.

A plan came to mind. He'd need a helper, though, to carry it out.

Yes, it would be worth a try, he thought. *I'll run it by Rod and Derek tonight.*

*

Rod had reached the pub first and waved to Don as he crossed the street from the station. The Highwayman had a beer garden alongside the main building and Rod had claimed the last vacant table. He also had a pint of lager waiting for Don. His own glass was half empty.

"Just in time, Sherlock. Another two minutes and I would've started on yours!" he joked.

"Cheers Rod, and thanks. Yeah, I misjudged how long it would take to get from Highgate back to Victoria Station. It's a good thing the London bus drivers don't get paid by the mile or they'd starve to death."

"Too right! There's been talk once again of charging to drive into the central core. That's probably what it will take to thin out the traffic."

"The sooner the better, I say," agreed Don. "So, you must have passed your check ride or you would've waited for me to buy, I'm thinking!"

Rod laughed. "Yes, managed to squeak through once more. Good for another six months at least."

"Don't know how you can screw up these days with the computers doing all the thinking and flying for you. Much more talent was required back when I was in the cockpit."

"A typical Neanderthal remark! But coming from a typical Neanderthal, not all that surprising," retorted Rod. "I think the real reason you gave up flying was to save yourself the embarrassment of not being able to cope with modern technology, oldtimer."

"Yeah, you're probably right," admitted Don, raising his hands in mock surrender.

He made short work of his beer and reached for Rod's glass. "Here, let me top us up and I'll fill you in on my day."

When Don returned from the bar, Rod slid a sheet of paper over to him. "Here's the info you requested on crew hotels. It was European destinations only that you were after, wasn't it?"

Don nodded yes, and studied the list for a moment. "Yep. This is exactly what I wanted. Good work. Thanks, Rod."

He folded the sheet and stuffed it into his pocket. He spent the next fifteen minutes recapping what he'd learned while snooping around Highgate Village, specifically at the Glory of Venice and the newsagent's shop. When he told Rod what he wanted to do next, his friend agreed that his brother-in-law would again be the one to turn to.

*

While they were dining at a moderately busy Indian restaurant near the pub, they discussed plans for the next few days. Rod was flying Wednesday and Thursday, and his wife and family were due back from the Lake District Thursday afternoon. He told Don that he was more than welcome to extend his stay at the Weathers' home, but Don shook his head.

"Thanks anyway, my friend, but I'll be able to make better use of my time if I'm staying in London," he said. He wanted to do some more legwork around Highgate, and a central location would give him more time on the job, as he phrased it.

Before they left the restaurant, bowed out by the three elderly waiters who had served them, Rod called Derek Houghton's home number. His wife answered and told him Derek was working, but expected home within the hour. They chatted briefly, mostly about family news. Yes, she agreed, she'd have Derek call as soon as he got in.

Rod and Don had been in the house for less than ten minutes when Derek called. The Canadian explained his thoughts about a stake-out to see if it would turn up Rosen's female companion. He suggested a time frame of three to five days. He asked Derek for his opinion, and if he might know of someone who could take on the job.

"An off-duty police officer, maybe," said Don, "and he'd be paid for his time, of course."

Houghton agreed the plan was worth a try. "As to whom to use, let me sleep on that. Finding a copper who wants to earn a few extra quid won't be a problem," he said, "but I can think of a better option. A chap we've used before. I'll try him in the morning."

"Great, I'll leave it with you, Derek," replied Don. "I'm moving into the city tomorrow. As soon as I get settled, I'll call you."

Derek gave Don his mobile number before they rang off and said he would have a name for him by midday.

6

HIGHGATE VILLAGE, WEDNESDAY, JUNE 25

"Good afternoon Mr. Carling."

The greeting took Don by surprise, even though he was expecting it. True to his word, Derek Houghton had come through, arranging for a likely candidate to help with Don's surveillance plan.

After checking into the Beech Tree Inn at Swiss Cottage, Don had called Houghton.

"What was the name of that pub in Highgate, Don?"

"Uh, The Morning Sun. It's on the left near the top of the High Street."

"Be sitting out front at two o'clock. A chap named James Coates - James, not Jim - will be along to meet you. He's a retired MI5 man. He's handled short assignments for the Met police a number of times."

Don let out a small chuckle. "I guess I don't have to ask how Mr. Coates will know me, do I? Sounds a bit furtive though," he said.

"What can I say? Once a spy, always a spy, perhaps. Anyway, I'm sure you'll hit it off with him," replied Derek.

He was right; Don took an immediate liking to Coates. At age 71, the former agent was slim and fit looking, five foot seven or eight, with thinning and still sandy-coloured hair. His warm smile showed off his remarkably white and even teeth. He was wearing brown trousers, a light-weight tweed jacket, and a dress shirt and tie. His footwear was a popular model of Clarks walking shoes.

He quickly accepted Don's offer of a drink, his choice a half pint of Guinness. A breeze had sprung up since Don had arrived shortly before two, and he suggested that they might be more comfortable inside.

"Oh no, dear boy! This is our summer after all! It could end in a heartbeat, you know." exclaimed Coates.

Don had to laugh. "Okay James, fine with me!" When he returned with their drinks, the two men exchanged brief, informal biographies.

Coates had joined the army in May 1944, a day after his eighteenth birthday. He finished training in time to take part in the British Army's advance on the Rhine in the spring of '45, and made sergeant before the war ended. After being demobilised in 1946, he took his university degree at Cambridge, graduating in 1950. He was recruited by MI5 in 1955 at the height of the Cold War, and retired in 1981. He added, with a touch of sadness, that his wife had passed away five years ago.

Don's favorite reading over the years had been anything to do with spying and espionage, and finding himself talking to a man who had actually worked in the field left him wanting to ask James dozens of questions. Maybe there would be time in the days ahead.

Coates listened carefully while Don described how he got to be a private investigator, why the pilot's federation had retained his services, and brought him up-to-date on what was known about the most recent killing. He ended with his hope that a watch on the neighborhood might turn up Bert Rosen's female companion.

When Don finished, James stroked his chin pensively before he spoke. "Yes, if she's still here. Worth a try, though."

"But you don't think it likely?" asked Don.

"No. If your assumptions are correct - and they seem quite logical - I too would have expected her to come forward by now." James paused and took a drink before adding, "I can see the woman wanting to remain anonymous if this Rosen fellow had been happily married, perhaps to save his family any further grief or embarrassment, but that wasn't the case, you say?"

"No, apparently not. He'd been divorced for at least three years, according to his co-pilot, who was also a close friend."

"Well, I'm game to give it a go. I'm free until mid-July when I'll be traveling up to Scotland to visit my brother and his family. I'll start tomorrow morning, how's that suit you?"

"Perfect, James! Glad to have your assistance."

"Well, I hope I can help. Now then, I'd like to hear more details about the previous deaths. There have been three, you say?"

"That's correct. In each case, local authorities concluded that the victim had died accidentally, although that verdict was quickly discarded in the death in Glasgow last New Year's. But maybe I'd better start at the beginning. Right after IPF retained me last February, I traveled to each of the locations for a first-hand look..."

7

CASE ONE - 'NEWSON'

Nᴀᴍᴇ/AGE OF DECEASED: Leonard L. Newson, 48, DOB 11/03/47

CITIZENSHIP/AIRLINE: Canadian citizen, Northern Flyer, DC-8 Captain, YYZ base

CIRCUMSTANCES OF DEATH: body found in Rhine river near cruise boat dock in Mainz, Germany at 2:20 A.M. local time, 24 June 1995. He had apparently spent the evening aboard the RHINE PRINCESS, a river boat that offered short trips to/from Mainz. Vessel had docked on schedule at 12:15 A.M..   Last passengers disembarked at 1 A.M.., after onboard bars closed. Body spotted by crew member as he was going ashore. It was wedged against a piling approx. 10 metres from the ship's stern. Wallet, money and wristwatch found on body.

CAUSE OF DEATH: Deceased had drowned, but how/when he entered river could not be determined. Body's alcohol level was .018, indicative of heavy drinking during previous 6-8 hours. Time of death between midnight and 2 A.M.

*

TUESDAY, FEBRUARY 11

The day after meeting in London with the IPF board, Don flew to Frankfurt. He was met by Werner Ruess, a captain for a German cargo airline and IPF's local representative. Don got acquainted with Ruess on the short drive to Mainz.

On this dreary winter morning Werner had no trouble finding a parking spot in the riverfront parking area. Carling shivered and tugged his light topcoat closed at the neck as they walked the short distance to the Rhine's bank. The raw east wind blowing off the wide expanse of cold, choppy water dropped the chill factor much lower than the air temperature of plus 3C, and the sodden stratus ceiling promised rain before long.

Three cruise boats were moored alongside, huddled together bow-to-stern to wait out the winter. The *RHINE PRINCESS* was the middle vessel, and the largest of the three. The Canadian studied the gangplank, now chained at both ends. He estimated its length to be about twenty feet, and the drop from the ship's deck to the quay at three to four feet.

Don studied his copy of the coroner's report. Photographs attached to the report, taken from the vessel's stern, showed the piling against which the body had been found. Carling slowly walked towards it. He bent down on one knee so he could look straight down. The dark water was less than four feet from the quay. In the photos it appeared to be much greater. Did the Rhine's level vary from season to season, he wondered?

Yes it did, according to Werner Ruess. It was normally lower in the summer months, he explained. Winter rains brought the level up noticeably and, with a brisk east wind, the level today was probably as high as it got in Mainz.

Satisfied with the explanation, Don turned his back to the wind and headed for the cruise line's ticket kiosk located a short distance away on the cobbled promenade. Naturally it was closed for the winter, but Don wanted to have a look at the sailing schedule affixed to the kiosk. The departure and arrival times for the *RHINE PRINCESS* dinner cruise were still listed as 8 P.M. and 12:15 A.M.., unchanged from the schedule for the summer of 1995.

Don wondered aloud how he might go about speaking to the captain of the vessel on the night Newson died. Werner thought for a moment and then took a cell phone from his jacket pocket. A tall man, he had to crouch to read the head office number in small print shown at the bottom of the schedule. After a long conversation in German which Don couldn't follow, he ended the call.

"So, I explained about your request, but the fraulein I spoke to was the only one in the office today, you see, and she was I think, ah, how do you say it?..." he paused, searching for a phrase. "Not very high up the post."

Don smiled. "The ladder - not very high up the ladder."

"Yes, the ladder. I will remember that. She was sorry, but she could not give me the captain's home number."

"Oh well, he probably couldn't add anything to what we already know," said Don.

"Perhaps, but I did convince her to call the captain - he lives in Mainz year-round - and ask him if he would be good enough to call me. So, I left her my number and maybe he will call. We will see soon enough, no?"

Don thanked him for his efforts as they retreated to the warmth of Ruess's late model Taunus sedan. Ten minutes later, just after they'd pulled onto the autobahn to Frankfurt, Werner's phone rang. He eased over to the right lane and slowed to 120 km/hr as he answered. The captain of the *RHINE PRINCESS* was on the line.

He explained the situation once again, then handed the phone to Don, assuring him that the captain spoke excellent English and would be glad to answer his questions. His name is Reiner Drader, he added. Don spoke to the skipper for ten minutes. Satisfied, he thanked him for his cooperation and hit the 'end' button before handing the phone back to Werner.

"Well, that was informative, I'm glad you were able to arrange it, Werner. Thanks again."

"You're welcome," he replied. "So, what did you find out?"

"It seems that the police weren't entirely convinced that Newson had fallen overboard accidentally, even though he must've been quite drunk. Drader didn't leave the bridge until after the body was discovered so he hadn't seen anything, but he was present when the police questioned the chief steward and the bartenders, he said.

"From their recollections, Newson was alone throughout the cruise, and spent most of the time drinking beer in the aft lounge. Apparently he didn't eat anything other than pretzels. The steward was sure he hadn't been in the dining lounge. The autopsy backs up their observations: his stomach contents were mainly liquid, with just remnants of sausage and pretzel residue present. He probably ate the bratwurst before he boarded the boat," he added.

"So how did the police think he ended up in the river?" asked Werner.

"Two possibilities were noted. They think he might have fallen from the gangway while leaving the boat. Stumbled, perhaps, and fell over the railing, which, as you saw, consists of two lengths of heavy rope." replied Don.

"Yes...if he was so drunk, that is not impossible, I think," agreed the German pilot.

"Or, it would have been quite easy for someone to push him into the water, either from the gangway or over the stern of the vessel, given his inebriated state," mused Don. "One solid blow to his back and he'd have found himself flailing helplessly about in the murky water with nothing to grab on to."

"So, did the police consider the possibility that he might have been attacked?"

"Yes they did, according to Captain Drader. But with no witnesses, and no signs of trauma to his body..." Don sighed.

"Ach so. I guess nobody saw him leaving the boat."

"No, apparently not. Most of the other eighty-five passengers had gone ashore soon after they docked. The steward told the police the last twenty or so drinkers in the bar were from a local football club celebrating someone's birthday. These guys were whooping it up and most were bombed, and weren't much help to the police. "

The driver chuckled. "Yah, I can imagine!"

"But," continued Don, "one fellow recalled bumping into 'an older American', as he described him, in the bar's urinal just before the boat docked. This was probably Newson." The threatened rain began just as Werner slowed to take the first exit to Frankfurt's sprawling airport complex. Don offered to buy him a drink to thank him for his help, perhaps in the hotel across from the main terminal. Werner begged off, saying he had a few chores to take care of at home. He was scheduled to leave next morning on a five-day trip to the Far East.

"I'll take a raincheck if we meet again," he said, braking to a stop in front of the terminal.

"Perhaps we will," smiled Don. "And thanks very much, you were a great help today."

"It was my pleasure! And best of luck with your investigation. Please say hello to Rod from me. If you come back, just have him contact me again," he said, as they shook hands. Don retrieved his briefcase and overnight bag from the back seat and headed for the nearest entrance, scrunching his shoulders against the steady downpour as he dashed across the taxi and bus lanes.

*

CASE TWO-KRANTZ

NAME/AGE OF DECEASED: Daniel G. Krantz, 51, DOB 29/6/45

NATIONALITY/AIRLINE: American citizen, B-747 Captain, International Airways, JFK based

CIRCUMSTANCES OF DEATH: Body found under stairs of Paris metro station near crew hotel at 3:30 AM on October 25, 1996. Discovered by public works crew. Heavy fog, visibility less than 50 metres.

CAUSE OF DEATH: broken neck and fractured skull consistent with a head-first fall from a height of 20 feet or more. No other significant trauma. Estimated time of death between midnight and 1:30 A.M. Victim's wallet containing credit cards, drivers licence and other personal documents found on his person, Pockets contained 400 French francs and 60$ US. No witnesses. Inquest did not come to a conclusion as to whether victim died accidentally or at the hand of a person or persons unknown. Police file 'OPEN' as of 31 December

The flight from Frankfurt to Paris took 90 minutes, almost half of it on the ground or holding for an approach time to Aeroport Charles de Gaulle. The congested skies of Europe must cost the airlines a fortune in fuel every day, mused Don. Arriving in Paris after 6 P.M. meant a quick trip into city's heart, though. After exchanging two hundred dollars in travellers cheques for francs, he called the Residence Roland, and booked a room. The small, three-star hotel was tucked away on a quiet side street close by the Champ de Mars. Fifty minutes after landing he had checked in and made his way up to his modest room on the third floor.

The day's travels had left him feeling quite grubby. He ran the shower to make sure the hot water supply was working before he stripped off his clothes. After a good soak, he felt refreshed and ready for his next move. He liberated a cold bottle of Kronenberg 1664 beer from the room's minibar and finished it quickly as he dressed.

He stopped at the desk to ask about coming in late.

"Pas de probleme, m'sieu," answered the concierge. Switching to English he added, "We lock the front door at 10 P.M., but just ring the bell, I won't be far away!"

It was just after 7:30 when Don stepped outside. The Parisienne evening was cool and dry. The weather system that had been drenching the Frankfurt area as he departed had obviously passed over northern France earlier in the day. As he reached Avenue de Suffren, Don glanced to his right. He could just see the top of the Eiffel Tower with its spot-lit flag rippling in the wind, further testament to the front's passage.

He crossed the tree-lined avenue and continued south through a warren of narrow residential streets. Ten minutes of brisk walking brought him to the busy intersection of Boulevard Grenelle and Avenue Motte-Picquet. The Dupleix metro station where Captain Krantz's body was found was not far from here, but Don decided to eat first. His stomach was rumbling, reminding him that he hadn't had much to eat since breakfast in London 12 hours ago. He was familiar with this area of the city from his airline days, and one of the restaurants he used to frequent was only a few minutes from where he was standing. His timing was perfect. He found a table on the upper level of the Cafe de Commerce without any trouble. Any later than 8 P.M. and the place rapidly filled up with local trade, he recalled, and by 8:30 all three levels would be packed. The restaurant was well-lit, pleasantly warm and appeared to have been redecorated since his last visit some eight or nine years ago. The tables on the upper floors were aligned around a large rectangular opening, and looked down on the kitchen and bar areas on the ground floor.

Don observed the busy happenings below as he worked his way through an appetizing meal of onion soup, a half roast chicken, pomme frites, and cheese and biscuits - all washed down with a half litre of the house red wine. His bill came to the equivalent of thirty Canadian dollars, including a generous tip.

His waiter offered a smile-less 'Bonsoir, m'sieu' as Don stood to go and quickly set about readying the small table for a waiting couple.

*

After leaving the restaurant, Don retraced his path along the rue du Commerce back to the busy intersection and crossed to the Motte-Picquet/Grenelle metro station, situated at street level below the elevated tracks. He deposited a ten franc coin in the vending machine to obtain a one-way ticket and used it get through the automated turnstile. Once inside, he took the stairs labelled DIRECTION PLACE CHARLES DE GAULLE leading up to the trains.

A half-empty train arrived shortly after he reached the platform. His destination was the DUPLEIX station only three minutes away, and the location where Krantz's body had been found. Don was the only passenger to alight once the train glided to a smooth stop at the much smaller station.

He walked to the end of the deserted platform and looked down the stairs leading to the street. The stairs were broken by a small platform approximately halfway down, no doubt designed to give elderly passengers a chance to catch their breath before continuing. The landing was shared with stairs leading up to trains heading in the opposite direction. After reaching the landing, the investigator stopped and looked back up. The upper platform was no longer visible, a partition near the top of the stairs hiding it from his sight line.

He turned around and moved the short distance to the top of the remaining stairs. To the right was a wall, consisting of a railing and a sheet metal panel, approximately three feet high. Don peered over it. He estimated the distance to the ground at twenty to twenty-five feet. It would be easy enough for someone to climb over, but a man would have to be falling down drunk to miss the top of the stairs and fall head first over the wall, he thought.

Yet that was one of the scenarios for Krantz's death put forward at the inquest. He made a mental note to re-check the report on the victim's blood alcohol level. He didn't recall it being particularly high, definitely not high enough to indicate that Krantz was hopelessly drunk.

After studying the scene for some time, Don felt a more likely explanation would have the victim being pushed or dropped over the wall. Could a single assailant have managed it? Most likely it would have taken two men, especially if the victim was able to put up some resistance, he reckoned.

There was almost no light reaching the area beneath his vantage point. One would have to stop and look down - as he was doing now - to see anything directly below.

He descended the rest of the stairs and pushed through the exit bars to reach the street. Turning to his right, he followed the iron railing that closed in the station at street level. The vertical bars were close enough together to prevent a person from squeezing through to bypass the turnstiles, but still allowed one to see inside. The fence completely enclosed the area under the stairs. He edged his way along the fence, mindful of the vehicles driving along the street paralleling the overhead tracks.

A number of heavy plastic rubbish bins sat clear of the street at the corner of the fence. The sanitation crew must have been collecting them when they spotted the body, he realized....

8

WEDNESDAY, FEBRUARY 12

Don had called British Airways last night and made arrangements to fly to Glasgow today. He'd thought about staying over and trying to contact the Gendarmerie that had investigated Krantz's death, but decided not to. At this point it would probably be a waste of time. If he did come up with evidence to connect Krantz with the other victims, he could always return. Rod Weathers had provided him the number for Claude Lejeune, an Air France captain who had agreed to assist him, much as Werner Ruess had in Frankfurt. He called Lejeune's number, got his answering machine, and left a short message saying he would contact him if he needed to return to Paris.

After checking out of the Residence Roland, Don grabbed a taxi to the Gare des Invalides and caught the shuttle bus to the airport. He made it to the BA departure lounge just as his flight was called.

The weather over southern England was clear and arrival delays at Heathrow were of short duration. After one circuit in the holding pattern southeast of the airport, the Boeing 757 was vectored over the British capital for an approach to 27 Right, the northernmost of Heathrow's two 12,000 foot runways. The senior BA first officer handling the controls of the twin-engined jet 'greased it on' despite the gusty west wind. In pilot parlance, a 'greaser' was the ultimate smooth landing.

It was only a short taxi to the gate at Terminal One. The captain set the aircraft's brakes, turned off the seat belt sign and shut down the engines at 12:02 P.M., eight minutes ahead of schedule. Immigration and customs formalities went quickly, too. At 12:30 Don stepped off the escalator onto the departures level. A check of the overhead screen confirmed his connecting flight to Glasgow was on time. With thirty minutes to kill before he needed to check in, he decided to try and reach Rod.

It took him a few minutes to locate a pay phone, and the display indicated the phone card he inserted still had two pounds, thirty pence available. *Should be more than enough for a call to IPF's headquarters, even it's long distance,* he thought. Don dialed the number shown on Rod's business card. After two rings a pleasant female voice answered.

"Captain Weathers' office, Jenny speaking. How may I help you?"

"Uhh, Jenny, hello...this is Don Carling. Is Rod in today?"

"Oh, Good Day Mr.Carling! Rod said you might call. Unfortunately you just missed him. He and a colleague left for lunch fifteen minutes ago, but you can reach him on his mobile," she added. "Would you like the number?"

"No, I have it, but thanks anyway, Jenny," he replied. "I'll give it a try."

"You're most welcome, sir. Cheerio!"

*

"Hi Rod, Don here. What's for lunch? Your all-time favorite 'bangers and mash'?"

The Englishman chuckled. "No mate, today's gourmet fare at the Tudor Rose is Shepherd's Pie. Where are you calling from?"

"I'm at Heathrow heading for Glasgow. I hope to get back tonight - tomorrow at the latest. What's your schedule for the rest of the week?"

"Hmm, I'm not flying until Friday. Yes, Friday and Sunday this week," he replied.

"Okay then, let's meet tomorrow. If all goes well, I should only need a few hours in Glasgow. Could you set me up with a room near the airport? Make it for tonight and Thursday. I'll head home on Friday."

"Yes, no problem. I'll have Jennifer arrange it. How did it go on the continent, by the way?"

Carling hesitated a few seconds before answering. It was too early in his investigation to come to any conclusions. He needed to make thorough background checks of the victims first. Until he could back up his suspicion that the deaths were somehow connected with hard facts, he was going to keep his thoughts about them to himself.

"Fine. I had a good look around both the Mainz and Paris locations. Your friend in Frankfurt was a great help," he said.

"Werner Ruess, yes, very nice chap. He's been a safety rep almost as long as I have."

"Yeah, anyhow, I'll give you a full rundown tomorrow, Rod."

"I'll look forward to it. Call either Jennifer or me from Glasgow for your reservation info. See you tomorrow."

*

CASE THREE-FLORES

NAME/AGE OF DECEASED: Ramon [Ray] Flores, 46, DOB 14/11/50

CITIZENSHIP/AIRLINE: American citizen, DC-8 Captain, Globe Wide Cargo, MIA based

CIRCUMSTANCES OF DEATH: body found near Glasgow Central Station in early hours of New Year's morning, January 1st, 1997. Body was crumpled against a steel support pillar for overhead rail lines. Appeared to have been the victim of a 'hit and run'. No witnesses. Body discovered by derelicts. Overnight temperature was -2C and light snow had fallen, accumulation less than 2 inches.

CAUSE OF DEATH: Body suffered severe trauma, with two skull fractures listed as the fatal injuries. In addition, body had two leg fractures, broken ribs, broken left shoulder, and multiple facial lacerations. Left hand and fingers also badly broken.

*

The next low pressure system sweeping in from the North Atlantic Ocean had already spread its moisture-laden tendrils inland. Combined with Glasgow's northern latitude, the overcast had drained most of the daylight away from the city by the time Don's taxi crossed the Kingston Bridge. It was only 3:30 in the afternoon.

"Cheers guv!" acknowledged the cabbie, touching his cap brim, as thanks for the two pound tip.

He'd asked to be dropped at Central Station, and he was now standing at the main entrance to the imposing edifice. A steady stream of people was heading in, the vanguard of the evening commuter traffic. He followed along and stopped beneath a large overhead information board, looking for directions to the LEFT LUGGAGE office. The counter was tucked into a corner of the cavernous interior, but easy enough to find. A harried-looking clerk exchanged his overnight bag for a claim ticket. Don's remark that ' it would only be for a few hours' received a non-committal grunt in reply.

He found an empty bench, and sat down to look over his file on Ramon [Ray] Flores. The captain's body had been found near the station in the early hours of New Year's Day. Flores had taken the train from Prestwick to Glasgow, arriving in the city on the afternoon of the 31st. He had flown into Prestwick from Miami on December 30th and wasn't due to leave again until January 2nd, after the New Year's holiday.

He was probably on his way back to this very station when he was killed, reasoned Don. The return portion of his ticket was found in his pocket.

This wasDon's first visit to Glasgow, and before he went any further he needed to orientate himself. He found a large scale map of the city centre on the wall near the exit to Hope Street. The street where Flores' body was found appeared to run under the station near its southern boundary, not far from the River Clyde. *'Should be easy enough to find if I just go out to Hope Street and turn left,'* he told himself.

Only a few vestiges of daylight remained as he descended the surprisingly steep hill and crossed the busy intersection at Argyle Street. From this point it was easy to see why the tracks were elevated as they fed into the station. The river Clyde was only a few blocks away, but ground level along its banks was noticeably lower than at the northern end of the station. The short street he was looking for was just another hundred yards towards the river...

"Ah shit!" he exclaimed out loud when he reached the corner. The street was barricaded off. A large sign headed 'Closed to Pedestrian Traffic' was affixed to the barrier. He stepped closer to read the smaller print below.

'Due to the fire, Southland Street is closed until further notice,' it read. Persons requiring access were directed to call the listed number for the City of Glasgow Public Works Department. The notice was dated 15 January1997, just over a month ago.

Carling continued to mutter curses as he peered down the darkened street. From what little he could make out it wasn't much more than a wide alleyway, barely space for two cars to pass.

He shivered against the cold wind blowing up from the river as his eyes strained to make out features under the tracks. The north side, to his left, contained a row of now boarded-up shop fronts. The south side was lined with nothing but support pillars for the overhead track system. If he had interpreted the police report correctly, the captain's body must have been found at one of these posts.

There was nothing further he could accomplish from the barrier, so he turned and retraced his steps back to the station, pondering his next move.

He checked the list of possible contacts that Rod Weathers had provided. The most likely possibility was the officer who had headed the investigation into Flores' death. He found an enclosed phone booth with a bench seat and dialed his number.

A recorded message told him he had reached Glasgow Police Headquarters, and if he knew the extension to dial it now. He punched in 115 and waited hopefully. After six rings he was about to hang up rather than get an answering machine when he heard a resigned sigh on the line, seconds before a tired sounding voice spoke...

"...DCI McGrath."

"Chief Inspector, hello, this is Don Carling speaking," and getting no response he continued. "I'm a private investigator from Canada. I was given your number by Captain--"

"Aye," the Scotsman cut in. "The American pilot case. I took a call from London about it a few weeks back," he said, in a more civil tone.

"Yes, that was Captain Rod Weathers from the International Pilots Federation."

"Yes, yes, that's the chap."

"Well, I'm here in Glasgow and I was hoping to ask you a few questions. Pick your brain, so to speak, about Flores..."

He was interrupted again. "Where are you now, Mr. Carling?"

"Uhh, I'm in the Central Station."

"D'ya know the area?"

"No, never been here before."

"I'll meet you at my local in ten minutes, you're only a short walk from it. That's if you don't take a wrong turning," he cautioned. "Here's what you do..."

Don listened carefully to McGrath's directions. "Okay, I'll find it. See you there," he replied, when the Scotsman finished. He didn't think he needed to ask how they would recognize one another.

Don took the Hope Street exit once again, this time turning right, heading away from the river. He crossed Bothwell Street and, as instructed, turned left into a lane halfway between Bothwell and St Vincent Streets. Thirty yards along he came to the unobtrusive entrance to the Nook Bar.

*

The old pub was rectangular-shaped with the bar to his right. The place was crowded, noisy, and smoky. His entrance went unnoticed except by a shabbily-dressed elderly gent seated alone just inside the door. He was busy with a 'roll your own' cigarette and stopped in mid-lick to squint suspiciously at the stranger who had entered his sanctum.

Don threw him a friendly nod and continued towards the near end of the bar. Two barmen were busy behind it. The nearest, a beefy red-haired man in his late-twenties, was drying the last of a tray of pint glasses. "Be right with you, sir," he said.

"No hurry," replied Don. He had a casual look around while he waited. No, he thought, Inspector McGrath sure won't have any trouble picking me out of this lot!

"There, that's done with! Now, what'll it be, sir?" asked the barman cheerfully.

"I'll try a pint of Tartan Special, please," replied Don.

"...And the same for me, Davy. My Canadian friend here will look after it!"

Don turned to find a smiling, brawny man extending his large hand towards him.

"Des McGrath," he offered, as they shook hands firmly.

"Four pound forty, sir," said Davy as he set their drinks in front of them. Don slid a five pound note across the bar and waved away the change.

McGrath raised his glass, and offered "Cheers!"

"Your health," responded Don, raising his own pint. He watched as McGrath quickly quaffed half of his beer, and decided he wouldn't want to go up against him in a drinking contest.

For a few moments McGrath and the barman engaged in good-natured banter. Don stood by quietly, sizing up the Scottish policeman.

McGrath was a good four inches taller than Don, at least thirty pounds heavier, and in his early 50's. He was wearing a dark blue, well-worn anorak over his tweed jacket and tie, also showing their age. His brown wool cap, in the traditional style worn by most men over forty in the UK, looked new in comparison. *Probably got it for Christmas*, Don figured. The cap complimented the detective's full head of brown hair, now peppered with grey.

"So Mr. Carling, let's you and I get a refill and find us a seat," he said, handing his empty glass to Davy and urging Don to finish his.

*

Fresh pints in hand, the two men claimed an empty table near the back of the room.

McGrath got right to the point, and asked Don what he hoped to achieve with his investigation. The private investigator did so, emphasizing that his intention was not to discredit any of the local findings but to see if he could uncover any evidence linking the deaths.

McGrath admitted he knew nothing about the deaths in Germany or France, so Don explained why he wasn't ready to write off Newson and Krantz as accident victims. Satisfied that the Canadian's quest was valid, he agreed to talk about his investigation into the Flores killing.

Initially it appeared the American was a victim of a hit-and-run driver, he began. The poor weather, the Hogmanay festivities factor, and the location where the body was found all pointed to this as a viable explanation. After the post mortem though, the police had dismissed this theory.

The report implied his death was the result of foul play. Quite strongly, in McGrath's opinion. Flores *had* been struck down by a vehicle, but probably on purpose. Both legs were badly shattered just above the knee, indicative of his having been hit from behind by an SUV-sized vehicle - one with a high front bumper. The two skull fractures were not consistent with his being run down though, or as a result of being thrown against the pillar. These injuries had been inflicted with a heavy, blunt object, probably after he was lying helpless on the road. The injuries to his left hand - broken wrist and fingers - sealed the beating theory for the experienced homicide inspector.

"As pissed as he was," McGrath concluded, "this poor chap was desperately trying to ward off blows to his head as he lost consciousness."

"Son 'ova bitch," muttered Carling. "Was that street so deserted that no one would see or hear anything?" he asked.

"Ah, that's a good question, lad," he replied, and paused to take a drink before answering. "He was probably killed near on 11:30, on his way to the station to catch the last train back to Prestwick. That train left at 11:45 P.M. What with the inclement weather, most people were likely living it up inside as midnight approached."

"And you don't think he was killed by locals?"

"Nae, quite sure of it. I've thirty years chasing down the criminal element in this city and nothing says to me that this was a Glaswegian-style hit. Besides, even the local baddies would be too busy drinkin' their sorry souls silly on Hogmanay. Nae, definitely not a mugging gone wrong." he added, shaking his head.

Don had to smile at the Scotsman's alliterative description. After taking another swallow himself, he asked, "So you're saying it was probably a--"

"Professional killing, aye," McGrath said quietly, finishing the thought for him.

He went on to fill in some more blanks. Flores was found by two homeless derelicts who usually sheltered overnight in a nearby car park building. The police dispatcher logged a call from a taxi driver at 2:45 A.M. It wasn't possible to pin the them down on the exact time they'd discovered him. And they couldn't say how long it took them to get a taxi to stop. The coroner set the time of death between 10 P.M. and midnight.

Flores' wallet was found on his person, as was his wristwatch. The only thing missing was any sterling, assuming he still had some left. The two who first found him vehemently denied robbing him, suggesting that some other street people might have tossed his pockets while they were trying to flag down a taxi at the end of the street.

It would have been logical for Flores to cut through the deserted street on his way back to the station, particularly if he had been visiting pubs along the river east of the station. Don interrupted to ask about the fire and the street's closure. Was it in any way connected to the killing?

No, that had been ruled out, even though the fire occurred just days after Flores died. The fire started in a business that sold used car parts: tires, batteries and the like. Years of accumulated junk, oil-soaked rags and newspapers fed the fire, which gutted the place and the only other business still operating, a kebob take-out next to it. The street was still closed while engineers studied the overhead track support system for possible heat damage.

DCI McGrath had been called to take over the investigation at 7 A.M. on New Year's Day. The victim's wallet contained photo ID identifying him as a pilot for Globe Wide Cargo Services, based in Miami, Florida. This, along with the return portion of the Railink ticket to Prestwick pointed McGrath in that direction. By 9:30, he'd ascertained that Flores was registered at the Coastview Inn near Prestwick Airport, as were two other Globe Wide pilots.

The front desk clerk gave him the home number for Globe Wide's local operations manager, John Gibson, who lived in nearby Ayr. McGrath called Gibson to inform him of Flores' fatal accident. The news, quite naturally, shocked the fellow who was just about to sit down to breakfast with his family and a houseful of relatives.

The inspector allowed that he would have to come out and interview the other crew members and asked Gibson to contact them. He readily agreed, and advised McGrath that while the policeman was en route, he'd make his way to his office at the airport. He had a file there detailing company protocol to be followed in the event of an employee's death away from home base. He would be in his office by the time the inspector arrived in the Prestwick area, he told him.

McGrath thanked him and said he would stop in to see him after he had interviewed the other pilots.

Carling had listened carefully, making mental notes to himself. When McGrath paused to finish his beer he asked, "Did they say why they hadn't come to Glasgow with Flores?"

"Oh, aye, no mystery there. Unlike Flores, they were both keen golfers and Mister Gibson had arranged for them to play that afternoon at Royal Troon. Even set them up with borrowed clubs. Flores told them he was going to head into Glasgow to take in the New Year's festivities during the afternoon and evening. Said he expected to be back in time to celebrate at midnight with them. When he didn't show up, they assumed he'd decided to stay over in the city and they would meet him for lunch the next day as planned ..."

"I see...yeah, that's all quite plausible," said Don. "But if his killing was a set up, how did they--"

"How did the killer - or killers - know Flores would be in Glasgow?" said McGrath, finishing Don's thought once again. "Or even in Scotland at that time? Was he followed from Prestwick? Must have been. Definitely looks as if the chap was targeted, if your conspiracy theory holds water, doesn't it?"

"I'll say," was all Carling could reply, his mind quickly registering more questions, questions that would take a lot of digging on his part before he could answer them.

McGrath conceded that at the present his investigation was stalled. None of the bar staff in pubs in or around Central Station could recall serving Flores; there hadn't been any leads from informants; no trace of the vehicle used to run him down; no likely suspects booked into hotels in Glasgow, Ayr or along the Ayrshire coast. Nothing at all...

"Well, if I come up with anything that might be relevant I'll give you a call, Des," offered Don.

"I'd appreciate that. Not much to go on so far, is there?"

"Just that all three men had spent their last hours alone, two of them probably to the point of being pissed, and on the surface their deaths appeared to be accidental," Don told him.

*

Carling had finished his beer, and declined his host's offer of a refill.

He rose and extended his hand once more, and thanked Des for meeting him. He assured the inspector he would keep in touch and pass on any lead, however slim, that might have a bearing on the Flores case.

Rain bordering on sleet was slashing down as Don made his way back to Central Station. After retrieving his bag, he headed for the taxi rank at the main entrance. He was thoroughly chilled by the time he reached the head of the silent queue, even though his wait was less than ten minutes. By 7:30 he was on his way to the airport, hoping to catch BA's last shuttle flight back to London. His luck held, and he was assigned one of the few seats available: a middle seat in the last row. Don dozed most of the way, firmly wedged between two portly businessmen. Neither of them was any more inclined to conversation than Don, which left him undisturbed to digest what he'd learned from DCI McGrath.

A few minutes after midnight the shuttle bus dropped him off at the **Heathrow Radisson** hotel. Ten minutes after reaching his room he was sound asleep.

9

THURSDAY, FEBRUARY 13

Carling arose fully refreshed after eight hours of solid sleep and a long shower. The full English breakfast he ordered from room service arrived just as he finished shaving. He drained a cup of black coffee before tucking into the hot food.

'That takes care of my monthly grease intake', he told himself as he swiped the plate clean with the last slice of tepid toast. But he'd enjoyed every mouthful.

Don had spoken to Rod last night before leaving Scotland, and they'd agreed to meet this morning at eleven. He'd finished breakfast by 9:30, and spent the next hour reviewing the information he'd gathered over the past two days. Most of the new information he entered into his computer pertained to his discussion with Des McGrath about the Flores killing. Once he was happy with his updated files, he decided to get some fresh air before Rod arrived. He shrugged into his top coat, took the stairs to the spacious lobby and crossed to the front entrance. Outside, the morning mist was dissipating rapidly as the sun gained altitude. Don took a few deep breaths before setting out along the sidewalk, heading east.

The modern hotel was on the Bath Road in the centre of the airport strip, which bordered Heathrow's north side. At mid-morning the roadway was a bustle of vehicular activity in both directions. Lorries, buses and airline catering trucks vied for space en route to the service entrance to one of the world's busiest airports. Ten minutes and a half mile from his starting point he reversed his course and returned to the hotel.

He felt better for the short workout, in spite of the diesel fumes. He needed to exercise as often as possible while away from home, he knew, even if it was only a brisk walk. Keeping his weight below two hundred pounds was a never-ending struggle: Ideally he would like to carry no more than one hundred and eighty pounds on his five-foot ten frame, but that number was long gone. He'd been closer one ninety or more since he turned forty.

He stepped inside and looked around for Rod. His friend hadn't arrived yet, so Don slipped off his coat and plunked his body in a box-like leather armchair near the reception desk. For the next few minutes he watched as an attractive young lady from *Plants for Pleasure*, according to the logo on a mini-wagon holding her supplies, lavished her attention on a large potted floral arrangement, one of four spaced around the foyer.

"You're way too old for her, Sherlock." Don turned to see Rod smiling down at him from behind.

"Don't I know it. But watch, it's amazing! She even dusts the leaves - top and bottom!"

"Well, if you any inkling about plant life you'd understand the necessity."

"Hah! If I only worked a couple of days a week like you I might have time for some serious gardening," retorted Don, rising from the chair. "Where'd you park, by the way?"

"In the rear lot. Why?"

"Just leave it there then, and follow me," said Don. He steered his English friend towards the front entrance and out to the street.

*

Five minutes later they were among the day's first customers at the Air Hostess pub on the north side of the road. Pints in hand, they moved to a table near the room's small gas heater. The pub had been a fixture since the early days of Heathrow's development. Don had first been introduced to the establishment while flying with a senior Wardair captain named Wesley Bayliss. He had emigrated to Canada soon after the war, but never lost any of his quirky British affectations during his forty- odd years 'in the colonies', as he referred to his adopted home. His stated aim on UK layovers was to educate the younger Canadian pilots in the 'finer traits expected of a gentleman'.

'Rule number one young man', he would intone to a new boy with mock seriousness, 'a gentleman must be able to finish at least three pints of beer before taking a piss'.

Don smiled inwardly at his recollection, and silently offered a toast to Wesley's memory. Captain Bayliss died in 1985, just a few months after retiring.

"So...I think your suspicions are well-founded," began Don, after the two men had settled into their chairs, "certainly in the Glasgow case."

"Really? That's rather disconcerting. What makes you so sure?" Rod asked.

Carling recounted his meeting with Inspector McGrath, ending with the disclosure that Flores' death was now being looked on as the work of professionals. Then he back-tracked to his trip to the continent and his first impressions about the cases in Germany and France. Although both deaths could have been accidental, he cautioned, the similarities with Glasgow meant that foul play couldn't be ruled out.

"The more I think about it, the more I'm convinced they were murdered. These men were stalked - they had to be - with the killers waiting until the victim had finished his pub crawling, or whatever, and then making their move."

"Taking your theory one step further then, do you think it likely they were all killed by the same person?" asked Rod.

"Good question. And yeah, I seem to be leaning that way. But it's really just conjecture at this stage," answered Don. "It's likely more than one person was involved, though. At least in the Glasgow killing, and probably Krantz's in Paris. And they're not just ruthless, they're clever."

"In what way?"

"Well, by knocking them off in different locales. McGrath hadn't heard anything about the German and French deaths until you mentioned them. I'm sure the same applies to the police who investigated those cases. If I can come up with a common thread or two, they might want to rethink their findings," said Don.

"It's all rather alarming, to say the least. Let's hope you can uncover a link."

"Well, it's out there somewhere. A few questions need to be answered first. Did these men get involved with the wrong crowd? Were they gamblers? Unable to pay their debts? Or maybe screwing around with the wrong woman?" Don shrugged, then added, "And just maybe there isn't a connection at all."

"Plenty of possibilities, it would appear," Rod said. "So what will you do next?"

"Nothing more I can do on this side of the pond for now. When I get home, I'll start digging into their backgrounds. Len Newson was based in Toronto, so I'll start there. Shouldn't take too long to put together a profile of him," said Don, thinking out loud.

They ordered another pint and, changing the subject, chatted about skiing, golf and flying while they drank. Don used Rod's mobile phone to call Air Canada and book a return flight for that afternoon, using the flexibility his executive class ticket allowed.

"I'd offer to stay the night and treat you dinner and drinks, captain, but since you're flying tomorrow morning you'd probably stick to one of those God-awful non-alcoholic drinks they serve over here. And you're pretty dull company when you're completely sober!" he joked.

"Thanks anyway, you great twit. I'll get you another time. Besides, I know you would only play the big spender and add it to your expenses!"

They shared a few more minutes of friendly banter before returning to the hotel. Rod retrieved his car from the parking lot and drove around to the front entrance while Carling checked out. Traffic had eased up and there were no tie-ups on the access routes to the airport. Even in the long tunnel under the runway that fed into the maze of roads leading to Heathrow's three older terminals, there was only a minor slowdown. A trio of traffic wardens was on duty in front of the Terminal Three departures area. One, a robust lady with her whistle firmly clamped between her lips, helpfully pointed Rod towards a curbside space just as a mud-splattered Land Rover pulled out.

He left the engine running while he stepped out to say goodbye.

"Have a good flight home," offered Don.

"And you have a safe flight tomorrow, Rod. I'll call you next week," Don told him as they shook hands.

10

FEBRUARY 20

Carling called Northern Flyer's office after his return from London, and spoke with Jack Hammond, the company's chief pilot. Hammond questioned his motives for wanting to dig into Newson's background. Once Don had outlined the similarities between Newson's apparent accidental death and the others - and reminded him that he was conducting his investigation on behalf of the pilot's federation - he reluctantly agreed to see Don.

When Don arrived, his greeting was more cordial than he'd expected. The reason soon became clear over coffee.

"I had a chat with Dick Gooden after your call, Don. He spoke highly of you, even if you were a bit impatient at times, to quote him," he smiled. Gooden had been a check pilot with Wardair when Carling started with the airline.

Don gave a sheepish chuckle. "Yeah, I suppose I was," he admitted. "How's he keeping? He retired some years ago, didn't he?"

"Yes. Dick has been living the good life for six or seven years now. He's in good health, enjoys his cottage on Lake Simcoe in the summer and spends a couple of months in Florida most winters."

The two men traded names of mutual friends while they sipped their coffee. Hammond showed a surprising interest in Don's career switch, and even pressed him for details of his more recent investigations. By the time they had finished a second coffee there was no fence between them. Hammond readily agreed to answer his questions and had no objections to Don talking to other company pilots about Newson.

*

"Well, I can't say I was completely shocked," replied Hammond, when Don asked for his reaction when he first received word about Len Newson's drowning in Germany. "He ah, did have a drinking problem, you know. A problem that he didn't have when I hired him."

"How long had he been with Northern before he died?"

"I'm not positive, but he must've been hired in '88 or 89. That's when we had our big expansion, you know. The six additional aircraft doubled our fleet. We needed more pilots, of course, and he was one of the ex-military types we took on," he said.

"Yeah, I remember those days. Some of the other charter outfits were looking for pilots too, I believe," said Don.

"Yes they were. We were probably lucky to get the experienced pilots we did. We hired seven or eight guys from Transport Command. If I recall correctly, Len had 707 command time, and after the DC-8 conversion course he was given a captain's assignment right away."

"So, there were no signs of any personal problems back then?"

"No, none at all. In fact I knew his former boss in the air force and he had nothing but good things to say about him. And he was very competent," Hammond went on. "I gave him his check-out flights and also a few of his annual instrument renewals. He handled the simulator as well as any of our pilots."

"So when did things change?" Don asked.

"Hard to say, exactly. Maybe some of his golfing buddies could answer that better than me. When I said he had a 'drinking problem', I didn't mean it affected his flying. No goddamn way! If he'd as much as showed up for work with booze on his breath I would've pulled his licence right then and there. I did a few spot checks myself, so to speak, at some of his pre-flight briefings over the last two, three years . After I got wind that he was drinking more than usual."

"I see. What about family? Was he married?"

Hammond paused for a few moments, gathering his thoughts before answering. "He divorced shortly after he joined us, and I believe it was what one would call 'a messy divorce'."

"In what way?"

"Well, I'm not going to get into what I heard, or what others were saying. He wasn't a personal friend and I never heard any details directly from Len," he stated.

"No, that's fine. I'm not asking for any hearsay info, that's for sure, Jack,"

"But I will tell you this. Back, oh, about four years ago, a court order was issued to garnishee his wages. I know because my boss - the company's chief executive officer - told me to advise Newson that his wages were going to be docked starting with his next pay check."

"Which must've meant he hadn't been making support payments or whatever to his ex-wife. Such an order is usually a last resort, I believe, so he was probably well in arrears," added Carling.

"Yes, that's my understanding. We've dealt with a few of them since I've been Chief Pilot," said Hammond. "Anyway, I had him in, gave him the bad news, and that was the end of it. He didn't offer any explanation and I didn't ask. He just acknowledged that he understood and left."

At this point Don got the impression Captain Hammond had said all he wanted to say about Len Newson. He decided the rest of his questions could wait until he talked to friends or colleagues who knew him better. Don rose from his chair, offered his hand to Hammond and thanked him for his cooperation.

"Glad to help, Don. And I'd be interested in hearing how your investigation turns out."

"Sure. It's going to take me some time yet, but I'll see that you get a copy of my report."

*

Don Carling had asked Northern Flyer's chief pilot for the names of the pilots who were with Len Newson on his last flight merely as a matter of form. He already knew who they were, but professional courtesy meant going through the company's chief pilot. It had been an easy call on Don's part, and the affable parting with Captain Hammond told him that it had been the right move.

He knew because Ralph Woods, who was also a former Wardair pilot, was a skiing buddy of his. Ralph had hooked on with Northern Flyer about the same time as Len Newson. The news of Newson's death wasn't widely reported in the Toronto papers - just a short paragraph or two referring to his accidental death while on a layover in Germany.

Carling had heard about it some weeks later while he was having a beer with Woods and a few other Northern pilots.

Fell overboard when he was all pissed-up, was the only explanation anyone seemed to have heard, and that was the last Don thought about it until Rod Weathers contacted him.

Don spotted Ralph right away when he entered the Briefing Room tavern, which took up one end of a strip mall a few miles north of the airport. Ralph was sitting with three other men at a round table near the entrance and waved a welcome to him. Don slipped out of his topcoat as he approached the group and draped it over the back of the only empty chair at their table.

"Good to see ya' Don!" smiled Ralph. "Say hello to these sorry excuses for pilots before they drink too much and get thrown out!"

His remark was answered with chortles of derision from the others as they reached to shake hands with Don. After the introductions, Don sat down and lifted the glass of draft beer that had been pushed in front of him. Ralph held the now empty jug up and a passing waitress swept it from his hand without stopping. There was no need for a verbal request for a refill.

"Cheers fellas!" Don toasted, "and thanks for meeting with me." His salutation was echoed around the table, as each man eyed the newcomer.

John Marciano, seated to Carling's right, had been Len Newson's first officer. Next to him was Sean Williams, a dark-haired man and by far the youngest present, probably in his late 20's, guessed Don. He was a flight engineer, the third man in the crew, a position still needed on the DC-8 aircraft operated by Northern Flyer. Later generation jets, from the Boeing 767 on, were handled by a two-man crew, a captain and first officer. With the advent of the 767, the aircraft systems - including hydraulics, fuel, electrics and air conditioning - were computer-controlled making the flight engineer position redundant. Sean held a pilot's license though, and, as seniority allowed, he would move up to a first officer position.

The third man seated across from Don was Ed Kirkham. Ralph had asked him to join them because, as he explained, Ed had not only been on the same air force squadron with Len but had flown regularly as Newson's first officer in the year before his death. Ironically, Kirkham had been promoted to captain to fill the vacancy in Northern's roster left by Newson's death. Don figured him to be in his mid-forties.

The three continued to jibe away at Ralph for his smart-assed remark as they finished their beers. The give and take bantering reminded Don of sessions he'd happily participated in during his airline days.

"What took you so long, Marge?" chided Ralph playfully, as the waitress plunked the fresh jug of draft beer down in front of him.

"Just thinking of your liver, old timer!" she shot back as she turned away.

The mood around the table took on a more sober note after Woods had refilled everyone's glass and suggested the private investigator explain why he was here. For the next ten minutes they gave Don their full attention as he outlined why IPF had hired him to look into the three deaths and why his checking into Newson's past was an important first step.

"First off, I've got to ask this," he said, glancing at each of them. "Does anyone think Len was suicidal?"

The question obviously shocked them, and it was a few long seconds before they reacted. The unanimous answer was clearly negative and summed up succinctly by Ed Kirkham.

"No fuckin' way," he scowled.

"I didn't think so, either," agreed Carling.

His first questions were directed at Marciano and Williams. Questions about the last flight. Rocky, a nickname that was a 'no brainer' for a guy with his surname, began with a full account from the time they departed Toronto until their arrival in Frankfurt the next morning. Their departure had been delayed three hours while maintenance changed a leaking fuel pump and they hadn't arrived in the German city until almost 10 A.M. local time. This was on May 24, 1995.

Newson would do the flying on the flight to Frankfurt, he told them at the pre-flight briefing, and Rocky would fly the return leg. It was their fourth flight cycle of the month and the routine had been the same on each trip. Actually, pointed out the first officer, this appeared to have been Len's standard way of dividing up the flying for the past year or so before he died. He looked to Kirkham for confirmation.

"Yeah, that's right. I flew with him for three or four months in late '94 or early '95," said Ed. "He flew eastbound and the first officer got the westbound leg. Most skippers alternated the flying more often then that."

After landing in Frankfurt, Newson bought a six-pack at the kiosk outside the terminal before they boarded the crew bus for the thirty-minute drive to their hotel in Mainz. They each drank a beer en route, which wasn't unusual, according to Rocky. Newson took the remaining cans with him when they arrived at their hotel at 11:30. The captain wanted them up to come to his room and finish the beer before hitting the sack, but both men declined.

He also suggested they just sleep for three hours and then go on a Rhine cruise. Rocky and Sean both begged off, saying they were going to sleep for at least five hours. That was the last either of them saw Len.

Rocky and Sean met at 5:30, wandered around for a while, then had a few beers at a sidewalk cafe. They ate dinner at a restaurant frequented by airline crews and were back at the hotel shortly after 10 P.M. Crew pick-up time for their return flight the next day was scheduled for 9:30 and they'd agreed to meet in the hotel's restaurant for breakfast at 8:30.

Marciano got the bad news first. His phone rang a few minutes after 6 A.M. It was the airline's station manager calling to tell him that Captain Newson was dead, having apparently drowned in the Rhine the previous night.

Their flight would be delayed at least 24 hours until another captain could get here, he advised, and he was on his way to Mainz to meet with the police. He requested that he and Sean remain at the hotel, as the police would want to interview them.

"So, Wolf, the station manager, and three policemen arrived about nine-thirty and we told them just what I've told you," said Rocky. "They asked us a bunch of questions about his drinking habits, where he normally went drinking, did he maybe have a girlfriend in Mainz, or other friends, that sort of stuff, but we couldn't tell them much." He paused, and turned to the younger pilot. "Anything I missed, Sean?"

"Nope, that's how I remember it," he replied.

Carling didn't want to be seen as disrespectful to the dead, but decided not to pussyfoot around with his next question.

"From what I've learned so far, Len did drink a lot, even on layovers. You fellas flew three previous trips with him that month, what condition was he usually in the next day? He must've been hung over," he said, more of a statement than a question.

The pilots exchanged wary glances, seemingly unsure of what sort of response Carling expected. It was Ed Kirkham who finally spoke out.

"Listen, I'll save us all some time. Len Newson had big problems over his last few years - personal problems - some he talked about and some he kept to himself. And he was drinking too much. *He knew he was drinking too much!* And even hung over he could probably get the job done. But that's probably why he had the first officer do the flying westbound. He was always completely sober at departure time from here," he said, rapping the table for emphasis. "Rocky, Sean, am I right?"

Both of them nodded their agreement. Rocky added that Len usually looked rough the next morning and drank a lot of coffee, but always handled the non-flying duties and the radio work without difficulty.

Don figured Newson's personal problems were the key to his demise, directly or indirectly. He needed to follow up on Kirkham's assertions but concluded that this was neither the time nor place. And he got the impression Ed didn't want to talk about them now, either.

Don offered to buy lunch but only Ralph Woods took him up on it, the others opting for another brew instead. Talk turned to what Carling knew about the other deaths he was investigating as he and Ralph tucked into their soup and salads.

He fielded their questions honestly, but declined to speculate on whether or not Len Newson had been murdered. They would have to wait until he finished his investigation, he told them. He gave all of them his business card and asked them to call him anytime if they thought of anything that might help his investigation.

As they settled the bill with the waitress and made ready to leave, Kirkham was the last to shake his hand. Fingering the business card, he told Don, "I'll call you."

11

D on was in his office when Ed Kirkham called the next morning. "I'll tell you what," he said, after they had exchanged the usual 'Good morning, how are ya?' greetings. "I think I know what kind of info you're lookin' for about Len. Rather than you ask, and me answer, why don't I just tell you what I know first? If I leave anything out, just ask when I'm finished, okay with you?"

"Why not?" replied Don, slightly bemused at Ed's directness. "Fire away..."

He and his wife had been neighbors of the Newsons' back at the base in Trenton before Len resigned from the Canadian Armed Forces, he began. That was in the summer of 1989. Ed took the same route the following year, joining the airline in October 1990 as a first officer. Len's marriage, which had weathered a few rough spots during his last years in the air force, was definitely on the rocks by this time. His wife, Sandra, was against his career change from the beginning, and after moving to Toronto, complained continuously about being parted from her close friends back in Trenton.

They separated in early 1991. His wife took their son and daughter, moved back to the Trenton area and rented a house. Soon after she filed for divorce, which was granted about a year later. She was awarded outright custody of the kids, which really pissed Len off, and he was saddled with hefty lawyers bills and a monthly settlement that took a fair chunk of his air force pension and his monthly pay at Northern.

He changed from an easy-going guy, happy to be still flying - instead of 'flying a desk' which is probably what he would've been doing if he'd stayed in the service - to a very bitter man who started drinking too much. At first he refused to make the support payments, and when he did start, wasn't paying regularly. Ed didn't hear this from Len, but his wife heard it through the wives' grapevine. This was late in '92 or early '93. There was a rumor that his ex-wife had resorted to having his wages garnisheed.

A few years before he died, Len's demeanor changed noticeably for the better. His money problems seemed to have vanished, he wasn't being hounded by his ex's lawyers and he joined the golf club, something he'd found too expensive up until then. He was still drinking on his days off, but not out of bitterness.

By the fall of 1994 he'd changed again. Something was bothering him, really eating away at him. He wouldn't say what it was and Ed never did figure it out. The last month they flew together was February '95 and Len had been more reclusive than ever.

"So, that's about it," he sighed. "Never opened up to me - or anyone else as far as I know - about what was bugging him."

Don had jotted down a few notes, mainly names and dates, as Ed spoke. He waited a few moments to see if the pilot was going to add anything.

When he didn't, he asked, "So he was still in that frame of mind when he died?"

"As far as I know. I only saw him once or twice after February. I'm not even sure if he renewed his membership at the club that year. I left a message on his answering machine a few times to see if he wanted a game - that would've been in April or early May - but he never got back to me," Ed replied.

"I see. This sudden end to his money problems intrigues me. He never let on how he overcame them? Was he a gambler? Maybe he got real lucky in a high stakes game, something like that?"

"Len a gambler? Oh shit no!" exclaimed Ed. "He'd play a 'two-dollar Nassau' with the guys maybe, but that was high stakes for Len. Don't think he even bought lottery tickets."

Don said he had a few more questions and Ed said he would try to answer them.

Did he know who handled his estate? Was there a funeral?

Newson had a brother, George, who lived in Windsor, Ontario and was the executor of Len's estate. Len's body was cremated after it was returned to Canada. A memorial service was held in Windsor a few weeks later, and Ed and three other pilots drove down for it. That was the only time he met George Newson. Len's son Fred attended, but his ex-wife and daughter did not.

Sandra had moved to Ottawa after Len died and was living with a retired air force officer who worked for the Ministry of Defence. This information also came via the wives' club network, he explained. He had not seen nor talked to Sandra since she left Len. His brother had come to Toronto a week after the memorial service and cleaned out Len's apartment. Ed had offered to help him, but ended up spending an extra two days in Vancouver when a mechanical problem grounded his aircraft and didn't get back in time.

Did Ed by chance have a phone number for George? What about the ex-wife?

Yes, he had both numbers. He had a business card from the brother, who was in real estate. His wife had supplied the number in Ottawa for Sandra. Don copied both numbers onto his note pad.

"Len's son. How old would he be and do you know where he lives?" Don asked.

"I think Fred attends university in London, Ontario, and he's probably 19 or 20 now," Ed replied.

Don looked over the list of questions that he had been checking off. Only one remained.

"Ed, what about female companions? Len wasn't a monkish type, was he? Did he have a girlfriend, maybe more than one? Was infidelity a factor in his marriage break-up?" he asked, trying not to sound accusatory.

There was a long pause. A very long pause. Don thought Ed wasn't going to answer.

"Listen..." he finally said, "I'm not going to comment on anything that might have happened before they split..."

Right! That's an answer in itself, Don thought. He put two big exclamation points after the word infidelity on his notepad.

"But yes, he did have a couple of short term relationships that I was aware of after Sandra left. Nothing serious, no live-in arrangements.

He wasn't a bad lookin' guy, after all, and he liked the ladies. Probably met them in bars, would be my guess," he added. "I never met any of them, though."

"What about overseas? Did he ever have a lady friend in one of your layover cities?"

"London. I think he knew someone there. Never mentioned her to me, but that was the scuttlebutt among the guys he flew with," Ed responded. "I know there was a time when he flew to London as often as he could."

*

His call to Sandra Coombs, Newson's ex-wife, was met with stony suspicion. Even when he brought up the possibility that Len's death might not have been an accident, her stance never softened.

"The cheap son of a bitch probably got done in by his drinking and skirt-chasing. That's what he blew most of his money on!" she denounced. "All I'm left with is half of his measly air force pension," she added bitterly.

He brought up the subject of his coming into money a few years before he died. She either didn't know or wouldn't say where it came from. Instead, she launched into another profanity-laced tirade about how he had cost her a small fortune in lawyers fees before he paid up, and had cut her off again about six months before he died.

"Was there any life insurance?" he asked.

"The bastard cut me out of that, too. Fred was the beneficiary, and it wasn't a big policy. Got him started at university, though," she said grudgingly, but quickly hardened her voice and added, "Good thing no one asked me to pay for his funeral. I would've told them to just dump him into Lake Ontario!"

Well, I certainly know where she stands! He decided there wasn't anything to be gained by prolonging the call.

He had one last question. Could she tell him how to contact her son? Fred was a first-year student at the University of Western Ontario in London, she told him, and gave him Fred's phone number.

*

Two days later, Saturday, Don set out to meet Len Newson's son. It was a picture-perfect winter's day in southern Ontario. The air temperature was -4C at 10 A.M. as Don turned onto the westbound lanes of the 401 Highway south of Pearson International Airport, heading for London.

With the cruise control set at 110 kilometres per hour, he reflected on his dinner date with Yvonne last night. It was the first time he'd seen her since before Christmas, when, by mutual agreement, they'd decided their relationship could use a breather. That, he recalled thinking, usually meant 'thanks, it's been nice knowing you' and that was the last they'd see of each other. At least that's how his flings with Karen and Joan had ended. They had been the only other women he'd dated for any length of time since his divorce.

He wasn't sure why, but he was glad he'd called Yvonne Thursday night. And she had seemed genuinely pleased to hear from him. They'd had dinner at the rustic Terra Valley Inn, a favourite of his ever since he had moved east to start his airline career.

The inn was nestled in a narrow rift in the Niagara escarpment just outside the hamlet of Mayville. Only his long-term patronage of the popular restaurant secured him a table on short notice for Friday night.

They had passed a pleasant evening, chatting comfortably while savoring their dinner: chateaubriand for two, garnished with sauce bearnaise. Don joked he could eat the sauce by the bowlful. They shared a bottle of red wine, as well as a dessert course: a local, tangy cheddar plate, complimented with crackers, grapes and apple slices. Their amiable mood continued on the thirty-minute drive back to Yvonne's apartment building in Brampton. Spending the night was never mentioned - or even hinted at - by either of them. This was fine with Don. Sex during their relationship had always been enjoyable, but in his mind it wasn't the main reason he'd called her.

Traffic thinned out quickly after he passed the second exit to Milton and Don reset the cruise control to 120. His two- year-old Buick Park Avenue settled into a quiet, effortless ride on the smooth, dry asphalt surface.

Face it buddy, you're not getting any younger, he sighed. *She could be the one after all.* The adage about not wanting to grow old alone seemed to crop up more often lately, he mused.

Yvonne had taken his face in her hands and given him a warm and lingering kiss before she let herself out last night. "Call me again. *Soon,*" she said. It was half-request, half-question. He promised he would. And he meant it...

*

Carling had never been to London before, but he had consulted a street map prior to setting out, and easily found the house Fred Newson shared with five other students in the city's north end. The two-storey, red brick dwelling had four vehicles parked end-to-end in the driveway alongside. The porch held as many bicycles, the alternative mode of travel for the inhabitants. Six or seven cases of 'empties' were stacked beside the front door, solid evidence that beer was still the beverage of choice for university students.

There was no mistaking the lean, good-looking and sandy-haired youth who answered the door bell as other than an offspring of the dead captain. The lad was definitely taller than his dad, though. Len's vital statistics listed his height at five feet, eight inches.

After introducing himself, Don asked Fred to suggest a good place for lunch, preferably one that might not be too crowded on a Saturday. The student thought for a moment, obviously eliminating a few before replying. "There's a bistro about ten minutes from here, sort've Italian-type food...that probably should be okay," he shrugged.

"Sounds great! I'm starving!" He indicated his car and said, "Just point me in the right direction and tell me when to stop." He hoped his levity would put the young man at ease. Fred had been surprised - even shocked - when Don had called him and mentioned the possibility that his father's death hadn't been an accident after all.

The purpose of the private investigator's trip to London was two-fold. First, he was hoping Len's son could shed some light on when and how his dad had acquired the money that he used to pay off the arrears in support payments to his ex-wife.

Secondly, he wanted to get his hands on the dead man's flight bag. There just might be a clue - a phone number, maybe a name or address - anything that could explain his sudden change in fortune that Ed Kirkham had made reference to.

During the drive to the restaurant and after ordering lunch, Don got the young man talking about his life at the university. Fred spoke freely about his courses in business administration, his roommates, and what he liked about the city. By the time their lasagna and salad arrived, he seemed quite at ease and said he didn't mind answering questions about his parent's separation and eventual divorce.

He was thirteen years old when Len left the armed forces, he said, and became aware of the almost daily arguments and shouting matches between his folks soon after they'd moved to Toronto. The bitterness increased on his mother's part after she took him and his sister and moved out. Things only got worse. Money, it seemed, was the major problem. His mother said it was because their father wasn't paying her as much as he was supposed to. This was after the divorce was final.

Don let him tell his story without interruption. He got the impression Fred hadn't spoken to anyone about his family's break up for a long time, but was glad for the chance to let it out.

When Fred finished, he asked him, "Did you see your Dad after the divorce?"

"Yes, but not very often. More at the beginning, I guess. He was supposed to have visiting rights to me and my sister Janey once a month, but not overnight. I know he was really mad about that."

His mother didn't want them to see their father at all, and eventually he stopped coming down to Fred and his sister. He'd phone though, and sent birthday cards and Christmas presents.

Did he remember when his Dad finally sent some of the money he owed? Yes, a few years before he died, he knew that Len had sent his mother a large cheque.

"Actually it surprised the heck out of her," he said, "she couldn't believe it." His mother paid off her lawyers' bills, and a bunch of other debts. "He started sending support payments regularly and Mom had finally landed a decent paying job," he added, "so she was a lot happier for a while."

Don guessed that the wage garnishee slapped on Len figured in there somewhere too, but decided there was nothing to be gained by mentioning it to Fred. He touched on his investigation into his dad's death, but just briefly. Before the young man could ask, Don assured

Fred he'd let him know if and when he came up any new information.

Well, it was worth the drive, Don figured, as he navigated his way back to the 401. He'd learned more about Len's unexplained improvement in his financial situation, temporary as it was. And the flight bag his son had lent him might provide even more revealing information. Don assured him he would return it as soon as he checked through it, but Fred told him there was no hurry.

*

While Don was recounting his February trip and the weeks that followed for James, they had moved from the pub to a small park not far from the High Street, and found a bench in the shade of a tall plane tree.

"Most interesting," James said. "Two seemingly planned killings, and two suspicious deaths. All related? Quite possible. But your problem is uncovering a conclusive link. Perhaps that's where this mystery woman comes in..."

"Yeah, that's why I'm hoping we can track her down. And soon..." shrugged Don.

They sat in silence for well over a minute before James spoke again. "And you haven't had much success to date profiling the other American victims, you say."

"No, but I haven't given up. I should hear from Krantz's best friend before too much longer. He quit the airline and moved to California soon after Krantz died, and has been sailing somewhere in the South Pacific. According to his sister, he was due back last week, and she promised to give him my message."

Their conversation turned to what Don had learned about the personal life of the Glasgow victim, Ray Flores, when he journeyed to Florida to meet the dead captain's father back in April...

*

Trying to get any useful information about Ray Flores by phone had proved futile. The airline he had flown for was in receivership and no one he spoke to had time to answer his questions. One of the company's managers suggested he contact Juan Flores, Ray's father. When Don called, Juan expressed his eagerness to meet him, even to the point of offering to pay for Don's airfare. That wouldn't be necessary, Don told him, and he arrived a few days later at the senior Flores' office.

He was greeted warmly by a slight, distinguished-looking man with unmistakable Latin features: dark brown eyes, copper-coloured skin, and a neatly-trimmed mustache. Don put his age at seventy-five, plus or minus a year or two. Juan Flores had prospered since arriving in Florida in 1963, one of thousands of boat people fleeing Castro's Cuba. His import/export fruit business had grown to a multi-million dollar enterprise, mainly as a result of the exhausting twelve-hour days he put in during the start-up years.

He had high hopes that his only son Ramon would join him and eventually take over the firm, but that was not to be. The younger man got the flying bug as a teenager, and that was all he ever wanted to do.

"So, what could we do?" he asked rhetorically. "Ramon paid for most of his flying lessons himself, money earned working in our warehouses. Apparently he was a good pilot, and he was overjoyed when he got a job with the cargo airline flying jets." Juan paused and stared out his office window. Don thought he saw a tear run down his weathered cheek.

He let the father talk on about his son, even though it was causing him pain. Ramon had been a changed man in the year or so before his accident, he admitted, and distanced himself from his parents. His father had begged him to open up to him and offered more than once to help him in any way possible.

Eventually Juan brought up his son's death, mentioning that he'd been told very little about it. What could Don tell him? Whatever it was, it couldn't cause him anymore grief than that which he already carried, he told him.

Don recounted what he had learned in Glasgow, specifically why the Scottish detective in charge of his son's case was no longer looking at it as an accident, but a deliberate assault. He commented on the similarities between Ray's death and those of Newson and Krantz. He stressed that so far he hadn't found hard evidence to link them, but felt it was only a matter of time. In summing up, he broached the subject that the pilots may have unwittingly been involved in something they shouldn't have, and left it at that.

Juan had taken it all in, his face an expressionless mask. When Don finished, he jotted something down on a note pad before he spoke.

"Thank you for being so candid, Mr. Carling. I will make inquiries. It may take time, but I have sources that I can call on. If Ramon was in trouble, I will find out why."

Before they parted, the father handed him an envelope. "That's to help your investigation. Please find out the truth about Ramon's death, for mine and my wife's sake. Good or bad, I want to know," he urged.

When Don began to protest and tried to hand back the envelope back, the old man wouldn't let him.

"No, no, please take it. If you need more just call." He all but tucked the envelope into Don's coat pocket for him.

Don's didn't open the envelope until his return flight had reached cruising altitude thirty minutes after leaving Miami. It contained a cheque for $25,000 in US funds.

The money was still untouched in his business account.

12

HIGHGATE VILLAGE, JUNE 25

Don and James had left the park and walked back to the High Street as the Canadian finished talking.

"Have I answered all your questions, James?"

"Yes, yes, that's put me nicely in the picture. I must say it's a most intriguing scenario, these chaps being knocked off like that," James said. "And who's to say there won't be more victims?"

"Yeah, that possibility has occurred to me," said Don. "More the reason to find this woman."

"Agreed. And you're quite right. This is the place to look for signs of her." The retired spy spread his arms to indicate the village around them.

*

Carling and his new partner exchanged phone numbers and agreed to touch base the next afternoon. Before they parted Don pointed out the newsagent's shop and the Glory of Venice restaurant. Coates said he would take a stroll around the area, much as Carling had done the previous day, to get the lay of the land.

Don headed for Mr. Patel's shop. His reception was no warmer than yesterday: his greeting acknowledged with an unintelligible grunt from the proprietor. He headed for the shelf containing the foreign newspapers. The Polish newspaper was gone, but the Sunday paper from Berlin was still there. Mr. Patel eyed him warily as Don approached the counter. He was busy setting out a pile of the latest edition of the *Evening Standard.*

"I see the Warsaw paper is gone. Did the buyer match the description of the woman I described yesterday?" Don asked.

"No, she was quite elderly," he admitted.

Don picked up a copy of the *Standard* and slid a one pound coin across the desk. He pocketed the change and asked, "If I give you a phone number Mr. Patel, do you think you could call me if someone comes in for the Berlin paper before the weekend?" When Patel hesitated, Don put a ten pound note on top of the card with his hotel number on it. "Just call and say she was in, that's all I need to know."

The proprietor picked up the card and the bank note and folded them into his breast pocket. "I suppose I could do that," he shrugged.

*

Back in his hotel room after dinner Don went over his notes, trying to draw a clearer picture of the possible connections between the victims. The dates of their deaths didn't seem to offer any clues; Newson in May '95; Krantz in October '96; Flores last New Year's and now Rosen's.

The fact they were all single or divorced was one thing they had in common. Newson and Rosen both had financial problems. Whether the same situation applied to Krantz or Flores wasn't known yet. And three of them had apparently been worried, withdrawn, or distracted, according to his findings, in the months prior to their deaths.

He looked over the information that Rod Weathers had collected for him. One important factor stood out: the Pembury House here in London was the only common hotel where all the airlines the four dead men worked for booked rooms.

At least two of the victims - again Rosen and Newson - were known to had a female companion here in London. Could it have been the same one? The woman he was hoping to find living in the Highgate area? And what brought them together in the first place? The hotel didn't have a bar or lounge open to the public, so it was reasonable to assume this lady didn't get picked up by the pilots at the hotel. There were plenty of possibilities near the Pembury, though. But if she initiated the contact, how would she know whom to target?

Don put his pen down, stood up and stretched. He gazed out his fourth floor window at the steady stream of cars passing along the tree-lined street below. *It's amazing how quiet traffic is in London compared to other large cities*, he thought. It was still relatively light outside, even at 9 P.M., with the sun still partially visible above the northwestern horizon. He debated going down to the hotel bar for a nightcap before turning in early. But he couldn't get the thought out of his mind that somehow there must be a connection between the Pembury House and the woman he was trying to find.

Maybe a chat with the night man there might provide some answers...

*

After he'd made the decision to visit the crew hotel, Carling consulted his pocket-sized London A to Z street atlas. It wasn't that far from the Beech Tree Inn, probably about a mile, and he quickly worked out the most direct routing. *If I walk at a leisurely pace, I should reach the Pembury House shortly after 10 P.M.*, he figured. According to Ruth Headley, the hotel's manager, that was when the night man started his overnight shift. He made one wrong turn en route, which cost him seven or eight minutes. Still, it was just after ten when he turned onto Pembury Road and approached the hotel from the east. The front door was propped open and Don could see a man's head bent over the reception desk as he stepped up to the entrance. The man looked up as the private investigator crossed the foyer.

"Are you looking for something?" he asked.

"Good evening," Don said, and handed him a business card. He gave the man time to look at it before he continued. "I'm investigating the death of Captain Rosen, the American pilot who was killed last weekend. I was hoping you could answer a few questions for me."

The night man went pale and fumbled with the card.

"Sir, you... you shouldn't be here," he stammered. "This is a private hotel for airline personnel only." He tried to give the card back to Carling. His reaction puzzled Don.

"Yes, I know that. But I've been hired by the pilots federation to--"

"Don! What the hell are you doin' here?" boomed a voice from behind.

He turned to see Ralph Woods approaching, his face flushed and smiling. One of Don's former pilot colleagues used to refer to it as the 'Guinness grin'. The Northern Flyer captain was followed by two younger men. Don took them to be Ralph's crew members. He was right.

"Hello Ralph," Don smiled, extending his hand. "I'm here on business. Looking into the death of the Atlantic Best captain."

"...Oh yeah, it made the Toronto papers earlier this week," replied Woods, more serious now.

"We had a drink with one of their crews earlier tonight up at The Crow. They were still pretty upset about it." Don had passed the pub a few minutes ago.

"That's only natural," offered Don

"Hey listen, come and have a beer with us! We're gonna grab a nightcap before hittin' the sack. We're not out until late tomorrow afternoon."

He put one hand on Carling's shoulder and indicated the way to the lounge. "It's okay Alf, he's one of us," he told the night man, who was still looking askance at Don.

Woods introduced Don to his companions, First Officer Jack Miller and Kip Beeston, his flight engineer.

The lounge was just behind the reception desk. In one corner sat an older refrigerator, which served as the unofficial bar. Ralph opened it and pulled out four cans of Tennents lager. The bar operated on the honor system. A hand-lettered sign read 'ONE POUND PER CAN'. Woods pushed a five pound note into the cigar box affixed to the door.

"An extra pound for Alf," he explained. The night man made a few extra quid keeping the fridge stocked.

The three pilots listened closely while Don told them why he was in London. When Ralph asked if he had made any progress, Don mentioned the woman. Back in February Ed Kirkham, another Northern Flyer pilot, had suggested that Newson had a lady friend in London.

Ralph Woods nodded. "Yeah, I'd heard that too. Maybe it's the same woman this Rosen fella was seein'," he ventured.

"It's a possibility alright" replied Don. "Finding her is my priority at the moment." Not wanting to get into what might lead to conjecture - and start rumors - he steered their conversation away from his investigation. By 10:45 Miller and Beeston had finished their beers and headed up to their rooms.

Don glanced around the lounge as they departed. The area was just a large open room to the side and behind the foyer and reception desk. Conversation, especially if it were loud or boisterous would easily be overheard by anyone at the desk. In fact, Don observed, even though Alf appeared to be engrossed in reading a newspaper, he'd been keeping one ear on their conversation. Don declined Ralph's offer of another beer.

"How about a coffee, then? Alf's usually got a pot goin' in the kitchen by now. It'll probably taste like mud, but at least it's wet," he chuckled.

With that unappealing description Don decided to pass on the coffee, too.

Don changed chairs so that his back was to the front desk. He wanted to ask Ralph a few questions regarding the night man, and he didn't want to be overheard.

What sort of chap was Alf? Friendly? Was he a busybody? Meaning did he take an interest in the personal lives of the hotel's regular crews, for instance? Who else works the night shift?

"Hmm, yeah, I suppose you could say he's a bit nosey at times," confided Ralph, matching Don's lowered voice. "Yes, he probably knows a fair bit about some of the guys' personal lives, now that you bring it up. Asking who's been divorced or separated since their last trip. That kind of thing, when they're sittin' around in here after the pubs close."

"Does he ever have a beer with the guys?"

"No, can't say I've ever seen him do that. Mind you, he gets invited to often enough, that's for sure. But no, personally I've never seen him take up the offer."

Don tried a few more questions, but Ralph didn't know anything about Alf's background. He was yawning now, his evening's alcohol intake catching up with him.

Don thanked him for the beer and the information. "Oh, one last thing, Ralph. The manager told me the hotel policy is no visitors after 10 P.M. You and I both know a rule like that never stopped a randy pilot before, did it?"

Ralph chuckled softly. "You wouldn't be referring to the old 'little head leading the big head around' adage, would you?" He laughed again. "Nah, nothing's changed since you packed it in, Don!"

Don couldn't help but laugh himself. "So Alf there would be the last bastion a fella would have to get by late at night then?"

"Well, I suppose so. But one could bring a friend in earlier. There's usually one of the gals on before Alf comes in."

"True. Anyway, I wouldn't mind a short talk with Alf. How about putting in a good word for me?"

Woods did as he was asked. He told Alf that his good friend was a former airline captain and that he was working for the pilots federation. He should feel free to answer Don's questions, he told him.

"I'll vouch for his discretion, you can be sure of that," he said, tapping Alf on the arm, and giving him a knowing wink.

"Good luck with your investigation, Don," he said as they shook hands. "And let's get together for lunch after you get back to Toronto."

After Woods entered the lift, Don turned his attention to Alf.

"Alf, I won't take more than a few minutes of your time. Just a few questions, that's all..."

As it turned out though, Don spent nearly fifteen minutes dragging information out of the him. They were only interrupted once, when the buzzer for the now closed front door sounded. Alf reached under the desk and pushed a button to unlock it. Two casually dressed men came in. Don pegged them for Americans, confirmed when one of them offered a friendly 'Howdy gents' as they approached. They gave Alf their room numbers and he retrieved keys from the row of boxes mounted on the wall behind the desk.

"They're with Cargo Swift International," he said, as they headed for the lift.

Alf reluctantly admitted that he had known Bert Rosen. He allowed that Rosen had stayed at the Pembury quite often over the last year, and that they had been on a first name basis.

Did he ever see Captain Rosen with an attractive woman, probably with auburn or brunette hair, age about forty?

His answer was too quick. An abrupt 'no'. Did he ever see him either entering or leaving the hotel with any woman? Once again, just a curt 'no'.

What about other pilots bringing female companions into the hotel after hours? Did that ever happen? Don assured the night man that he wasn't on a witch hunt and that any information Alf gave him would remain confidential.

"Against the rules, sir. Worth my job if the manager found out," was all he would say.

Don let it go. It probably happened, but it wasn't really pertinent to his investigation.

He switched tactics and got Alf talking about himself.

How long had he worked at the Pembury? Ever since it opened in 1977.

Was he looking forward to retirement? This was Don's subtle way of asking how old he was. He looked to be well over sixty.

No, not unless his health failed. Wouldn't know what to do with himself, no family, and he lived alone.

Don decided to butter him up. "You could be here for a long time to come then, you look pretty healthy to me!" he praised.

Alf swallowed the bait and finally cracked a smile. "Well, I'm almost 70, you know. But I don't overeat, not like a lot of people these days. And just the occasional drink."

Not likely, thought Don. Alf had the face of a long-time and regular imbiber. The collapsed veins in his purple-tinged nose and cheeks gave him away.

Don stuck out his hand. "Alf, thanks for your time. I'll be on my way."

He could almost feel Alf's relief through his handshake.

"Not'a 'tal, sir. Too bad about Captain Rosen. He seemed like a nice fellow. I'll unlock the door for you. Just push it open," he said.

"Great. Thanks again," replied Don. He turned away as if to leave and then stopped.

"Almost forgot," he said, reaching into his pocket. "Do you remember this chap?" He held out a palm-sized photo of Daniel Krantz. "He was a captain with International Airways, must of stayed here a few times..."

A cautious expression quickly returned to Alf's face. He fumbled on his reading glasses before replying.

"Nope, don't recall ever seeing him," he said.

"How about this man?" Carling had replaced the first photo with one of Ray Flores, the Glasgow victim. Alf leaned closer. A bead of sweat was now visible on his brow. "He was a DC-8 captain for Globe Wide. Flew to London often, I'm told. Friendly chap, too. Would've stayed here a couple of times last year, or even earlier," prompted Don.

Alf straightened up and removed his glasses. "No...can't say as I know him, either. Sorry," he said lamely. He lowered his eyes. His hands were busy now, apparently shuffling paper under the desk top.

Don had what he wanted. "Okay, thanks anyway. I'm off."

As he walked back to his hotel, he mentally filed away what he had just learned. He could accept that the night man might not have recognized Krantz.

But Ray Flores was a different story...

13

THURSDAY, JUNE 26

The message light had been flashing when Don got back to his room last night. Derek Houghton had called. He asked Don to ring him first thing in the morning.

Don put in a wake up call for 8 A.M., and was sound asleep when the steady ringing jarred him awake. He ordered breakfast from room service before dialing Derek's mobile. The inspector answered after the second ring.

"Morning Derek. What's up?"

"Don, the DCI in charge of this airline chap's killing wants a meeting with you. His name is Upton, Spencer Upton. Not much personality-wise, but a good copper. I thought I'd pick you up about nine and we'll run up and have a chat with him. Will that work for you?"

"Uhh, sure. Definitely. I'll be out front waiting for you," he replied.

*

By 8:40 Carling had showered and shaved. The Sky News weather gal was promising viewers another fine summer day with the afternoon temperature reaching 24C. Don would have preferred to dress casually, but went with a shirt and tie, knowing the British policemen would be similarly attired. He packed copies of his case files and photos in a soft-sided briefcase and locked his laptop in his suitcase before leaving the room.

He was enjoying the morning sun outside the inn when Derek drove up. He was driving an unmarked police vehicle, a slate-grey Ford Mondeo sedan. The two shook hands as Don settled into the front passenger seat and fastened the seat belt.

"Looks like another warm day in the making, Derek" he said, loosening his tie. "I'm beginning to think the UK's reputation for lousy weather is all a myth!"

"My pessimistic wife says it's all because of global warming. But you won't hear me complaining," said Derek. "How did you make out with James Coates?

"Just fine. He was an excellent call on your part. And he seems genuinely interested in my investigation. He's going to snoop around the area for a few days to see if there's any trace of the woman."

"Good show. He's quite the unsung hero, you know. You'd enjoy sitting down with him sometime and getting him talking about his MI5 days."

"I know I would, and I'm looking forward for a chance to do that."

*

The meeting with DCI Upton didn't get off to a good start. He kept them waiting for almost fifteen minutes after the desk sergeant buzzed his office to tell him they had arrived. Don could tell Derek was getting ticked off before he showed, and was even more miffed when Upton didn't offer any explanation for keeping them waiting.

He led them up to his office on the first floor. The large window behind his desk overlooked a busy intersection. He invited the two men to take the two hard wooden chairs across from the desk.

"Inspector Houghton tells me of you think there's a possible connection between Rosen's death and some other American pilots. What is it? Three others? Four?"

"Actually it's three, and one of them was a Canadian." He pulled out a file folder and placed it in front of Upton. "For what it's worth, you might want to have a look at these case histories I've worked up," said Don.

"I'll try and find time later," he said, sliding the folder to one side. "What I'd be most interested in is any hard evidence you might have that will help me solve this chap's killing. There isn't anything I can do about these cases," he said, tapping the folder, "at least until we are able to identify a suspect or two. Then we would pass their names on to Interpol. None of these other killings have been solved yet, I take it?"

"No, they haven't. But if you'll bear with me for a few minutes perhaps you'll see why I'm so certain they're connected."

Upton pushed his chair away from his desk and held up his wrist to check his watch. "Go ahead. You've got ten minutes," he replied sceptically.

Trying not to show his irritation with Upton's attitude, Don summarized what he knew about the three deaths prior to Rosen's.

"You won't see a connection from reading the police reports, or the autopsy results," Don said. "Accidental death was the verdict in the two on the continent, and initially the pilot killed in Glasgow was thought to have been the victim of a hit and run."

"What changed that?" Upton asked.

"The inspector who took over the investigation the morning after the body was discovered, a DCI McGrath, is quite certain the man was run down deliberately, and the coroner's report determined that the fatal injury - a fractured skull - was probably inflicted after he had been hit by vehicle. Flores was the victim of a professional hit, in McGrath's opinion."

"So we have two victims - this chap in Glasgow and now Rosen - who were deliberately targeted," said Upton.

"Right," answered Don, "and two of the four were seeing a woman here in London. There are a few other common, uhh, factors in their backgrounds that I'm looking into."

"I see, but if these killers have been so careful in the past, why did Rosen not get the same treatment?" asked Upton.

"Well, that's a good question, and one I can't answer yet. But, as I mentioned to Derek yesterday, the publicity resulting from the flight delay probably came as a surprise to his killers. They would have been under the impression that you, the London police, would have no reason to connect the case to any others," Don explained.

"That's the bit about a flight switch the killers wouldn't have known about?"

"Yes, that's right. Only cargo flights were delayed in the other cases, and that wouldn't have been especially newsworthy, is my thinking. The quote, unquote, accidental deaths only briefly made the local news."

To his credit, DCI Upton softened his stance after Don finished. "Hmm, most interesting," he said. Upton stood up, gazed out the window for a moment or so, then turned back to address Don again.

"So your take is that this woman is part of a conspiracy that used these airline chaps to carry out illegal work on its behalf, probably smuggling in some manner. And paid them sizable sums to do so. When they became a liability - for whatever reason - they were killed." He leaned on his desk, his eyes on Carling, inviting an answer.

"Yeah, that's it in a nutshell, Inspector," Don replied. "It may seem a bit of a stretch in some ways, I realize, but finding this woman just might lead us to the killers."

Upton turned to Houghton. "Any comments, Derek?"

"Well, sometimes it takes a bit of a stretch to make one's theories fit the crime, doesn't it Spencer?

"Yes, I'll grant you that. It's early days yet, but we haven't any leads to Rosen's attackers. Our informants have come up empty in spite of having sizeable amounts of lolly dangled in front of them. Doesn't fit the crime profile in the area, either. B & E's are the major doings of the local lads," said Upton. "Yes, could be the work of professionals all right."

Their conversation turned again to the woman Rosen had probably been with during the hours before he was killed.

Don laid out for Upton what he had learned about her so far. Attractive, dark-haired, about forty, and was known to have been in the Glory of Venice on more than one occasion in recent months, escorted by Rosen. This information came from Mrs. Rossani, wife of the restaurant's owner. Don also mentioned his chat with the newsagent next door to the restaurant. He thought it likely that the same woman bought a Sunday paper from Berlin every week from the shop - except this week.

"When you put this info together, I'm of the opinion that she probably lives in a flat within walking distance of the High Street," he added.

Upton's team had uncovered the same information except for the fact that she might be from Germany, or at least German speaking. "Good work," he acknowledged, "Mr. Patel never said anything to us about the newspaper."

'*One point for me,*' Don told himself.

Upton handed him a sheet of fax paper. "Here's something I received yesterday," he said, "I'll have a copy made for you."

It was a list of transactions on Rosen's Visa card for the last three months. It wasn't long, just seventeen transactions in all. He'd only used the card twice outside the States, both times in London. The most recent charge was on May 16th when he charged forty-seven pounds at the Taverna Santos. The 16th had been a Friday. The previous charge occurred the week before on Saturday, May the 10th.

"What sort of business is Mary & Friends?" asked Don.

"Well, it's not an escort service, if that's what you're thinking," replied Upton, with a short smile. "It's a pet shop. Located close by the Archway tube station. Nothing fancy - puppies, birds, fish and the like. Rosen purchased a six-week-old tabby kitten, along with a carrying cage. No other information asked for or given, according to the lady who owns the shop."

"So, a gift for his lady friend, maybe."

"No doubt, but untraceable. The Greek restaurant was a dead end as well. Large place over in Hampstead. Crowded on weekends. None of the staff remembered Rosen. Not surprising, unless he'd been a regular customer."

A buzzer sounded on Upton's intercom. "Mr. Wiggins is here now, Inspector," said a crisp feminine voice.

"Tell him I'll be a few more minutes. Thanks, Mona," answered Upton. "Finding this woman would appear to be the priority for both our investigations at this point, so this is what I'm going to do..."

The DCI said he would have his team canvass all the apartment buildings in the Highgate Village area. They would talk to superintendents of the larger places and each tenant in the smaller ones.

"How about surveillance tapes?" suggested Derek.

"Wouldn't hurt to check them out. Especially those from bank card machines. Might even get lucky and catch her and Rosen picking up some late night snacks in the 24 hour deli, eh?"

His last remark brought chuckles from Don and Derek. "You never know, it's worth a try," shrugged Houghton.

*

"Spence isn't a bad sort once he realizes the other fellow isn't out to upstage him," offered Derek as he and Don walked to the car park.

"Ahh, no offense taken. I've run into guys like him before. They just need a little stroking, don't they?"

As promised, DCI Upton had the clerk make a copy of Rosen's Visa card usage before they left the station. He also asked Don to pass on any information he came up with on his own. Carling agreed, and they had exchanged cards.

"Anywhere I can drop you, Don?" asked Derek when they reached his car.

The police station Upton worked out of was located on Holloway Road, a few miles from Highgate Village. Don had arranged to meet James Coates at 12:30. It was just after eleven o'clock now.

"Would Hampstead be taking you out of your way? I may as well have a look at this restaurant."

Mid-morning traffic up Highgate Hill and around the top of Hampstead Heath was light, and fifteen minutes later Derek braked smoothly to a stop just past the trendy borough's main intersection.

"It's up the street about fifty yards," he said, pointing to the left. "You can't miss it. We had a retirement party there a few years ago. Plenty of plate-throwing and too much ouzo!"

"I see," laughed Don. "Should be safe at this time of day, though! Thanks again, Derek, much obliged. And thanks for the invitation. I'll take you up on it if I'm still here."

Rod and Kate Weathers would be at the Houghton's for dinner on Saturday and Derek had invited Don to join them.

14

Don wasn't sure what, if anything, he expected to learn from visiting the Taverna Santos. But Rosen had been here last month and therefore it was worth checking out. Finding pieces of the puzzle he was hoping to solve was going to take a lot of legwork.

The first impression he had while standing opposite the restaurant was that it looked out of place. The tree-lined side street was home to estate agents offices, a dental clinic, an antique shop and three or four other small businesses. In contrast, the restaurant's wide street front facade, with it's floor-to-ceiling folding glass doors and brightly painted blue and white frames seemed to be imposing on its genteel surroundings.

It was warm now, and Don shucked off his jacket and threw it over his shoulder before he crossed the narrow street. Most of the doors were open giving direct access to the interior. A middle-aged waiter looked up from his table setting duties as Don walked in...

"Take any table you like, sir. I'll bring you the luncheon menu," he said.

"Actually, I'm not ready for lunch yet. Can I get a coffee, though? A large cappuccino?"

The waiter shouted back to someone Don couldn't see with the order. He chose a table set for two along the wall. Once his eyes adjusted to the lesser light inside, he glanced around. It was quite a bit larger than most London restaurants he'd been in. The main room in which he was sitting had at least thirty tables. An archway led into another room at the rear. To the left of the arch was a well-stocked bar. A small stage took up the space on the other side of the opening. Instrument cases and amplifiers were piled on it. A hardwood floor directly in front of the stage left no doubt that dancers would be able to hear the music.

The wall opposite Don was decorated with colourful murals depicting life in the Greek Isles. The wall he was sitting against was covered with photographs of patrons celebrating various occasions.

"Who takes the pictures?" Don asked as his coffee arrived, delivered not by the male waiter but by a vivacious young woman with unmistakable Mediterranean features.

"Oh, my Uncle Theo takes them," she smiled. "By the dozen. But only on Friday and Saturday nights."

"Does he sell them?"

"No, no, Papa won't let him! But some people give him money anyway, I think."

"So he just takes pictures of people having a good time and sticks them up on the wall?"

"Yes, that's exactly what he does. Sometimes he takes two: one for the customer and one for the wall. So when they come again they'll be reminded of other good times, he says. Some are old, maybe ten years or more."

"Long before you started here, right?"

She laughed. "Well yes, but not too long. I started helping out when I was twelve, you know. That was almost seven years ago."

"Really! I bet you'll be running the place before much longer."

"Never! I'm only working to pay for my university. After that, 'Ciao, baby!'"

"Well, good luck with your studies," smiled Don. "Mind if I take a look at the photos when I finish my coffee?"

"Of course not. Take as long as you want," she said, rewarding him with a dazzling smile of her own. "If you want anything else, just ask."

If DCI Upton and his team were on top of things, they would have checked to see if Rosen's photo was among those on the wall, thought Carling. Maybe they'd even interviewed this Uncle Theo.

Having finished the surprisingly flavourful coffee, he stood and slowly made his way along the wall. Most of the photos were of couples, all wearing big smiles. Obviously Uncle Theo waited until his subjects had been into the wine or beer before he pounced. Family parties were the second most photographed scenes.

Don had almost reached the last batch when he did a double take...

"Shit!" he exclaimed out loud. That's--"

He hurried back to his table, tore open his briefcase, and pulled out the photos of the dead pilots. He shuffled through them, his fingers having a hard time keeping up with his brain. When he found the one he wanted he rushed back to the photo that had stopped him cold.

He compared the 4 X 6 black and white glossy he held with the smaller, coloured Polaroid snapshot stuck on the wall.

There wasn't any doubt. He'd caught his first big break.

The handsome smiling Latino face in the photo was that of Captain Ramon [Ray] Flores - killed in Glasgow last New Year's Eve. And he had his arm around an attractive woman. She looked to be about forty, but could be younger.

There was only one drawback: the woman had blonde hair...

Don pulled the photo off the wall. It had been attached with double-sided clear tape.

He turned to find the waitress and the older man eyeing him suspiciously.

"Sorry folks, but I need this photo. I'll bring it back if you like but I haven't got time to explain right now," he apologized. "Here, this is for the coffee and the photo." He shoved a five pound note in the speechless young lady's hand, grabbed his briefcase and jacket and hurried out into the street.

*

Don walked quickly back to the intersection with Heath Street where Houghton had dropped him off. Five frustrating minutes passed before he was able to flag down a taxi.

"Where to guv?" asked the driver, as Don scrambled into the passenger compartment.

"Highgate Village, please! Uhh, just head for the High Street. I'll tell you when to stop." The bearded driver grunted his assent and pulled away from the curb. Traffic was much heavier now that it was past noon. He debated calling DCI Upton to tell him of his discovery, but decided to wait until after he'd talked to James Coates. He was going to be a few minutes late as it was for their rendezvous.

At12:30 the taxi was crawling up the High Street, trapped behind two buses on the busy two lane street. He tapped the sliding glass window behind the driver's head to get his attention. "Anywhere along here will do, driver. Thanks," directed Don. He was only a few blocks from his destination now and figured he could make better time on foot.

At the next corner the cab driver pulled over and turned off the meter. "Seven pounds sixty, guv," he said.

Don gave him ten pounds, and told him to keep the change. He wasn't going to waste time calculating a more reasonable tip. He half-jogged, half-walked the remaining distance to the restaurant. He stepped inside, and scanned the crowded Cafe Uno twice before he spotted Coates. He had to smile. The retired agent definitely blended in with his surroundings.

*

"James! Sorry to keep you waiting. Traffic, you know," he offered lamely, his breathing almost back to normal .

The retired MI5 man waved away his apology. "Think nothing of it, Don. You'll soon learn anything less than thirty minutes is considered on time by London standards. Beastly situation nowadays! Far too many vehicles dashing about!"

After ordering, Don told James about his meeting with Upton and the credit card information that led him to the Taverna Santos. He showed him the snapshot of Flores and the blonde woman.

"What do you think? Is this woman a real blonde or not? Flores was killed six months ago, so this must have been taken sometime last year, maybe earlier. If it's the same woman Rosen was seeing, maybe she's changed back to her natural color."

Coates put on a pair of reading glasses to study the photo.

"I'm no expert on women's hair, but it wouldn't be difficult to get a proper opinion," he said. "But first I suggest you get this enlarged. I recall passing one of those InstaPrint shops along the High Street and--"

"And I remember seeing a hairdresser's salon yesterday," interjected Don. "That should give us our answer, right?"

While they ate lunch, they discussed the other purchase Rosen had charged to his credit card in London last month. They agreed with the DCI Upton's supposition: the kitten was probably a present for his female companion.

"Interesting," murmured James. "I wonder what she did with it?"

"Pardon?"

"Nothing really. Just a thought. It'll keep. Let's get on with the task at hand, shall we?"

Don shrugged, and signalled their waiter.

While they were waiting for him to return with Don's credit card, Coates picked up the photo again and studied it. As he handed it to Don, he said, "We know one other detail about her from this, don't we?"

Don was up to the challenge. "Yeah, for what it's worth, she's probably left-handed."

The woman was holding a cigarette in the fingers of her left hand...

*

Carling had the print shop make copies in three different sizes. The copy with the best definition was approximately four inches by six. Two larger prints were quite grainy and the facial colors of Flores and his companion appeared washed out compared to the original.

Their next stop was only a few doors away. Two hairdressers in the Elite Beauty Salon were busy with customers, while two others were standing at the reception counter. One, who they soon learned was Mrs. Hodge, the owner, flashed Don a questioning smile and asked politely, "What can we do for you gentlemen?"

Don apologized for their intrusion and quickly explained what they were after. Bemused, they studied the photocopy he showed them. Their decision was quick and unanimous: the woman was definitely not a natural blonde.

"Out of a bottle, and not very well done at that," suggested the owner, the older of the two.

Don decided his cause wouldn't be advanced by knowing what she meant by her rather catty criticism.

"Do either of you recognize her?" James asked. Both studied her again before shaking their heads. Mrs. Hodge took the photo over and showed it to the other hairdressers and received the same answer.

"Sorry. She might use another salon. You might try Margie's just up the road. You can't miss it," she told them, handing the photo back to Don.

"Why not?" shrugged Don. "We'll stop by there. And thanks, ladies. Appreciate your help. Cheerio now!"

Ten minutes later they emerged from Margie's Salon. No one there recognized the mystery woman either.

Outside, Don pondered his next move. Coates left him, saying he wanted to get on with his check of the area. "Talk to you later, old boy," he said, as he strolled away.

Don wanted to get the photo into DCI Upton's hands that afternoon. If the photo was re-touched, giving her hair a more brunette-like coloring, they would then - theoretically - have a more recent likeness of the woman they were searching for. A police lab would have the capability to handle the task.

It was only 2:25 though, according to the large clock over the doorway to the NatWest bank, and Don decided to follow up on one of his earlier leads first. He crossed the street and made his way to the Glory of Venice.

The restaurant wasn't busy. Just three customers left from the lunch crowd, businessmen lingering over their coffees.

"Good Afternoon, Julia," he said. The restaurant owner's wife was busy at her desk sorting through a collection of credit card slips. She glanced up briefly, not recognizing him immediately. "Can you spare me a few minutes?"

When she looked up again, her memory locked on, and she flashed him a winsome smile.

"Ahh, Mr. Carling! You come about the lady? Have you found her yet?"

"Yes, that's why I'm here. But no, I haven't found her. But I have something to show you..."Julia peered closely at the blown-up copy of Flores and the woman. She echoed the hairdressers' remarks about the woman's hair not being her true color. She didn't recognize her, though.

Could she visualize her with dark hair, and if so, was it the woman she remembered coming in with Rosen last month? he probed.

Maybe, she offered hesitantly, but she couldn't be any more definite than that. What about the man? Any recollection of him? Not necessarily with this woman.

She was more definite about Flores. "Him I don't know. He is very handsome, yes? But I don't see him before. But let me check with Antonio. He is on his lunch break in the kitchen. Let me get him," she said, handing the photo back to Carling.

Don remembered her telling him that Antonio was a relative of her husband and their only full-time waiter. She returned a minute later with a slight young man in his mid-twenties in tow. He was wiping pasta sauce from his mouth with a large white napkin. Julia introduced them and Don apologized for interrupting his lunch.

"Is okay," he shrugged.

First, Don showed him a picture of Bert Rosen.

"This is the American who was killed. I see his picture in the newspaper," stated Antonio.

"Yes, that's right. But do you remember him eating here? Julia says you probably would have served him."

He shrugged again. "Si, I remember him. Last month, maybe..."

Don showed him the photo of Flores and the blonde woman. His reaction was immediate.

"Si, si! She I know!" He ran his fingers through his thick head of curly black hair. He pointed at the cigarette in her hand. "Always smoking! And she wants ashtray changed all the time! Only two cigarettes finished, she ask for clean one!" He flicked his hand the way Italian men do to show disdain.

Was there anything else he could remember about her, Don wondered. Antonio gave another noncommittal shrug of his slim shoulders, and looked at his watch. Don kept eye contact with him. "Nothing?" He asked again.

"She have good figure for a woman her age, I guess. She have nice brea--"

"What do you mean, *her age?*" demanded Julia, slapping him on his shoulder. "She same age as me!" She rattled off something in their native language and swatted him again. Antonio flinched and broke out laughing.

"Si, si, you are good looking too, Aunt Julia!"

Don joined in the laughter and they parted on friendly terms. He would drop in again after he had a retouched photo of the woman, he told them. For now though, he was satisfied with what he'd learned.

He could place the mystery woman in the Glory of Venice - at least more than once during the past year or so. The waiter recalled her with bleach-blonde hair but didn't recognize Flores. Both remembered Rosen dining with a dark-haired woman in recent months, but couldn't say for sure if she was the same woman. He would also tackle Mr. Patel again after he had a better likeness of her. If he could come up with a positive visual identification, it should make it easier to put a name to her.

He called DCI Upton and told him about the photo. The inspector asked where he was calling from. "Wait in front of the restaurant. I'll have a patrol car pick you up," he instructed. "Should be one in the area."

Five minutes later a silvery-grey police car with the distinctive checkerboard striping along its side panels braked to a stop in front of him. Don identified himself to the uniformed driver and was dropped off at the Holloway Road station soon afterwards.

*

Upton was waiting for him and ushered Don into his office. A younger man seated inside rose as they entered and Upton introduced him.

"This is my sergeant, David Ross, he's my right-hand man on the Rosen case," he explained.

"A pleasure, Mr. Carling," smiled Ross, gripping the Canadian's hand firmly.

" Don will do just fine, David."

"So what have you found, Don? And I wonder how *we* missed it?" Upton added, casting an accusing glare at his subordinate.

"You didn't miss it, Inspector. Maybe I didn't make myself clear on the phone. It isn't a photo of Rosen, it's a picture of another one of the victims, Ramon Flores, the American who was killed in Glasgow last New Year's." He laid the Polaroid and the copies on the DCI's desk. "So you didn't find a photo of Rosen because there wasn't one."

Carling quickly explained his latest suppositions about the woman and her relationship with more than one of the dead men, and how a better likeness of her might give them a positive ID.

"Your tie-in based on the assumption that this blonde and the dark-haired woman are one and the same," said Upton, summing up Don's rationale.

"Exactly."

"Right then," he said, bundling up the photos. "Take these downstairs Ross, and make more copies. And treat this Polaroid like gold. If anything happens to it, I'll have your 'you-know -whats' for bookends!"

His half-serious, half-jesting remark brought a mock salute from the sergeant.

"Yes boss! And yes, I will be glad to take it down to the Yard as soon as possible," he came back, anticipating Upton's next order.

"Damned right you will! Deliver it to McKechnie personally. No one else, you hear?"

If he's gone for the day, be waiting for him in the morning. And wait until he's finished. I want them by noon tomorrow at the latest. In fact, I'll call and tell him to expect you. Off you go!"

While Sergeant Ross was making the copies, Upton was on the phone to the crime laboratory at New Scotland Yard. He caught Graeme McKechnie just as he was about to leave his office. The man was an expert in all aspects of facial imaging, ranging from Identikit drawings of suspects from victims memories to re-constructing the face of a decomposed body, Upton told Don.

Carling was impressed by how quickly and succinctly the DCI explained about the photo he was sending him, and how important it was to his murder investigation. Before ringing off Upton had wheedled a commitment from the technician to make it his first priority in the morning.

"Good man, McKechnie, the best there is. We'll have exactly what we're after by noon tomorrow, perhaps sooner. I'll ring you as soon as I get the package back from the lab," he promised.

*

Don declined Upton's offer of a lift back to his hotel. "Thanks anyway, but I'd rather walk, at least for a mile or so," he said, patting his stomach. "Need the exercise!"

The Canadian investigator didn't exactly fall into the fitness buff category, and the two or three beers he'd been enjoying each day since his arrival in London had already translated into a weight gain, he was sure. He vowed to get to the training room at his hotel for a strenuous workout in the next day or so. The alternative was unappealing: give up the beer. He did belong to a health club near his office in Toronto and worked out there at least twice a week. But his favourite exercise was riding his bike around the deserted side roads near his home early on a weekend morning. The terrain had just enough ups and downs to leave him pleasantly tired after an hour's outing.

But for now, a good walk would have to do, and he set off at a brisk pace. If he headed in a generally southwesterly direction for about thirty-five or forty minutes, he figured, he should end up close to the hotel. If all else failed, he could always grab a taxi.

Only ten minutes after he left the police station, though, he found himself passing right by Mary & Friends, the pet store where Bert Rosen had purchased a kitten last month. On a whim he decided to go in. A question had been nagging him ever since he'd left DCI Upton's office that morning...

If Rosen *had* bought the kitten as a gift for his lady friend, where would she take it if got sick, or needed a rabies shot, for instance? Mary & Friends didn't advertise veterinary services, but presumably they would recommend one if their customers inquired. The shop must use a vet for their own young animals, he thought.

His assumption was right. Without identifying himself, Don put his question to the teen-aged clerk who was busy cleaning out a rabbit cage. She wore a name tag on her jumper that proclaimed 'I'm not Mary, I'm Sarah'.

Sarah opened a drawer on the cluttered sales desk and pulled out a mimeographed sheet. It was a list of veterinarian services and kennels in the area that they recommended to new pet owners. There were six establishments listed for small animals. Three offered both vet and kennel services, and three were boarding kennels only. In answer to Don's next question, Sarah told him that if they sold a kitten that had been to a vet, the name and date would be supplied to the buyer.

"What sort of pet are you thinking about, sir?" she asked, as he looked over the list.

"Nothing at the moment, just doing some research first!" He folded the sheet and tucked it into his carrying case. "Thank you, Sarah," he smiled.

It will take some digging, but the list might provide a lead, he was thinking as he resumed walking. *If the woman has registered the cat for shots, the service she used should have her address on file.*

15

By 5:30 Don realized he wasn't on course to reach his hotel any time soon. He'd been walking for almost an hour and he was now hot and thirsty from the afternoon sun. He was on Chalk Farm Road, and, having left his street map behind that morning, not sure how far he had to go. If asked, he would never admit that he was lost, just 'temporarily unsure of his position'.

As it turned out he wasn't too far off course, and the taxi he flagged down had him back at his hotel less than ten minutes later. During the ride he made a mental list of calls he needed to make once he got to his room...

'Priority one', though, was a cold beer. After stripping down to his briefs, he opened the minibar. He had a choice: Heineken lager or Bass ale. He went with the Dutch beer and quickly drained half of it.

The red message light was blinking on his bedside phone. His secretary Joanne had called at 9:30 Toronto time, and asked that he call her back as soon as possible.

Contacting his office was number one on his list anyway. He dialed the toll-free Canada Direct number, punched in the numbers of his personal calling card, followed by his office number. Joanne answered on the second ring.

She had two messages for him. The Crown Prosecutor's office had called to remind him that he was due to testify next week, probably

Monday. KayRoy had solved a bogus airline ticket scam for a large travel agency and the trial of the defendant - a former employee - was slated to begin on Monday, the 30th.

"With any luck, he'll change his plea before the trial starts," Don told her. "There's no doubt he's guilty. But I'll be home in time to testify, I'm just not sure exactly when yet. Let me know if there are any developments, will you?" Joanne assured him she would.

The second message was from Jerry Wahl. He had just recently picked up his mail, and was responding to Carling's request that he get in touch concerning the death of Roger Krantz. He had been crewing on a friend's yacht, he'd told Joanne, and had been more or less out of touch for the last three months while they sailed the South Pacific.

*

Jerry Wahl was with Captain Dan Krantz on his fateful last trip. Carling had been trying to reach him since last winter, soon after he began his investigation. International Airways operated out of both JFK and Newark, New Jersey airports. Most of their pilots were employed on a contract basis and their flying times fluctuated with the company's fortunes. Naturally this had a direct bearing on their incomes. Don hadn't learned much about Krantz when he spoke with the airline's acting chief pilot in March. He was just filling in for the chief pilot, who was in the hospital recovering from injuries suffered in a car accident, he'd told Don. He had only met Krantz once or twice in passing and didn't know anything about his personal life, but if he could leave it with him for a few days he would try and track down the crew members who had been with Krantz when he died.

The next day a woman called from the airline's administration office. She informed Don that Jerry Wahl had left the company a few months previously, in November '96, apparently to take a corporate flying job on the west coast. He had left a forwarding address, but no phone number.

The flight engineer was still working for them, she said, and gave Don his name and number.

Don recalled his short conversation with Charlie Moore.

"Krantz was a real jerk," he began, after Don had explained why he was calling. "He had the personality of a parachute but wasn't nearly as useful," he said. Don couldn't help but chuckle. Moore added that he'd only flown with Krantz a few times before the Paris flight.

"Talk to Wahl," he suggested. "They must've flown together a lot. Not too many guys wanted to work with the prick if they had a choice, but he and Krantz seemed to have a history."

Speaking ill of the departed didn't seem to bother Mr. Moore, thought Don after their brief conversation ended.

*

Wahl's forwarding address was to a suburb of Los Angeles, California. After failing to trace him by phone, Don sent a letter to the address in the hope that it would eventually catch up with him. After not getting a response for so long, he had more or less written him off. The eight hour time difference meant it was a few minutes after 10 A.M. in California when Don dialed Wahl's number. A cheery male voice answered. "Good morning! This is Jerry."

"Jerry, Hi. Don Carling here. Thanks for getting in touch."

No response for a moment, then, "Oh yeah, the private eye! Well, you're welcome. Sorry it took so long, you know. Just got back on dry land last week and picked up my mail from my sister's place."

"That's okay. So where are living now?" Don asked.

"Well, I'm uhh, sorta just settin' up a pad here in El Sugundo. Got me another corporate job startin' next month. Flying a Lear out of Long Beach. Hope it's lasts longer than the last one. Not too many slots around for a forty-something dude like me anymore. Least anything that pays worth a damn," he said. "Are you in LA? Want to come by for a beer?"

"Wish I could Jerry, but I'm calling from London. Another American captain was killed here last weekend. Fellow named Rosen, flew for Atlantic Best. Definitely not an accident. Including Daniel Krantz, that makes four suspicious deaths in just over two years, all happening on layovers in Europe or the UK."

"Well I'll be a beached whale! What a bummer, " sighed Wahl. "Yeah, well, Dan's death was sure suspicious, at least to me. The friggin' French cops kept on about suicide. Why would he kill himself? 'He must have been depressed', they said. Why? Over and over, they seemed to want to call it suicide and wash their hands of it. Odd way to kill yourself - diving thirty feet to the pavement! I was really pissed off with their attitude."

Don let him talk it out without interrupting. Wahl finally told the inspector in charge that he wasn't going to put up with anymore questioning, even when they threatened to keep him in France until an inquest was held. They relented though, and he and the flight engineer flew home three days after Krantz's death. He'd tried to find out more about the police investigation through the airline, but never heard 'squat', as he put it.

Wahl left International soon afterwards when it appeared there wasn't going to be much flying available that winter. "Did they ever issue a final report on Dan's death? I haven't heard anything since I moved out here."

"No, the file is still open," Don assured him, and, changing the subject, said, "I was told you and Dan had known each other for a long time. Am I right?"

"Yes," Wahl confirmed. They had both been with Eastern Airlines at one time. Jerry was twenty-two when he was hired 'off the street' in 1982. He trained as a second officer on the Boeing 727, which comprised a large part of Eastern's fleet at the time. 'Off the street' referred to a pilot hired with minimum flying hours under his belt, normally on light aircraft, compared to ex-military pilots with plenty of hours and jet experience.

Krantz, he went on, had just been promoted to captain and seemed to have the world by the tail. They flew together regularly, the older man tutoring Jerry in the finer points of airline life, both in the air and on the ground. They'd partied hard at times, especially on the longer layovers in the Caribbean. Wahl turned to pilot-speak again.

"Danny boy had a well-deserved reputation as a 'stick man', that's for sure," he said. A good stick man meant a pilot who was smooth on the controls, and handled a plane well in all conditions. It also had a sexual connation...

"Yeah..." Wahl went on, "A real 'tail hound' on layovers. Cost him his marriage, though. Right about the time Eastern folded. Real bitter divorce. She got everything and Dan's high flyin' days were over for quite a while."

What about the last few years before he died? Did he seem better off financially by then? What about his frame of mind? Was he contented?

Happy? Unhappy? "Any aspect of his situation you can shed light will help my investigation, Jerry," Don said.

There was a lengthy silence before Wahl spoke again. "Look, it might be better if I didn't say any more. It won't bring him back, will it?"

This was the third time Don had run into resistance at a critical point when talking with friends or colleagues of a dead man. He knew he could get more out of Jerry if he played his cards right.

"Jerry, I can understand your loyalty to Dan, and not wanting to say anything derogatory. And I don't blame you. But let me tell you what I think got these other guys killed, and maybe Dan as well. When I'm finished, you can decide if he fitted the profile. Okay?"

It took him five minutes. Wahl never said a word the whole time.

"So there you have it. Anything sound familiar?" asked Don.

"Son'ova bitch! Yeah, you're probably right. I can see him gettin' involved with something not quite on the level. Especially if it paid well. He was a big time gambler, an addict even. I know he spent a lot of time in Atlantic City those last years, even lived down that way. Had a condo on the Jersey shore. I was there a few times," Jerry recounted. "Maybe he was into the loan sharks for a bundle, who knows?"

"Possibly, and like the other victims, a prime candidate for manipulation if he were offered what initially seemed like an easy, low risk way to make his money problems disappear," replied Don. "But as I said earlier, this is still just conjecture for the most part. I could be wrong."

"Well, I sure hope so." sighed Wahl, "However, if Dan was into shady doings, I'd bet my last buck she was involved, too."

She, he explained, was a woman named Lori Wilson. Lori had moved in with Krantz two or three years before he died. This would have been around 1993, maybe a year earlier. But the two had a history long before then, recalled Wahl. As a vivacious young and impressionable flight attendant, she was one of his conquests at Eastern. Her lengthy affair with the older Krantz had been a poorly-kept secret among the Atlanta-based crews.

Until she resigned - read *fired* - in 1985. Her sudden departure fed the rumor mill. Some thought she'd been caught pilfering alcohol once too often from aircraft supplies, the miniature bottles in popular use at the time. Others hinted she had been suspected of propositioning well-heeled businessmen and meeting them on layovers.

Wahl thought she was a druggie, and her habits had been her downfall.

"What type of drugs?" asked Don.

"Well not heroin, I'm pretty sure. But probably anything else going around. It was about the time that 'doin' coke' was becoming the in thing, you know?"

"Any idea where she is now?" he inquired.

"Nope, can't help you there. I'm not even sure she and Dan were still together when he died. He hadn't mentioned her for a while, now that I think back," was his answer.

"What about overseas? Did he have girlfriends over there?"

Wahl chuckled. "Well, he never really changed. He was Danny Boy right up until the end! Never stopped looking for a chance to score!"

"No steady girlfriend? How about in London, ever see him with anyone there?"

"No, but then we didn't lay over in London that often. If we landed in the UK, it was usually en route to or from Paris or Brussels. He had someone in Paris for a while, though. He used to meet her at a bar across from the hotel."

"Really! So he spoke French, did he?"

"Oh hell no! If they didn't have menus in English he would've starved to death!" laughed Jerry. "No, the woman wasn't French."

"Did you ever meet her?"

"Not really. Saw her a few times. They were just leaving a bar once when myself and the engineer were heading in for a beer. Dan waved but didn't introduce us. She was a looker though. Great body!"

"So how do you know she wasn't French?"

"Well, I was kiddin' him about her on the flight the next day. He said she was German, just working in Paris for a few months. That's all he knew about her. *All he needed to know*, was the way he put it."

"Do you remember when this would have been?"

"Hmm...six, maybe eight months before he died? Yeah, that would be about right."

"Anything else you remember about her? Approximate age, height, hair color, that sort of thing?"

"Jeez, well, I'd say she would've been in her late thirties, maybe five-foot six or seven. And as I said, nicely put together. Not too heavy, but not thin either. Blonde like Madonna. Yeah, that's why she didn't look French. Too brassy."

*

The call to Wahl had taken almost forty minutes. Don took another ten minutes to straighten out the notes and comments he'd jotted down, and what his follow up action would be. He told Jerry Wahl he would e-mail him a copy of the photo of Flores and the woman. If Wahl could identify her as the woman he saw with Krantz in Paris, he would have another piece of the puzzle...

The only thing he had forgotten to ask Jerry about was the remark made by Moore, the flight engineer, about Krantz apparently being unpopular with most pilots. Obviously it wasn't a concern for Wahl.

*

"Good show! Look forward to seeing you Saturday afternoon. Come by about four and we'll slip down to the pub for a chat," said Derek. Don had phoned to say he would still be in London and would gladly accept the dinner invitation. "That way we'll escape the wrath of my dear wife by not talking shop during the meal!"

Just as he was deciding what to do about dinner, the phone rang. It was Rod Weathers, just back from his flight. Don brought him up to date on his investigation and his plans for the next few days.

"Excellent. We'll see you at Houghton's on Saturday. If there's anything I can do for you tomorrow just call me at IPF," said Rod before ringing off.

*

The restaurant off the lobby was still open and Don studied the menu posted on the door. It won't win any gastronomic stars, he mused, but the steak sandwich and baked potato caught his eye.

A rack of complimentary newspapers stood beside the cashier's desk. Don realized he hadn't looked at a paper for a few days. He selected a copy of the *Daily Mail* and, following the bored waitress's invitation to 'sit anywhere you like, sir', took a table near the window. He scanned the paper while he waited for his meal to arrive.

Bert Rosen's killing had been relegated to page nine, no longer headline news. The reporter had interviewed a Superintendent Welch, who, Don figured, must be DCI Upton's superior officer. Since the crime was still unsolved, most of the quotes attributed to him were of the predictable variety: pursuing a number of leads, still early, appeal for anyone with information to come forward, etcetera.

When asked about speculation that the victim may have been visiting someone in Highgate Village, Welch would only say that *'police had not as yet ascertained why Mr. Rosen was in the area where the attack occurred.'* He would not admit they were seeking a specific person or persons, let alone a woman.

Don knew the superintendent's reasoning. It would only be a matter of time before an enterprising reporter found out who they were looking for. Then the tabloids would have a field day. The longer the police could search for her on their own the better.

He folded the paper and tucked into his dinner. It was hot and filling, if nothing else. The glass of house wine, a Common Market red of indeterminate lineage, did little to improve on it.

*

After signing his bill he sauntered outside, pondering whether to make another evening visit to the Pembury House. He was curious to see what the night clerk's reaction would be if he showed up again. And he did want to do check on the dates that Ray Flores had stayed there. However, he decided, it would probably be best to wait until next morning and approach the manager with his queries.

A better time to confront Alf would be when he had the photo of Flores and the woman together to flash at him.

16

8:30 A.M., FRIDAY, JUNE 27

The weather had changed noticeably overnight. A weak low pressure area was stalled over the English Channel, and the resulting southeasterly flow had swept a relatively cool and damp blanket of fog up the Thames and over Greater London. From his window Don estimated visibility to be no more than a hundred yards. When he opened the door to his small balcony the moist air seeping in seemed to have a physical quality. A barely perceptible drizzle was falling, evidenced by the hissing of tires on the pavement below.

The first item on Don's list was a call to Glasgow. He wanted to check on something concerning Ray Flores with DCI Des McGrath. He was in luck. The Scotsman answered on the second ring.

"Good morning, Inspector, Don Carling calling."

"Ah, morning to you. Thought I might be hearing from you one of these days."

It had been over two months since they'd last spoken. "Yeah, well I'm in London again. I presume you heard about the American captain's death last week?"

"Aye, indeed I did. No chance of it being an accident, according to the papers."

"No, definitely not. He was targeted."

"Uncovered any evidence that I might be interested in?"

"Not directly, at least not yet. But maybe down the line. For now I was hoping you had something for me."

"That being?"

"The address book found in Flores' personal belongings. You mentioned it contained some UK phone numbers."

"Yes, that's correct. Not many as I recall, and most of them were for numbers at Prestwick Airport. Company numbers, the weather office and so on. They all checked out."

"I'd like to know if there were any London numbers in the book."

"Aye, I believe so. They checked out as well. Why?"

"Just a hunch, but it's worth checking." Carling quickly explained about the picture of Flores and the unidentified woman.

"I'll pull the file. Hang on a sec." Don could hear him asking a junior officer to fetch the Flores file. "Won't be long, Don," he said. "We've had a wee break in the case since we last talked. Got a lead on the vehicle that was probably used to run down this Flores chap."

"Really? So when did this happen?"

"Late last month, it was. I'd sent out inquiries further south. When nothing turned up around here I got to thinking about your conspiracy theory," said McGrath.

"How so?" asked Don.

"If Flores was hit by the same killers as your previous victims, the odds are they were from somewhere on the continent, and probably flew to the UK to do the dirty deed. The logical airport, I thought, would be Manchester. Flights to and from a number of European cities, and not that far by road from Prestwick. Follow me so far?"

"Yeah, easy in, easy out, and no traces locally," replied Don.

"Exactly! Anyway, my initial inquiry to Manchester came up empty. Same results from a few other cities in the Midlands. Mind you this was some time after New Year's, and I'm not sure how thoroughly some of the larger car hire firms checked their records. Finally called a mate of mine with the Lancashire force. Asked him to check with some of the small operators, just a fishing expedition, so to speak. He said to leave it with him, and he'd have a nose round." McGrath paused, and Don heard him say, 'that's it, thanks'. "Got the Flores file now. What is it you're after?" he asked.

"It'll keep for a few minutes. I'd rather hear about the vehicle," replied Don.

"Right. Well my mate called back a week, ten days later. This was on May twenty-second,"

Don listened closely, taking notes, as McGrath related what the Lancashire detective had discovered. On December twenty-ninth, the day before Flores and his crew flew into Prestwick, two men rented a Land Rover from HIRE 4 LESS, a small firm that stocked used vehicles, most of them three to five years old, at their lot on the outskirts of Manchester. They hired a black, 1994 model, completely rigged for off-track operation, and the only SUV class unit available.

They paid cash for a week's rental, the firm's minimum hire period. One of the men did all the talking and spoke reasonable English. He presented a French driver's licence for the paperwork, but the manager didn't think he was French. He conversed with his companion in a language the manager couldn't place. The vehicle was not returned at week's end. It was located three days later in a parking garage at Manchester Airport. The left front headlamp was badly cracked, and the moulding around it noticeably dented. There was no other damage. The Land Rover was locked and the keys were inside. The ticket from the automated machine used to gain entry to the garage was found crumpled under the seat. It was date-stamped 9:22 A.M. on January first, New Year's Day.

Even though the rental had been paid for in cash, the hire firm had insisted on a credit card imprint before they released the vehicle. When the manager tried to bill the credit card to recoup the substantial parking fees incurred at the airport, it was rejected.

"Did this fellow contact the police?" asked Don.

"No, apparently he just decided to write it off. Said he didn't think the local coppers would make much of an effort for the hundred odd quid involved," said McGrath, "and no doubt he was correct in his assumption."

"Yeah, not something Interpol would want to be bothered with, I'd bet."

"No, but my colleague followed up," replied McGrath.

He contacted the Prefecture of Police in Paris and asked for a trace of the name and address on the driver's licence used to hire the Land Rover. The licence was a fake, as was the credit card in the same name.

"Do French licences have the driver's photo on them?" asked Don.

"Yes, they do, but the manager didn't make a copy of it. Not that he is required to do so. However, he was able to give a reasonable description of the men. I'll fax all this info to you as soon as we ring off. Maybe it will be of use to you or the London Bobbies." Don hadn't heard that term for years, and wondered if the Scotsman was using it facetiously.

"Thanks Des, I'll alert the front desk to watch for it," said Don.

"Now, it's a phone number you're after, is it? Let me have a look." Don heard the sound of paper being shuffled. "There was only one we couldn't trace. Apparently it's a mobile number, and it had been disconnected. Got your pen handy?" McGrath asked.

"Yessir, go ahead." The Glasgow policeman read off a number beginning with the 0171 London prefix. "Got it. I'll be in touch in a few days. Thanks, Des!"

*

Don expectantly compared it to an 0171 number he'd copied from Len Newson's address book. The book he'd found in Newson's flight bag after his visit to his son ,Fred, last winter.

Bingo! It was a match!

Don remembered trying to call the number from Canada, but it wouldn't go through. At the time he'd seen no reason to pursue it further.

Now he thought he knew why: the number had been disconnected on January fourth, a few days after Flores died. The phone's owner probably canceled it just in case the police did try to trace it. But with this new evidence linking two more of the dead men, it might be worth another look. He'd run it by Derek tomorrow.

*

The fax arrived while Don was having breakfast in the dining room. The concierge held it up to catch Don's attention as he crossed the lobby. He signed for it, and then sought out an empty chair away from the busy front desk. The fax was three pages in length. Don scanned it quickly, looking for information that DCI McGrath hadn't mentioned on the phone.

He underlined the section about the driver's licence used to hire the Land Rover, and the descriptions of the two men.

The bogus licence had been issued in Paris to a Pierre Louis Seguin. DOB 12 Mars 63. Black hair and eyes. The hire firm's manager described him as about six foot tall, and estimated his weight at fourteen to fifteen stone. He had a full moustache, but was clean-shaven in the photo on the licence.

The second man was a few inches shorter, but heavier. He had thinning, greyish-blonde hair and a goatee beard, neatly trimmed. His name was never mentioned. Both men were wearing dark turtle neck sweaters and well-worn, short black leather coats. A style, he remarked, that said 'east European' to him.

When found, the vehicle had 634 additional miles on it. This was consistent with a round trip journey from Manchester to either Prestwick or the Glasgow area, plus some local mileage, noted McGrath.

Don re-read the fax and added a few notes of his own before heading back up to his room. He wasn't expecting to hear from DCI Upton until closer to noon, which left him time to make another visit to the Pembury Hotel. No call from James Coates either, but he'd check with him later.

*

Ruth Headley's greeting wasn't exactly cordial, but she agreed to spare him a few minutes. She ushered him into her office and bade him take a chair. His attempt at small talk didn't change her mood, so he switched tactics. He quickly explained why he wanted to check the hotel records for names and dates. The hotel manager listened without comment. When he finished, she pushed an intercom button.

"Yes ma'am?" inquired a pleasant female voice.

"Jane, would you step in here for a moment, please?"

Don rose as the door opened and a woman in her early thirties entered. She returned Don's smile as they were introduced. Jane Redan remained standing beside Don while her boss told her who he was and why he was at the Pembury.

"Please show him the crew rosters he is interested in," she directed.

"Certainly ma'am," Jane answered. "Please follow me, sir, " she said, flashing the visitor another smile.

Don thanked the manager for her cooperation and closed her office door. Jane's office was a small but tidy room off the passageway leading back to reception area. The room had one window which looked directly onto the brick wall of the building next door. It did, however, let in a reasonable amount of sunlight and was fitted with an air conditioner.

She pulled a folding chair out from a table that held a bulky copying machine and invited him to take it, once again calling him sir.

"Enough of that 'sir' stuff Miss Redan. How about just Don?"

"Fine, Don it is!" Her quick smile was really quite charming. "But only if you call me Jane."

She insisted on getting him a coffee, assuring him it wouldn't be a bother as there was always a pot brewing in the staff lunch room. He could imagine what that would do to the taste, but gave in rather than decline the young woman's hospitality.

"Sure, just a bit of milk in mine, please," he said, as she picked up an empty cup from her desk and hurried out of the office. She was back in less than a minute, and handed him a cup, apologizing for it being plastic.

"We've got a few extra real cups," she explained, "but they've been here for ages, and they're all chipped and discolored. Lord knows what's been in them besides tea and coffee!"

"This'll do just fine, Jane, and thanks." He took a sip, and managed not to grimace.

"Now, what is you wish to see?" she asked.

For starters, Don said he'd like to have a look at the daily crew rosters for 1996 for Globe Wide Cargo, the airline Ray Flores flew for. If the records didn't go back that far, the period from July to December would suffice.

Jane told him that paper records were kept for two years so it wouldn't be a problem. She explained that the information was entered into the computer as well, but only after a crew checked out. This room tally was used to bill the individual airlines at the end of every month. The computer records only had the number of rooms used, not names.

Don said he would need to see the paperwork then. Jane turned to the filing cabinet next to her desk and pulled out a surprisingly small file folder. It was labeled **GlobeWide Cargo, Jan-Dec 1996**. He remarked on its size.

"Ah, yes. Well they don't have crews here every night like some of the other airlines.

I believe it's only a few nights a week," she said.

"Okay, that should make it easier for me," smiled Don.

"Can I get anything else for you?"

"How about the Atlantic Best rosters for the last six months. Could you pull those, please?"

Don set the Globe Wide folder on the table and opened it. The daily roster the hotel kept was straightforward enough. It recorded the date, crew member's name, arrival time at the hotel, room number assigned, and the date and time the pilot or flight attendant checked out.

It didn't take him long to find the information he was looking for. Ray Flores had laid over quite often at the Pembury in the early months of 1996; three times in February; twice in March; and three times again in May and July. In July, the layovers had been for two nights. After that, there was a gap before his name showed up again, a single layover in September. According to the rosters, his last trips to London were on the 15th and 22nd of October, two months before his death.

As he leafed through the folder, Don jotted down the dates on a note pad. He also noted the names of the other crew members who had flown with Flores on the October trips.

He closed the Globe Wide file and reached for the thicker one for Atlantic Best Airlines. Starting with January of this year, he searched for Captain Bert Rosen's name. The O'Hare- based airline ran a daily cargo flight to Stansted, as well as the occasional passenger charter. On a few dates starting in May, AB had two crews laying over at the Pembury.

The London flight appeared to have been a favourite of Rosen's. He'd overnighted at the Pembury most weeks for much of the past four months.

But he wouldn't have been staying here next month, would he? Don mused. Bob Lewis, Rosen's co-pilot, had mentioned that Rosen had bid to fly to Brussels and Frankfurt for the month of July. Don re-stacked the roster sheets, and closed the folder.

"Thanks very much, Jane. That's all I need to see. You've been a great help."

"Oh you're most welcome." she answered, and then asked, "Do you think the police will catch whoever killed poor Captain Rosen?"

"Given time, I'm sure they will. Not too many murders go unsolved in Britain, you know. And they've got a good team working on it," he assured her. Before she could ask him anything further, he put a question to her.

"Jane, how well do you know Alf? Been working here for quite some time, I'm told."

"...Alf?" A puzzled look crossed her face. "Oh, you mean Mister Heard! Funny, none of us girls ever refer to him by his first name. But I know all the pilots do, don't they? Yes, he's been here for simply ages! Long before my time, anyway."

"Do you ever chat with him?"

"Oh, hardly ever. Just occasionally when I've come in early. I don't usually start until nine, you see, and he's off at eight. Just said hello, really. Is there something he..."

"No, no, don't even know why I brought it up. Forget I ever mentioned him. But I'll need his home address. Miss Headley said you looked after the personnel data." This was stretching the truth, but he didn't expect he would be caught out over it. Jane consulted a Roladex file, copied out the information onto a slip of paper, and handed it to him.

"Thanks again for your help, Jane," he said. "I'll be on my way."

Don found his way out, and waved a farewell to the two women manning the reception desk. They were roughly Jane's age, and if his instincts were right, his interest in Alf Heard's background would be a topic of conversation among the female staff by lunchtime.

*

The fog had burned off while he was in the hotel, giving way to partly cloudy skies. The temperature had risen too, but would probably top out at four or five degrees cooler than the past few days.

His phone beeped as he was walking back to Finchley Road. The call was from a Police Constable Raines: he had a message for Don from DCI Upton. He was leaving copies of the re-touched photos with the constable and Don could stop by the station at his convenience to pick them up. End of message. Don thanked him, and said he would be by within the hour. It was now 10:40. Don spotted a Seattle Coffee Company shop just up the road and made for it. He needed a place to sit and make a few calls.

The shop was nearly empty and he took his cup of dark roast coffee to a table well away from the counter. Rod Weather's number at IPF produced a busy signal. His second call was answered by James Coates after the first ring.

"You must be psychic, old boy, I've been trying to call you."

"Sorry James. I had my phone turned off while I was checking out something. Just left there ten minutes ago," apologized Don.

"Not to worry! I'm on a bus taking me up to Highgate and was hoping to meet up with you. Might have a lead on our quarry," said Coates.

"Good show! I've got to stop at the Holloway police station to pick up a package," replied Don. He paused, checked his watch, and did a quick calculation. "But I'll be up that way in about forty, forty-five minutes. Noon at the latest. Where do you want to meet?"

The retired spy gave him directions to a small park up the road from the Morning Sun pub. He would wait for him there. Don quickly drained the strong coffee and stepped outside to hail a taxi. He'd try Rod's number again while he was en route to the police station.

*

The first four taxis heading his way were all occupied and it was almost ten minutes before a southbound cab driver acknowledged his energetic arm waving and made a U-turn to pick him up. Rod's number was still busy and Don decided to leave his next try until later.

He had the driver wait while he went into the police station.

Constable Raines was a strapping young man, and probably fairly new to the job, thought Don, as he watched him approach. He was almost marching down the hall. He politely asked the Canadian to sign a form acknowledging he was in receipt of the sealed manilla envelope from DCI Upton. Don scribbled his signature, and thanked the constable.

"Would you see that this gets to DCI Upton? Tell him I'll check with him later today." The envelope he handed Raines contained a copy of the fax from DCI McGrath.

17

Don had the driver drop him off across from the pub. He got his bearings and headed up the leafy street James had described, moving away from the High Street. The park was no more than a good-sized rectangular patch of green space, its neatly-trimmed lawn bordered by a narrow bed of colorful annuals, most of which Don couldn't identify. There were three wooden benches, one at each end, and one in the middle facing the row of elegant Georgian houses opposite the park.

An elderly lady sat on one of the end benches, chatting away to her companion, a short-haired terrier seated at her feet. The dog was paying close attention to her, mainly to ensure the tidbits she was doling out continued to come its way. Don smiled at the pair as he passed, and waved a greeting to James, who rose from the far bench.

James was attired much as he'd been the previous two days. Dark blazer, grey trousers, light blue shirt with a matching tie. In deference to the cooler temperature, he was also wearing a light woollen vest. Anyone noticing him would register a smartly-dressed pensioner out for a stroll.

Don sat down and pulled the package of photos out of his case. The crime lab had crafted three new images of the woman in the picture with Ray Flores. One was a replica of the two together, but showing the woman as a brunette. The other two were 'stand alone' shots of her head, cropped from the original. They were 4 X 6 in size and displayed her as a brunette in one and with a light shade of brown in the other.

The copies that Don had taken to DCI Upton were also in the package. Both men studied the images carefully. Don explained about the hostess and waiter at the restaurant and why he wanted them to see the new images of the woman. His hope, he said, was that they could identify her as Rosen's recent dinner companion at the Glory of Venice.

"If they can, then we can tie her to both Rosen and Flores," he told James, "and probably to Newson."

"What's the connection to him?" asked Coates.

Don explained about the London phone number found in both Newson's and Flores' personal effects. A number that was disconnected not long after Flores was killed.

"No phone number in Rosen's possession?"

"Not that I'm aware of. Upton hasn't mentioned it. If Rosen had a written record of her address and phone number you'd think the police would have traced her by now, wouldn't you?"

James agreed, and then said, "Well my friend, I think I have found the building where this mystery woman lives. Or did until she disappeared. With these," he went on, indicating the touched-up photos, "we should be able to confirm that. It was the bit about the American chap purchasing a kitten that provided the lead. Let's take a little walk and see what happens."

*

James led him back to the top of the High Street and then left onto Mulberry Street. Two short blocks along he stopped in front number 214, the middle of three identical five-storey buildings. At a quick glance, Don figured there must be at least eight flats on each level. The front entrance was approximately nine or ten yards from the sidewalk.

Don shot his partner a quizzical look, as if to say 'Now what?'

"Just be patient," Coates cautioned, a wry grin on his face. Taking the Canadian by the arm, he led him up to the front entrance and pushed the buzzer for flat number one. The intercom crackled a few times before an elderly-sounding female voice answered.

"Hello Mrs. Whitt, how are you today? It's James Coates. We met yesterday, remember?"

There was further static on the line and then the sound of the main door unlatching electronically. James pulled it open and entered the small foyer, followed by Don. Mrs. Whitt's flat was the first on the right.

"This is my colleague, Mr. Carling," said James to the woman who peered at them from her door. "Thank you for seeing us today, Mrs. Whitt. We'll only take a few minutes of your time."

The lady motioned for them to come in and, after closing the door, led them through to her living room. Charlotte Whitt was as old as she sounded, somewhere in her eighties, guessed Don. She eased herself into a large stuffed chair with her back to the window. Her visitors sat on the matching sofa facing her.

James led off, politely inquiring after her health.

"Oh, I feeling the same as always, no better, no worse," she answered without much enthusiasm. " It's my eyesight, you see. Nothing they can do about it, they say." She sighed and added, "Thank the Lord I can still hear. If I didn't have my radio for company I don't know what I would do."

James commiserated with her and said to Don, "Mrs. Whitt is legally blind, even though she still gets around on her own most of the time, don't you, dear?"

Don's mother had suffered from macular degeneration in her last years, and he was fairly certain that Mrs. Whitt was afflicted with the same condition. He'd noticed a white cane leaning against the wall just inside her front door. From where she was sitting, he and James were probably just two shapes, their facial features indiscernible. Only from close up would she be able to identify someone. Reading was impossible, he knew, without a powerful magnifying glass. He spotted one lying on the coffee table to her right.

James asked Don for the large, retouched photo of the mystery woman. He reached across and handed it to Mrs. Whitt. The image showed the woman with dark hair.

"Is this the lady the kitten belongs to?" he asked her.

Mrs. Whitt picked up the magnifying glass and squinted through it to study the photo. She held the glass just inches from her eyes.

"Yes, that's her. Renate, that's her name."

"And that's your neighbor across the hall, is it? The owner of the kitten?"

"Yes, although she hasn't been taking very good care of it if you ask me. Just gone off and left the poor soul. If I hadn't taken it in, heaven knows what might have happened to it."

Don was still in the dark, and looked to James for an explanation.

"Mrs. Whitt, why don't you tell my friend here how you came to rescue your neighbor's pet? Just the way you told me yesterday," he said.

Charlotte Whitt set her magnifying glass down on the table, and told her story.

Don listened closely - and patiently. Her rambling took almost ten minutes, when a concise report would have taken less than three.

Mrs. Whitt was a widow and had lived in her flat for fifteen years. She and her husband had purchased it when he retired in 1982. Mr. Whitt died of heart failure only six months after they had moved in, leaving her with a modest pension. The woman she identified as Renate - she didn't know her last name - had lived across the hall for less than two years. She spoke quite good English, but Charlotte thought she was either Dutch or German. The flat belonged to an agency, and was rented out fully furnished. None of the tenants had lived there for longer than two years, she recalled, and most a lot less. There were other flats in the building belonging to the same agency, but the majority of the units were privately owned. There wasn't an on site superintendent.

Renate was often away for extended periods, she said, occasionally as long as three weeks. Mrs. Whitt had tried to be a good neighbor in the first months after she moved in, but her invitations to come for tea were always politely rebuffed, and the only times they spoke was when they happened to cross paths in the hallway. Renate didn't appear to work at a regular job, but did leave her flat most days, usually for three or four hours.

She didn't even know that her neighbor had acquired a pet until a few weeks ago. On that particular day she was just about to let herself in the main entrance when the kitten came prancing playfully around the front corner with Renate close behind. The pet stopped when it saw Mrs. Whitt, allowing it's owner to scoop it up. It had been a gift, Renate said, and left it at that.

That was the last she saw of it until Tuesday when it showed up on her balcony, which was only a few feet off the ground and accessed through her kitchen. It appeared to be hungry and wouldn't go away once it caught sight of Mrs. Whitt inside. She knocked on Renate's door, but got no answer. She tried a number of times that day with the same result. That evening she took pity on the animal, let it in, and fed it. The happy feline showed its appreciation by curling up on her sofa and sleeping for twelve hours. By yesterday morning, Thursday, there was still no one home across the hall. She decided to call a nearby boarding kennel, hoping they would take the creature in until its owner returned.

"And that's where I came in," said James. "I happened to be passing by when the chap from the kennel was making the pick up. Couldn't help overhearing him tell Mrs. Whitt that she would have to give him a deposit."

"He was ever so helpful," chimed in Mrs.Whitt. "Mr. Coates gave the man the twenty pounds he wanted before he would take it away. Wouldn't take my cheque, you see," she told Don. "Don't know why she would just go off and leave the poor thing to fend for itself like that."

Don had a pretty good idea why, but there was no reason to confuse her even more.

"Well, you did the right thing, Mrs. Whitt. And she'll be darn thankful when she comes back," Don assured her. James knew what was coming next and gave him a slight nod as if to say, 'Go ahead'.

"Mrs. Whitt, from what you've told us, your neighbor obviously keeps to herself. Do you recall seeing any of her visitors? Friends, maybe?" he coaxed.

"She didn't have anyone living with her, if that's what you mean. But she did have gentlemen callers...different ones. Not that I kept track, mind you. But I have seen her going out of an evening with an escort on more than one occasion."

Don searched through his case and took out the picture of Bert Rosen and handed it to her. "Have you ever seen her with this man?" he asked.

Once again she reached for the magnifying glass.

"No, I couldn't say. They have always been too far away for me to make out their faces, you see. But they weren't Englishmen, I can tell you that."

"Really? How could you tell?" asked Don.

"Because I heard them! When I'm making my supper. Occasionally

I leave my door ajar to get a breeze from the hallway. Heard them speak when she lets them in, and sometimes when they go out."

Her kitchen was the first room on the right as one entered, and her entrance door was directly opposite her neighbor's. The kitchen window was a good vantage point to observe people entering or leaving the building.

"What kind of accent did her callers have. European, like hers?"

"Oh no. Not at all! They were definitely from America. You hear enough of them on the telly these days. Much like yourself, in fact."

Mrs. Whitt wasn't the first Londoner to mistake him for an American this week, but he didn't correct her. Nor was he offended. He looked at James to see if he had any questions.

"Mrs.Whitt, did you see or hear her with anyone last Friday evening? Or at any other time on the weekend? I know I asked you that yesterday and you said you weren't sure, but said would sleep on it. Anything come back to you?" asked James.

"No, I don't recall seeing her on the weekend. I do recall seeing her going out one afternoon last week, but that's the last time I saw her. I'm sorry to be so vague, a few years ago my mind and eyesight were much better," she said, a tinge of sadness in her voice.

Both her visitors were quick to assure her they weren't disappointed, and James told her once again how helpful she'd been. Mrs. Whitt offered to make them a cup of tea, but they politely declined. Don had one final question for her as they rose to leave.

"Did she ever see Renate with blonde hair?"

Mrs. Whitt clasped her hand over her mouth in surprise. "Yes, I'd forgotten that! It must have been about the time she moved in, now that you mention it. Yes, blonde hair. But only for a short time, as I recall."

Don complimented her on her memory, and thanked her for seeing them. When she started to rise, James motioned that she should remain seated.

"We can see ourselves out, my dear. You've been most helpful," he told her.

He also mentioned that she would probably be getting a visit from the police before long, and they would no doubt be asking her the same questions about Renate. When she showed surprise, he quickly assured her that it had nothing to do with her handling of Renate's kitten. There was a slight possibility, he said, that the American killed nearby on the weekend had been an acquaintance of the woman, and the police would probably want to question all the building's residents, not just her.

*

After they left her flat, Don and James conferred in low voices in the corridor.

"How do you suppose the damned cat got out?" asked Don.

"Through the bathroom window. I had a look round the exterior of her flat yesterday afternoon. She'd left it open about six inches, just wide enough for the cat to get through. Which it probably did after it got hungry."

"Yeah, that makes sense." Don glanced at the door to Renate's flat. "Well, I suppose I should let DCI Upton know what we've learned from the widow Whitt," It was a half question, half statement.

"But it wouldn't do any harm if we had a look round her flat first, would it?" said James, reading his mind. Don nodded his agreement.

James fished a small handful of tools out of his pocket. Before he went to work Don rapped on the door. There was no answer, and no sounds from inside. James had the simple lock open in thirty seconds. They slipped inside and closed the door quietly behind them. The flat was a mirror of Mrs. Whitt's. The small kitchen was on the left, and the short hallway opened into the living room. The patio doors, covered by heavy drapes, were straight ahead. Another short hall led away from the living room. The bathroom and bedroom were on the left of this hall. Both these rooms were against the exterior wall. Opposite them was a bank of cupboards and closets, along with a washer and dryer.

At first glance the flat looked normal, nothing out of place. No visible damage to the modern furnishings, and nothing to indicate that the occupant wasn't coming back.

Until Don opened the closet doors: they were empty. Just a jumble of hangers dangling on the rack. The dresser drawers in the bedroom had also been cleaned out. The bathroom had also been stripped of any personal items; no toothpaste or brushes; no make-up items; nothing to indicate someone had been living here recently. Don noticed the open sliding window above the toilet. No challenge at all for a cat bent on escaping...

Everything that one would expect when renting a fully-furnished flat was there, though. Bedding and towels, cleaning supplies, kitchenware and appliances were neatly stowed in cupboards.

The kitten's dish was sitting on the counter beside the kitchen sink. It had been licked clean. Three foil wrappers scrunched up near the dish bore the logo of a popular cat food.

"It would appear she left enough to keep the animal fed for a few days," said James.

"Uh huh," agreed Don. He pointed to a plastic container full of used kitty litter in one of the kitchen corners. "Good thing it was toilet trained before she abandoned it."

One side of the double sink had three inches of water in it. Other than that - and the open window - the woman hadn't made any effort to ensure her pet's survival.

James, using his handkerchief, opened and closed drawers looking for any clues as to the woman's identity. But there weren't any. No photographs, no bills or bank statements. Nothing at all.

Don checked the refrigerator. It was lacking obvious clues, save for a few unopened containers of dairy products that might yield fingerprints. But that would be a task for the police.

It didn't look as if the woman had subscribed to any land line phone service: the jacks in the living room and bedroom still had security locks over them.

Don checked the time. They had been in the flat for almost fifteen minutes. *We should get out of here soon,* he thought, and was just about to say so, when, with a last look around the kitchen he spotted the only mistake Renate had made...

"Here we go, James!" he enthused. "Check this out!" He was looking at a calendar tacked to the inside of a kitchen cabinet door. Coates tucked his handkerchief into his pocket and took out his reading glasses.

" B for Bert, eh?" Don was pointing to the box for Friday, June 20. There was a capital B written in it. There was another B under June 6th. "These are the last two dates Bert Rosen was in London, "Don stated.

"..Ah yes. But even more important are these N's - on the third and seventeenth," said James. "Who might he be? You haven't come across an N yet in your investigation, have you?"

"Nope! But I think we're onto something. He could be a live link to our mystery woman."

Using a pen, he flipped up the sheet to reveal the calendar for July. "And look at this. Whoever he is, she was expecting him again next month."

The letter N was penciled in for three successive Tuesdays, starting on the fifteenth

Don was rapidly making notes of the dates when James glanced out the kitchen window and tugged on his arm. "Time's up, old chap!"

A police car had just pulled up in front of the building.

*

Don and James were standing outside the front entrance when the policemen approached. Two were in uniform, the third in plainclothes. Don recognized the detective.

" Good Day, Sergeant Ross."

Slightly startled, it took DCI Upton's assistant a few seconds to respond.

"Oh, Mr. Carling. Hello, sir," he replied warily.

Don ploughed ahead before Ross could ask him why he'd been inside 214 Mulberry Street. "I think I can save you and your men some time. The lady you're looking for lives in Flat 102, but she isn't there. Apparently she's been gone since earlier this week." The puzzled expression on Ross's face told Don that he was a step ahead of the police investigation. "You'll probably want to speak with Mrs. Whitt in 101. We've just had a chat with her, and for what it's worth, this is what she told us...."

After Don had given them a quick summary of their conversation with Mrs. Whitt, Ross said, "Most interesting sir, I'll see that DCI Upton is informed of this development straight away."

"Okay Sergeant. And I'll try and get in touch with him myself later today," Carling told him.

*

Ten minutes later the two investigators were seated in a quiet corner at the Morning Sun, pints in hand, waiting for their lunch orders. Don had suggested the convenient venue for a brainstorming session to plot their next moves.

Tracking down N would now be a priority, and he'd already thought of a few options as they walked back towards the High Street. He ran them by James, inviting his input.

With this latest break he'd prefer to remain in London, but with the court date looming in Toronto next week that might not be possible. He made a mental note to call his secretary later.

One possibility, suggested Don, would be to wait until July fifteenth and see who checked in at the Pembury with a name beginning with N. But three weeks was too long to wait, he admitted, and James pointed out other drawbacks as well.

"There might be more than one pilot with the initial N on that day. Didn't you say there are forty or more pilots staying over on any given night?"

"Yeah, that's about the average," Don acknowledged.

" Or," continued James, "He might be with an airline that stays at a different hotel."

"True enough. I see how we could miss him, that's for sure." Don took a large swallow of his beer. "Rod Weathers might be able to help. He should be able to get me rosters from airlines with scheduled layovers for the fifteenth. Yes, that would be a good starting point."

They wrestled with how N would make contact with Renate now that she had apparently left the flat on Mulberry Street for good. How would he know she'd moved out? Could she contact him before he arrived in London? Possibly. If not, she might leave a message for him at his layover hotel, they agreed. Or most likely, N would have her mobile number and he'd call her. Then again, maybe she'd never return to London...

*

By 1:30 they had finished lunch. A light drizzle - barely enough to wet the pavement, had started while they were in the pub.

"Thanks James, I really appreciate your help," offered Don as they made ready to get on with their separate plans for the afternoon. "Call me later and let me know how you made out."

The senior citizen waved off the praise. "Haven't enjoyed myself so much since my dear wife passed away. We'll see this through old chap, trust me," he vowed.

Coates was going to chase down the property management firm that let the flat to Renate. A small placard fixed to the lower corner of the entrance door at 214 Mulberry Street named *Ascot Executive Leasing* as agents for rentals and James had made a note of the firm's number.

For his part, Don was going to make another call at the Glory of Venice restaurant.

'Damn, I should have taken James there for lunch,' he chastised himself. *'Next time,'* he muttered.

But first he had to make a few calls. To stay dry he stepped into the broad entrance way to the local post office, a few doors from the pub. First, he called Rod Weathers, and told him that they had located the mystery woman's flat and learned her first name.

"Well that's progress, isn't it, Don?" marveled Rod. "Do the police know this?"

"Upton's deputy does. We ran into him as we were leaving. I'll call the inspector myself later today."

"Good stuff. Is there anything I can do for you before I pack it in for the day?"

"Actually there is. It may not be possible, but here's what I would like you to try and get for me."

He wanted crew lists from the cargo carriers with planned layovers in London on the nights of July the fifteenth and the twenty-second. Could Rod have a go at that? He promised to tell him why when they met at Houghton's for dinner tomorrow.

"Sure thing. I'll contact their crew scheduling departments. Some of the bigger outfits with monthly bid systems for pilots should be able to provide names. "Worth a try, mate! I'll get right on it. Probably be next week, though, before we get any replies."

"No sweat, and thanks."

"You're welcome. By the way, I've managed to get you a pass to Toronto on British Airways. Are you still planning to leave on Sunday?"

"Yeah, I'm afraid so. I've been waiting until office hours in Toronto to call my secretary."

"I'll bring the pass along tomorrow. See you then. Cheers!"

*

The drizzle had turned into light rain while he was talking to Rod, so Don elected to stay in the sheltered entrance while he called Toronto.

Joanne had already talked with the Crown Prosecutor's office. "Good news and bad news," she proclaimed. Rather than start the trial on Monday, the day before the July First federal holiday, the judge had rescheduled opening arguments for Wednesday, the second, and expected the case to be wound up by next Friday.

"Well, that gives me a little breathing room, doesn't it?" said Don. "I'll plan on flying home on Sunday or Monday. I'll be in touch on Monday in any event, okay?"

"Right boss. There are a few other things that need your attention but they'll keep until you get back. Stay out of trouble over there!" She teased, signing off.

18

By noon Saturday a high pressure system had moved over southern England, bringing clear skies, just a wisp of a breeze and another warming trend. The temperature had climbed to 23C by the time Don set out on foot for Little Venice. After his conversation with Upton, he'd spent the rest of the morning in the hotel's health club. He now knew how many stone he weighed - fourteen. He did the math while he was on the treadmill.

Fourteen squared equals one hundred and ninety-six. Therefore, I've put on three pounds since I arrived in London. So I want to lose what? About a fifth of a stone? Never heard a stone spoken of in that manner. Were the Brits the only race that used stones? And why, one wonders?

He got bored with the treadmill before he came up with any plausible answers. But the moderate workout followed by a soothing sauna left him feeling very refreshed, both in mind and body. 'Oops! Time for a haircut.' He was studying his visage in the mirror as he finger-brushed his full head of dark brown hair. The greying at his temples was more evident every time he looked in a mirror recently, as were the crow's feet around his eyes. Up until now, he'd paid little attention to these inevitable aging signs, but he knew they weren't going to disappear. 'Oh well,' he sighed, 'I've always wanted to be described as distinguished-looking.'

As he strolled leisurely along side streets heading towards St John's

Wood, Don was cognizant of how quiet the British capital was on a Saturday afternoon. *Where is everybody? Have they all fled to the countryside?*

The other thing he noticed was the alarm systems on the exterior of most of the stately residences along his route. The reason for such precautions was obvious once he reached St John's Wood. He spent ten minutes browsing the 'homes on offer' listings in Estate Agents windows. Most of the detached homes for sale were priced between a half million and a million pounds. Luxury flats commanded six figures as well. *'And I thought Toronto was pricey!'* he chuckled.

With time to kill before he was expected at the Houghton's, he window-shopped along the fashionable High Street, looking for but not finding a suitable gift for Yvonne.

'There's always the airport for shopping,' he rationalized.

*

"Don't worry ladies, I wouldn't dare take the plunge again without your blessings!" Don laughed, lifting his arms in mock surrender.

He'd been bantering with Kate Weathers and her sister, Sonya Houghton, about his personal life. They had cornered him soon after his arrival. The two of them homed in on his relationship with Yvonne. Was it going to lead to marriage, and if not, why not, they wanted to know?

He was rescued by Derek. "Enough you two! Leave the poor chap to his single life of misery. We're off to the Arms for a pint before dinner. Back in an hour."

*

Don stood the first round, thankful to be spared from further grilling by the well-meaning wives. The Lock Keepers Arms was only a stone's throw from the Grand Union Canal, but rarely did a stranger venture in. The pub was hidden from passersby strolling along the waterway because of its location: it was hidden from view by a sharp bend in the narrow passageway leading from the canal. *A local in the true sense of the word*, was how Derek described it. The building housing the pub itself was of relatively recent construction in comparison with its neighbors, having been erected in 1949. A German bomb intended for the rail yards at Paddington Station had missed its mark and wiped out the original structure in 1942.

The pub was busy though, and the men were halfway through their pints before Derek noticed one of the two picnic tables in the forecourt being vacated and quickly claimed it.

"Good eye, Derek!" complimented Rod, as they seated themselves around it.

Talk turned to Don's investigation, and his conversation earlier with DCI Upton.

"Yeah, you could say he sounded slightly pissed off," admitted Don, in response to Derek's probing. "Maybe I should have told him I had someone working with me, but I hadn't seen any need for it just yet. Don't see why he should be complaining to you, though."

"Oh, he wasn't really complaining. Just wanted to know why I had put you onto James, I think. Anyway, he's in the loop now, as you chaps are wont to say. Shouldn't be any further bother over it," explained Derek.

The police had learned about Coates's involvement when they interviewed Mrs. Whitt. She told them the story of the kitten and the visit from Don and James yesterday morning.

"I think he's just a bit put off that we found the photograph at the Greek restaurant and the apartment of this Renate woman before they did," said Don.

"No doubt. But do your best to stay on his good side, my friend. I'll say no more about it." Derek drained the last of his tankard and stood up. "Drink up! We've time for another before we rejoin the ladies."

While Derek was inside, Rod confirmed that he had sent queries to the airlines requesting crew rosters for the July dates Don was interested in.

"Should have something for you by early next week. I've left word with Jennifer to forward the info to you immediately it arrives if I'm off flying."

"That's great, Rod. I'll wait until Derek comes back to explain what I'm looking for." Derek was weaving his way towards them through the throng of happy imbibers crowding the pub's front terrace.

"Thanks, Derek. Cheers!" said Don, raising his glass.

"Cheers, mate," added Rod.

"And the same to you gents," replied Derek, reclaiming his seat. "Now, Rod tells me you've uncovered some solid leads tying these deaths together. I'm all ears..."

"Right. And feel free to poke holes in my thinking," urged Don.

He started with Renate, surname unknown. Two people at the Glory of Venice confirmed that she had been to the restaurant recently - at least twice in the past three months - with Bert Rosen. Julia, the hostess, remembered them when shown the touched-up photo of Renate with darker hair, and Antonio, the waiter, also recalled them dining together. He had received this confirmation when he stopped by the restaurant yesterday afternoon.

He told them about finding the Polaroid snapshot of the same woman with blonde hair at the Greek restaurant in Hampstead, accompanied by Ray Flores. Antonio also recalled serving her as a blonde, but couldn't place Flores.

"Do you have a time frame for her blonde days?" Rod asked.

Don hesitated for a moment, pondering whether to mention the blonde woman seen with Dan Krantz in Paris in late '95 or early '96. This according to his buddy, Jerry Wahl. But he decided against it. Better wait to see if Wahl could identify her first. He'd faxed a copy of the photo of Flores and his blonde companion that morning to Wahl in California. He quickly brought his mind back to Rod's question.

"Not exactly," he answered. "If we work back from the date of Flores' death, it had to be sometime before the first of this year. This Antonio fella isn't sure when he'd seen her with blonde hair, but he's only been working at the restaurant since September of '95, less than two years ago. Oh, and Mrs. Whitt, who lives in the flat across from Renate's, remembered her with blonde hair about the same time."

"Using those dates, then," Derek said, "she could have been a blonde from the time she moved into the Highgate flat - let's say late '95 - until she changed her hair color sometime after Flores was killed and she took up with Rosen. Sometime earlier this year, perhaps..."

"Yes. It may not matter whether we know for sure. Probably worth checking with other tenants in the building, though," Don replied.

"Upton and his team will be chasing down those details today, I'm told. He'll also have a warrant to search her flat. And the rental agency should provide them with her full name," said Derek.

"You mentioned a connection to the Canadian captain who died in

Germany, the first victim. What's that all about?" Rod asked.

"A phone number. Both he and Ray Flores had the same London number in their possession. It was for a mobile phone that was disconnected earlier this year. I think it was probably hers."

"That would be shortly after Flores' death, then. How did you find that out? About it being disconnected?" Derek asked.

"DCI McGrath in Glasgow. He had all the London numbers in Flores' address book traced. This particular number was the only one he couldn't put a name to, and left it at that. Do you think it's worth pursuing?"

The London policeman shrugged. "Well, yes. Could be another lead. Even old information is better than no information in a murder investigation. Perhaps she changed numbers to avoid being traced."

"Yeah, that was my thinking too," said Don.

"May take some digging, but we should be able to find out which company the number was assigned to, and her name might still be on file. Yes, worth a try, get me the number and I'll put someone on it first thing Monday morning."

Don pulled a small piece of paper from his wallet and handed it to Derek. "Here it is," he smiled. "I wouldn't be surprised if she'd used a false name and address, though."

"You're probably right," Derek nodded. He tucked the paper into his shirt pocket. Their deliberations were interrupted for a few minutes when an acquaintance of Houghton's stopped by their table to say hello. Rod had met him before, and Derek introduced Don as a visitor from Canada without further explanation. After a few polite questions about how Don's trip was going he wished them a good evening and left.

"Well Don, I'd have to agree that your findings suggest quite strongly that this woman knew all these chaps at one time or another. Any idea how she would have met them?" Derek asked, once his friend was out of ear shot. "Highly unlikely they all met her by chance, wouldn't you say?"

"No, that doesn't hold water. Nothing I've uncovered suggests she's a prostitute, or even a high-class call girl. And I don't think she would have picked them up in a pub or restaurant near the Pembury, either. I have a theory, but I need more time to check it out."

"Why don't you run it by us then?" urged Derek.

Don thought it over for a moment before deciding. "Why not?" he shrugged.

He told them about his chat with Alf Heard, the night man at the Pembury House, and the man's obvious uneasiness when questioned about the dead men. In particular, his denial that he didn't know Ray Flores when his reaction said the opposite. Then he mentioned Alf's known nosiness when pilots were discussing their marital or financial problems while they were drinking in the hotel lounge late at night.

"So, you think he might be the link between the woman and the victims?" asked Rod.

"Well, it's a possibility that keeps running through my mind. Alf is definitely lying. Why, I don't know yet. I'd like to have another chat with him, but not at the hotel. Pressure him a bit, if you know what I mean," Don said, looking directly at the London police officer for his reaction.

"And how would you go about that?" was Derek's cautious reply.

"Well, I have his home address. Thought I might pop by there, see what happens."

"Tell you what. Before you do that, let me run him through our computer. See if he's got a history, that sort of thing." Derek said.

Don nodded. "Sure, that's a good idea."

"I'll have to let DCI Upton know, of course. I don't imagine these are avenues he's pursuing, but, if your assumptions are right, eventually there will be a tie-in with the Rosen case."

Their glasses were almost empty. Derek checked his watch and said, "Time to go. Must'n keep the cook waiting."

"Just one more question, Don," Rod said. "You were going to tell me why you wanted the crew lists. What's that about?"

Carling was hesitant about bringing up the unauthorized search he and James had conducted at Renate's flat yesterday, and the clue they'd found to another possible suitor. He was saved by a phone call. James Coates was on the line...

"No, no, go ahead. I'm just having a pint with Derek Houghton and my buddy Rod," said Don. He listened to the former MI5 agent for a good two minutes, nodding occasionally, before he spoke again.

"Excellent job, James," he commended. "Tell you what, let's get together tomorrow morning. Maybe Derek will join us. Call you at nine. Cheers!" He ended the call and offered his companions a Cheshire cat's grin. He made a production of draining the last drops from his glass before he ended the suspense for Rod and Derek.

"Gentlemen, we have a last name for our mystery lady. Neumann... Renate Neumann. The flat was leased and paid for by a Brussels-based firm."

19

SUNDAY, JUNE 29

Saturday evening had been enjoyable on all counts. Sonya loved to cook, and her pork roast, homemade applesauce and vegetable medley attested to her background in the culinary arts. The Moselle wine Derek had served was a perfect accompaniment to his wife's tasty meal. By the time Don had devoured two helpings of trifle, he was sure he had negated his morning workout twice over. Their occasionally animated conversation during and after dinner ranged from past ski holidays to Princess Di's alleged affairs. After coffee - liberally laced with Drambuie - Don was in an exceedingly mellow mood when he stumbled into the taxi Derek had called for him. Rod and his wife were staying overnight and both couples waved happily from the front steps as the taxi pulled away.

Derek Houghton had taken him aside last night while they waited for the taxi. He assured Don that he would definitely be along to sit in on his meeting with Coates the next morning.

"Nonsense! I'll be there. Count on it. I'm finding this case of yours most intriguing," he'd said, brushing aside Don's suggestion that he might want to spend the morning with his wife.

*

They met in Don's hotel room just after ten. After a brisk walk earlier, followed by a light breakfast, most of the Canadian's cobwebs had evaporated. Don had ordered a six-cup carafe of coffee from room service, and he and Derek sipped on the hot brew while they listened to Coates.

His account of how he had obtained the information about Renate and the flat rental left them both impressed and amused. James had called the agency that managed the building at 214 Mulberry Street and arranged a meeting with their leasing agent.

He passed himself off as a well-to-do widower looking to rent one of the vacant flats, possibly with an option to buy. The agent, a chap in his mid-thirties named Wallace Grover II, was a bit full of himself, and no match for the retired spy's wily manipulations. After being shown a flat on each of the top two floors, James said that he would much prefer one on the ground floor. Did he, by chance, know of anything that might be coming available in the near future? A flat similar to his friend Mrs. Whitt in 101? Perhaps 102 opposite?

Over lunch - and warmly effusive after drinking most of the twenty-four pound bottle of '93 Beaujolais that James had ordered - Grover had revealed the information Coates was seeking. The lease on 102 expired at the end of August, and so far hadn't been renewed. The lessee was a company headquartered in Brussels, Belgium. The flat had been rented for two years, ostensibly to house one of their employees while she was on assignment in London. Grover had only met her the one time, when she first moved in. He'd been on hand to give her the keys, provide her with his firm's contact number, and get her signature on some paperwork pertaining to her occupancy. The name she signed was Renate Neumann.

Before they parted, Grover vowed he would contact Coates as soon as he knew if 102 would be available at the end of August. Actually James never expected to hear from the agent. He'd given him a phony name and phone number.

When he'd finished his report, Derek asked, "Did you get the company's name?"

"But of course! Something called Flanders Holdings," answered James.

"How should I handle this info, Derek?" Don asked. "I suppose I should try and contact Upton today..."

After mulling it over, the policeman suggested that tomorrow would be soon enough. If the police had acted on the search warrant, they should come up with the same information on their own, reasoned Houghton.

"Yes, let's leave it at that. Call him in the morning," Derek told him. "He'll no doubt want to know how you acquired the information, but I'm sure you'll have come up with a logical explanation by then."

"Yeah, I'll work on that," Don smiled.

*

As it turned out, Don didn't have to wait. Upton called him later that afternoon.

"Her last name is Neumann. She works for a Belgian firm. In what capacity, we haven't discovered yet. She apparently cleared out of the flat late last Sunday, between 10:30 and 11 P.M.. A tenant who lives above her flat saw her getting into a minicab. She had two large cases and a few smaller ones." Upton related all this is a clipped voice before Carling had barely said hello.

"Uhh, I see...thanks," was all he could get out.

"But you smart guys already know this, don't you?" Upton continued sarcastically. "Or was the elderly gentleman with all the subtle questions about the occupant of flat 102 just a figment of Mr. Wallace Grover the second's imagination? A man who bears a remarkable similarity to an ex-MI5 officer we both know...

Don was about to offer some sort of apology for not contacting Upton with the information about the woman - didn't want to bother him on the weekend, thought it would keep until Monday, etcetera, etcetera - but he didn't.

'Screw you, Jack,' he decided, *'your chippy attitude doesn't warrant an apology.'*

"Just doin' what I've been hired for, Inspector," said Don in an even voice. "The firm's name is Flanders Holdings, by the way."

"I know. We've already checked it out. Doesn't exist, apparently."

"Ah, well that doesn't really surprise me. But thanks anyway." With that, their short conversation ended.

The confirmation that Renate had probably left the flat for good strengthened his take on her. Either directly or indirectly she was connected to Bert Rosen's killing. And she was going to great lengths to prevent anyone from finding her.

DCI Upton's revelation that Flanders Holdings didn't exist wasn't news to Carling. James Coates hadn't been able to find any trace of the company, either. But he'd contacted a former colleague who was now working for a private security firm in the Belgian capital.

"If there's any trail to this sham company to be found, Beck's the lad who'll find it," James had promised at their morning meeting.

*

Later Sunday afternoon Don phoned Rod Weathers to confirm he'd be leaving tomorrow, preferably on an afternoon flight.

"Right then, give me an hour to set it up. I'll get back to you," said Rod.

Don put his feet up and watched a telecast of the final round of a golf tournament being played in Holland. The only names he recognized were those of pros who also played the American tour - Singh, Montgomery, and Ernie Els. A Danish player he'd never heard of was clinging to a one stroke lead when he dozed off.

The phone rang before he was completely under...

"Okay mate, the best I could do was Flight 24 at 1500 hours. Arrives Toronto at 1750. Forty seats open, so it shouldn't be a problem. There's an evening flight at 1900 but it's almost full," explained Rod.

" Great. Three o'clock suits me just fine," answered Don. "By the way, how did you manage a pass on BA?"

Laurence Ashby, a British Airways captain and a member of the airline's flight safety committee, was a good chum of his, Rod told him. After earning their wings, the two young pilots were posted to the same RAF Squadron, and enjoyed three memorable years flying Tornado strike aircraft. They had kept in touch since joining their respective airlines.

"Larry and I talked about these deaths back in January, even before I contacted you. He offered to help any way he could, so, when I approached him a few days ago, he made a few calls and voila, the pass is the result. It's 'space available', of course, but I shouldn't think the flight will sell out in the next twenty-four hours."

"Good. Be sure and thank Captain Ashby for me," replied Don.

20

Don was on the phone to DCI Derek Houghton when he heard his name paged.

"Would passenger Carling please check with the desk," intoned a pleasant female voice over the public address system in the departure lounge for British Airways Flight 24.

"Okay then, Derek," said Don, "let's leave him until I return. I've gotta run. Thanks!"

The background check on Alfred Heard, the Pembury Hotel's night man, had been negative. The man did not have a criminal record.

*

Don edged his way past the line of passengers being pre-boarded and approached the desk. "I'm Carling," he said.

"Good afternoon, Mr.Carling. We've had a few 'no shows' in first class today. Perhaps this will make your flight with us a just a little more enjoyable." She exchanged his boarding pass for seat 39D for a new one. His new seat number was 4A.

Don glanced at her name tag."Well, thanks very much, Mandy," said Don, returning her smile. "I'm sure it will be!"

"You can board anytime now, sir. Through the door to your left."

Don gathered up his carry-on bag and computer case and thanked her again.

"You're welcome," she said, and with a slightly mischievous grin, added, "Captain Weathers says to go easy on the single malts!"

Don chuckled to himself as he strode along the boarding bridge, and made a mental note to bring back a duty-free bottle for Rod's buddy when he returned to London.

There were only four rows in the forward section of the 747's first class cabin, and 4A was a window seat on the left side. Directly to Don's right was a bar and galley area. Behind that a circular staircase led to the upper deck. Because of the unique shape of the jumbo jet's nose section, his seat was almost directly beneath the flight deck. Don glanced around the cabin as he was stowing his bag in the overhead bin. The only empty seat appeared to be 4B, the one next to his. That was fine with him, as he hoped to use the flight time to at least make a start on his report for the IPF's board. They were meeting in mid-July and Rod thought it prudent that Don have a progress report for the board, including an accounting of his expenses so far.

He also needed to plan his next moves. The court case he was to testify at could end quickly. If it dragged on though, or was recessed again, it could become a real pain in the ass for him. He planned to return to the British capital at least a few days before July fifteenth. The date - if he was right - that Renate Neumann would be expecting a male companion to arrive in London. If either the police or James Coates traced her before the fifteenth, he'd have to move earlier...

Once he was finished in court, he would have time to travel down to Atlantic City to see what he could learn about Daniel Krantz from his ex-girlfriend, Lori Wilson. That's assuming she's been traced and would be willing to talk about him.

He put a question mark after Bob Lewis's name. He'd told Lewis, Bert Rosen's co-pilot, he'd let him know how his investigation was coming along. *Wait until after possible meeting with Wilson,* he penned. He made the same notation beside Fred Newson's name. Even though Fred's mother had told Don in no uncertain words that she didn't care how he'd died, Len's son wanted to know. And he would check with Juan Flores in Miami...

*

Don set aside his notes when the crew started the meal service. The dinner was excellent in every aspect: choices, preparation, taste, and quantity. By sheer willpower he passed on offerings from the dessert trolley, opting instead for a second glass of fine Port.

He slipped the audio headset over his ears, pushed the selector button in his armrest until he got the light classical music channel, reclined his roomy seat and closed his eyes.

So just exactly what have I found out so far. What will you tell the board that will ensure their continued support?

You can tell them that you're 99 per cent certain the deaths are connected. That their deaths were meant to appear accidental, other than the last one. That you can tie three of the four victims to a woman named Renate Neumann, who bolted soon after Rosen's killing.

He would no doubt be asked a number of questions, questions he couldn't answer yet. What made them expendable, for instance? If he suggested that money - big money - was involved, he'd be asked what he thought the victims did to earn that money. And who paid them? He stared out the window, frowning. Something - or someone - caused these aircraft commanders to lose sight of their primary mission: transporting their passengers or cargo safely from A to B.

Diverted them, in other words, to a personal point of no return... down a path that ultimately cost them their lives...

His thoughts were interrupted by the chief steward leaning over the empty aisle seat to get his attention. "Anything from our duty-free offerings, sir?" he inquired politely.

"You bet," Don exclaimed, removing the headset. He'd been late getting to Heathrow and hadn't had time to browse through the shops in the departures area. "Perfume or pearls, I think. Let's have a look..."

21

BRUSSELS, MONDAY NIGHT, JUNE 30

As Don's flight cruised over the North Atlantic sixty miles from the southern tip of Greenland, three people were meeting in a small office a short distance from the Belgian capital's Grand Place.

"Why did you send such incompetents to London?" the lone woman present demanded, addressing her question to the younger of the two men. "This has seriously jeopardized my mission!"

"Calm down, Olga! They were the same men who carried out the previous assignments. Somehow this, ahh, 'target', became aware of their presence and they lost the element of surprise. He put up a struggle before they dispatched him," he told her. "At least there were no witnesses."

"Well, they have made it very difficult for me," she said, her anger turning to frustration. "I'm sure the police knew he must have been seeing someone in the area. Before long they would have found out where I lived. I had to abandon my flat in a hurry." She took a deep drag on the cigarette she had been waving about as she spoke.

"My dear Olga, not every day ends with the perfect sunset, as your parents no doubt told you many times when you were growing up," he said. "If I had known about the change to the captain's flight before hand, I would have postponed the operation," he added, a hint of censure in his voice.

"Don't you dare try and blame me for the publicity his murder caused, Vlad! I didn't know his flight had changed until he arrived at my flat that evening. How could I let you--"

"That's enough! Pointing fingers is not going to change anything, is it?" interjected the second man, raising his hand.

"Sorry Uncle," mumbled Olga."You are right, of course."

The other man nodded and reached for the pack of cigarettes.

Sixty-year-old General Georgiy Ivanovich Kravitchkev was the leader of Circle 17. The name stemmed from the number of original members who formed the secret group after the demise of the Soviet Union. All were former officers of the KGB who had survived the dismantling of that once vast Soviet intelligence service. Most of them were now employed by the new Russian security service. While they paid lip service to the ideals of detente with former enemies of the USSR, each of them hoped for a return to an authoritarian regime: one that would restore the power they once wielded over the populace. Power they lost with the collapse of communism in the USSR.

Circle 17's main goal was to continue the struggle against the Western alliance, and their individual determination was fostered by their continued loathing for the American government and all it stood for. With the limited manpower available, the group's leadership soon realized that they weren't going to be very effective on their own. Uncle Georgiy was the first to suggest that helping other organizations bent on wreaking havoc on American and Jewish interests around the world would be a better use of their resources - and also extremely lucrative.

It wasn't long before Kravitchkev had a client list eager to pay for the munitions, arms and intelligence that Circle 17 had access to. The buyers were mostly from Arab nations: terrorist organizations that mushroomed in numbers after the 1991 Gulf War. Raising money to pay for their purchases was not a problem: donations from sympathizers around the globe swelled their coffers, already amply funded by certain Arab government agencies under the guise of humanitarian aid.

To help hide the money trail between Circle 17 and its clients, the general had turned to the so-called Russian Mafia. Personally, he had utter contempt for their dollar-driven ways, but the mafia's expertise in money laundering made the alliance necessary.

Small cells of trusted agents, hand-picked by the general and his deputy, were recruited and inserted into cities worldwide to facilitate contracts. Pavel Fedorovich Nadrony, code name 'Vlad', was the head of the cell based in Brussels.

Renate Neumann was 'Olga', his most important deep cover agent for the past three years. Her real name was Tatiana Leonidovna Kravitchkevna, and the older man present really was her uncle.

Her father Leonid, a colonel in the KGB, had been killed while he was on an espionage assignment in West Germany in 1975. He was only forty-five when he died. Although never proven, his execution was suspected to have been the work of a double agent in the German intelligence service. But it must have been sanctioned by the CIA, of that the KGB had no doubt.

Tatiana, an only child, was born in Moscow in May 1959, When she was ten her father was posted to East Berlin. The family was still living there when he was killed. Her mother, German by birth, and with no real ties to the Soviet Union, decided to stay put. Tatiana had just graduated from university in 1981 when Uncle Georgiy came calling. Georgiy had followed his older brother into the intelligence service, and had been promoted to colonel shortly before Leonid was killed.

He offered his niece a chance for a prestigious career in the intelligence service. Such a position would bring her further education, good pay, and the promise of the many perks available to undercover agents stationed abroad. It only took the attractive twenty-two-old a day to make up her mind.

She said 'yes', much to her mother's chagrin.

The constant anti-west propaganda drummed into her by the Communist East Germany school system was a contributing factor in her decision. The clinching argument was the notion that a career in the KGB might in some way avenge her father's death: a point her uncle kept hammering at while they dined in East Berlin's most expensive restaurant, surrounded by the drab city's communist elite.

By 1984 Tatiana had completed all the courses and training the KGB required of new recruits. The next few years were spent working in the service's Moscow headquarters. Her duties were not especially challenging, and certainly not dangerous. Tatiana spent days and weeks shadowing foreign embassy staffers, and chatting up the same men and women at social events, searching for likely candidates who could be turned against their countries. It was her schooling in the 'dirty game', all part of the Cold War played out by regimes on both sides of the Iron Curtain.

Her Uncle Georgiy had never specifically mentioned sex when he recruited her. But soon after moving to Moscow the young agent-in-training realized that sexual liaisons would be an effective tool in the roles she was being groomed for.

Her virtue was tested a number of times in her first year in Moscow, and she was positive that some - if not all of the approaches - were part of her training. They ranged from hints of friendly seduction to what could only be termed attempted rape. A few days after each encounter she was offered a subtle chance to quit, usually along the line of 'if you've had enough, just say so, no one will think less of you' etcetera, etcetera.

She let the offers pass without ever acknowledging them, and finished the course. During her third year in Moscow Tatiana had her first real love affair, an affair that might have led to marriage. She would never know if her uncle had a hand in what brought it to an abrupt end. Her handsome beau, also a KGB trainee, was unexpectedly fast-tracked and posted back to his native Hungary three months before the end of training. She never heard from him again.

*

Tatiana didn't know how many others were in her cell, and she knew enough not to ask. Vlad had been her only direct contact since the start of her present assignment. He made the arrangements and paid for the apartments she used in Paris and London, and supplied funds for her everyday living expenses. The forged passports and other documents she carried were also supplied from Brussels.

Olga was on her own once the arrangements for her stay in London had been made. She was responsible for her own cover story, and keeping to a daily routine that ensured a low profile. In her present assignment, she was posing as Renate Neumann, a customer relations representative for a firm marketing women's fashions. Once she was supplied with the name and description of an airline pilot who might be vulnerable, how and where to orchestrate a 'chance' meeting with him was up to her. This had been the easy part, her attractiveness and training ensuring success with her planned seductions. Deciding when her relationship with each captain had progressed to the point where she could suggest that her cousin in Brussels might be the answer to his financial problems was a bit trickier.

But the carefully crafted ruse had succeeded admirably with four captains so far. She'd never been completely at ease with their deaths, but she knew that there was no point in her asking questions as to why they'd become expendable.

Renate didn't know who supplied the names. He - or she - never communicated directly with her. The information was always passed to her by an anonymous cell member. But it wasn't too long after her second affair began that Renate was certain that the informant must have some connection with the Pembury House Hotel.

*

"Olga, are you listening?" Kravitchkev said gruffly.

His niece brushed at the cloud of cigarette smoke that their combined chain smoking had produced.

"Sorry Uncle, I was thinking. What did you ask?"

"We still have one last contract to carry out. You know what I'm referring to. Then you can come home for a while. Can you still manage it?"

"Yes, Uncle. It should be completed by the end of July. It will take me a week or so to set it up once I get back to London," she answered, throwing Vlad a cold glare.

"Good. The end of next month. No later". It came out as an order, just the way the head of Circle 17 intended.

22

Moments after the meeting in Brussels ended, Captain Norman Holt finished packing his overnight bag in his Brampton condo. He too was thinking about next month and London.

Norman Holt was the N on Renate Neumann's calendar. Holt was a 747 captain with Northern Flyer, and the destination of his flight tonight was Brussels. After a twenty-four hour layover, he would be flying directly back to Toronto. He would much rather be heading for London and Renate. He had no way of knowing that she would be in Brussels when he landed tomorrow morning. Nor did Renate have any intention of surprising him, even though she was aware of his schedule. London was the only venue for their affair. The success of her mission depended on it.

*

British Airways Flight 24 arrived in Toronto ten minutes ahead of schedule at 5:30 P.M. There were long queues in front of the customs and immigration inspectors though, and it was another thirty minutes before Don reached the baggage hall. At least his checked bag was already on the carousel when he got that far, and there was only a short line waiting for taxis after he exited the terminal.

He directed the driver to KayRoy's office a few miles away, and received a disgusted scowl in return. *'There's goes the bigger tip I was planning to give you for the short ride, sport,'* decided Don.

His car was covered in a layer of fine grit, testimony to the drought-like conditions still persisting in the Great Lakes region. The car's interior resembled a sauna bath, and Don started it and turned the air conditioner to maximum before entering the office.

Joanne had scribbled WELCOME HOME BOSS on a sheet of paper and left it on his desk. She included a phone number where she could be reached if he needed to talk to her before she returned to work after the holiday. He sorted quickly through the phone messages, and decided most would keep until Wednesday. The only message he took with him was one from Wilson Halpern, a private eye based in New Jersey. Halpern had called last Friday afternoon, he noted.

Don rang Yvonne's number before he left for home. Her answering machine cut in after the third ring. Disappointed, he left a message saying he was home and would try again later.

23

TORONTO, JULY 1

Canada Day dawned bright and sunny and Don was up early, enjoying the peaceful beauty of the view from his sundeck. His five-acre property was only twenty kilometres from the expanding suburbs north of Pearson International. But it was far enough from the busy Airport Road to give one a genuine sense of living in the country. The deck faced south. A dense wood lot bordered his acreage to the east and his neighbor's house on the west side was barely within shouting distance.

Don had his own stand of trees, a line of tall Lombardy poplars along the small stream that defined his lot's southern boundary. With the early stillness he could hear the water trickling down the stream's shallow grade. Four huge weeping willow trees and a number of small shrubs accounted for the rest of the yard's foliage. The only sizeable patch of grass was in front of the ranch-style home. When it needed cutting, his Lawn Boy riding mower made short work of the job.

There had only been one message on his private line when he arrived home last night, and it was from Yvonne. She had been invited to spend the Canada Day holiday at a friend's cottage on Georgian Bay, she said, and would be home either tonight or first thing Wednesday morning.

She left the number for the cottage, adding 'I miss you' in a soft voice. Three words that made him wish he had flown home for the weekend. He'd definitely call her later this morning. If he was lucky, he'd hear her say she was driving back tonight.

*

Don puttered around while he brewed more coffee. He found a half loaf of whole wheat bread that he'd remembered to put in the refrigerator before his hurried departure for London. There were still a few slices untouched by mould. He salvaged the best two and slid them into the toaster. By the time he'd finished his spartan breakfast of toast and jam and a third coffee he was feeling much perkier. Still in his bare feet, he padded out to the mailbox at the corner of his driveway and retrieved last week's mail. It took him a leisurely thirty minutes to go through it, browse the community newspaper he subscribed to, and write cheques for bills that should have been mailed last week. It was still only 8:45 when he stepped out of the shower and toweled himself dry. He decided shaving could wait until he talked to Yvonne. If he wasn't going to see her today he would just 'grub it out' until tomorrow.

*

At nine o'clock Don dialed Wilson Halpern's number.

"This is Will, what can I do for you this fine morning?" A cheery voice inquired.

"Mornin' Will, Don Carling here. You're up bright and early for a night owl. Been to any good Irish pubs lately?"

"Avoiding them like the plague, pal! Almost joined the Temperance Society after that evening!" he chuckled.

"That would've been the end of that fine organization," Don laughed.

The two had first met in 1994 at a convention for private investigators held that year in New York City. They'd spent one night trying to hit all the pubs within a four- block radius of their hotel that had Irish names. Had they been twenty years younger they might have succeeded. Their mission ended in the smoky confines of their seventh or eighth stop, the Blarney Castle Pub not far from Madison Square Garden.

'"Too far between pissers," declared the American, returning from another pit stop. "Couldn't agree more," burped his drinking companion. "Bartender, two Bushmill's if you please. And make them doubles!"

His head was still throbbing painfully at noon the next day and, not for the first time, Don vowed to drink in moderation forever after.

They'd exchanged cards when the convention ended and Halpern was the first person Don thought of after his long conversation last week with Jerry Wahl. He had called him from London and asked him to try and find Lori Wilson: the woman who, according to Wahl, had been Daniel Krantz's longtime girlfriend.

"So what have you come up with? I didn't expect to hear from you so soon," said Don.

"You caught me on a slow day, Don, and the info you had on her was still current. Led me right to her, in fact. Hold on a sec while I find my notes," he said. "Ah, here we go..."

Don made notes while Halpern spoke. Lori Wilson was still living and working in Atlantic City. She worked for a small airline that ran gambling junkets from cities up and down the East Coast, ferrying dedicated high rollers to the beckoning casinos on the Atlantic shore. The company operated two well-used 727s and Lori was on their flight attendant roster, he reported.

"Actually, they call them hostesses," said Will, correcting himself. "And some of them look rather well used, too!"

Don let the chauvinist remark go. No matter what their appearance, they would have been trained to FAA standards, he knew.

Halpern continued his report. The flights only operate three days a week: Friday, Saturday and Sunday. He had the address for her apartment, her home phone number, and the make and model of her car. He hadn't had time to find out how she spent her days off yet. Did Don want him to check that out?

"Hmm, sure, may as well," he replied. "If I decide to come down and talk to her I suppose a Tuesday or Wednesday might be the best time."

"Probably. I'll see what I can find out in the next few days. I haven't had a chance to look her over in the flesh yet anyway. What say I get back to you by Thursday night?" Don agreed, and gave Will his pager number.

He had one more request. Did Halpern have any contacts in the Chicago area? He did, and Don added the name and number of a private investigator in Wheaton, Illinois to his notes. Wheaton, Halpern explained, was a small city to the west of the metro area and not that far from O'Hare.

"Thanks again, Will. Hope to see you next sometime next week."

*

After hanging up, Don weighed the pros and cons of calling Lori Wilson. And not for the first time, he wondered, what, if anything, he could expect to find out by talking to her. Jerry Wahl was fairly certain that she and Krantz had split up sometime before he died. If that were true, then Lori might not be interested in helping him. He had no reason to believe she would know anything about whatever Krantz had been involved in. But then again, he knew very little about Krantz, period.

Leave no stone unturned, was one of the principles to live by in a homicide investigation. Don recalled his criminology professor stressing the point repeatedly. Yes, he decided, he would try and talk to her, but not on the phone. If she had any hesitation about answering his questions, it would be much easier for her to say no if they weren't face-to-face.

Just after ten o'clock, nine in Illinois, Don dialed the number for the Ronan Agency. Tim Ronan, the gravelly-voiced owner and only employee, answered. After explaining who he was and his connection with Will Halpern, Don outlined the investigation he hoped Ronan would handle for him.

*

By one o'clock, Don was settled in his Lazy Boy chair, planning to kill a few hours watching a baseball game. He was half watching, half listening to the announcer and color commentator prattle on about the importance of today's game between the Toronto Blue Jays and the visiting team, the powerful New York Yankees and their lineup of millionaires. His phone rang just as the playing of the National Anthems ended. It was Yvonne...

"Hi gorgeous! I was just about to call you. I've been on the phone most of the morning." *Liar! You're a rotten liar!*

She didn't let on whether or not she believed him. "Well, I just checked my answering machine and got your message. So how did your trip go?" she inquired.

He was making progress, he told her, but couldn't see the light at the end of the tunnel just yet. They chatted for five or six minutes about nothing in particular before Don popped the question he'd been trying to phrase properly all morning.

"I suppose you're having such a great time that I can't entice you to come back today, especially when all I can offer is a quiet dinner on the patio deck? Just the two of us?" he wheedled, hoping she could picture his hang-dog expression.

She left him hanging for long seconds. "I'll be there by six - make sure the wine is well-chilled," she vamped. "I'll be hot..." She hung up before he could reply.

Don clicked off the television and mentally 'high fived' himself. *Now I'd better get my ass into town and hope I can find a store open!*

But first he needed to shave...

*

With Yvonne's arrival still a few hours away, Don decided to make one more call. He phoned Miami just after 4 P.M. and was put right through to Juan Flores.

"Ah, Senor Carling! How good of you to call," the gracious Cuban-American responded to Don's greeting. "Have you any more news about our son?"

"Well sir, unfortunately I'm still not positive why Ramon and the others were killed, but I'm getting closer."

He told Flores how the latest death in London had provided a number of promising leads, about the two suspects the Scottish and London police were trying to trace, and the hunt for a woman that seemed to have been acquainted with all of the victims.

"I'll be returning to London in a few weeks and should have more news for you when I get back. The British police are very thorough and I am working with them on it," said Don. "I'm sorry that's all I have for you so far," he added.

"No, no senor. I do not expect miracles. From what you have told me I am sure your investigation will succeed. How about money? Do you need more?"

Don thanked him for the offer, but assured Juan his investigation wasn't being hampered for lack of funds. Flores made him promise to call him first if he ran short and then switched the subject.

"Senor Carling, I have found out a little more about my son's problems..."

Through his influence in the Little Havana community he had been able to confirm the rumors he'd heard concerning Ramon's gambling, mainly at two of the area's major racetracks. His son had run up large debts with a Mafia-backed loan sharking organization. In early 1996, he had been given a 'final' deadline to repay his loan. According to the elder Flores' sources, Ray had started paying down his debt shortly after the warning. This hadn't satisfied his debtors though, as their onerous interest charges meant his debt was still climbing.

Sometime that summer Ramon was roughed up to the point that he had to book off a couple of his flights. Neither Juan nor his wife knew of this beating. He had secluded himself until his wounds had healed, it seemed. His sources told him Ramon had come up with a big payment in August or September - enough cash to get them off his back for a while - and assured the sharks he would pay off the balance by year's end.

"Uhh, do you know how much they were talking about?" asked Don.

"Yes, he paid back over twenty thousand dollars. And none of it came from me."

*

BRUSSELS, JULY 1

Norman Holt and his crew crammed themselves into their transport, a Peugeot utility van. They all agreed it must have been designed for midgets. The driver made good time for the first nine or ten kilometers en route to their hotel in the centre of the city, but conditions changed abruptly when they turned off the ring road. The heavy morning traffic degenerated into a bumper-to-bumper crawl, and the last few kilometers seemed to take forever to the three tired pilots. Their rooms were ready when they finally reached their hotel though, which wasn't always the case. By a quarter to nine, Norman had unpacked, stripped and stretched out on the comfortable, queen-sized bed.

He thought of calling Renate, but, with the one hour time change, decided it was too early in London. His lover wasn't a morning person. From experience, he knew a call later in the day would get a much warmer response,

Am I actually falling in love with this sexy, secretive woman? was the last thought the Englishman had before drifting off to sleep.

24

BRUSSELS, WEDNESDAY, JULY 2

Norman Holt had tried to call Renate three times last night. There had been no answer at her London number. This was a bit puzzling, because he'd told he would call from Brussels. He had hoped to make a flight switch that would get him to London before the fifteenth, but hadn't been able to manage it, and wanted to let her know.

He'd tried again early this morning, also without success. She didn't have an answering machine, which had amazed him when he'd first found out. He'd suggested he would like to buy her one as a gift, but she had been quite adamant that it wasn't necessary, and he eventually dropped the subject.

As fate would have it, less than a mile separated Holt and Renate as he recalled that discussion. Both were traveling towards the Brussels airport; Renate in a taxi; Norman's crew in the same van that had carried them into the city the previous morning.

*

Renate Neumann never traveled using a passport in that name. For this trip to and from Brussels her German passport identified her as Katrina Mueller, born in Heidleberg on the second of May, 1959. Her cover story - which had never been challenged - was the same. She was a customer rep for a women's clothing firm. Her briefcase contained letters of introduction, catalogues, and various business cards of real persons connected to the fashion industry in European cities, theoretically more than enough to satisfy an inquisitive immigration or customs official.

By 11:15, Holt and Renate were even closer to each other. She was seated in a middle row seat in the economy class cabin of a Sabena 737, second in line for takeoff on Runway 25R. Onboard their 747, less than fifty yards behind her flight, Captain Norman Holt, First Officer Gene Rudd, and Flight Engineer Jack McCarron were busy running down the Before Takeoff checklist. Jack was reading off items, and either Norman or Gene flicked the appropriate switch, or checked for the correct setting on the flight instruments. When the Sabena flight received clearance to taxi onto the runway, Holt released the brakes to let his aircraft roll forward. From their vantage point on the 747's flight deck thirty feet above ground, they had a bird's eye overview of the smaller 737.

When the 737 began its take-off roll, the tower controller cleared Northern Flyer 225 to 'line up and hold' on the runway.

"Position and hold, 25 Right," acknowledged Gene Rudd.

Using the nose wheel tiller to steer the giant 747, Holt maneuvered the plane from the taxiway onto the runway. Once he had it positioned on the center line, he set the brakes again, and the crew completed the last items on the checklist.

"Before Takeoff Checklist complete, Norm," confirmed the flight engineer. Holt acknowledged and called off the pertinent speeds he would observe to get airborne.

"...142, 148, 168. Runway heading to 1,500 feet, then a right turn to a heading of 285. We're cleared to 5,000 feet," he said, reviewing the sequence of headings and altitudes he would fly to comply with their departure clearance routing.

"Northern 225 cleared for takeoff. Contact departure on frequency 135.5 airborne," said the tower controller.

As soon as Gene acknowledged the clearance, the captain released the brakes, placed his right hand over all four throttles and eased them forward towards the pre-computed power setting. Rudd reached under the captain's hand and fine-tuned the throttles until they were all reading the same, then called, "Power set!"

Thirty-nine seconds later the giant bird lifted gracefully off the runway...

*

Thirty minutes after taking off from Brussels, Northern 225 was over the North Sea, approaching the southeast coast of Scotland. Their altitude was 31,000 feet, and the auto-pilot was engaged. Norman called for the Cruise Checklist. From memory, the first officer called out the items to be checked and Norman or Jack responded.

"Cruise check complete, skipper. Time for a drink, doncha' think?" said Gene, unbuckling his shoulder straps.

Jack left his seat and stepped back into the galley area behind the flight deck, poured three coffees, and brought them forward.

"Just right, too strong!" Gene grimaced, after taking a sip. He was drinking his coffee black, both Norman and Jack being cream and sugar men.

"I made it that way just to keep you awake, smart ass!" retorted Jack. "Aren't you glad this is the last trip we have to put up with him, Norm?" Jack and Holt were scheduled to fly together again on their next trip, but with a different first officer.

"Yes, flying with Gord Chalmers should lead to a higher level of conversation," smiled Norman. He reached over and gave Gene's shoulder a light punch. "Just kidding!"

"I'm hurt. If that's how you guys feels about me I shall desist from other than operational talk for the rest of this flight," Gene huffed theatrically.

"Wish I could believe that," muttered Jack, getting in the last word.

*

An hour after reaching cruise altitude the 747 was over the North Atlantic Ocean , 200 miles west of Scotland's Outer Hebrides Islands. In London, Katrina Mueller had just cleared immigration and customs after the arrival of her flight from Brussels. Her passport had only received a cursory glance from the officer manning the line for EU passport holders. She offered a casual smile to the two customs officers observing passengers using the green 'Nothing to Declare' exit and seconds later she was swallowed up by the waiting crowd of greeters in the Terminal Two Arrivals area.

Shunning the temptation of a convenient taxi trip into the city, she made her way across to the Airbus loading zone. She wasn't taking any chances. It was possible, she knew, that the police might have discovered her identity and connection to Bert Rosen by now. If so they might have put her description on a watch list that would have been circulated to include taxi drivers.

The half-full bus to Victoria gave her a comfortable sense of anonymity, and she was able to concentrate on the task ahead. After her hurried departure from the flat in Highgate Village, Renate had taken a room in one of the many bed and breakfast hotels near Victoria Station. She had spent three nights there before flying to Brussels for the meeting with her uncle and Vlad.

Her first priority now was to set herself up in another flat, and the Circle 17 agent had already prepared for just such a move. She had scouted out suitable venues during her early days in London, and had kept the list of possible new addresses updated. That groundwork would now pay off...

The requirements were fourfold. One, the flat must be far enough from her previous location that she wouldn't run into someone who might recognize her. Two, the building should cater to short-term rentals. Three, it should have a good-sized shopping area within walking distance, and finally the area should be easily reached by either bus or underground, preferably both.

Renate had decided on her first three choices by the time Airbus One shuttle bus pulled into the busy station just before noon. She bought four London newspapers before she called a nearby B&B and booked a room for two nights, but not at the same hotel she had stayed at after fleeing her Highgate flat. Two days should give her enough time to arrange for a new flat. The newspapers were to be scanned for any mention of Rosen's killing or, even more important, any reference to her.

Once she'd found a suitable flat, she would contact Vlad and have him make the necessary leasing arrangements.

25

THURSDAY, JULY 3

Don had arrived at his office just after 8 A.M. and was studying the fax from Rod Weathers when Joanne swept in at 8:20.

"Coffee's ready. Hope you like it strong," he greeted her.

"Well, I'm impressed! How come you're here so early, boss?" she asked, running a brush through her hair. "Geez, it's breezy out there!" A line of thunderstorms had rolled through just before dawn and the weak cold front behind it was kicking up gusty north winds. "How did the trial go? Did you get to testify?"

"That's three questions and you're only allowed one before I get my second fix," he said, joining her at the coffee maker. What passed for Joanne's lunch area was a small table in an alcove opposite Don's office. The coffee maker sat on one end of the table. "C'mon in and sit for a few minutes. You're not on the clock yet, either." Her normal hours were from 8:30 to 4.

The thunderstorms woke him up, he couldn't get back to sleep, so he decided to come in early. "Simple as that!" Don told her. He didn't get called to testify because the defendant decided to plead guilty just before opening arguments were to begin. The defence attorney asked for a consultation which, after a further two-hour adjournment, resulted in a plea bargain arrangement.

"So, after twiddling my thumbs for three or four hours, I was out've there. Not that I'm complaining, mind you. Anyway, give me an hour to go through this," he told her, indicating the phone messages he'd left behind on Monday night. "Then we'll talk about what needs to be addressed in the next week or so."

*

Don flew to Atlantic City on the following Tuesday, July the eighth. Wilson [Will] Halpern had gained a few pounds since Don had last seen him. The former state trooper's grip hadn't lost any strength though, and the Canadian flexed his fingers after they shook hands, checking for damage.

Halpern's large and tanned bald head wore a patina of perspiration, courtesy of the ninety degree temperature and even higher humidity on the New Jersey coast. He'd been waiting in a No Parking zone in front of the terminal, chatting amiably with an airport cop.

"Hop in friend, let's get out of this steam bath! It's a lot more bearable down near the shore," he said. Don stashed his briefcase and overnight bag on the rear seat of Will's two-year-old Ford Crown Victoria. The air conditioning was on max and the leather seats were cool to the touch. "Thought we'd stop at my office first and then go from there," he said once they were underway. Fifteen minutes later Halpern wheeled into a small plaza a mile south of the casino strip. His storefront office was sandwiched between a State Farm Insurance office and a health food store. When Don stepped out of the car he felt the sea breeze immediately, even though he couldn't see the ocean.

"It's a half a mile that'a way," said Will, pointing east. "Knocks about ten degrees off the temperature," he added.

His office was smaller than Don's. It had one main room containing a desk, two chairs and a small table with a cheap plastic plant sitting on it. A short hallway in one corner led to a washroom and a storage area at the rear.

"Don't need one most of the time," said his host, reading his visitor's mind. "Got a gal to do the books when necessary and send out invoices. *This* is my secretary," he continued, indicating the latest in desktop office communications systems. "I can be reached anytime of the day or night through this. Doesn't matter where I am. All the bells and whistles, too."

"Sounds like the ideal set up, Will," said Don. "I'm sure most of your time on the job is spent outside the office, anyway. I know mine is."

Don scanned the photos and citations on the office walls while Will went to get them coffee from the café across the parking lot. When he returned, the two investigators talked shop while they drank. Even though there was plenty of business in Atlantic City, he told Don, he was being squeezed. Halpern's biggest beef was the new guys on the block who grew in number every year.

"All most of them have ever done is write parking tickets for some hick town force down south and all of a sudden they're private investigators in AC. I have to charge ten bucks an hour less than I did five-six years ago just to stay in business," he griped.

Don commiserated with him as he sipped the very hot, but also very weak coffee. When they were interrupted by a phone call, he slipped back to the washroom and dumped the rest of it in the sink.

Will's pessimism was gone when he hung up. "That'll keep me busy this weekend. Thank the Lord for referrals, huh?" He smiled. "Now let's talk about this gal of yours." He reached for the lone folder on his desk, slid a photograph out, and passed it over to Don.

"What's the big deal that brings you all the way down here to interview a run-of-the-mill call girl who plays stewardess on weekends?"

*

Don studied the image, an enlargement of a photo that had been taken with a telescopic lens. It was in black and white, and snapped as she was getting out of a car. From a distance, Lori Wilson's face showed no signs of aging. A stranger looking at the photo would probably guess her to be no older than thirty.

Will read from his notes. "Lori Wilson - which is her real name, by the way - age thirty-seven, five seven, a hundred and thirty-five pounds, brown hair and eyes, no visible scars or markings, lives alone. Two priors, both times received suspended sentences and probation. Last time was--"

Don interrupted him "Whoa! What was she charged with?

Prostitution?"

"Nope. Possession of an illegal substance - cocaine."

"And when was this?"

"First time was back in 1986 in Atlanta, Georgia. A year's probation and a two thousand dollar fine. Stayed out've trouble until she was busted in Philadelphia in August '95." He was still reading from his notes. "Actually, she was charged with trafficking. Must've had a sharp lawyer, though. Ended up pleading guilty to the lesser charge of possession."

"Is that a normal occurrence?" asked Don.

"Hard to say. Sometimes the prosecutor doesn't think the evidence the police have is sufficient to get a conviction. Or she wasn't viewed as a major dealer and the state didn't want the expense of a trial," shrugged Will. "But in this instance, a condition of her probation was that she get treatment for her habit, which, apparently she agreed to. Probation was for two years, so she's still got a few months to run. Yeah, here it is. Doesn't end until October fifteenth."

"Interesting," commented Don. He was doing the math in his head. That was almost two years ago, and Krantz was killed just over a year later. "Do you know if she's clean now?"

"Well, I didn't see any sign she was using, but I can't say for sure. Does it matter?"

"No, I suppose not. But her previous drug use could have played a part in this web I'm trying to untangle," said Don. "Let me fill you in and see if you agree."

*

Don laid out what he'd learned so far about the suspicious deaths. By checking into Daniel Krantz's background, he hoped to fill in more of the blanks. Lori Wilson's relationship with the dead man was what he wanted to ask her about.

"So Lori and this pilot lived together, but split up sometime before he died. You don't know when. And he was - hypothetically - being paid big bucks to smuggle goods of some kind into the US. Then he became a liability, or whatever, and they took him out. And the same scenario applies to these other victims?"

"Yeah, that's how it looks to me. Maybe drugs were a part of it and she had something to do with Krantz's problems," suggested Don.

"Well sir, there's one way to find out. Let's go talk to the lady!" said Will.

*

"You didn't seem surprised when I said she was a working girl. Did you know that already?" asked Will. They were on the coast road heading away from the strip. It was 11:45, traffic was heavy and they were hitting every red light.

"No, not exactly. Jerry Wahl hinted at it. But that would've been a long time ago. How did you find out?"

Will took a business card from his shirt pocket and handed it to Don. It was embossed with gold-colored lettering. *Lorraine, Discreet Companionship for Gentlemen of Means,* it read, along with a phone number. Halpern had tailed her the previous weekend after the flight she was working arrived back in Atlantic City. On both Friday and Saturday evenings she had returned home, changed clothes and shortly afterwards drove to a hotel on the strip. She met her date in one of the bars, had a drink or two with him, and they eventually took an elevator upstairs, presumably to his room. About an hour later she would reappear alone, and head for home.

"On Saturday, she went to two different hotels to meet johns. Didn't get home until after two," said Will. "I had a little chat with one of her customers afterwards. Flashing a badge still works wonders. He handed over her card without too much persuasion."

"Jeez, she must be dragging her butt on the flights!"

"Well, they're not exactly dawn patrols, you see, and mostly short flights. Usually don't depart AC until after lunchtime, and arrive back here two or three hours later, with another load of eager beavers," explained Will. "And some of them are after beaver themselves," he chuckled.

Don had to laugh too. "So she lives around here, does she?" They had just passed a *Welcome to Ventnor City* sign.

"Actually we passed her townhouse complex about a mile back. She goes to a health club a few mornings a week, today being one of them. Thought we'd catch her when she comes out. Which should be soon," answered Will, checking his wrist watch. He turned into a nearly empty parking lot in front of the Forever Young Fitness Center and Spa.

"Yeah, she's still here. That's her car." He was pointing at a white Grand Am, as he drove towards it. He parked beside it, shifted into 'park', and left the engine running. The outside temperature was showing eighty-four degrees, but the interior was a comfortable seventy-two.

From their vantage point, they had a clear view of the building's large plate glass entrance doors, about twenty yards away. All of a sudden the parking lot began to fill up. Car doors slammed and people with gym bags climbed out and hurried inside, no doubt to work out on their lunch break. So far only a few people had come out of the building, young mothers with pre-school kids in tow.

It was ten minutes past noon when Will announced, "Here she comes now."

Don studied the woman striding towards them. She was dressed in a peach-colored, nylon track suit and wearing white running shoes. Under a black ball cap her hair was pulled back into a pony tail. As she got closer Don could see the cap's DKNY logo. Lori Wilson was a very attractive woman, he observed.

Halpern turned the engine off and both men got out.

*

Don smiled at her. "Miss Wilson? Lori Wilson?" She stared at him, but didn't reply. "My name is Don Carling. I was hoping you could help me out." He handed her his card, which she reluctantly accepted. "I'm investigating the death of Daniel Krantz," he added quietly while she studied it.

"He died accidently in Paris. That's all I know," she said quickly, handing him back the card. She turned her back on Don and fumbled with her car keys.

"He was murdered, Lori," said Don. "It wasn't an accident."

Taken aback, she froze for a few seconds. "I...I...don't know anything about that," she said. There was fear in her voice, though. "So I can't help you."

"Lorraine, I think you'd better talk to my friend." Will had been leaning against his car's trunk. He moved closer before he spoke to her again. He dangled her business card in front of her. "Your parole officer might not look too kindly on your sideline business. Prostitution is still illegal in these parts, as I'm sure a bright gal like you is well aware of."

"Bastard! How did you get that?" She grabbed at his hand but wasn't quick enough. Halpern held the card behind his back and said, "Just give my Canadian friend here a few minutes of your time and I'll tear this up. You'll never see me again. Okay?" He started towards the building. "I'll just go and check out the action inside while you two have a little chat."

"Honest, I'm not here to cause you any problems," said Don, holding up his hands, as Will strode away. "Why don't we go over and sit in the shade?" He pointed to a picnic table under a large willow tree to the left of the building. Lori shrugged as if to say 'why not?'

After they were seated on opposite sides of the table, Don began, "Miss Wilson, I..."

"Oh pul'eeze, call me Lori. This isn't a court room."

"Okay, thank you. Lori it is. Lori, Dan Krantz wasn't the only airline captain killed on a layover in Europe. There have been three others, the latest less than three weeks ago in London. I'm trying to find out why." He paused to gauge her reaction.

Eventually she spoke, still somewhat defiantly. "Still don't see what any of this has to do with me." She didn't sound totally convinced, though.

"Maybe nothing Lori, but let me tell you what the others had in common in the year or so before they died and then--"

"We weren't living together when he died," she interrupted, doodling on the table top with her keys.

Don knew that, but not the why and when. "When did you break up?" he asked, trying to sound surprised.

"*We* didn't break up. He basically told me he didn't want me around anymore. Threw me out, to be exact."

"And when was this?"

"October twelfth, nineteen ninety-five. The day before I started my rehab. I'm sure your smart-assed buddy told you all about that too, didn't he?" she challenged. "He obviously knows that I'm still on probation, the prick."

"Will's also a licensed private investigator, and I hired him to find you. That's all. No one is going to be calling your parole officer, you have my word."

"I'd like to believe that," she offered softly, making eye contact for the first time. "I've been clean since they discharged me. But I've got to make a living and flying three days a week doesn't bring in enough, so I..."

Don held up a hand. "You don't need to explain. I know kicking an addiction isn't easy - or fun. I know because my sister went through the same thing," he said. This was a lie. He didn't have a sister. But he knew sympathy would gain him more than strong arming.

"Really? Is she still okay?" Lori asked, an unsaid plea for support.

"Doin' great!" he smiled, "And it's been over three years. You just have to make a fresh start, don't you?"

"Yes, yes, that's what my counselors kept saying! And I'm trying, believe me. I just need time. As soon as I have enough money saved up, I'm heading back to Georgia. A girlfriend in Atlanta wants me to be her partner in a pet grooming business. I think I'd like that," she said, her voice trailing off.

"I'm sure it will work out for you, Lori. I'd say you're over the hump already."

She mumbled her thanks. To her credit, Lori didn't make excuses for her past. When prompted, she talked openly about her on-again, off-again relationship with Dan. Her story was tinged more with sadness than bitterness.

Lori had moved in with Krantz in 1992. The pilot had rented a one-bedroom beachfront condo in Atlantic City soon after he had been hired by International Airways. He either drove the hundred or so miles to JFK or caught a commuter flight. They moved to a larger townhouse a few months later. This was the first time they had actually lived together, and all went well for the first few years. They went out to the casinos a lot to have dinner or see shows. Dan's passion was gambling, and quite often he would play poker all night. On some nights, Lori would take a taxi home after dinner. On other occasions she stuck around and partied with the other non-gamblers. Dan won more often than he lost at first, she recalled.

"But then he started to lose. And lose big. He stopped being nice to me, as if I was the cause of all his problems. And I was using..."

"Lori, stop for a minute," he placed his hands over hers, which were still fussing with her keys. "See if I can finish your story. Then you tell me if I've got it right."

She gave him a puzzled look. " How do you--?"

"Just bear with me," he urged. "Eventually Dan was desperate for money, the sharks were threatening him, then all of a sudden his financial situation improved." He had her full attention now. "He paid off his debts, and was his old cocky self again. Only problem was how he got the money. He was involved in something illegal - probably smuggling. Bringing contraband into the US from abroad. Then the people that set him up wanted him to do something a little more risky. Carry something more valuable, maybe even a passenger. But realizing that if he were caught it would mean the end of his flying career - and probably jail time - he told them 'no'. And that's when he became a liability to them." He paused, waiting for her reaction.

Lori remained silent, but she'd stopped fiddling with her keys.

Then he added, "And he was involved with another woman, probably in Paris."

She was now on the verge of tears, and nodding her head ever so slightly. He had her now. Just needed to phrase his next request so it wasn't a threat.

"Lori, please help me out with this. Tell me what you knew about his dealings. There are striking similarities between Dan and the others. You can help me put a stop to it. What you know might keep other guys from the same fate."

He wasn't sure if was his approach, or her just wanting to get it off her chest, but Lori opened up and told him more than he ever expected she would. Reflecting on it later, he figured it had been a bit of both.

*

An hour later Don and Will were sitting on the deck at Lonnie's, a popular beach bar overlooking the surf a few miles from Lori's health club. They'd ordered burgers and a pitcher of Miller Genuine Draft. The jug of cold beer almost empty by the time Don finished telling Will what he'd learned from Lori.

Don's assumptions about Krantz had been mostly right, Lori admitted. He hadn't been particularly secretive with her about how he was making extra money.

'Just doing the odd favor for a friend in Brussels,' he'd told her.

He'd have a package to deliver when he returned from a trip, she said. Not every trip, but at least five or six that she knew about. This was in the summer of 1995, two years ago. The first ones she saw were envelopes and she presumed he just mailed them. The others she knew about were small packages, about the size of a box of chocolates. She'd wondered how he had managed at customs, but never asked.

She thought he probably just carried them in his flight bag. That was feasible, Don figured. Any time he'd been spot-checked by customs, he could only recall one time when his flight bag had been given more than a cursory inspection.

"So whatever this guy was smuggling must've been quite valuable to someone, huh?" said Will. "Porn photos, maybe?" he mused.

"Nah, I can't see that. Ten, fifteen years ago, maybe. Now you can download all that shit off the internet. No, I'm thinking more like stolen bonds, counterfeit bills, some sort've money laundering scheme, that kind of stuff," said Don.

"Makes more sense. How did he get rid of it?"

"Ah, this is where it gets interesting," answered Don. "She'd only been with him once when he delivered a package. Apparently he'd made a call and set up a rendezvous. The meeting place was the lounge bar of the Gulfstream Casino. They were--"

Will noticeably sucked in his breath, causing Don to pause.

"What?" he asked

"Tell you when you finish. Go on with her story," Will replied.

" Okay. So Krantz was still nursing his beer thirty minutes after they arrived and getting antsy," she said. "Eventually he suggested she make a visit to the ladies room, which she did. When she returned, Dan stood up, said 'Let's go', and ushered her out. After that he always went alone to make his deliveries."

"So she never saw who he was dealing with?"

"Nope. The transaction took place while she was in the john."

"Yeah, well, that's not surprising, is it?" shrugged Will. "So you don't figure she was involved in any of his activity then?"

"No, I think he was acting alone," replied Don.

"So how did she get money to feed her habit? Let me guess - she was peddling her cute ass around town when her boy was off on a trip, right?"

"Not exactly, but you're on the right track," answered Don.

He'd asked about her drug problems and Lori had been quite open with him. When she needed cash, she confessed to working occasionally for an escort service in Philadelphia, not that long a drive from Atlantic City. Her arrest for dealing and possession had occurred in Philly while she was with a client. She figured the guy lied when he told the police she had sold him the coke in able to protected his identity. As far as she knew, Krantz never heard about her arrest and her plea bargain to the lesser charge of possession.

He was aware of her more than social use of the drug though, and her addiction led to their break up. Her main supplier was a dealer at one of the casinos where Krantz did most of his gambling. When she was short of cash, her drug buys were added to what Dan owed them for his gambling debts - at the same exorbitant interest rates.

"That was the last straw for Krantz when he got wind of it. He told her to pack up and move out. She never saw him after that," explained Don.

"And he was killed how long after they split up?"

"About a year. She only heard about it months later. Jerry Wahl phoned to tell her."

"Remind me again how he fits in?"

"He was a good friend of Krantz's. A pilot who also worked for International Airways. They were flying together when Krantz was killed."

So what's with the Gulfstream Casino? Not your favorite spot, I take it."

"Mafia, my friend, as in Russian Mafia. Their foothold into the bright lights of AC."

"You don't say," murmured Don. His mind raced through the inventory of facts he'd heard or read about the expanding reaches of the Russian criminal element. Was it possible, he wondered, that the two suspects in the UK killings were members of the mafia as well?

Will indicated Don's empty mug. "How about another beer?"

"Uh, no thanks, Will, not for me. Had enough for now."

"Yeah, me too, probably. Listen, why don't you stay overnight? That'll give us a chance to check out the Gulfstream? Poke around a bit, you know. Maybe Krantz spent more time there than his girlfriend knew about."

Don was already thinking along those lines. Time-wise he didn't have a problem. He'd booked to fly home tonight at 7 P.M., but there was also a morning flight departing at 8:30.

"Why not?" he decided. "There's something else I'd like to check out, too."

26

WEDNESDAY, JULY 9

As it turned out, his overnight stay in Atlantic City hadn't been particularly productive. After returning to Halpern's office, Don phoned the airline, switched his flight, and booked a room at the Hampton Inn near the airport. His next call was to California, and Jerry Wahl picked up on the second ring.

"Hi there, Don! Didn't expect to hear from you so soon. What's up?"

Don gave Jerry a run down on his meeting Lori Wilson. "I've got a few follow up questions for you."

"Shoot!" said Wahl.

He asked Jerry about Krantz's supposedly doing favors for someone, probably bringing packages back from Europe. When Wahl hesitated, Don told him that Lori had confirmed his suspicions about Krantz's smuggling, but didn't know who his contact was.

"Yeah, well I thought she must've known something about it. And I do recall seeing him shove envelopes into his flight bag a few times," admitted Wahl.

"Jerry, did you see who gave them to him? Was it at your crew hotel, or maybe someone from your company?"

"No, I think he must have picked them up at the airport. But I never saw who he got them from. Sorry, that's all I remember."

"Which airport? Do you remember?" asked Don.

"Brussels. Yeah, it was definitely Brussels."

Wahl didn't hesitate when Don asked his second question. "Did you get the photo I faxed from London?"

"Oh, the other captain and the blonde. He flew for Globe Wide, didn't he?"

"That's right, Jerry. His name was Ray Flores."

"Flores, yeah. Well, I wouldn't swear on a stack of bibles, but she sure looks like the woman I saw with Dan in Paris."

*

Lori had given Don the address of the townhouse where she and Krantz had lived together. Will was familiar with the complex, which wasn't that far from his office. When they arrived, Halpern gave the superintendent - a retired navy petty officer named O'Donnell - a song and dance story about investigating an insurance matter involving the late pilot's estate. Don didn't think the guy completely bought it, but grudgingly agreed to answer a few questions.

Krantz's townhouse was sold by the bank holding the mortgage, he told them, and the new owners moved in a few months after he died. Yes, he remembered the attractive woman who had lived with him for a few years, but thought she had moved out some time before his death.

"Don't know how she put up with the jerk for that long," he commented. "He was a real sour type, always had a bitch about something around here."

O'Donnell didn't have any information to offer about what happened to the contents of the place, or even who had cleaned it out. As far as he knew everything was handled by the bank, or someone working for them. He didn't know anything about family or friends who might have visited them, and couldn't say if Krantz had been close with any of his neighbors.

That was all the time he had to answer questions, he told them rather brusquely, and closed his door without further comment.

"Hope he was more useful onboard a ship," muttered Will as they turned away.

Knocking on doors adjacent to Krantz's former address hadn't turned up anything new. The elderly widow on one side had trouble remembering Krantz and Lori, let alone recall seeing any visitors. They went out a lot, she told them, and, with a not very subtle hint of disapproval, added that his wife went out quite a bit when he was away, too. The young couple on the other side had only moved in four months ago and had no knowledge of Krantz.

*

Their visit to the Gulfstream Casino hadn't provided a wealth of information, either. Nothing about it suggested to Don that it was other than it what it looked like: a low budget gambling venue on the fringe of the downtown area. It reminded him of the generic casinos on Fremont Street in Las Vegas. Plenty of twenty-five cent slots and black jack tables with two or three dollar minimums, at least until 9 P.M. No lavish floor show, just a run-of-the-mill trio providing non-offensive music for people who weren't there to listen to them in the first place. Nothing said 'Russian' to him, either. The muscle lounging near the entrance, with their shaved skulls, ears that didn't match, and biceps that stretched the sleeves of their of cheap suit jackets, looked like a pair of World Wrestling Federation 'wannabies'.

They were seated at the short end of the dimly-lit, L-shaped bar. Most of the fifteen or twenty stools were occupied - all by men - and the two bartenders were busy keeping up with orders.

For an hour Don and Will munched on taco chips and mixed nuts while nursing their drinks. Will had been over tipping the thirty-something, well-endowed blonde tending their end of the bar. When she finally took a break, she perched on a stool across from them, lighted a cigarette, and let out a sigh. This gave Halpern the opening he'd been waiting for.

"Bet you could do with a foot rub, huh?" he said, putting on a sympathetic smile. From their seats they'd had ample opportunity to notice her curvaceous thighs and calves as she moved about on her three-inch stiletto heels.

Will kept up the small talk for a few minutes, feigning a more-inebriated state than the weak drinks could have induced. The blonde listened politely, the big tips paying their intended dividends. Her smoke finished, she stood up and stubbed it out in the small ashtray she'd been holding.

"Say Debbie, meant to ask ya," said Will, as he reached over and placed his hand on her forearm. "Have you seen ol' Dan around lately? Dan Krantz. I used to drink with him in here before I moved back to Philly. He was a regular, know what I mean? Usually came in about this time when he wasn't flyin'."

"Never heard of him, hon," she replied quietly.

"Would've been, oh, at least a year ago. Yeah, I left here last June. Haven't been back since." Debbie was still shaking her head no. "Good lookin' guy. 'Bout my age?" She tried politely to pull away from Will but he had tightened his grip.

"Sorry mister, don't think I knew him," she said, trying to keep a civil tone.

"How about askin' your partner down there," he persisted, indicating the male bartender who was now watching Will. "Ask him if he's seen Dan lately, will you?" Almost as an afterthought he added, "Please?"

He released her arm and sat back on his stool. The male bartender was a good eight inches taller than Debbie and had to bend over to hear her above the din. He'd weigh in at about two twenty-five, and none of it was fat, observed Don. He listened to her message, still watching Will. When Debbie finished, he set down the glass he'd been drying and sauntered down to their end of the bar.

He leaned close to Will and asked, "Who wants to know?" His body may have said twenty, but up close his lined face said thirty-five or more.

Halpern went into his good old boy routine once again. It might've rung true with Debbie, but Don could tell the hulk wasn't buying it.

"No one by that name has ever been a 'regular', as you put it, in this bar." He leaned even closer to Will, held his large index finger an inch from his nose, and whispered just loud enough for Don to hear, "And I don't recall ever seeing in you in here before either, *buddy*."

'That's a threat if I ever heard one,' Don thought.

*

Don replayed their visit to the casino as his flight was crossing Lake Ontario, descending towards Pearson International. They'd left the casino shortly after the brush off from the bartender.

Will vowed to go back again some other night, just to show the bartender that he couldn't be scared off that easily. Don could understand his wanting to save face, but suggested it might be better just to give it a miss. He'd been pissed off at Will's rather clumsy approach because they hadn't discussed using Krantz's name beforehand.

"I'd rather that my investigation didn't become public knowledge around here, Will, at least not yet," Don explained.

Halpern reluctantly agreed. He said he would stay away from the Gulfstream Casino until he heard from Don again.

I just hope the damage hasn't already been done, Don thought, as the aircraft eased to a stop at the gate.

27

Joanne picked up on his somber mood as soon as he stepped into the office.

"Okay, how much did you lose?"

"What makes you think everyone who goes to Atlantic City loses, Miss 'know-it-all'?"

"Because losers come back wearing a frown, just like yours, boss!"

"Ah, well, just thinking about something, that's all. Didn't go near a slot machine the whole time," he said, smiling now.

He'd had a number of calls since yesterday morning she informed him, handing him the message slips. He thumbed through them quickly.

Joanne glanced at her watch, then said, "I suggest you try Captain Weathers first. He'll only be at his office for another twenty minutes."

"Okay, make the call. I'll take it in my office," he instructed. "Thanks, Jo."

*

"Afternoon Rod, how goes the battle at IPF today?" inquired Don.

"Situation normal, just the way I like it! I've just been finalizing my report for next week's board meeting. I'm assuming you'll be back in time for it, right?"

Don assured him he would, and then asked, "How much lead time do you need to get me on a flight? I'd like to use the return portion of the pass on BA if possible."

"No problem. My chum set it for a round trip. I just have to call and list you for a specific flight. Got a date in mind yet?"

"Not exactly. I want to be in London no later than Monday though, which means leaving here Sunday night," He was thinking out loud more than answering Rod's questions. "Probably should try and get there sooner. Tell you what, I should know by tomorrow morning. Can I get back to you then?"

"'Sure, just call the office, I'm flying Friday and Saturday, but Jennifer will look after it for you if I'm out."

Rod had called to let Don know that he was forwarding more crew rosters for the following week. These were in addition to a short list he'd faxed on Monday. Don shuffled through the paperwork that Joanne had left on his desk.

"Yeah, I've got them in front of me, Rod. I'll be going through them this afternoon," he said. "I see a message here to call Derek, too. Do you know what that's about?"

"Not exactly. But I gather the Met police have made some progress in the Rosen case and he has the latest info for you."

"Great! I'll call him after we sign off. Anyway, I'm hoping take care of some loose ends here by Friday, and that'll free me up to head back your way on the weekend. I"ll confirm tomorrow. Cheerio!"

*

Derek had left his home number, and his wife Sonya answered Don's call. Derek had just phoned to tell her not to expect him for dinner, she said. In fact he told her not to wait up, as he expected to be quite late.

"Police business, you know," she added dryly . They chatted about the weather - rainy in London, hot and humid in Toronto - and Don gave her his unlisted number.

"I'll be home all evening, so Derek can call me when he gets in. If I don't hear from him tonight, I'll call him tomorrow." He tried to end the call quickly but Sonya wasn't having it.

"How are things with the lady Yvonne? Paying her proper attention since you got home, are you? And when are you going to get over your fear of flying again and propose? Any progress on that front?"

Don sighed. "Tenacious, that's the only word for you, Sonya! But since you've inquired, my dear, I've been showering her with attention since my return." He was chuckling now. "In fact as soon as we ring off I intend to call the florist and send her another dozen roses. An almost daily occurrence since I got home, I might add!"

"Oh please. I can see your nose growing from here!"

"Goodbye, Sonya. Can't wait to see you again!" Don hung up and reached for the Yellow Pages. He found the number for a nearby florist and ordered a dozen roses. After ordering the flowers, Don rang Yvonne's home number. He left a message inviting her out for dinner tomorrow night. *Better not leave it until the weekend - I might be on my way to London by then,* was his thinking.

*

His next call was to Tim Ronan in Illinois. An answering machine picked up after the third ring. He'd just identified himself when a male voice cut in.

"Hold on a sec... I'm here now." The speaker sounded out of breath, and then he heard what sounded like a chair scraping on the floor. He pictured an overweight guy settling heavily into a well-padded seat.

"I was just leaving, just locking up," he explained, still huffing. "So how're you doin', Don?"

"Hello Tim, glad I caught you. I was down in Atlantic City with Will Halpern when you called yesterday. He sends his regards, by the way," he replied.

"And how is our east coast buddy? Still burning the candle at both ends, I'd wager."

"Yeah, he's a hard guy to keep up with," Don concurred. "It was worth the trip though, and Will's groundwork saved me a lot to time. How 'bout you tell me what you came up with and then I'll tie it all together for you?"

Carling hadn't given Ronan a complete account of his investigation when he'd contacted him last week, deeming it unnecessary. He had only spoken of his interest in Bert Rosen, and, after a brief conversation, hired Tim to check into the Chicago-based captain's personal life.

Don had given Ronan the number for Bob Lewis, Rosen's co-pilot, and suggested he might be a useful starting point. As it turned out he was, albeit indirectly. Lewis told Ronan that a group of Bert's friends, including some other pilots from Atlantic Best Airlines, were holding a wake for Bert at the golf club where he'd been a popular member. The wake was held on the previous Saturday evening, the fifth. Lewis had invited him along, and introduced him to a few of Bert's close friends, ones that he'd had business dealings with. Ronan had waited until the wake was well underway, numerous toasts had been made, and most of those in attendance were feeling no pain, before he asked a few questions.

Don had no trouble picturing the gathering. Friends might be more inclined to discuss their late buddy with a stranger after they had a drink or three under their belt.

Tim continued his tale. "So these two fellas - I don't suppose their names are important - who described themselves as Rosen's business partners, told me they would set me straight concerning rumors about Bert's financial difficulties. A few years ago, they had put together a complex real estate deal that was projected to make huge profits for a select group of investors. Bert Rosen was a member of the group. It was all above board, but to make a long story short, for various reasons it never got off the ground and most of their investment went down the drain.

"Anyway, Bert's share was fifty grand. When the dust cleared, he was on the hook for most of it. Money that these two gentlemen had loaned him because he was a good friend and they wanted him to be part of it. They knew his divorce had cost him most of his assets, and with little or no collateral, the banks wouldn't touch him for such an investment. Bert's word was all the collateral his partners needed, so he was in."

"Nice to have friends like that, isn't it?" Don commented.

"You bet. But he must've been a good guy to warrant this treatment," said Tim.

"Oh, I'm sure he was," agreed Don. "Did he ever repay any of his loan?"

"Yeah, almost half. Most of it in two installments, the second about six months ago, they told me. And they were adamant that they hadn't been pressuring him for the balance, either."

When Tim paused, Don said, "And I'll bet they didn't have any idea how he came up with the money, right?"

"You got it. That's all I can tell you, Don. Hope it's what you were after."

He assured him it was and, more out of professional courtesy than necessity, Don told the American about his broader investigation and how Rosen's situation fit the pattern.

*

Don decided to put off calling James Coates until he had studied the crew lists Rod Weathers had faxed him. He might come up with a name that the MI5 man could check on from his end, although it wasn't very likely. He buzzed Joanne for more coffee and set to work.

The fax listed all the airlines with rooms reserved at the Pembury Hotel for the nights of July fourteenth and fifteenth. Don was surprised at the number: seventeen different airlines were on the list. Five of them Don had never heard of. Obviously, he surmised, there was still a dollar to be made flying cargo about in older aircraft.

Ten of the airlines had supplied crew names. Don culled four N's from the rosters. Two he discarded immediately. One was that of a crew member flying for a company based in West Africa, which looked like a tribal name starting with Nj. The second was a Captain Nassar, no initials supplied, flying for a Lebanese carrier.

That left two possibilities, neither of which sounded like prime candidates: an N. B. DeGroote, and an N. A. Jensen. Degroote was a captain on a Trans-Caribe flight arriving on Monday, July fourteenth, and departing on the sixteenth. The second name, Jensen, was booked in on the fifteenth, but also departing on that date. He was shown as captain for a Scandinavian charter airline Don recognized. At first glance, he thought the departure date must be a mistake, but on reflection, he figured it out. A crew could arrive in the early morning hours, take a legal crew rest, and still depart that same night. If that were the case though, he didn't think it likely Captain Jensen would have scheduled a tryst with a lady that day or evening. Or would he?

Don put a check mark beside Jensen's name. He was a long shot, but he'd have to be checked out. He also put a mark beside the name of the Trans-Caribe captain, and made a note to ask Rod what he might know about the airline.

One other name had caught his attention, although the first initial wasn't an N. He thumbed through the list until he found it again. A Northern Flyer crew scheduled to arrive in London on the fifteenth listed an R. N. Holt as the captain. Don had never heard Holt's name mentioned by Ralph Woods or any of the other Northern pilots he had golfed with, but decided he'd better check him out. Maybe he was hired recently? Ralph would know. He looked up his number and dialed it. It was mid-afternoon, and Ralph was in.

"Hey Don, what's up? When did you get back?" Woods asked.

"Early last week, Ralph. Been busy though, no time for golf. How about you? Still two or three rounds a week?"

"Yeah, about that. It's a steam bath these days, with this damned heat and humidity. A few cool ones at the nineteenth hole make it all worthwhile! How's your investigation coming along?"

Don allowed that it he was making progress, and hoped for a breakthrough soon. At the first opportunity he changed the subject.

"Ralph, Northern has a captain named Holt. Do you know him at all?"

"Norm Holt. Yes, I've met him a few times. Not socially, but he--"

Don's heart skipped a beat. "Excuse me, did you say 'Norm'? Is that what he goes by?"

"Uhh, yeah. Norm. The guys tell me he prefers Norman, though. Why?"

"Well his initials are R. N. At least that's the info I have."

"Oh, I see. No, I've only heard him referred to as Norm or Norman. He's a Brit. Been around for maybe three years or so. But I heard that he was thinking of going back to the UK. That's if he can find a suitable job. Why do you ask?"

"I'd like to keep my interest in Holt confidential for now, Ralph. I'll fill you in as soon as I can. That's a promise." Woods didn't push him. Don thanked him for understanding and hung up.

Don pushed his chair away from his desk, leaned back and put his hands behind his head.

Could this really be happening? Was the N he was seeking right under his nose here in Toronto? Was Holt the latest captain to be caught up in Renate Neumann's perilous web?

*

Don spent the next half hour deep in thought, wondering how he could best exploit this new information. One thing for certain: if indeed Holt was N, he needed to find out all he could about him before the week was out. If it was just an eery coincidence, it might become evident and Holt could be eliminated from the list of 'possibles'. He weighed numerous options before making his next move. One question that popped into his mind was quickly answered by a call to Ed Kirkham. Ed had been a close friend of the first Canadian captain killed, Len Newson.

No, Ed told him, he was certain Newson never had any connection - social or otherwise - with Norman Holt. The Englishman hadn't been with the company that long before Len died, and he didn't know of any Northern pilot who might be termed a close friend of Holt's. He moved to Canada on his own, Ed knew, which led him to believe the man was either single or divorced. Ed didn't know where Holt lived, but he could probably find out, he told Don.

" No, that won't be necessary, Ed. I can do the leg work myself. But thanks for your help. And you'll be among the first to know when I've worked it all out."

Just like Ralph Woods, Ed had been curious about Don's interest in Norm Holt.

He felt like a bit of a heel deflecting their questions, even though both men seemed to understand his reticence. He vowed to give the Toronto pilots a personal report when the time was right.

*

Thirty minutes later Don had even more to think about, and they were disturbing thoughts. James Coates, the retired British intelligence agent had been noticeably somber while relaying his report. Understandably so, Don realized. Beck, James's contact in the Belgian capital, had been digging for information about Flanders Holdings, the Brussels company that had leased the flat for Renate Neumann. The details he'd manage to uncover were scanty, but alarming nonetheless.

It seems that the holding company was a front for a previously unknown organization headed by ex-officers of the KGB, the former Soviet intelligence apparatus. Headquartered in Moscow, it was able to function unnoticed, mainly because of the political instability plaguing the new Russian republic.

The holding company was set up to move money from Brussels to their agents working in other European cities, including London.

It had all the earmarks of similar operations established in Western Europe after the break up of the Soviet Union. In other words, well-financed, borderline legal, and whose principal officers were untraceable once their charters had been approved. Their life spans were invariably short, averaging twenty-four to thirty months. Long enough to fund their shady businesses, and short enough to elude detailed analysis of their bogus financial reports by EU banking authorities.

In addition to paying the two-year lease for the Highgate flat used by Neumann, Flanders Holdings made a monthly transfer of funds to a Barclays bank branch in the City, the heart of London's financial district.

"I don't know how he got this information, but it must of come from someone with close ties to Interpol. He didn't say, and I didn't ask. But reading between the lines, I should think an organization like this would have no qualms about sanctioning killings to protect their profitable undertakings."

Coates paused to give the Canadian investigator a moment to digest the implications of what he was telling him.

Don didn't need a further caution, the message was loud and clear. It was the second time in less than twenty-four hours that he'd heard reference to this burgeoning criminal organization. He told James about Krantz's connection to the casino in Atlantic City with supposed ties to the Russian Mafia.

"Ah well, that does send us a warning doesn't it, my friend? You must watch your back from now on. These are not people to take lightly, you see," offered Coates.

Don agreed with his assessment and advice. Not that he had come across the Russian criminal element personally, but he was aware that their tentacles had spread worldwide, including Canada. According to a recent report in a Toronto newspaper, a few so-called king pins of the organization had apparently bought expensive houses in the city. He asked James if they had come to public attention in Britain.

"Well, they are certainly here, perhaps not as visible as in some countries. As I'm sure you know, London is a major financial center and it's highly likely that some of their money laundering operations, for instance, pass through here. Very difficult to trace that sort of thing in this high-tech era, at least that's what I'm led to believe," James said. "Most of this organization's growth outside Russia has occurred since I retired. I was never involved in any ops concerned with it."

Their conversation turned to the hunt for Renate Neumann. Coates had been trying unsuccessfully to track her down using the scant information involving the wire transfers from Brussels. He was working on the assumption that Flanders Holdings funded her living expenses in this manner.

"If we need to pursue this, it will no doubt require subpoenas or warrants that only the authorities can provide. I suggest you set up a meeting with your Inspector Upton as soon as you get back, Don," he said.

"Good thinking. I'm waiting to hear from Derek Houghton. Apparently he has some new information for me as well. I'll mention it to him."

Don told James about the possible lead to N. They discussed a few options that Don might explore regarding Holt before he returned to London.

"Thanks James, always good to have your input," Don said before he hung up. "See you soon!"

*

It was 5:30 when Don locked up the office and headed for home. A call to Yvonne got her answering machine again. Then he remembered that Wednesday was 'girls night out' for Yvonne and her co-workers. That meant it would probably be at least nine o'clock before he heard from her, assuming they didn't take in a movie after dinner and drinks. Unsure what he had at home in the way of food, he stopped at the fish and chip shop at the intersection of Airport Road and the county road he lived on. The meal was still hot and deliciously greasy when he got the newspaper wrappings off it ten minutes later. He was just finishing up when the phone rang.

"Not too late for a quick chat, I trust?" inquired the unmistakable British voice. Don's watch read 7:20.

"No, no, good timing actually, Derek. Just finished dinner. A bit late in London though."

"True enough. We had a stake-out going for a dastardly chap who did his wife in a few nights ago. Used a machete, if you can believe it. Very messy. However, he's under lock and key at Paddington now." Derek quickly got to point. "There's been a development in the Rosen case," he told Don. "They've ID'ed one of the suspects in his murder."

"No kidding! How did they manage that?"

The key turned out to be the initial descriptions of the men who had hired the SUV in Manchester: the vehicle thought to have been involved in running down Ray Flores last New Year's in Glasgow. DCI Upton noticed the similarities with the descriptions of the two foreigners a young waiter in Highgate had given his team. He conferred with McGrath and fine-tuned, for want of a better word, their depictions of the suspects. Upton had a team check the video tapes taken as passengers flying to Europe passed through immigration control at London airports on the day after Rosen's killing and found a possible match. Interpol, was contacted and asked to run the image through their extensive data banks.

"Interpol came up with a name, that of a known Bosnian Serb mercenary. Suspected of war crimes during the civil wars there, but never charged," said Derek. "That's all the info Spence Upton had as of Monday."

"Well, that's not to be sneezed at, is it?" enthused Don. "But what's with the waiter in Highgate? That's the first I've heard of him."

"Ah, well. Apparently he got in touch with Upton sometime last week. He'd left for a hiking trip in Wales on the morning Rosen's body was found. Didn't hear about it until he returned to London. He works at the pizza shop on the corner of Mulberry Street and the High Street. His boss told him about the police coming around and asking if they'd had any suspicious customers on the Friday night. Seems he remembered having two men who weren't locals hanging about that evening. Drinking coffee mostly. Anyway, the lad obviously has a good memory and provided Upton with usable descriptions."

A flood of questions came to Don as he listened to Derek. Questions that would have to wait until he could speak to DCI Upton in person, he realized.

*

Don sat on his deck, quietly sipping Scotch on the rocks. He was once more thinking about the pilots, and what they'd done - or maybe not done- that made them marked men. Desperate men often took the easy way out, whether it was illegal or not, unfortunately. And, he had to admit, pilots were no different than other men in that regard. He just hoped there was more to it than just greed on their part. He was still trying to make sense of it all when the night's first wave of mosquitoes descended on him, driving him inside.

28

THURSDAY, JULY 10

Don Carling had spent a restless night, his mind rejecting deep sleep while it wrestled with all the ramifications of the latest reports from London. He struggled from bed shortly after six o'clock and put coffee on to brew while he showered. Ten minutes later he felt much better, most of his grogginess washed away. By the time he'd shaved and dressed he had mapped out what he needed to do in the next forty-eight hours. Then he would be free to fly to London on Saturday night, assuming there was a seat available on BA's flight.

Rod was in a meeting when he called, but his secretary made note of Don's request. Captain Weathers would get back to him later that morning with flight details, she told him.

*

Before he left for the office, he made a list of the questions that had kept him awake. He wanted to ensure he didn't overlook anything that could be checked out in Toronto before he left.

The answer to one very big question had probably been answered though - who the victims had been involved with. All indications pointed to the Russian Mafia , both in Europe and on this side of the Atlantic.

Did these men know they were being used by the mafia? Probably not. Were they aware that whatever they'd been carrying was contraband? If not initially, then somewhere down the road? Seems a logical assumption, Don felt. Why else would they have been paid? And not mere pittances, either.

Were they asked to carry anything on their flights to Europe? He didn't know yet, but hadn't uncovered any evidence to indicate that was the case.

Did they 'want out' after they'd realized what they'd been lured into? Perhaps after being asked to carry something that meant a much larger risk of discovery? If so, was their decision enough to mark them for elimination? To prevent them from talking? Ruthless, but probable, he figured.

Finally his thoughts turned to Renate Neumann. She had to be a key figure in the conspiracy. All the victims had been involved with her, that he was now certain of. But did that necessarily mean she was supplying them with the shipments? That didn't seem logical. In the scheme Don envisaged, her involvement would have been limited to the seduction of the vulnerable pilots, and, after gaining their confidence, steering them to whomever would pay them for their help.

If this were so, the pilots probably picked up their shipments somewhere other than London. But where? Jerry Wahl had mentioned Brussels. Realistically, there weren't too many options. The airlines the victims flew for only operated out of a few common European cities.

Another nagging question: someone must have fingered these men for Renate. He - or maybe she - had to somehow 'vet' them for her. Once again, there had to be a common link. Was it the Pembury Hotel? London was the only city where all the victims laid over at the same hotel. This Rod Weathers had ascertained and double-checked.

A number of other unknowns he could only speculate on. Why would the Russian Mafia need to use pilots to carry contraband for them in the first place? Wouldn't using couriers, sometimes referred to as mules, be easier? Perhaps, but maybe the Russians were just the middlemen, being paid by some other clandestine group that thought using pilots was a better option. Perhaps an option that they deemed less likely to be discovered by authorities.

This brought him to Norman Holt. Was he a recent addition to this dangerous woman's stable? He hoped to find out before he flew back to London. He had a plan in mind, and he'd worked out the details by the end of the day. Friday had been set aside to meet with an new client.

*

Friday was a good day on all fronts, and by 5:30 P.M. Don was definitely thinking TGIF. The morning meeting in KayRoy's office with the prospective clients had gone well. Once they were satisfied that Don's plan to tackle the criminal activity costing them a great deal of money was viable, the firm's two principals gave him the go-ahead. The contract was finalized over lunch at Roberto's Steak House on the airport strip. The first step would be getting Don's undercover men in place, a process that would be completed over the next few weeks and didn't require his presence. Their sizable retainer sealed the contract and Don assured them they would receive regular updates, even though he would be in London for a few more weeks.

For the rest of the afternoon Don and another of his operatives, Ricardo Martini - known as Baldy, for obvious reasons - discussed how they would best be able to keep track of Norman Holt over the weekend. They were hoping to either confirm or eliminate him as N. Yesterday, using his contacts at Northern Flyer, Carling learned that Captain Holt was still in Europe and wasn't due back until Saturday. He was still scheduled for a flight to London on Monday night, the fourteenth.

*

Holt's address and phone number were unlisted, but this had been a 'no brainer' for Don's secretary Joanne. At Don's urging Joanne had been taking night courses towards a private investigator's certificate. Posing as an employee of a laboratory that analyzed blood samples drawn from pilots during their annual medicals, she had called Northern Flyer's Personnel Department. A letter they'd sent to an R.N. Holt had been returned with the notation 'moved' on it, she told the young clerk who answered her call. Could she please have his current address and phone number to update their records?

"Well done, Joanne," lauded Don, taking the slip of paper from her.

"Guess I'll fund you for another term."

Baldy and Don settled on a plan and made a list of equipment he would need. By five o'clock a rental van had been delivered and parked at KayRoy's rear door. Don packed a small case with a variety of tools and electronic gear taken from the storage cabinet in the back room and locked it in the van. Baldy wouldn't need it until later that night.

After a call to Yvonne to confirm he would pick her up at seven, he checked the paper files and computer disks he wanted to take with him to London. After Joanne and Baldy left, he made a final security check of the office before locking up.

He had just enough time to drive home, take a quick shower, and change of his clothes. He listened to his Dire Straits tape as he made his way up Airport Road, happily strumming his fingers on the steering wheel in time with the music.

29

SATURDAY, JULY 12

Norman Holt was on his way back to Toronto after spending the better part of three days in London - an unexpected three days. He had flown into Brussels last Tuesday as scheduled, and awoke Wednesday morning to find a message from Operations advising him that his return flight was canceled. Tuesday night's flight from Toronto had been scrubbed due to a major maintenance problem and the aircraft would be out of service for another forty-eight hours, perhaps longer.

This meant a major reshuffling of flights and crews. Captain Holt and his crew were to deadhead to London and await further assignment, probably a flight from Stansted to Toronto on Friday, the eleventh. Holt was elated with this turn of events: his first officer and flight engineer were not. They weren't any happier when their stay in London was extended until Saturday.

For Holt, the company's misfortunes worked in his favor. For the past week he had been baffled by his inability to reach Renate by phone, either from Brussels or Toronto. The second time he'd tried from Toronto, a few days after his return, a recorded message advised the number was no longer in service. She had never mentioned a business number to him, so his only alternative was to wait until his next scheduled flight to London, and then go around to her flat. Much to his relief, the mystery was cleared up after they arrived in London on Tuesday afternoon.

As a service to crew members, the Pembury Hotel kept a box available for them to receive personal mail. Those who took advantage of the service, including Holt, used it to receive brochures, magazines, and notices of upcoming aviation-related events in and around London. Holt had his subscription to Flight magazine mailed to the hotel, for instance. As soon as he had registered, he rummaged through the mail box. He found an envelope addressed to him, with no return address. It was from Renate. The short note told him she had changed mobile phone companies, and gave her new number. No other explanation. Norman hurried up to his room and called her.

*

He wasted no time getting to Renate's new flat. He'd traveled by tube to the Westbourne Park Station and then, with the aid of his pocket-sized A to Z, navigated his way through the maze of short streets to find Simcoe Terrace Gardens. The gardens weren't much larger than your average golf green, mused Norman, as he took in the crowded yet colorful jumble of shrubbery.

Number 12 Simcoe Gate was an inconspicuous four-storey block of flats set among similar buildings bordering the south side of the gardens. Norman pushed the buzzer for number six. He couldn't help but notice that there wasn't a name card in the slot for Renate's flat. But the door unlatched before the question 'why' registered and, in the anticipation of seeing her, he forgot all about it as he took the stairs two at a time to the first floor. Her door opened as he reached the landing and two strides later he swept Renate up in an amorous embrace.

"I missed you darling. I thought I might never see you again! What happened?" he whispered, as he nuzzled her neck and hair. She'd changed her hairstyle, he noticed. More reddish in color, and shorter too, as he ran his fingers through it.

"Later Norman. Later I'll explain. Take me to bed, please. Now..." She knew by his evident arousal that he wouldn't object.

*

Thirty minutes later they were stretched out side-by-side on the crumpled sheets, both covered in perspiration. Renate reached for a small towel and softly patted her lover's brow.

"That was wonderful, Norman," she praised. " You see, I missed you too."

The Russian agent had played her cards perfectly. Relaxed in sexual bliss - and with the anticipation of more to come - Norman was more unlikely to question her forthcoming explanation. The story she had fabricated to explain away her new surroundings.

Her employers had decided to move her back to the continent at the end of June, she began. The expensive lease on her flat in Highgate Village was expiring and they thought she could manage her job just as well from a city on the continent, probably Dusseldorf, Germany. She balked at this proposal and had to fly on short notice to the firm's head office to discuss it with them. That's why Norman couldn't reach her from Brussels, she said.

Her employers were adamant about moving her from London. After some serious contemplation, she decided to end her contract with them. Fortunately she had other contacts in the industry and a few days later had negotiated a new contract with a French company as their representative in London.

"I wanted to be somewhere I could still see you, Norman," she murmured seductively, running her fingers through his chest hairs. "So I'll be here for another year at least. And this flat is closer to your hotel, isn't it?"

"Yes, I could probably walk it in less than thirty minutes," he answered, his breathing now returned to normal. "But why couldn't I get you on your phone?"

"Oh that was my fault!" she lied. "In my haste to move from the flat, I misplaced it, lost it somehow. I had to have it canceled and get a new one. I had no way to tell you."

"...I see. Well that won't happen again. I want you to have my number in Canada. Then you can let me know if you're going to be away. Understood?"

"Yes, I promise," she said sheepishly.

He had more unanswered questions running around in his head, but concluded they weren't really that important. He had her now, and her passion for him seemed more genuine than it ever had before. Her warm hand began slowly stroking his eager penis as she finished her explanation.

She had read him perfectly, as she knew she could. When he was hard, she rolled over and mounted him. Her urgency as her warm wetness engulfed him cut off any further thoughts he had about the gaps in her mysterious background.

*

Thursday night they went out to dinner and Norman stayed over again. Renate insisted they eat in on Friday, and prepared a meal with a continental flavor, mostly from dishes she bought at the a nearby delicatessen. With Norman's crew call scheduled for 6:30 A.M. Saturday morning, she understood when he left early to return to his hotel. Their relationship had reached a new level this week. Norman sensed Renate had begun to return the passion that he had felt for her ever since they'd first met.

Even more encouraging, she hinted that once he returned to the UK for good, she would give serious thought to his suggestion of a more permanent arrangement. A suggestion she had more or less thrown cold water on when he first proposed it a few months ago. Her attitude had changed after he'd reluctantly agreed to make one more delivery. Like the last two, it would originate from Stansted.

He hadn't been entirely surprised when Renate made the proposition. From day one Norman had doubts about the Brussels connection, her 'cousin', Karl. But he'd gone along with it, and once he started taking the money, he gave less thought to how involved his lover was with the whole set-up. She obviously played some part in it though, however minor. And he had considered what might happen if his bags were searched at customs: he would have a lot of explaining to do, at the very least. But so far the risks had seemed minimal, and he'd decided to cooperate just a little longer. He knew he hadn't carried anything dangerous, like drugs. Mainly it had just been envelopes or small packages easily concealed in his flight bag. At least one envelope had contained computer disks, the ones known as floppies. He could tell by the feel. All he had to do was mail the envelopes a day or so after his return to Toronto. But now Renate's direct involvement troubled him, and he told her of his concerns.

"Darling," she told him, as they laid entwined together before he left for the hotel, "Karl and I have a business arrangement that is making us both a lot of money. And I want to share it with you. One more delivery, that's all we're asking, I promise. Trust me?"

'In for a penny, in for a pound,' he sighed. The money being offered, $50,000, was more than a year's net salary.

This alone should have been cause for alarm - for that kind of money the risk to him was probably going to be much greater. When he pushed Renate for more information, she told him not to worry. Even if the shipment was discovered, no one would be able to connect it to Norman. *Easy for you to say,* he thought.

"Our man at the airport will look after everything, darling," she cajoled. She promised to give him more details after the final arrangements were set.

And if I don't like what I hear, I can still back out. Or can I? That was his last thought before he drifted into a troubled sleep.

*

He was still mulling over the pros and cons of what his continued cooperation might lead to as Northern Flyer Flight 213 cruised over northern Quebec. They were six hours out of Stansted Airport, after their lengthy stay in London. One thought that hadn't surfaced for months was bothering him today: how he and Renate had first met. Had it been strictly by chance, as he'd always assumed, or was it planned? Their meeting in the wine bar near the Pembury had seemed innocent enough at the time. Probably because the euphoria the welcome relationship brought him blocked it out. Until later...

He'd been delighted with how well they seemed to get on with each other, and their rapid move to intimacy was a bonus he didn't question. He really did look forward to London flights and the chance to see her. And it wasn't just the sex. He enjoyed taking her to concerts, or even just a Sunday stroll along Bayswater Road to browse the art work. Things that Norman did on his own before meeting Renate. Her enthusiasm for their outings appeared genuine enough, and he welcomed the opportunities to answer her many questions about Britain and the British way of life.

*

He couldn't recall exactly when his lover first mentioned her cousin in Brussels. It must have been after their fourth or fifth date, he figured. He hadn't stayed overnight at her flat until their third night out. Yes, it was a few trips later - when spending the night was a given - that Renate had suggested that Norman say 'hello' to Karl on his next trip to Brussels. By this time, Norman had known her for three months and there wasn't much about his private life that she hadn't pried out of him.

"Get to know Karl," she'd urged him. "He could help you out financially."

Once he'd taken the bait and agreed to carry packages for Karl, it didn't seem to matter whether or not he and Renate were in fact related. They did speak English with the same accent though, he noted.

After he'd made this next delivery and the fifty thousand was deposited in his bank account on the Isle of Man, he'd call it quits. Once he resigned from Northern Flyer he wouldn't be any use to them anyway.

*

Norman's unexpected appearance in London had taken her by surprise, but Renate realized that it had been a blessing in disguise. By playing the ardent lover she had been able to confirm Norman's reluctant agreement to make one more delivery. It was to be the final shipment for the group Circle 17 was acting as middlemen for. Renate was completely in the dark about the unnamed group: she had no idea of who they were, or what their goals might be. Her Uncle Georgiy had cut her off abruptly when she had dared to ask about them. But her part had been made a little easier by Norman's unexpected visit. If he hadn't returned until his next scheduled layover on the fifteenth, she would have had only the one night to work on him. Now, with the extra breathing room, it might be possible to advance the timetable for the shipment to his flight on the sixteenth, instead of his last flight of the month on the twenty-third. At the very least, meeting the end-month deadline she'd been given shouldn't be a problem.

As he was preparing to leave last night, Norman mentioned the blank name card next to the buzzer for her flat. She was going to leave it that way, she told him, to prevent unwanted calls from door-to-door canvassers. Another lie. 'Renate Neumann' had left London for good. The name on the lease for her new flat, arranged by Brussels, was Katrina Mueller. The same name she'd used to acquire her new mobile phone. Only to Norman Holt would she still be Renate Neumann.

At least she hoped that was the case. She assumed the police were still looking for Renate Neumann in connection with Bert Rosen's death. If all went well, her assignment in London should be completed before anyone discovered her new identity.

In the mean time, and despite her altered appearance, she planned to lie low as much as possible until Norman's return. And be extra vigilant when she did go out.

30

SATURDAY EVENING, JULY 12

Don's cell phone rang just after his hand baggage had passed through the x-ray machine at the security checkpoint. He'd only brought it with him was so he could call Yvonne while waiting to board his flight.

Had she beaten him to it? he wondered, as he quickly shoved his laptop computer back in its case and moved away from the security screening area.

"Hi! Good timing. I was just..."

"Mr. Carling?" It wasn't Yvonne, but the voice was slightly familiar.

"Uhh, yes, this is Don Carling," he replied. He checked the number but didn't recognize it.

"It's Lori Wilson." Her distress was evident. "I had to call you!"

Don recalled his last words to her in Atlantic City as he had handed her his card. 'I won't bother you again, but you can call me anytime if you think of anything that might help my investigation.'

"Oh, Lori, yes. How are you doing?" A dumb question, he knew, but the best he could come up with.

"That man you were with when you came to see me? The other detective?"

"Yes, Will Halpern. He hasn't been bothering you, has he?"

"No, no. He's dead!" Her voice was only slightly higher than a whisper now.

"Oh, shit," muttered Don. "What happened to him?"

Seconds passed before she answered, her voice was a little steadier now.

"It was just on the news. I just got back from my flight. They found his body this morning on a back road between here and Philadelphia. They showed his picture, that's how I knew who it was." Her voice trailed off again. " They said he was a former state trooper..."

Don checked his watch. They would be boarding in ten minutes. "Lori, I'm just about to board a flight to London, otherwise I'd fly down to see you." He wanted to say something to allay her fears, but he couldn't find the right words.

"They say he was murdered...shot in the head."

"Listen, Lori. Had he been in touch with you since I was there?"

"No..."

"Good. I don't think his killing has anything to do with our coming to see you," he told her. He hoped he was right. "But I'll try and contact the police once we get airborne. And I'll call you from London tomorrow. Can you give me your number?"

There was another long pause as Don reached the departure gate. Pre-boarding was underway and he heard his name being paged as he got within ear shot.

"Lori? Are you still there?"

"I won't be here tomorrow, I don't want to stay here any longer. I'm going to leave for Atlanta."

"Okay, listen. Once you get to Atlanta, call my office and give my secretary a number where I can reach you. Will you do that?"

"Maybe, probably. I just thought you should know about your friend." She sounded very tired now.

" I'm glad you did. And thanks. Don't worry, Lori, there's no reason for anyone to harm you. Just leave a number for me once you get to Atlanta, okay? I'll get in touch." She hung up without another word. Don slipped the phone into his pocket and approached the check-in desk.

*

"We've got a problem, Don." This from Derek Houghton. Both he and Rod Weathers had been waiting for him at Heathrow. They were in Rod's car and had just turned eastbound on the A4 north of the airport. It was a glorious morning, not a cloud in the sky as Rod accelerated smoothly past a string of tour buses carrying day-trippers into the city.

"Not another one," sighed Don.

Rod glanced at him in the rearview mirror. "What do you mean?"

The Canadian shifted his weight, trying to give himself more leg room in the back seat.

"Well, just before I boarded last night, I had a call from Lori Wilson, Krantz's former girlfriend."

Don gave them a run down on his trip to Atlantic City, his interview with Lori, and Will Halpern's clumsy attempt to learn about Dan's connection with the Russian Mafia-backed casino. "He was murdered a few nights ago," he said, stifling a yawn.

Derek asked, "You're thinking the bartender fingered him?"

"Yeah, that was my first thought. He certainly didn't buy into Halpern's spiel about being a friend of Krantz's," said Don. "But it could've been another case he was working on that pissed off the wrong people."

"But only if you believe in coincidences, eh?" said Derek, finishing his thought for him.

"Yes. Anyway, I called from the plane and got through to one of the detectives working the case. Told him about our visit to the casino. Maybe it'll help them, maybe it won't. I told him I'd check with him again sometime this week."

Rod made good time until they reached the Hammersmith flyover where the now two-lane traffic slowed to a crawl. Derek suggested Rod take the next road to the left and route via Kensington, Bayswater and Sussex Gardens.

"It will be quickest route on a Sunday morning," he assured his brother-in-law.

"So what's the problem at this end?" Don asked once Derek had finished giving Rod directions.

"DCI Upton called me yesterday. Needs to talk to you. I suggested tomorrow morning, and he'll expect us between eight-thirty and nine at Holloway Road." Don nodded his agreement, and Derek continued. "Seems you and the Met force aren't the only ones with an interest in this Neumann woman."

"Really? And why is that a problem?" Don asked.

"Well, I'm not exactly sure yet. Upton wasn't too forthcoming, saying he preferred to wait until you got here to go into details. But it sounds as if he's been told to back off, at least for the time being."

*

Derek was right. Traffic was reasonably light once they reached Kensington High Street, and it took them less than thirty minutes to wend their way to the Beech Tree Inn after exiting the Great West Road. Rod and Derek had a family obligation that afternoon and Don politely declined their half-hearted invitation to join them.

"You're sure now, Don," kidded Rod as he pulled the Canadian's luggage from the boot. "Kate and Sonya were positive you'd want to come to their niece's christening. Lots of non-alcoholic punch, tea and cookies. Broaden your horizons, it would!"

"Please tell your caring wives that I would have been delighted but I forgot to pack my morning coat. Or is it an evening coat? And go easy on the fruit juice or you'll end up with acid indigestion!"

*

After he'd checked in and unpacked, Don changed into casual clothes and headed out for a brisk walk. He wasn't tired enough to sleep yet, and he hoped the exercise would help to keep him awake until a decent time tonight. As he walked along the quiet streets, he pondered what tomorrow's meeting might bring. He couldn't come to any rational conclusions though, and eventually turned his thoughts to his own plans.

An hour later, having been to Primrose Hill and back, he opened a beer from the mini bar, flicked the television on, and stretched out on the bed. The final round of the British Open was unfolding, the last pairings on the back nine. He managed to finish the beer before falling asleep, and didn't wake up until 6:30. It wasn't until the next day that he found out who had won the coveted trophy.

*

Before he'd dropped off, he had decided that there was nothing to stop him from having another chat with Alf Heard at the Pembury House. Now that he was wide awake, he planned to do just that.

He watched a classic Pink Panther movie on television, occasionally chuckling out loud at the antics of Peter Sellers in his Inspector Clouseau role, until it was time to leave the hotel. At 9:45 he set out on foot, heading for the Pembury House. He figured Heard should have settled in for his overnight shift by the time he reached the hotel. As he turned onto Pembury Road he noticed three men walking approximately twenty yards ahead of him. He took them for pilots heading for the Pembury, and this was confirmed a minute later when they mounted the steps to the hotel's entrance. Rather than arrive at the same time, he crossed to the street's south side and watched as one of them rang the buzzer. They were let in, approached the reception desk where Alf was seated, exchanged a few laughs with the older man and then trooped off towards the lift.

From his vantage point it didn't appear as if there were any other guests sitting in the lounge area behind Heard. He waited another five minutes before he crossed the dark street and pushed the buzzer. The night man peered over his reading spectacles at Don. He seemed to be trying to identify him before unlocking the door. Don gave him a friendly wave, and heard the door unlatch.

"Evening, Alf," he said with a smile.

"Oh, it's you again," said Alf reprovingly. "You shouldn't be here, I've nothing to tell you."

"Just a few questions, Alf. I 'm still on the case, you see, investigating Captain Rosen's death. So--"

"I'm not speaking to you. I want you to leave right now!" Heard was visibly agitated.

Don had expected some reticence on Alf's part, but not this vehement rebuff.

"Nice to see you too, Alf. Okay, I'll come right to the point. Are you acquainted with a Captain Holt? From Northern Flyer? He's due in on Tuesday morning, I believe."

"Out! Or I will call the police. You've no right to be here!"

"Oh, I'll leave peacefully, Alf. Calm down before you give yourself a stroke, why don't you?" Don said evenly, turning to go. As he reached the door, he turned back and said just loud enough for Heard to hear, "You must know Renate Neumann, too. The German woman - Holt's girlfriend. She was a friend of Bert Rosen's too, wasn't she?"

Carling's remarks brought an immediate look of pure hatred to Heard's face: a look that turned to fear as Don made his exit.

'Got you now you lying old bugger,' Don said quietly as he strolled away.

#

Ten minutes after the Canadian detective's departure, Alf Heard fumbled a folded piece of paper out of his billfold and dialed the number written on it: a number he had never called before. A number, he had been sternly instructed, was only to be used in an emergency.

An answering machine picked up immediately. 'Leave a message', was all it said. The voice had a foreign accent, but that didn't surprise him.

The rattled night man hadn't expected the recording, and stumbled through what he wanted to say.

"Uhh, uh... This is Heard. They know about me and...uhh, I don't mean the police, just this one detective, a Canadian, his name is Carling. He mentioned the woman's name. I never admitted anything, you must believe me, but I thought I should let you know. Uhh, that's all."

'That's it for me. I'm finished helping these buggers for a few bloody quid!' he told himself after he hung up.

31

MONDAY, JULY 13

Renate had every right to be wary. Even though Katrina Mueller had entered the country without setting off alarm bells, Vlad's activity in Brussels had apparently come to the attention of Interpol. At least that was the impression Don Carling came away with from this morning's meeting.

The venue had been changed, Derek told him when he picked him up, and it was just after nine o'clock when they were ushered into a third floor conference room at New Scotland Yard. The reason for the change was soon apparent. This was not just a meeting with the Metropolitan Police. DCI Spencer Upton was the first man he recognized, though. He reached for the detective's outstretched hand and nodded a greeting to the other familiar face, Upton's partner, Sergeant Ross. Upton welcomed the Canadian back to London, and then introduced Don and Derek Houghton to the others in the room.

The strange faces were all from different agencies. Jean-Marc Rousseau was Interpol's assistant-director for Europe, based at the parent body's headquarters in Lyon, France. He was the oldest man present. His full head of neatly trimmed grey hair contrasted with his bushy and remarkably black eyebrows. Clean shaven, Don placed him in his early 60's. Don returned the Frenchman's smiling 'Bonjour' with one of his own as they shook hands.

The second man was British, and his name was Harold Watson. He was closer to Don's age, and the regimental tie he wore was the brightest part of his attire. "Harold is with MI5," was all Upton offered by way of introduction. The youngest man was introduced last, and brought a surprised look to Carling's face.

"Wait a sec! I know this guy, don't I?" Don said, smiling broadly as he grabbed the man's hand.

"Good to see you again, Don!" said Brian Roberts. "I didn't know until this morning that you'd become an international detective."

The others looked on, waiting for an explanation. Don spoke first, telling them that he and Brian had worked together a few years ago on an investigation in Canada.

"He's being far too modest, gentlemen! Mr. Carling here broke a major smuggling ring responsible for bringing large quantities of drugs into Canada through Toronto airport. All the RCMP and local police had to do was round up the bad guys. Bagged almost all of them early one morning - fifteen or sixteen of them, wasn't it?" Roberts said, looking to Don for confirmation. "And they all received long jail sentences, thanks to the solid evidence he and his team had amassed." he lauded.

"I had good help, don't forget. And we had a few lucky breaks, too," offered Don. He deflected further talk of about KayRoy's first major case with a question for Roberts.

"So what brings you to London, Brian? The Mounties' musical ride isn't in town, is it?" Roberts was the only one who got the joke, and acknowledged it with a loud chuckle before explaining his presence. Sergeant Brian Roberts was the RCMP's liaison officer to Interpol's UK division. His assignment was for a two-year period, and he was six months into it.

The pleasantries over, Rousseau invited everyone to be seated at the round table. The highly polished oak surface and the well-padded swivel chairs around it took up almost half the room's floor space.

The director had obviously been well-briefed on his investigation to date on behalf of the International Pilots Federation, Don soon discovered. Rousseau praised Don's efforts that had helped the British police to identify the suspects in the killings of the latest two American victims - Rosen in London and Flores in Glasgow. Both had now been identified, he went on, and were linked to a group that Interpol had under surveillance in several European countries. The suspects themselves were still at large. In a friendly manner, Rousseau grilled Don about his findings. He specifically wanted to know if Don had any information about what the airline pilots might have been smuggling. Had he uncovered any evidence along these lines?

"We are interested in anything you may have learned while you were in Canada, Monsieur Carling," he asked.

"Please, call me Don," invited the Canadian, "and I did make some progress last week. But I must admit that so far a lot of it would fall under the heading of circumstantial evidence."

"Eh bien, 'Don' it is," smiled the Frenchman. "And believe me, Don, most of our ultimate successes are the result of many circumstances adding up to fact."

It took Don fifteen minutes to brief them on his investigation on both sides of the Atlantic. He rhymed off the similarities in the victims' personal lives, and his thoughts on why they had been singled out. Watson and Roberts made notes as he spoke. In particular, Carling's telling of the most recent event, the slaying of Wilson Halpern in New Jersey so soon after his visit there, raised eyebrows around the room.

"As far as what these men carried on their flights, I can't say for sure. I'm guessing laundered money, maybe counterfeit or stolen bonds, forged passports or documents," he shrugged. "For whose benefit, I don't know." He paused to see if Rousseau or Watson had any comment, and when none was forthcoming, he added, "But you gentlemen probably know more about that sort of thing than I do."

They weren't about to say, though. Rousseau shuffled the papers from the folder in front of him.

"Don, thank you for this information, it will be of great help to us," he said. "We were umm, unaware, that the group we have under surveillance was using airline pilots in the manner you suggest, or that they had resorted to murder."

On the subject of Renate Neumann, Rousseau was just as evasive. He wouldn't say if she was now on their 'watch list', but inferred that they had no reason to doubt Don's assumptions that she was a key player in the conspiracy. Here again, he admitted, the woman's existence had previously been unknown to Interpol, and finding her could have a positive impact on their investigation.

Then Rousseau dashed the Canadian's immediate plans. Despite the good work Don and the Met Police had accomplished, they were now being asked to put their search for Renate Neumann on hold. In fact it was more an order than a request.

"To not jeopardize our investigation at a sensitive stage", was the way Rousseau phrased it when asked why. He wouldn't elaborate, and politely but firmly refused to go into details. Don was about to object, when a look from Derek told him to go slow.

Nor would he admit the group receiving Interpol's attention was the Russian Mafia, or at least linked to them, even when Don again mentioned the probable connection between the mafia in Atlantic City and Daniel Krantz. With an apologetic shake of his head, Rousseau rose, offered his hand to Don, and ended their meeting.

*

"Do they have the authority to do that? Legally, I mean?" asked Rod Weathers.

Rod was waiting at the Beech Tree Inn when Carling and Houghton returned from New Scotland Yard. The three were sitting in the small bar in the corner of the main lobby. Don had just finished a recap of the meeting and what Rousseau said -or didn't say. He looked to the his brother-in-law for an answer.

Derek shrugged. "I don't think it's a matter of legality per se, Rod. More of a question of a senior body pulling rank, if you will. It would appear that these deaths - and this woman -are now just one aspect of a larger Interpol investigation. One that probably involves police forces in more than one country."

"And we're being asked to steer clear until...until they--"

"Probably just temporary, Don," interrupted Derek, holding up his hand. "Remember, Interpol doesn't have their own police force. They'll probably need cooperation from the local coppers at some point."

"With Upton, you mean," replied Don.

"Well, yes, of course. But I would hope that Spence Upton will share any developments with you."

An uneasy silence settled over the hotel room, broken when Rod asked about the two mercenaries.

"Do they know where these suspects are now?"

Don answered. "Rousseau wouldn't say, but I got the impression they're on a Most Wanted list of some sort, didn't you, Derek?"

"Yes, that would be the procedure. By now Interpol should have provided all ports of entry here and in Europe with their photos, names, perhaps aliases they might be using," agreed Derek.

"Did you say there was a representative from MI5 at the meeting?" Rod asked. "Aren't they usually concerned with spies or terrorists?"

"Yes, well, it's obvious it's more than a murder investigation they're running," replied Derek.

"So it seems," said Don. He mentioned James Coates's remarks about the mystery woman's actions and how they reminded him of the old KGB ways.

"You don't say!" exclaimed Rod.

"Well, he'd be the one to know," remarked Derek, "and that might explain why British Intelligence is involved." Another silence settled over them.

Finally Rod asked, "Where do we go from here, then?"

"Well, for starters you'd better hold off on sending out anything to the airlines for the time being," sighed Don.

*

In the aftermath of Bert Rosen's slaying, Rod had suggested that a notice be sent to all IPF members, emphasizing the risks involved in carrying unauthorized shipments on their flights. Although Don could understand where Rod was coming from, he had numerous misgivings about the plan. Most airlines already had rules to that effect in their Standard Operating Procedures - SOP's for short - that their pilots should be conversant with. He didn't feel such a caution would get the necessary attention unless a specific reason for issuing it was mentioned.

"Okay," Rod had suggested, "what about circulating the woman's name, then? Ask for anyone with knowledge of her to come forward?"

Don could see problems with that approach as well, he told his friend. A notice posted on a bulletin board in a flight operations environment, and intended for pilots eyes only, would no doubt become public knowledge somewhere along the line, he felt, and when it did, it might alert the conspirators that the net was closing around them.

They had discussed the issue last week while Don was still in Toronto, and Rod agreed to wait and see what happened if and when N showed up on the fifteenth before acting.

"Right, then. Still no notice to the airlines at this time," said Rod, "and you're in limbo until you get the green light again from this Rousseau chap. In other words, steer clear of you know who. Am I right?"

Once again, Don deferred to Derek for an answer. The inspector appeared to be searching for the right words before he spoke.

"Yes Don, that was made quite clear, wasn't it? No further attempt to trace this woman directly."

The Canadian shrugged his agreement. "But I still have an option or two, don't I?"

"And those would be?" prompted Derek.

"Well, for one thing, we haven't positively identified who Renate's present beau is, have we?" He allowed a sly smile to creep over his face. "We only know that his initial is probably N, and he should be arriving in London tomorrow."

"He wasn't discussed this morning?" asked Rod.

"No, and I didn't think it was the right time to mention him, either," said Don.

"Does DCI Upton know about him?"

"If he does, he hasn't said so," answered Don. "Has he said anything to you, Derek?"

Derek shook his head. "But the next time you speak to him, it might be a good idea to mention it."

"I'll do that. As soon as I can positively identify him. I'm hoping we'll have that info some time tomorrow."

"Assuming the lady in question is still in London, and he contacts her," added Derek quietly.

"Exactly," said Don, in the same pensive tone.

"What else can you do? Within bounds, of course," asked Rod.

"Alf Heard. I didn't hear anything this morning to suggest that he's part of their investigation. But it would've been too late anyway. I dropped in to see him last night."

Don told them about the night man's hostility, and his guilty reaction when Don brought up Renate's name. When he finished, he offered Derek a weak smile.

"I know I'm asking a lot, Derek, but I think flashing a badge might loosen his lips a bit."

"Don't see how that could be construed as interference," Derek answered slowly. "When do you want to do it?"

Don's spirits lifted immediately. After last night he was more positive than ever that Heard was somehow involved in the deaths. Even if Heard himself wasn't entirely aware of it.

"Great! I was hoping you'd agree," enthused Don. "How about tomorrow? That's his regular night off, so once he leaves the hotel in the morning he'll probably be home all day."

"Right then, I'll keep the morning open. Call me when you're ready to go and I'll pick you up."

32

MONDAY, JULY 14

Tatiana Kravitchkevna, a.k.a. Olga, a.k.a. Renate Neumann, and now masquerading as Katrina Mueller, studied herself in the full-length bathroom mirror. She had just stepped out of the shower and was shocked to see that she looked as confused and lost as she felt. Quickly she pulled the large towel around her, sank onto the commode and dropped her head into her hands.

Ever since Friday night, her mind had been a whirlwind of uncertainty. Her self-confidence, that had buoyed her during the long undercover assignment her uncle's Circle 17 organization had trusted her with, was beginning to fade.

How much longer can I go on like this? Do they expect me to live a life of lies until I'm no longer capable? Then what?

The image of her nakedness; hips that were starting to spread; breasts that weren't sitting as high as they were just months ago; and lines at the corner of her mouth only added to her dilemma. She was being quite hard on herself, though: passing males were still sneaking second looks at her on the street. She switched thoughts again.

Am I really making a contribution to our cause? To be honest, the ideals she'd so eagerly embraced during her KGB training, the same ideals that buoyed her through her first undercover assignments, no longer seemed particularly relevant. For instance, during her time in London, she'd never heard anyone in public say anything derogatory about the new Russia. It was basically the same in the press and on television newscasts. And it was no different in western Europe: any lingering barriers to detente had for all intents and purposes been pushed aside.

And what does the future hold as far as Circle 17? Will they have a new assignment, just as lonely as this one? What would my option be? Return to live in Germany or Russia, over forty and on my own?

She couldn't think of one positive reason for going back. She had no real family ties to draw her back, that was for certain. Her mother had remarried, and her second husband had taken no interest in Tatiana or shown her any affection on the three occasions they'd met - just the opposite, in fact. Her mother had stopped answering her daughter's occasional letters, and sadly Tatiana had given up her attempts to keep their bond alive five or six years ago.

Slowly Renate struggled to her feet, made her way to the bedroom and willed herself to dress. Over her third coffee of the morning she forced her mind to deal directly with the issue that led to all this troubling soul searching - Norman.

His unexpected appearance in London last week - and the passion their being together generated - had been the stimulus. For the first time with her string of lovers, her affection for Norman wasn't feigned. This surprised to her. At first she tried to analyse what made him so different from the others. They were all confident men, which wasn't surprising given their profession and status. And each of them had been going through a rough time in their personal lives when she entered the scene. But here the similarities ended.

The Canadian, Len Newson, drank too much and, as a result, wasn't much of a lover even though she let him think he was. He was the easiest to recruit for money.

Dan, the American, was the biggest chauvinist she had ever met. And she had encountered plenty in her younger years in East Germany and Russia. Fortunately their relationship was fairly short and she wasn't sorry when he was eliminated.

She had mixed feelings about the Cuban-American, Ramon Flores. He at least had a sense of humor and was a caring lover. His need for money made him easy prey, though. She was shocked when Vlad informed her she wouldn't be hearing from him again. Vlad wouldn't elaborate, but hinted that Flores' demands had become unreasonable.

She liked Bert Rosen, too. The burly American was an unpretentious man, and probably would have dropped her after their first few dates if he hadn't owed so much money to friends. He seemed to know he had been duped into abetting illegal activities, though. Once he had collected a few large fees, he'd made no bones about telling Vlad he was finished.

And, like the others before him, this sealed his fate with the ruthless men behind Circle 17.

*

The Englishman Norman Holt had touched a part of her that no man had reached for many years - her heart. From her very first contact with him, she knew he was different from her previous conquests.

Flattered as he was by her coy, yet well-rehearsed approach, he was a gentleman from the start.

Unlike the others, he didn't see their seemingly innocent meeting as a lucky opportunity to bed her right away. He'd taken a genuine interest in her, asking many questions about her job in London. Almost too many, actually. She'd had to be sharp to make her fabricated life sound plausible, leaving no holes in it that he could question. Nor was he as exploitable as the others when she 'learned' that first evening that he was an airline captain.

"Actually it's not as glamorous a job as you make it sound," he had told her modestly. "There are many of us doing it, and it's just a matter of good training and experience. It's fairly routine after that. One just had to stay with the standard procedures every flight."

A few of the others had eaten up her exaggerated awe and admiration and almost dangled the key to their room in front of her. She allowed herself a quick smile at the recollections.

But unlike the others, Norman was not in debt, and the terms of his divorce meant his financial obligations weren't onerous. The divorce settlement was reached before he left for Canada and the job with Northern Flyer. There had been one child from the marriage, and he was more than happy to pay most of the cost of his daughter's schooling. This left him neither rich nor poor, he confided to her on their third date.

He was, therefore, harder to recruit than the others. Renate didn't make her pitch until Norman allowed that he would like to give up his job in Canada and return to the UK permanently. 'I'd do it in a flash,' he'd confessed, 'if I had a nest egg to see me through until I landed a decent flying job in England or Europe.'

Once she was privy to this disclosure, she had him. It helped that Norman saw his cooperation as a means to bring them together much more often.

*

And now, months later, she realized she definitely wanted this to happen. Whether it was her growing disillusionment with her role, or her feelings for Norman, she wasn't sure. Probably a bit of both.

But getting her Uncle Georgiy to agree with her would be a hard sell. Maybe she could suggest that she could still be of some use to Circle 17 if she were to live permanently in Britain. Sort of a semiretired mole, so to speak. She would try and bring it up the next time she met with him.

With a renewed resolve to concentrate on the next few days, she dressed quickly and left her flat, heading for a restaurant in the nearby shopping district. She realized she was quite hungry, not having eaten anything substantial in the past forty-eight hours. She was expecting a call from Norman to confirm he would be arriving tomorrow as planned, but that wouldn't be until sometime this afternoon.

33

It was 1:15, and Rod and Don had just finished lunch.

"Got any plans for the rest of the afternoon, Don? If you haven't, how about coming out to Milne's Marsh for dinner? I know Kate would be more than happy to throw a meal together for us." Derek Houghton had been paged by one of his sergeants and left them before they'd entered the hotel restaurant.

"I'll take a rain check, Rod," apologized Don. "I should try and get together with James Coates and bring him up to date. He spent some considerable time in the past week or so checking out Alf Heard. I'd like to get his report before Derek and I approach him tomorrow."

"Just be careful, Sherlock," warned Rod. "Remember what Derek said about Interpol's involvement. Could be a big plus. Maybe they're close to wrapping up their investigation and our murders will be solved at the same time."

"Yeah, and maybe I'll still be on hold weeks from now."

*

When Don called, James suggested they meet at five at his club. Don gladly accepted the invitation and jotted down the address.

"Jacket and tie?" he inquired.

"Not strictly adhered to, but I'll be so attired," said James.

Don got the message. He showered and donned a dress shirt and tie to go with the sports coat and trousers he'd worn to this morning's meeting. At four-thirty he took a taxi to the address James had given him.

*

The call from Norman came just after 4 P.M., which left Renate plenty of time to make a pre-arranged call to Vlad. A call that she was going to place from a public phone some distance from her flat. After their last meeting in Brussels, Vlad had cautioned her to be extra careful when communicating with him. Although he hadn't said so in as many words, he'd hinted that he thought his activities were being monitored. He told her that as soon as the shipment she was working on had been dispatched, he would be closing down operations in Brussels.

With that warning in mind, Renate took a circuitous route to reach Paddington station. She boarded an eastbound train from Westbourne Park to Great Portland Street station. After alighting and studying a wall map of the underground system, she crossed to the westbound platform. It was now the middle of the evening rush hour and trains were arriving and departing at one to two minute intervals. She let three pass before joining a crowd boarding a crammed Circle Line train, and got off again two stops later at Edgware Road.

She took the escalator up to ground level and entered the busy Marks and Spencers department store opposite the station entrance. After finding her way to the cosmetics section, she spent five minutes browsing around the counters full of health and beauty products. Finally she chose a small container of hand cream that she didn't really need. After paying for it, she left the store by the same door she'd entered by, now certain she was not being followed.

She walked the rest of the way to Paddington along Praed St, pausing only as she passed St Mary's Hospital. A siren from an ambulance turning into the emergency entrance had startled her. At the cavernous rail station Renate purchased a phone card and sought an empty booth, the end one in a bank of five. From her handbag, she took out a Sabena Airlines boarding pass. Before leaving Brussels, Vlad had supplied her with a new number to use when communicating with him. She'd jotted the number down on the boarding pass. She waited patiently for her call to be answered...

"Yes?"

"Is the shipment ready? I can send it Wednesday."

This pre-arranged wording told Vlad that the airline captain Olga was running was still expected in London tomorrow and would be flying out on Wednesday.

"Good, yes, the shipment is ready. Advise me when it has been dispatched so I can let our cousin know to expect it."

"Yes, I will call as soon as it's gone."

"By the way, did you know Uncle Ted is sick? He called last night to say he had taken ill at work."

"No, no I didn't. I haven't been in touch lately. Should I visit him?"

"Not necessary. I'll let you know when he is better."

*

After hanging up, Renate let out a worried sigh. She was about to slip the boarding pass back into her handbag when suddenly she gasped.

What are you doing you stupid cow? Carrying the boarding card around with the contact number broke a cardinal rule for an undercover agent. It would spell disaster if she were apprehended with it in her possession. She closed her eyes and repeated the number from memory three times. Satisfied she would now remember it, she tore the boarding pass into small pieces, and left the phone booth. With no rubbish bin in sight - a security precaution left over from black days of the IRA bombings in London - she scrunched the scraps of paper in her hand until she could dispose of them. After a casual glance around the station interior to make sure she was still unobserved, she headed for a coffee bar. She ordered an expresso and took it to an empty table, disposing of the boarding pass remnants in the coffee bar's rubbish container.

As she sipped the bitter liquid, she wondered what had unnerved Alf Heard. His use of the emergency number meant trouble. 'Uncle Ted' was the code name for the Pembury's night man. It wasn't the police, or Vlad would have used the phrase 'Uncle Ted is seriously ill' instead of just 'sick'. But who was it?

Heard didn't know Olga's phone number or address, and they had never met in person. She made the calls to him after he had left word with another cell member regarding a possible contact. And then only spoke long enough to get the pilot's physical description, and the dates he was expected to be laying over at the Pembury House. Even if he were questioned about her, she was sure he would be unable to provide them with any useful information as to her whereabouts.

34

At 4:55 P.M. Don arrived at 231 Belgrave Circle, a leafy crescent a short distance off the busy Knightsbridge.

A discreet, one foot-square, weathered bronze plaque on the solid looking entrance door gave the only hint to the building's use. THE TRANSVAAL CLUB read large letters in the center of the plaque. Beneath the name in smaller script were the words *Members Only*. Beside the door a more recent sign advised tradesmen that deliveries were to made via the mews entrance only.

Don straightened his tie and gave the buzzer a short burst. Seconds later the door was opened and he was greeted, not as he had expected by a formally-clad butler, but by a smiling and attractive red-headed lady.

"Please come in sir, and welcome to the club. You must be Mr. Carling!"

Taken slightly aback, he admitted he was.

"Hi, I'm Susan Hyde-Morgan, the club secretary," she explained, extending her carefully manicured hand. "Just go straight along the hall. The bar is on the left, you can't miss it. You'll find Mr. Coates waiting for you there. Enjoy your visit with us."

*

"Very nice James, very nice indeed," enthused the Canadian as he surveyed the trappings in what was once the formal drawing room. Three large chandeliers hung from the high ceiling in the narrow but lengthy space. The room's only windows were at the rear, and looked out on the mews.

"Good to see you, Don, welcome back to old blighty," said James, rising to greet him. "Take a chair, I'll have Reynolds fetch us a libation." Reynolds the barman was already approaching their table and took their orders. "Didn't think you were a high tea man or I would have asked you to come earlier."

"No, you're right about that. Not much on cucumber sandwiches, either. And I never could hold my pinkie finger the proper way."

"Ah, well. There are some things better left to we British," chuckled his host.

Don asked about the history of the club while they waited for their drinks.

"It was founded by officers returning from the Boer War, in 1903, I believe," James began, "and continued as a sanctuary of sorts for them until some time between World Wars One and Two. Once they began dying off, the membership was opened to assorted bods with military ties. I've been a member since the early seventies, I suppose. Have to be put up by a present member, of course, and vetted by the board. All very structured, you see!"

"Are many of your former colleagues members?"

"Oh, yes. Nothing like old warriors telling tales over a few large gins, is there?" It was a rhetorical question, but Don smiled and nodded his agreement anyway.

Their gin and tonics arrived.

"Cheers!" said James.

"Cheers yourself, and thanks," responded Don.

The club had four bedrooms upstairs for use by out-of-town members. The modest kitchen provided breakfast for the guests, and other meals were limited to lunch and High Tea.

"Nothing fancy really, and that keeps the dues at a reasonable level," said James. He went on to tell Don a few tales about well-known members, and pointed out their portraits adorning the room's damask wall coverings. James signaled the barman for another round as he finished talking about the club's history. Once the fresh drinks were delivered, he said, "So, tell me about your meeting. I take it from your phone call we're not alone in our search for the mystery woman who has been seducing these airline chaps."

Once again Don recounted the main points from the meeting at New Scotland Yard. When he finished, he looked to the retired intelligence officer for his comment.

"Can't say I'm too surprised. When my friend Beck in Brussels tried to follow up on the bogus holding firm he met with a dead end. His contact at Interpol told him obtaining more details on Flanders Holdings required a higher security clearance than his."

"Hmm. And taking that one step further, we can assume whoever is behind her is using another front now."

"Right. And if she's still in London, she'll be using a new identity as well."

Just then Don's borrowed mobile phone beeped. "Excuse me, James." The call was from Canada, and for two minutes Don just nodded his head and offered the occasional 'uh huh'.

Finally he said, "Great work, Baldy! I'll be in touch."

He closed the phone and gave his companion a 'thumbs up'. "That was my guy who's been watching Holt. Captain R. N. Holt of Northern Flyer Airlines, is confirmed as N. He just called our elusive Renate here in London."

"Wonderful news, old man! Shall I assume by the satisfied smile on your face that it took a little subterfuge to get this information?"

"Just a little, one could say. Baldy got into N's apartment two nights ago and planted a listening device in his phone. Not terribly high tech, but enough to let him eavesdrop on Holt's calls. It meant sitting in a vehicle nearby for the better part of the past forty-eight hours, but that's what I pay him for. Holt placed the call an hour ago." Don checked his watch before continuing. " That would've been half past eleven in Toronto. He confirmed his arrival here tomorrow morning. Looking forward to seeing her, would call once he got to the hotel, etcetera." Don got all this out hurriedly, then leaned back and let out a satisfied sigh.

"Excellent. I don't suppose he had any way of ascertaining the number called, or did he?"

"No, and the device he was working with doesn't have a recording capability, either."

"No matter," said James. "At least we now have two positives to work with. N's identity and the fact that Renate is still here in London."

"But, as you suggested earlier, she's probably using a new alias, and Holt probably isn't aware of it."

"Precisely. Obviously she's still Renate to him," agreed James.

"Yeah, that's the way I see it. Now we have to decide if we can use this info without stepping on Interpol's toes. But I suppose I should let them know as soon as possible, eh?"

"Oh yes, no other option, Don. You say that N wasn't discussed this morning?"

"Not directly. I told them I thought Renate was probably involved with another pilot, but so far I hadn't been able to identify him. But now..."

Coates interrupted him. "But now we know. And you've got too much to lose by trying to go it alone at this stage. You could end up getting your arse kicked all the way to Heathrow and handed a one-way ticket home."

Reluctantly Carling agreed with James's 'no nonsense' assessment. He took a business card from his wallet, and placed a call on his mobile phone. After three rings, an answering service picked up.

"Hello Brian, Don Carling speaking. Time is 5:40. I've just received pertinent info that I want to pass on to you. Call me as soon as possible." He read off his number and hung up.

"That's Brian Roberts, the RCMP officer working with Interpol," he explained to James. "Hopefully I'll hear back from him tonight and we'll go from there, okay?"

"Yes, I think that's for the best. I have an idea that might keep us on the scent, so to speak, without stepping on toes."

"You do? Let's hear it."

"Well, we could–," A wall clock chimed a quarter to the hour. "My goodness! Look at the time. I must be on my way, I'm afraid. Walk with me, Don. I'm meeting friends for dinner at a restaurant near Harrods. Not that far from here, actually. I'll explain on the way. Oh, and I must tell you about your Mr. Heard, too."

James signed a bar chit and they left the club, heading towards Knightsbridge.

*

While Don was in Toronto, Coates had shadowed Alf Heard for the better part of a week to get a good reading on his daily routine. He'd been watching for any sign that Heard was in contact with Renate Neumann, or met with any airline pilots outside the Pembury. Heard lived in the basement flat of a row house on a street just off the West End Lane, the main road through the borough of West Hampstead. He didn't own a vehicle, and used buses or the underground for transportation. He traveled to and from the hotel on the Jubilee Line. When he finished his overnight shift, he walked to the St John's Wood station and caught a northbound train to West Hampstead. It was a short trip, normally ten to twelve minutes. After alighting, he was left with a six or seven minute walk to his flat. In the evening he reversed the journey.

Heard was a man of habit, and Coates was quickly able to pin down his routine. Once he got home - no sooner that 8:30 and never later than 8:45 - he remained there until near ten. Then he emerged via the rear entrance to his flat, passed through the back garden to the lane way behind the house, and followed it to The Orchard pub. Until opening time at eleven, Heard was seen to help with sweeping up, emptying ashtrays, and gathering glasses left by the diehards after last call the previous evening.

By the time the front doors were opened to the day's first drinkers, Heard was perched on a stool at the bar, halfway through his first pint, a racing form in front of him. He nodded or mumbled a greeting to the first three or four regulars, mostly OAPs, who had been standing outside when the doors were opened.

It was a local in the most defined sense and James's appearance three days in a row didn't go unnoticed. Not just by the publican himself, but by the regular customers. In answer to the owner's not-so-subtle probing, he told him in a voice loud enough for all to hear that he was down from the Lake District visiting his daughter for a few weeks.

Once they were satisfied the stranger's presence wasn't a threat to their orderly and humdrum existence, conversation returned to normal and he was ignored. This left him free to eavesdrop while pretending to be completely engrossed in his newspaper. In this manner he picked up a few interesting facts about Alf Heard.

Heard's main interest, apparently, was betting the horses. On one occasion, when he returned from his third or fourth trip to the betting shop a few doors from the pub, one of the regulars kidded that perhaps he should just move in above the shop and save on shoe leather. This drew loud guffaws from the others who, by this time, had downed a few drinks. When the laughter subsided, James had casually asked a bewhiskered slip of a man smoking alone at the table next to his if Heard ever hit a big payoff. He was rewarded with a half-laugh, half-coughing fit before the man answered.

'Not in relation to amount he must be wagering,' he'd told James, because he couldn't remember the last time Alf had stood the lads a round.

The pub name derived from its proximity to a long since built-over apple orchard. The pub had definitely seen better days, James observed. The table tops were scarred and stained, and the chair and stool coverings were worn and faded. The only part that appeared to get regular attention was the bar area itself. The dark wood was highly polished, and the mirrors behind the rows of bottled spirits were clean and unmarked. The glasses were still being hand-washed by the owner and a female helper, who, James soon learned, was his wife.

She took no part in the conversation around her, speaking only to take an order and make change. She looked to be a decidedly unhappy person to James, and he never saw her smile. In contrast to her hefty husband, she was rail-thin and smoked steadily, lighting a fresh cigarette from the stub of the previous one. He figured the days were numbered before she was diagnosed with emphysema, if she hadn't been already.

Alf Heard left the pub each day between 1:30 and 2 P.M., returning straight home, once again by the back lane, presumably to sleep until it was time to get up and have his evening meal before leaving for the Pembury. He wasn't seen to visit the pub in the evening, even on his night off. James finished his report just as they arrived in front of the Indian restaurant where he was to meet his friends.

"He appears to live a very predictable existence, from my observations. The only thing that might have changed in recent years is his increased betting at the local Ladbrokes. If your hypothesis that he may have fingered these pilots for the woman is true, one would expect that he's been paid for the information. That might account for his extra cash."

Don thanked him and they shook hands. He declined James invitation to join him and his party for dinner, pleading fatigue. Before they parted, Don told him that he and Derek Houghton were going to call on Heard the next morning.

"So that's it, then. I'll leave a message on your machine once I hear from Roberts," said Don. "If not tonight, I'll call you tomorrow morning. We'll talk about what to do about N after I've had a good night's sleep."

He grabbed a taxi that had just dropped a couple off and headed back to his hotel. He wanted to touch base with Derek now that he knew more about Alf Heard. And he hoped to hear from Roberts.

*

There hadn't been any messages for him while he was out, so he elected to take a quick shower before calling Derek. He *was* tired, he realized, and hoped the shower would refresh him, at least for a few hours. And it did. He was feeling much livelier as he used a large fluffy towel to dry himself. He'd just settled into one the room's two armchairs when his mobile rang.

Brian Roberts was on the line. "What's up, Don?"

Carling wasted no time with his report. "This morning I mentioned that I thought this woman we've been seeking was probably involved with another pilot, but I hadn't ID'd him yet."

"Yes, I remember."

"A couple of hours ago I had a call from one of my agents in Toronto. I now have a name for him, and he's due here tomorrow morning."

"You're positive about this?"

"Definitely. No doubt at all."

Don told him about the bug on Norman Holt's phone, and his overheard call to Renate confirming his flight.

"So this fellow, a captain with Northern Flyer, placed a call to the woman you know as Renate Neumann, and this is the same woman you've connected to the previous victims. Have I got that right?"

"Yes, that's what I'm telling you. If you guys put a tail on him after he lands tomorrow, he'll probably lead you to her. At least that's what I would be doing if Rousseau hadn't told me to lay off this morning."

Roberts took a long time before he spoke again. "Don, right now all I can say is thanks for this information. I know you were pissed off after the meeting, and I can't say I blame you. But I'll get back to you in the morning. I might have better news for you then."

What could he say? It wasn't Robert's fault. "Okay by me, Brian. I'll have this mobile phone with me at all times. Good night."

His call to Derek Houghton was a short one. From the information supplied by James Coates, they agreed that the best time to catch Heard alone would be before he left his flat for the pub. Derek said he would come by the hotel for Don at 9:30. The drive to West Hampstead would take fifteen minutes at most, he told Don.

35

TUESDAY MORNING, JULY 15

Carling had put in a wake-up call for 6:30, but was awake long before then. He eventually rolled out of bed just before six. For the last half hour or so his stomach had been growling. Whether from hunger or anxiety he couldn't tell - probably a bit of both. He ordered a full English breakfast from room service and had just finished shaving when it arrived. He was on his second cup of coffee when the phone rang.

"Morning Brian. No, I've just finished breakfast." The RCMP officer had apologized for calling so early. "Any good news for me?"

"Well, I passed on the information you gave me about Holt and his call to the woman," Roberts said, "but..."

"But what?" asked Carling rather impatiently.

"I gave it to Commander Watson last night, and I assume he informed Rousseau. Don, things are happening very fast now. I got a call a few minutes ago telling me to drop everything and be at the Yard for a top level meeting at eight." There was an audible sigh over the line. "And even though I urged my superiors to bring you into the ah-h, 'operation', they didn't see it my way." Before the private investigator could respond, he added, "But I'm going to stick my neck out. Can we get together later today?"

"Yeah, I don't have a problem with that," Don replied cautiously.

"Good. Well, I've gotta run. I'll be tied up until late this afternoon at the earliest, but I'll call as soon as I'm free. Should I call your mobile number?"

"Yes, that would be best."

"Okay...and Don?"

"...Yes?"

"Keep this to yourself. No one else is to know."

*

The weather girl on Sky News was advising viewers to keep their umbrellas handy today, and Don found out why when he opened his drapes. A steady yet silent rain was already falling from the leaden skies. "Damn!" he muttered. He hadn't packed a raincoat, and he detested having to carry an umbrella around. He didn't fancy getting soaked, either, so he obtained a loaner from the front desk before he stepped outside to wait for Derek.

*

The rain had lessened somewhat as they reached Alf Heard's neighborhood in West Hampstead at 9:45 A.M. Derek reversed the unmarked police car into a parking space between two delivery vans, directly across from The Orchard pub. A brewery firm's panel van blocked the lane on the north side of the pub. Heather Street branched off along the two-storey building's south side. After locking the car, Derek led the way across the street. Don was glad now that he had the umbrella. Derek was wearing a light nylon raincoat over his suit and didn't seem to mind the rain on his head.

The address they were looking for was the fifth in a line of drab row houses that stretched to the next corner. Although not noticeably steep, the roadbed declined steadily from the main road to the bottom of the street. The rivulets of water running down the gutters attested to the slope. The houses had been built in the years after the Great War, and most looked their age. Many of them showed signs of decaying mortar, and broken chimney pots were the norm. The whole row of brick exteriors had weathered to a dirty and depressing shade of dingy brown. The grey overcast only added to the overall gloominess Don felt as they stopped in front of number 142. A rusting wrought iron fence guarded its front. A gate at the end of the fence allowed access to the steps that lead up to the front door.

Derek was up the steps in two strides. He had to squint to read the faded nameplate on the door frame.

"Here we go, 'A. Heard, basement', it says."

Don was still standing in the gateway, next to a set of spiral steps. "Must be down this way then," he offered, and lead the way to the stairwell, which took them down five to six feet below the sidewalk. The solid wood door confronting them was unlocked, and ajar a few inches. Carling shoved it fully open. They peered into an empty hallway. The only illumination - other than what the open door let in - came through the glass panes on the door at the far end of the corridor. Even on a sunny day Don doubted whether it would be much brighter inside. It took a few moments for their eyes to adjust to the dimness.

"Hello? Mr. Heard?" called the policeman. "Are you there?" When there was no reply they moved into the hallway and Derek rapped on the flat's door. After ten seconds he knocked again, harder this time.

"Doesn't appear to be in, or else he's a hell of a sound sleeper," opined Derek. "Right then, let's see if there's a landlady about."

As they gained the street level once again they were challenged by a sixty-ish, stout woman standing at the front door.

"Who might yer be lookin' for gents?" she asked warily.

"Morning, mum!" smiled Derek. "Seen Mr. Heard this morning?"

"Nah, ain't seen 'im. 'Eard 'im though, comin' in at his usual time."

"What time is that, luv?"

"Well now, it's just after half eight 'e gets 'ome. 'Es me alarm clock, ya see. Me bedroom's right over the entrance there. I 'ear 'im open and close that gate yer leanin' on," she said, addressing Don now. He wasn't actually leaning on the gate, just backed up against it.

"Would he be sleeping then?" Derek again.

"Nah, yer knockin' woulda' woke the dead! Say, why are ya lookin' for 'im then?'

"If he's not in his flat, where might he be now, luv?" asked Derek, ignoring her question.

"Oh, where 'e always is in the mornin', up at the Orchard. Helps the guvner sweep up, then 'as a few pints at openin' time. Sleeps in the afternoons, 'e does."

"Did you see him go up this morning?"

"Nah, usually don't though. 'E goes out back and up the lane. I'm in me front room watchin' the telly by then. Is it the police yer from? Is 'e in any trouble?"

"No, no, just want a word with him. Thanks luv, won't take any more of your time. How does one get to the back lane from here?" he asked, cutting off any further questions.

"Two doors down," she said brusquely, pointing to her left. "There's a passage way, you'll see." She closed her door on them without further comment.

*

The narrow opening she had directed them to was a minefield of dog feces, empty cans and candy wrappers. The two men stepped carefully through it and along the short path separating the adjacent backyards. The lane was paved and surprisingly clean compared to the alley way they'd just come through. The delivery van they'd observed earlier was pulling away as they reached the pub. A burly individual was lowering the metal covering over the cellar storage room. He looked up as the strangers neared.

"Good Morning. Are you Mr. Lansdowne?" Derek inquired, using the name shown as proprietor on the sign behind the man's head.

"Yes, that's right. What can I do for you?" he answered, mopping his brow with an oversized blue handkerchief.

"DCI Houghton. And this is Mr. Carling." The pub owner studied the badge Derek held out to him. "Is Alf Heard about?"

"No. No, he isn't. Haven't seen him yet this morning." He wiped his forehead again, not from the rain, which had stopped, but perspiration from the effort he'd put forth while handling the beer kegs. "Not like him, though. Should think he'll be along soon. He's always here by openin' time."

"Any idea where he might be? He's not in his flat."

"Well, er-r, could be at the laundry up the road, I suppose." He thought for a few seconds and then said, "But he usually pops in on his way by. As I said though, haven't seen him yet. Nothing serious, I hope?"

"No sir, nothing really. Just want a word with him concerning something we're looking into." Derek flashed the publican a short smile.

"Ah, well then. Can't see our Alf in trouble with the law," chuckled Lansdowne, smiling now himself. "Say, why don't you come in? Have a coffee, or even a pint? On the house, of course. I'll be openin' before long and I'll bet old Alf will be in soon enough."

Houghton and Carling exchanged glances that said 'why not'. "Very kind of you, sir. I'll settle for coffee, but I'm sure my friend here can handle a pint." said Derek.

They followed Lansdowne inside and took two stools near the end of the bar. He pulled a pint of bitter and set in front of Don, and then a half pint for himself.

"Coffee won't be long," he told Derek.

The investigators watched silently as Lansdowne busied himself behind the bar, cleaning ashtrays and washing glasses. Shortly before eleven he dried his hands and came around to unlock the double doors that opened onto the intersection. An elderly gentleman studying a racing form was the first one in. He was followed in quick succession by three or four other regulars, who, after ordering their drinks, staked out their favorite spots in the pub. None had exchanged more than a few perfunctory words with the publican. Most noticed the strangers at the end of the bar but only the first man in had acknowledged them with a nod.

Lansdowne asked if anyone had seen Alf about this morning, but no one had.

"Not in the laundromat, just come from there meself," said one, stubbing out his cigarette and shaking another out of a package.

Don and Derek waited patiently until 11:20 before deciding Alf wasn't going to show anytime soon. By now there were ten or twelve patrons in the pub. Unlike the first batch of pensioners, the latest arrivals were either local shop keepers or tradesmen in for a drink before lunchtime. Derek and Don had finished their respective libations.

"Most unusual, Alf not being here by now," offered Lansdowne, glancing at the clock on the wall.

"Well, we'll have another check at his flat, sir. And thanks again for the coffee," said Derek.

*

Don's phone rang just as they stepped into Heather Street. Don had been expecting the call from Rod Weathers, and he huddled under his umbrella before answering.

"Go ahead, Rod."

"Holt's flight landed an hour ago. I should think they'll be arriving at the Pembury any minute, if they're haven't already," he reported. Rod had called the tower at Stansted Airport to get Holt's arrival time. "Where are you?"

"Up in West Hampstead. Derek is with me and we're trying to find Alf Heard. Just heading back to his flat again."

"Check that. Do you still want to meet later?"

"Uh, yeah, probably around one-thirty or two."

"Good enough, mate. Call me when you're free and we'll set it up."

Don hit the 'end call' button. "Holt's flight has landed, and he should arrive at the Pembury House anytime now. Let me check in with James."

Before turning in last night he'd spoken to James about how they might monitor the captain's movements today without interfering with the Interpol operation. James had assured him he could manage it. "After all, that was my calling, you know," he'd reminded Don.

Coates answered on the first ring. "Hello James. Our party landed an hour ago. Should be with you soon."

"Just showed up, my boy. Will call you as soon as there's any activity."

"Thanks, I'll keep in touch. Should be back that way around one o'clock."

*

Neither man looked up at the landlady. She was watching them from the edge of her faded window drapes. Houghton led the way down the stairs to the door to Heard's flat. They entered the hallway and Derek rapped loudly on Alf's door. There was still no sound from inside. The detective tried the door knob. It wasn't locked, so he pushed it partially open and called, "Mr. Heard? It's the police. Are you okay?" Still no reply. He swung the door fully open and took a few steps inside.

"Hello? Oh, bloody hell!" he uttered just loud enough for Don to hear.

Carling stepped in beside him to see what Derek was staring at. "Jesus! What a mess."

The landlady was wrong - knocking didn't wake the dead...

Heard's lifeless body was stretched out grotesquely in his ancient armchair. His head lay awkwardly on his blood-drenched shoulder.

Derek flicked a light switch, which turned on a reading lamp behind and to the body's left. Its brightness gave them a clearer look at the gruesome murder scene.

Most of the dead man's blood appeared to have been pumped out by his dying heartbeats. The blood had congealed in pools on the thin carpet and on a newspaper lying beside the chair. There was even a spray of crimson on the wall a good fifteen feet from the body.

Houghton and Carling surveyed the rest of Alf's living room in shocked silence. Don finally said, "Doesn't look like a robbery, does it?"

"No, nothing appears to have been disturbed," agreed Derek, stepping as close to the body as possible without disturbing the bloodstains. He squatted down to get a better look at the corpse.

"I'd say the killer slashed the poor bloke's throat with a very sharp knife, probably from behind."

They retreated to the basement corridor. Derek made two calls. The first was to the Finchley Road Station requesting a detail of uniformed officers. The second was to Scotland Yard. After taking down Houghton's terse report of the murder, the dispatcher told him a site squad would be on the way within the hour. The squad's specially trained officers would be responsible for fine-combing the scene for physical and forensic evidence.

*

A police cruiser arrived seven minutes later, siren wailing and lights flashing. Two young constables jumped out and rushed up to DCI

Houghton.

"Slow down lads, the chap's dead, so let's do things slowly and by the book now that you're here," counseled the senior officer.

Derek had just positioned them - one in the backyard, and the other by the door to the victim's living room - when a second car arrived. Three uniformed constables climbed out, two men, and an anxious looking WPC. The older of the two males wore sergeant chevrons. Derek explained the situation to him, and they set about securing the dead man's flat until the site squad arrived. The sergeant's first move was to have the female officer place a plastic evidence bag over the inside door knob.

"Mind you don't touch anything in there, Townes!" he warned her. "And don't throw up inside, either," he added, as she started down the stairs.

"There's nothing I can do here, Derek. Maybe I should make myself scarce," Don said, after the others were out of hearing range.

"Yes, no need for you to stick around," agreed Houghton. "A detective from Finchley Road is en route to take charge of the investigation. Once I've briefed him, I'll be heading back to Paddington. I'll give Spence Upton a call and put him in the picture. I'll summon another car to give you a lift."

"No, no, don't waste the manpower. I'll head up to the main road and grab a taxi. Just call me when you get a chance." He hurried up the street past gathering knots of curious neighbors, wondering what sort of emergency had brought so many policemen to number 142.

*

By 12:30 Don's taxi was wending its way through the weave of roadways at Swiss Cottage when his phone rang. James was on the line again. Norman Holt and the other two pilots had emerged from the hotel twenty minutes after checking in, he reported, and made their way to the pub on the corner.

"Holt was in the pub for thirty minutes, and he's just returned alone to the hotel," said James.

"Good. If he doesn't come out again, he's probably gone to bed. I don't think he'll surface for at least three hours. Any sign that others might be watching him?"

"No, Haven't made anybody yet. What are your plans?"

Don didn't want to tell him about Heard's death while he was in the taxi. If Holt had bedded down for a few hours, he and James could rendezvous somewhere in the area.

"Tell you what James, stay put for another twenty minutes. I'll call you then and we'll meet nearby. Okay?"

"Righto. If he moves, I'll let you know."

*

Don had the driver drop him opposite the St John's Wood tube station. He remembered passing a pub along the road when he'd walked through this area on his way to the Houghton's a few weeks ago. One with a beer garden that would do nicely for a meeting place now that the rain had stopped and, contrary to the forecast, the overcast was showing signs of breaking up. The temperature had risen significantly, too.

Three short blocks east of Wellington Road, Don found the pub he was looking for. The Regimental Arms on Ordnance Road was a combination pub and restaurant, bordered by the leafy forecourts of the private homes on each side. The venue was well within walking distance of the Pembury Hotel. Don stopped on the corner opposite and called Rod for the second time since he'd left the murder scene, and told his friend where he was.

Rod was already heading into the city and cut Don off when he started to explain exactly where the pub was located. "No need Don, I've been there before. See you in twenty minutes."

Don crossed the narrow street and entered the pub via the lounge bar. The lunch crowd was thinning out. A party of smartly-dressed women was filing out of the restaurant, laughing easily with each other as they said their goodbyes. A neatly lettered sign on an easel informed patrons that the restaurant had been reserved that noon for the monthly meeting of the Marylebone Women's Volunteers Association.

36

Rod and James Coates arrived within minutes of each other shortly after 1 P.M. James had wanted to maintain his watch on the Pembury, but Don convinced him that Holt had almost certainly gone to bed for a few hours. If he were rushing off to meet his lady friend, he wouldn't have dallied to have a beer with the boys first, he reasoned. At Don's urging, James ordered a full lunch, while Rod opted for a sandwich.

"You're not eating?" asked Rod, after the waitress had taken their orders.

"No, had your famous full English breakfast this morning and I'm still stuffed," answered Don.

In fact he was hungry, but his stomach was still churning from the discovery at 142 Heather Street. He was also troubled by the thought that his visit to Alf two nights ago - and the accusations he'd thrown at him - were in some way responsible for his murder.

Too much of a coincidence for there not to be a connection, was the thought that kept running around in his head.

The three were seated around a metal patio table in the corner of the pub's fairly sizeable garden area. The garden was enclosed by a whitewashed brick wall adorned with hanging floral baskets. The tables and chairs were being wiped dry when Don arrived and so far they were the only customers taking advantage of the now sunny weather.

Don had ordered a beer, but hadn't touched it yet. Rod soon picked up on his peculiar mood.

"No luck tracking down the night porter?"

"Oh we found him all right - dead. He'd been murdered."

This brought astonished gasps from the other two, and a sudden end to their eating. Rod could only shake his head in disbelief as the Canadian recounted what had transpired in West Hampstead. The retired MI5 agent recovered his stride more quickly.

"Hmm, yes, I see. I would venture that his slaying confirms your suspicions about his involvement in this dreadful business."

"Yeah, there seems no doubt about that now, James. But I don't think he would've been the brains behind it."

"No, no, his role was probably along the line that you had deduced, that of a 'go-between' of sorts."

"But why kill him?" wondered Rod.

Don let James answer first. "Someone must have thought he'd become a liability, perhaps they were afraid he was getting cold feet."

"But he must have told someone that I had made the connection between him and Renate Neumann," said Don.

"Certainly. But that is what an underling such as Heard would have been instructed to do under the circumstances, you see."

Their discussion turned to whether or not Heard's death meant that Norman Holt was in imminent danger. A question that none of them could answer.

They decided that short of going directly to Holt - which was quickly dismissed - all they could do was watch from the sidelines when he surfaced again. Plus ensuring they didn't get in the way of whatever Inspector Rousseau's team was planning to do about Holt. Don hoped he would have a clearer picture of their intentions once he heard from Brian Roberts.

James left to resume his vigil near the hotel, once again assuring Don that he was quite content to stay until Holt arose. Don said he would spell him off later in the afternoon.

*

2:20 P.M.

Derek called while they were deciding what to do next. "Okay, we're not too far away, maybe twenty minutes. See you then."

Rod gave him a questioning look when he ended the short call. "We're off to Holloway Road Police Station. DCI Upton's turf. Derek will meet us there," said Don.

Rod had parked around the corner from the Regimental Arms, and studied his London map briefly after they strapped themselves in. "Hmm...routing via Camden Town looks like our best bet," he said, handing the map to Don. His estimate had been close: they arrived at the station at 2:38.

*

3 P.M.

Renate took the last cigarette from the package and lit up: a package that had been almost full when she got up this morning. She'd been killing time since Norman's call just before noon, and it was still too early to set out to meet him. However, now that she was out of cigarettes, she would have to allow extra time to pick some up before she kept the rendezvous. Norman was a non-smoker, and gently chided her for her addiction. She made a real effort to stretch out the time between smokes when they were together. But today she needed her crutch.

She slowly and meticulously applied her make-up, a practice that took a good five years off her facial features. Finished, she changed quickly into a figure-flattering navy blue pant suit and gathered up her purse and keys. At the last moment she grabbed her small umbrella, having learned the hard way about London's notoriously changeable weather.

This would be her first journey from her new address to St John's Wood, and the roundabout routing she followed gave her more than one opportunity to spot a tail. By the time she settled into a nearly empty car on the northbound Jubilee Line from Bond Street, she was confident that no one was following her. The quick run to St John's Wood left her with thirty-five minutes to spare before meeting Norman and his daughter at five. But she wasn't planning to show up much before five thirty.

If the authorities had somehow tied Alf Heard to her - and from his call to the emergency number on Sunday night that appeared to be the case - then Norman might be under suspicion as well. As of last night, Vlad had not been able to say if that were so. She knew there were probably other cell members operating in London, but their identities had never been revealed to her. Presumably Vlad would have had someone check with Heard to see why he had been spooked. In any event, the operation involving Holt's flight tomorrow was still on as of this morning. Renate was to give a final confirmation after spending the evening with Norman.

*

3:25 P.M.

The meeting at Holloway Road had centered around two issues, the murder of Alf Heard and whether or not Captain Holt was in immediate danger. Derek Houghton was on the phone receiving an update from the crime scene when Don and Rod arrived. Initial canvassing of the neighborhood hadn't found anyone who had seen strangers in the vicinity of 142 Heather Street that morning. Nor could anyone remember a vehicle that looked out of place.

"It isn't likely the killers would have driven close to the house, rather they would have parked along the busier High Street and approached on foot," offered Houghton, "probably via the back lane."

"Yeah, those fences along the lane are about six feet high and would allow them fairly good cover," added Carling.

"Could it have just been the work of a burglar or drug addict looking for quick cash from a man who lived alone?" Rod Weathers wondered.

Don answered. "No, I think we can rule out that scenario, Rod. This has to do with his job at the Pembury and his connection with the pilots who've been killed. That I'm sure of." The policemen agreed with his assessment.

"Don't suppose the medical examiner has made his report yet?" Upton asked.

"Nothing on paper. But off the record, he told Harrington the victim had been dead for approximately six hours." Harrington was the detective from Finchley Road in charge of the investigation.

"What time did he get to see the body?" Upton asked.

"Just before one o'clock," answered Derek. "According to the landlady, Heard arrived home at eight-thirty, give or take a few minutes. Harrington figures, and I agree with him, that the killer must have showed up shortly after, or he was already waiting inside."

"Killer or killers?" asked Carling.

"I don't believe that's been determined yet, Don."

Don asked if the Interpol representatives had been informed of Heard's death and if so, how they had reacted to the news.

"Yes, I called Commander Watson right after Derek contacted me," answered Upton. "From his reaction, I'm of the impression this development might be a problem for them. But in what way, he wouldn't let on."

"Humph! It sure became a problem for poor old Heard, didn't it?" said Rod Weathers, shaking his head disgustedly.

"Yes, well, I don't know what they're up to. Watson's main concern was that the police not make any suggestion of a possible connection between Heard's death and the killings Don is investigating when speaking to the press."

"Has the media got on to it yet?" asked Don.

"No, but it will probably be on the evening newscasts and in the morning papers," said Derek.

No one spoke for a few moments until Rod, changing the subject, once again voiced his concern for Holt's safety. He addressed his remarks to his brother-in-law and DCI Upton.

"Don doesn't think Captain Holt is in any immediate danger. I'm not so sure, given this ring's propensity for violence. If they're trying to wipe out anyone connected to them, why wouldn't they go after him just like they did the others?" Rod's worried tone left no doubt of his concern.

"We were talking about that before you arrived, Rod, and I understand where you're coming from," Derek said, "but I think we've got to assume the Interpol bunch know what they're doing vis-a-vis Holt and this woman, and trying to warn him off would only be interfering with their operation."

IPF's safety chairman was still not completely convinced, but resignedly offered no further argument.

"Are they using any of your lads in their operation?" Derek asked his colleague.

"No, haven't had any requests for men at all. Which leads me to think they're only using bods from Special Branch."

"Yes, probably," agreed Derek, and then asked Don, "Has James seen any sign of others watching the Pembury?"

"No, not at last report." Don looked at his watch. "Holt is probably still sleeping. I don't expect he'll surface much before four-thirty or five. I'm going to relieve James once we're finished here."

Upton expressed surprise at their surveillance. "We were told not to approach the Neumann woman, and we won't. Even if she turns up," Don told him, almost challenging him to object.

Upton got the message. "Yes, well I'd be most careful if I were you, Mr. Carling. And if you do come up with anything new, I trust you'll let Commander Watson know immediately."

"I don't have his number."

"Then please contact me and I'll relay it to him."

"Sure, no problem, Mr. Upton," replied Don, with an emphasis on the 'Mr.'.

*

4:45 P.M., ST JOHN'S WOOD

Renate hadn't been overly keen about meeting Norman's daughter, especially today. Norman had mentioned Alison, of course, but had forgotten that she was going to be in London on this particular day. He couldn't very well put her off, and he had no intention of doing so. He truly loved his only child and didn't get to see her that often.

"She's catching a train around seven from Paddington, so we'll have the rest of the evening to ourselves," he assured Renate when he'd called this morning. "I think you'll like her. I haven't been a very good long-distance father, I'm afraid. I'm hoping to make it up to her when I move back here for good."

"I'm sure we'll get on well, darling," she'd answered, injecting forced sincerity into her voice.

'I couldn't very well have said no, could I?' she asked herself after his

call. *'And if Norman and I do end up living together...'*

She'd quickly pushed aside any further contemplation about her future. For the next twenty-four hours she had to be fully focused on her mission, not wistfully pondering options with a man she had known for less than six months.

*

Café Kos was located half a block down from the T-junction of Allitsen Road and the High Street, on the west side. This meant that Norman would have to approach it from either the north or the south, assuming that he would walk to it from the Pembury. The logical direction was from the north, the shortest route from the hotel. Now, fifteen minutes before five, Renate was watching for Norman from a vantage point in a coffee shop on the east side of the street. A Greek restaurant and a wine bar occupied the space between the coffee shop and the corner.

The Circle 17 agent had figured correctly. It wasn't long before she spotted Norman and his daughter walking down the opposite side of the street. She studied the young woman as they passed. Renate was surprised at how tall she was: at least five-foot eight, only a few inches shorter than her father. She wore the uniform of choice for students - faded blue jeans and a tight, scoop-necked T-shirt that accented her trim figure. Even if either of them glanced her way, they wouldn't be able to see her. Renate's table was off to one side of the shop's window, which shielded her from view.

Once the pair reached the café, they sat at an outside table. Norman checked his watch, a move that brought a quick smile to Renate's face. She'd never known her latest beau to be late. Most of the time he was annoyingly early. She glanced at her own watch. It was 4:55.

*

4:55 P.M.

Don and Rod continued to debate what to do about Holt after the meeting ended. As they approached his hotel, Don said, "If nothing comes of this Interpol operation before his flight tomorrow, I'll fly home and confront him. There'll be nothing to stop me from doing that. Tell him everything we know about the woman, and her ties to the previous victims."

Rod nodded. "Yes, and then, if he's smart, he'll come clean and help you get to the bottom of this."

"Carling," said Don, answering his mobile just as Rod pulled into a parking spot.

"Our subject is on the move. I've just tailed him and a young lady from the Pembury to St John's Wood High Street. They've stopped at a sidewalk café," James reported.

"A young lady?"

"Definitely. Less than twenty, I should think. She entered the hotel about ten minutes before they exited together. She's toting one of those nylon carryalls the younger generation haul around these days."

"A backpack, you mean?"

"Yes, that's it. I expect she's a family member, a daughter perhaps, or a niece."

"Could be, Holt is British so having family here isn't that surprising, I guess. And it's just the two of them at the café?"

"That's right. But they've only just arrived. Where are you now, Don?"

"Just got back to my hotel. I was going to make a quick change and then head your way. Maybe I should come right now."

"No need to rush. They've ordered something, so I should think they'll be here staying put for a while," said James. "In fact it's starting to rain again and they're moving inside."

"All right then, I won't be long. I'll get Rod to drop me off near you."

" Righto. Call me when you get close and I'll tell you how to find me."

Don explained the situation to Rod, who said he'd wait in the car while Don changed. There were no messages for him, and Don wondered why he hadn't heard from Roberts. If the RCMP officer still wanted to meet with him, it might interfere with their watch on Holt.

Just have to cross that bridge when I come to it,' he told himself.

He quickly changed clothes, donning dark grey slacks and a long-sleeved navy blue polo shirt. He stuck with his black walking shoes. It wasn't an outfit he'd normally choose for evening wear in London, but fine dining was not in his plans.

*

5:25 P.M., ST JOHN'S WOOD

"Cheers, James," toasted Don. "Are you sure you don't want to call it a day?"

James shrugged off the suggestion. "I'm fine really, sitting and watching isn't physically tiring, you know. And I don't think we'll have to keep at it much longer. I'll wager you'll have some answers to this mystery of yours before much longer," answered the elder man.

The two were sitting in The Armada, a spacious wine bar at the bottom of the High Street, opposite the park and garden behind Saint John's church. As per James's instructions, Rod had dropped him off a hundred or so yards south of the pub. As he walked towards the wine bar Don spotted the sign for the Café Kos further ahead on the west side of the street. He soon learned why James had instructed him to approach from the south.

"Do you see the fourth vehicle up from the corner, Don? The dark blue sedan?"

Don peered over Coate's shoulder and through the pub's large north-facing window.

"Uhh, yeah, I've got it."

"There are two chaps inside, probably coppers. They must have been watching the Pembury from further up the street from my location. They drove past me just after I set out after Holt. They made two slow passes up and down the street before they parked."

"Ahh. So Interpol did decide to shadow him."

"Most certainly. Like us, they must think he'll lead them to Neumann."

"Or maybe she'll turn up here. He could be waiting for her, couldn't he?"

"True, that's a possibility. Anyway, that's the situation at the moment."

37

It was the Russian agent in her that spotted the telltale signs that Norman was being watched, not the Renate wondering what life with the Englishman who was so enamored with her would be like.

She'd first noticed the blue car driving slowly along the street a few moments after Norman and his daughter had passed her. Not the car in particular, but the two men inside. When they drove by again five minutes later, warning bells went off. She was able to observe them more closely the second time when the driver stopped to let an elderly pedestrian cross the street in front of them. Both men appeared to be in their mid-thirties, clean shaven, and wearing suits. It's possible, she thought, that they were just a couple of businessmen. But her instincts told her she'd spotted policemen at work.

Her spirits sank when she saw them pull into a parking space three car lengths from the Café Kos. That was fifteen minutes ago, and both men were still inside their vehicle.

This was a major setback: there was no way she could keep the rendezvous with Norman now. They *must* be following him. Even if their presence was just a coincidence, she couldn't take the chance. *But what to do? I'm thirty minutes late, Norman will probably phone me before much longer. Or maybe I should try and call him at the café? What excuse can I make? I can't tell him the truth...*

She finished her second coffee, now cold, and turned her thoughts to getting away from St John's Wood. She daren't step outside to flag down a taxi. Too much of a chance that Norman would pick that moment to come out of the café. He'd mentioned that his daughter had to catch a train that evening, she recalled, so they wouldn't be able to wait much longer for her to show up.

On foot, at least initially, was her only option, she decided. Fortunately the coffee shop's location was in her favor. She paused briefly at the doorway for a final glance towards the Café Kos. It was still raining lightly and there was no sign of Norman or his daughter. She could just make out the two men sitting in the front seat of the car a few doors from the café, even though the vehicle's windshield wipers were idle. Renate raised her umbrella and tipped it down to cover her face. A young man about to enter the shop held the door for her, and she smiled a 'thank you' to him. She turned left, and seconds later turned left again onto Allitsen Road. Now that she was out of sight of the café, she slowed to a reasonable walking pace. This was unfamiliar territory for her, but her sense of direction told her that turning right at any of the next corners would take her towards Regent's Park. She wrestled with what to do next as she hurried along the sidewalk.

If her phone rang, should she answer it? It would be Norman, and she still hadn't come up with a reasonable explanation for her 'no show'.

Perhaps he would see his daughter off before trying to contact her. Then again, if he was going to do that, logic said he would call her first to tell her he'd left the café. An even more threatening thought struck her and brought her up short.

Damn! I must contact him somehow! What if he decides to come looking for me at the flat? I can't let that happen while he's being followed. She had no choice, she realized: if her phone rang, she would have to answer it.

*

Norman had insisted Alison order something to eat, knowing she would only snack on the train back to Bristol. In spite of her protestations that she wasn't very hungry, she ordered two items from the list of starters: calamari and a small Greek salad. Her father ordered a glass of red wine.

Over their drinks, he broke the news that he was planning to move back to England sometime soon.

"What will you do? Will you be able to get another flying job?" Her questions reminded Norman of her mother's practical side.

"Oh, I should think I'll find something eventually. It will be easier once I've made the move," he told her.

Alison instantly made the connection: the woman they were waiting for must be the reason for her father's decision. Now she was really curious to meet her.

Alison had been eight when her parents separated, followed three years later by the divorce. Her father had moved to Canada soon after. At first she had hoped they would reconcile. She didn't ever recall them fighting, and her mother had never spoken unkindly about her ex-husband, at least not in her presence. Oddly, she'd never had the inclination to know exactly why their marriage had ended, and consequently had never asked either of them for an explanation.

"How's your mother?" Norman asked politely, shortly after the rain had forced them to move inside.

Alison smiled. *He always asks that,* even when he phones. And it always sounds as if his question is more of an apology for his leaving...

"Oh, she's okay, still working at the dress shop," she answered. "Goes out occasionally, but doesn't seem to mind being alone." And at other times, Alison knew, his casual *'How's your mother?'* was his polite way of asking if her mother was seeing anyone.

"Well, be sure and say hello for me, won't you?" Norman offered lamely.

They chatted quietly about her studies, and her plans once she graduated next year. As always, he asked how she was doing financially, specifically if the funds he sent to pay her tuition costs were sufficient. And, as always, she assured him she was doing just fine. Her part-time job as a waitress provided her with the extra cash for her not overly busy social life.

By 5:55 they had run out of things to talk about and Alison was ready to leave.

"Dad, I can't wait much longer. If I miss my train, I'll have to wait two hours for the next one." She pointed to her watch for emphasis.

"Yes, I understand," he told her. He signaled the waiter for the bill. "I don't know what might have held her up. She said she was looking forward to meeting you."

"Well, I'm sure there'll be another chance soon," smiled his daughter. Her father's face registered his disappointment, and she reached over and squeezed his hand.

Outside, Norman insisted she take a taxi to Paddington, even though Alison told him she had plenty of time to get there by bus or tube. She gave in only because it was still raining. She waited under the awning while her father hailed a taxi. As he hugged her goodbye, he folded a twenty pound note into her hand.

"Safe journey, dear," Norman told her. "I call you again in few weeks."

She waved, and blew her father a kiss as the taxi pulled away.

*

"Here we go," said Don when he saw Holt and his daughter coming out of the café. "Looks like they're trying for a taxi."

James turned to get a better look. They had already decided that if Holt did leave the area by taxi there would be no point trying to follow him. That would have to be left the watchers in the unmarked police car.

They watched as Holt helped the young woman into the taxi, and wave as it pulled away, heading north towards the corner at Circus Road.

"Must be his daughter, eh? And the police don't seem interested in her," observed Don. Their vehicle hadn't moved.

"No, it's definitely Holt they're on," replied James.

The target of their attention glanced uncertainly both ways a few times before he made his move. Suddenly he started down the street towards their vantage point.

The rain had tapered off once again, giving them a clear picture of Norman Holt as he approached the corner.

"Does he know you by sight, Don?" asked James.

"Not as far as I know. This is the first time I've laid eyes on him myself. If he comes in, he won't make us." The wine bar had gradually filled up since Don's arrival and it was standing room only around the bar.

It soon became apparent where Holt was heading: a bank of

telephone kiosks directly across the street from the Armada. Not the sturdy red call boxes so popular with tourists, but plexiglass booths open at both the top and bottom. Holt stepped into an end booth, next to one occupied by a woman and a toddler, who had her hands full trying to keep the youngster from straying away while she talked. Holt's back was to Don and James as he placed his call.

"Oh what I wouldn't give for one of those wonderful gadgets the lads at MI5 have at their disposal nowadays," commented James.

"Would that be a directional receiver you're referring to?"asked Don.

"Exactly," murmured James.

*

"Renate? It's me. What happened?" asked Norman.

"Oh darling, I'm so sorry! I tried to call you but you had already left the hotel and I couldn't remember the exact name of the restaurant." She began her contrived spiel, feigning distress. She'd pulled together a story as she walked towards Regents Park, where she'd found a dry bench under a leafy chestnut tree just before Norman called.

"I was just leaving to meet you when my manager called," she continued hurriedly. "I didn't even know he was in London. He insisted I come immediately to a meeting with one of our customers and--"

"Slow down, Renate! Take it easy. It's not the end of the world. Just take a deep breath and tell me about it."

The practiced liar did just that. Her lover listened sympathetically to her tale of woe. She had made a terrible and expensive mistake with an order for one of her firm's best West End customers, and Monsieur Laporte, her boss from head office in Paris, had thought it so serious he had flown over on a moment's notice to straighten it out. She had been severely chastised and told to drop everything until she had rectified things to the customer's satisfaction.

"I can't get away tonight - I'll be hours contacting suppliers to try and fix things. You do understand, don't you darling?" she pleaded.

"Uhh, yes, yes, of course. These things happen. I could come by later if..."

"No, no darling! It could be midnight before I'm finished. You'll be back next week. I'll make it up to you then."

"Yes, all right... I'll call you in the morning before we leave for Stansted."

"Oh yes! I'll be up early tomorrow. Promise you'll call me as soon as you get up. And Norman, everything is arranged at the airport for tomorrow. The same contact will handle it for you."

6:30 P.M.

'The same contact' was a man named Terrence McDuff, Terry for short. McDuff was a foreman with Fleet Cargo Handling, a contract company that serviced Northern Flyer flights at UK and European stations. His job was to oversee the loading and unloading of Northern's flights at Stansted Airport. He was responsible for 'signing off' a flight before it departed, and was normally the last contact the captain had with the ground crew before the aircraft doors were closed.

Holt was thinking about Terry over a glass of Beaujolais in the Duke of York pub at the top of the High Street. After his plans for the evening were dashed, Norman first inclination was to head back to the pub near the Pembury to hook up with his crew. Gord Chalmers, his first officer and Ozzie Novak, the flight engineer, were planning to meet there at six, he knew. As he walked up the High Street though, he decided he didn't really want to spend the evening with them. He'd told them this morning he would be seeing a friend tonight. No, after he finished his drink, he would stroll up to Swiss Cottage and have dinner at one of his favorite restaurants.

Terry. At first Norman hadn't thought much about him. It had been Karl, Renate's so-called cousin in Brussels, who first suggested that if he was going to be flying out of Stansted on a regular basis, then Terry would be a profitable contact for him.

'Just let Renate know if you're interested,' was the way Karl had put it.

That was almost three months ago. Karl knew why Holt preferred London, of course. Olga had played him well, and it wasn't long before she reported that Holt was cooperating with Terry. Now, after three deliveries from Stansted, he was increasingly worried about what he'd let himself in for. So far he'd only carried relatively small packages - ones that fit into his flight bag. A day after arriving back in Toronto, he mailed them from a local post office.

When he told Terry last month not to count on him in the future, the Scotsman wanted to know why.

Was it more money he was after? Had he run into trouble in Canada? When Norman told him the answer was 'no' on both counts, Terry told him to think it over. When Renate had made the surprise offer - one more delivery for $50,000 US - he was staggered.

'Just as risk-free to you as any of the previous shipments,' she assured him.

Her subtle yet insistent pressure during their last three days together had sealed his commitment. But he'd vowed once again that it would be the last time.

Norman left the pub and started walking north towards Swiss Cottage. The rain clouds had moved off, leaving clear skies and a crisscross pattern of contrails high over the city. Norman tried to close his mind to any more thoughts of how Renate, Karl, and Terry McDuff were connected for the rest of the evening.

Or what the consequences might be if things went wrong...

38

As soon as Holt entered the restaurant, Don headed off for his hotel, which was less than a kilometer from Swiss Cottage. He figured it would be at least forty-five minutes before Holt finished eating, probably longer.

Don and James had separated once Holt entered the Duke of York. They'd concluded that he probably wasn't going to lead them to Renate: something must have come up. James half-heartedly suggested that perhaps they never had planned to meet that night, but Don reminded him of the phone call Holt had made to her yesterday from Canada - the call that his operative had listened in on.

*

Two different plainclothes policemen were watching Holt now. The new team had switched with the original pair before Holt left St John's Wood. Don hadn't spotted anyone else following Holt on foot, but moments after he entered the restaurant he saw the surveillance vehicle parked nearby.

Don was undecided as to whether or not there was any point in taking up Holt's trail again after he finished eating. His mind was made up for him soon after he reached his room and saw the message light blinking.

There were three messages. The first message was from his office in Toronto. Joanne told him Ralph Woods had called. Woods had learned that Norm Holt had given notice to Captain Hammond, Northern Flyer's chief pilot, that he was quitting effective the first of October. Holt had submitted his letter of resignation before he left for London last night.

*

Before he could dial again, his mobile phone rang. It was the call from Brian Roberts he had been waiting for.

"I'd just about given up hearing from you," said Don.

"Yes, well, this is the first chance I've had to call you, I'm afraid." There was an audible sigh from Roberts. "We got the word about the hotel porter's murder, of course. I gather you were there when he was found?"

"Yeah, myself and DCI Houghton."

"What's your thinking? Is it connected to the other killings?"

"Fuckin' right it is! And it's tied in with whatever you guys are doing. I hope your boss realizes that now!"

"Take it easy, Don. Believe me, we're on the same page," said Roberts calmly.

"Well, the sooner you track down this woman, the sooner we'll get some answers. And if you don't, I'm going after her before Holt becomes the next victim," stated Carling.

"Just keep your distance for another twenty-four hours," Roberts advised.

"Give me a good reason to and I'll think about it," he replied, more bluster than bravado. He knew he didn't have a choice.

"I'll tell you why, and I'll trust you to keep it to yourself until after Holt's flight leaves tomorrow." Don listened carefully to the RCMP officer's explanation. He - Roberts - was going to be on the flight. Authorization for him to travel in the jump seat was being arranged. Interpol was investigating the transportation of illegal drugs on certain cargo flights to North America, he went on, and was about to close the noose on those behind them, both here and on the receiving end.

Northern Flyer Flight 213 - Holt's flight - was expected to have a shipment of drugs on board. Robert's role was to watch for anything out of the ordinary during the loading and unloading of the aircraft. A combined RCMP and Canada Customs team would take over surveillance once the flight landed in Toronto.

"What about Holt? Is he to know what you're up to?"

"Not necessarily..."

"Meaning?"

There was a pause before Roberts spoke again. "I have a cover story. If it doesn't hold up, it won't really matter."

His hesitance lead Carling to believe there wasn't anything to be gained by prodding him further. He decided to lay his cards on the table.

"Okay Brian, I hope you can wrap up your investigation in the next few days. Because if you don't, I'm going to confront Holt before his next flight and warn him about this girlfriend of his. She's a definite danger to him and I don't think he realizes it."

*

Don called Room Service and ordered a meal before he returned Derek Houghton's call. He filled the Londoner in on Holt's actions from the moment he'd left the Pembury this afternoon until minutes ago when he entered the restaurant.

"Doesn't seem to be any point in my trying to watch him any longer tonight. The locals are still on him," explained Don.

Derek agreed. "No, I suppose we'll just have to see what tomorrow brings, then."

"That's more or less the conclusion I've come to."

Don then told him that he'd heard from Roberts, omitting the part about his being on Holt's flight tomorrow.

"Well there's no doubt they're mounting a major operation. I've been on to a good friend of mine at the Yard, and he let on that a number of their top undercover lads are seconded to Rousseau at the moment."

"Let's hope they get results, then. I made it quite clear to Roberts that if they don't have answers soon I'm going to warn Holt about the Neumann woman. Rod and I both agree he has to be told before it's too late."

"Well, let's hope that won't be necessary," said Derek. Then he told Don why he'd called.

"Heard's murder is all over tomorrow's papers, " he said, "but there isn't any mention of a possible connection between him and Rosen."

"Any leads yet?" asked Don.

"Not really. I spoke with Harrington an hour ago. His men had completed their door-to-door canvass of Heather Street with negative results.

"Can't say I'm surprised," said Don, "these are professional assassins we're dealing with."

"No doubt. But Harrington's team now has photos of the two suspects in the Rosen case and they'll show them to shopkeepers along the High Street tomorrow. They're a more likely source to have noticed an outsider," suggested Derek.

"Assuming the same killers were used."

"Most certainly. In any event, a full-scale watch for them is in effect at all embarkation points in the southeast, including airports."

He asked the Canadian investigator if he had any plans for the next morning.

"Well, I guess we're just going to wait and see what develops. No other choice really," Don replied.

""Yes, that's the smart thing to do. I'll let you know if I hear anything."

"Thanks again for your help, Derek. I'll be in touch for sure," said Don, before wishing him good night.

*

His last call was to Rod Weathers. He covered the same ground as he had with Derek, emphasizing his commitment to confront Norman Holt before his next trip if nothing tangible happened tomorrow.

A thought crossed Don's mind while they were talking.

"Are you free tomorrow, Rod?" he asked.

"Definitely. What do you need?"

"Do you have a pass that'll get you into secure areas at Stansted? The cargo areas or the control tower, for instance?"

"Sure. As IPF's Safety chairman I have access to all restricted areas at UK airports."

"What about me? Could you get me authorization? Just temporary of course."

"Hmm, yes, I should be able to swing it. Why?"

"Well, rather than sit around here tomorrow with nothing to do, I think we might see more of what goes down if we're at the airport, don't you? I'll fill you in on the drive out. Can you pick me up around nine?"

Puzzled, but trusting his friend's instincts, Rod agreed.

"I'll make much better time if I leave home before seven, though. I'll get there about eight. Breakfast is on you!"

*

After making his calls, Don turned his attention to the dinner tray that had arrived while he was talking to Rod. He picked at the club sandwich and chips, not that hungry all of a sudden. He slumped into the room's lone upholstered chair, his mind a turmoil of emotions: frustration, resignation, and eventually thoroughly pissed off.

Frustration because he was so close to finding this woman who, he was sure now, bore responsibility for the deaths of four men. Men she had somehow lured into a smuggling operation, seemingly one of some magnitude.

Not that the victims were innocent bystanders, not by any stretch of the imagination. Not when the evidence indicated that they had all been paid for their help. They weren't just doing favors for a mysterious lady they'd all been romantically involved with...

No, even if she was just the bait, her accomplices used - and then killed - these pilots. Her guilt was confirmed as far as Don was concerned when she disappeared after Captain Bert Rosen's body was found.

Resignation because the Interpol operation that Rousseau was heading took precedence over the search for the killers of the pilots. The search that he and the Metropolitan Police had been doggedly making progress with.

'Guess I just don't have the big picture, or I might've been able to play my cards differently,' he thought, and that's what really pissed off him off.

At least they can't stop me from approaching Holt once he's back in Toronto. He was trying to decide when he should leave London when he dropped off to sleep.

He awoke two hours later with a painfully stiff neck, shrugged out of his clothes, turned off the lights and stumbled into bed.

*

Carling wasn't the only one wrestling with the future as darkness cloaked the British capital. In his room at the Pembury, Norman Holt was staring at the television screen. He was watching two expressionless snooker players take turns running eight or ten balls in a row. With the sound muted he had no idea who was winning, or even their names. He wondered if chalk dust was easy to get off the starched white shirts and cummerbunds they were wearing.

If he hadn't been so engrossed in his own thoughts, or if he had recognized any of the crew members gathered around the reception desk when he'd come in, he might have stopped to see what all the fuss was about. It would be next morning before Holt heard about the night porter's death.

What was on his mind - and had been most of the evening - was Renate's 'no show'. Her explanation was plausible enough. And her expressed regret at missing the chance to meet Alison seemed genuine as well. No, it was her poorly-veiled afterthought just before they said goodbye that bothered him.

Her relief that he was still willing to carry the shipment tomorrow seemed to outweigh her disappointment at not seeing him.

The worried captain fought his negative thoughts. *'Ah, let it go, I'm probably reading things into it that aren't there. And I've already decided that tomorrow will be the last time, anyway.'*

He too dozed off in his chair, and awoke a few hours later with the same stiff neck that Don Carling had sustained. Luckily he fell back to sleep in his bed before the unanswered questions surfaced again.

39

9 P.M., NEW SCOTLAND YARD, JULY 15

Jean-Marc Rousseau rapped the table to get the attention of the others gathered in the conference room. The room was now the operations center for the present investigation on British soil. Two long tables placed along one wall held an array of telephones and two-way radios. The communications setup was being monitored by two uniformed officers.

Commander Watson from MI5 and the RCMP's Brian Roberts occupied chairs to Rousseau's right. There were five other men seated at the table. Four of them were with the Metropolitan Police covert operations branch. Each of them commanded a six-man team. Two of the teams were already involved and the other two were on standby.

The other man had flown into London that afternoon. Franck Willbroek was an Interpol agent based in the port city of Antwerp. The forty-four-year-old Belgian had spent fifteen years as a welder in the shipyards before Interpol recruited him. He nodded unsmilingly to those around the table when Rousseau introduced him.

"Gentlemen, let's get underway," began Rousseau. " I would like to keep this as brief as possible so that you may get off to dinner and a good night's rest. Tomorrow will be a pivotal day and we all need to be sharp, n'est ce pas?"

Rousseau had Willbroek begin. The newcomer's voice was decidedly raspy, and his heavily-accented English had the others around the table straining to take in his report without appearing to do so. He had been keeping tabs on the Dutch lorry driver who had transported a suspected drugs shipment to the UK, he told them. The driver was a known cocaine addict who probably supported his habit by smuggling goods across the channel on his regular run. He had observed the handover near the dockyard in Antwerp, and forwarded the information that allowed the British police to pick up the trail once the ferry docked at the channel port of Felixstowe.

He would be tailing the driver on his return trip to the continent, where he would be taken into custody along with a number of others suspected members of the ring operating in the Low Countries.

In his report Willbroek mentioned a carload of men of mid-eastern appearance, and one of the Scotland Yard officers asked him to elaborate. Rousseau interceded before he could answer.

"I don't think we need to go there, Inspector. Suffice to say they are part of the investigation in Europe. They are not believed to have a direct connection with what is happening here. In other words, we don't expect you will see the men you have under surveillance come in to contact with anyone from that region."

He glanced around the table to see if there were any other questions. When none were forthcoming, he turned to another of the team leaders, Inspector Gerald Pitcairn. His men had followed the lorry from Felixstowe.

"Two hours after the vehicle rolled off the ferry, the driver pulled into a layby on the A12 north of Chelmsford. Ten minutes after he parked, a blue Ford van with UK registration stopped alongside it. The van's driver approached the Dutchman.

'Any Dutch cigarettes for sale, mate?' he asked. The words were picked up via a directional microphone. The phrase was obviously the code the lorry driver was expecting, because he climbed into the back of his rig and emerged a minute later with a small carton. The other man took it, stowed it in the back of his van, and drove off. A few minutes later the lorry pulled onto the motorway once more and proceeded towards London.

"The van was tailed to Barton Glen, a small village ten miles east of Stansted Airport.

It is now parked outside a house rented to one Terrence McDuff, identified by the van's registration and confirmed by the owner of the house."

"What do we know about this man?" Watson asked.

"We're still delving into his background as I speak," said Pitcairn, "but he does not have a criminal record. He's fifty-three, divorced, and is presently employed by a company named Fleet Cargo Handling at Stansted. At the moment, he is well on his way to getting pissed at the only pub in Barton Glen. Fortunately for Mr. McDuff, he's within walking distance of his place of abode. He's due to start his next shift at Stansted at seven tomorrow morning."

*

The next report concerned Captain Holt's movements. The police watching him had just radioed in, said their team leader, Detective Sergeant Reasor. Holt was dining at a restaurant in Swiss Cottage, and was still alone.

"That has me a bit baffled," admitted Reasor, "I was under the impression he would be meeting with this Neumann woman."

Rousseau turned to his MI5 liaison for comment. "Yes, well, that was the gen we received from a reliable source running a parallel investigation."

"Mr. Watson is referring to the work of a Canadian private detective who is investigating the deaths of four airline captains. The victims were apparently involved in the same type of smuggling as Holt," explained Rousseau. "All four also knew this woman. We have only recently become aware of his investigation. It is probable that the woman is a covert agent for the organization we are targeting, but her existence was unknown to us until a few days ago. We're not sure yet if these pilots were directly related to the international ring. More likely, our analysts think they functioned as a separate resource, a tentacle, if you like, of the broader conspiracy." Rousseau paused and took a few sips of water. "So, that is why we are watching this captain so closely while he is on the ground. Finding this agent may be a bonus we hadn't counted on, especially if there are others working with her here in Britain.

He shuffled through the few notes he had in front of him and was about to speak again when he was interrupted.

"Excuse me, sir," said one of the constables as he approached the table. "There's a call for DS Reasor." He handed a mobile phone to the policeman. Reasor identified himself and listened to the short report.

"Understood, Grimes, we'll watch the hotel all night in any event. I'll send another team to relieve you at midnight." He passed the phone back to the constable and turned to Rousseau. "That was the lads on Holt. The man has returned to his hotel, still alone."

"Hmmm...interesting," offered Watson. "Stay with him though, Sergeant. He's still our best lead to the woman at the moment. And she might yet arrive for a late night tryst," he added, a remark that drew a few knowing chuckles from the men around the table.

"And if she doesn't?" asked Rousseau.

"His telephone was bugged while he was out. We should be able to trace any calls he makes or receives."

"Excellent!" lauded the man from Interpol. "Gentlemen, thank you all for your cooperation. If there are any changes to your assignments for tomorrow you'll be advised in the morning. Otherwise carry on as planned. Bonsoir."

*

Renate was exhausted by the time she returned to her flat, even though it was only a few minutes past 8:30. Mentally tired, more than physically.

After Norman's call, she had taken a taxi to Paddington, and found a seat in the waiting area opposite the departure gates to the trains. There were about forty to fifty people seated around her. She glanced around, using a newspaper to hide most of her face.

She wasn't exactly sure what had prompted her decision to come here. If Norman did come to see his daughter off, she certainly couldn't approach him after the lie she had fed him. But it would give her another opportunity to see if he was still being watched. Even with hundreds of passengers milling about she was confident she would be able to spot a tail. After fifteen minutes she hadn't spotted Norman or his daughter.

She was beginning to think she was wasting her time when Alison passed within five yards of her. She was responding to a public address announcement advising passengers that the 7:15 train to Bristol was ready for boarding at platform six. The young woman had appeared from behind her. Startled, Renate pulled the newspaper closer to her face. She didn't dare turn her head. Involuntarily she held her breath as the young woman joined the orderly queue heading for the train. There was no sign of Norman.

'Stupid ! If Norman had been with her, he might have recognized me, even from behind!' she chastised herself. And that would have meant game over.

The shaken agent remained seated until the gate closed and the Intercity train pulled away. Once her heartbeat returned to normal, she folded her newspaper, stood up and followed the signs to the Paddington underground station. She boarded an almost empty car on the next westbound Hammersmith and City line train. Two stops later she alighted at Westbourne Park and walked quickly towards Simcoe Terrace Gardens. She made a circuit of the small park before entering her building. The six cars parked around the garden all displayed residents' stickers, she noted.

After locking her door and securing the safety chain , she used her mobile phone to call Vlad and tell him the operation could proceed tomorrow. She hoped she was right. The call to her cell leader had taken less than thirty seconds.

*

BRUSSELS, TUESDAY NIGHT, JULY 15

"Fucking Arabs! I'll be happy when we're finished dealing with these self-righteous assholes!" uttered Vlad.

He was on the phone to General Kravitchkev in Moscow. The head of Circle 17 had instructed Vlad to call him after he heard from Olga, no matter how late the hour.

"Tut tut, Pavel! This is business. I've told you that a number of times."

"Well, business with these Islamic bastards could bring us all down. Four of them arrived in Antwerp yesterday with the delivery. Four! They stand out like Orthodox Jews at a Neo-Nazi rally, for Christ's sake!"

"You weren't followed?"

"No General, *I* wasn't followed. I took extra precautions both before and after the handover. But any policeman with half a brain would have been suspicious of that crowd sitting in a car near the harbor. Fortunately I don't think they were noticed," said Vlad. "I made the transfer to the lorry driver shortly afterwards."

"Da, good. Anyway my friend, I have received their payment. That is the important point. That is the last time you will be dealing with them."

"Amen to that. I'll bet these fuckers are part of the same Allah-chanting fanatics causing so much grief in our southern states."

"Perhaps, but that is Yeltsin's problem, not ours. And you may be pleasantly surprised how our...ahh, 'cooperation' with them pays off eventually. The only enemy that matters to us may be in for a large setback and we will have had a part in it."

"I'll believe it when I see it," the younger man replied.

The men were speaking Russian, and Vlad, taking no chances, had placed the call to Moscow from the busy main rail station in the center of Brussels. He had chosen the phone booth at random from the eight designated for international calls, and paid cash for the charges when he finished.

Before he ended the call, Vlad assured his chief again that Olga was confident the shipment would leave London tomorrow.

40

WEDNESDAY MORNING, JULY 16

Norman Holt had not slept well. He'd tossed and turned until almost 4:30 A.M. before falling into a deep sleep. The alarm jarred him awake two hours later. By five minutes to seven he had showered and shaved and was debating who to call first. He decided it was too early to ring Renate.

Instead, he dialed the number for Fleet Cargo at Stansted to check on his flight's status. Even though crews were supposed to be advised of any long delays, from experience he knew that wasn't always the case. Too often they had been picked up at the normal time only to arrive at the airport to find their departure time had been delayed, either for a mechanical problem or because the inbound flight had been late arriving. Delays they would rather take at the hotel.

Today though, he was assured by Reg Wardlaw, the duty dispatcher, that his flight was on time.

"Flight 212 just updated his ETA. Should be on the ramp by 0940, ten minutes early. We'll have you ready to go on schedule at 11:30, Captain."

"Thanks Reg. By the way, is Terry McDuff working today?"

"Yes, I saw a few minutes ago. Want to speak to him?"

"Oh no, that won't be necessary. I'll see him when we get to the airport. Thanks."

Holt was just about to ring off when the dispatcher said, "By the way, Captain, you're going to have a jump seat rider today. His authorization was telexed here overnight."

'That's strange,' thought Holt, *'company employees or personnel from other airlines wanting to ride the jump seat are supposed to clear it with Northern's crew scheduling department at least five days in advance.'*

"You don't say. Do you have a name for him?" He asked, his annoyance showing.

"Let me check. Ah, here it is. A chap named Brian Roberts, Canadian citizen, authorized by Captain J. N. Hammond, Chief Pilot and Flight Operations Manager," read Wardlaw.

"Never heard of him. Does it say what company he's with?"

"No Captain, that's it, other than his passport number."

Holt hung up, and considered this unexpected development. As captain, he still had the final say on whether or not to carry non-flight crew personnel. But he realized he'd have to have an ironclad operational excuse before he went against his boss's okay.

'Maybe I should contact McDuff and tell him to cancel the shipment today...'

After further thought he decided that wasn't necessary. There wouldn't be anything at this end to connect him to it. And he would still have an opportunity to warn McDuff off after he met this Roberts chap and found out more about him.

*

7:15 A.M.

"Good morning, darling," answered Renate warmly. She had picked up on the first ring. "I'm so sorry about last night. I hope I'll get another chance to meet your daughter soon."

"I'm sure you will. How did you make out with your problem?"

"Oh, I could kick myself for being so stupid!" Her accent was quite noticeable when she spoke quickly or showed anger. "I was busy until nearly midnight and still didn't get it all straightened out. My boss is being most unreasonable about it. Maybe I should not have changed my job."

Norman was about to suggest that when he returned to the UK they could live together and she could give up her work. But a lingering warning signal in the back of his mind went off and he rejected the notion. Instead, he tried to soothe her frustration, telling her to forget about last night, and think about seeing each other next week.

"I'll take you to dinner somewhere special, somewhere you've never been before," he told her.

Renate let out a long sigh. "That sounds wonderful. I will count the days."

They sweet-talked each other for a few more minutes until Norman broke it off, saying he was going to take a walk before breakfast.

"Of course, darling. I won't keep you any longer. Have a safe flight." He thanked her, said good bye, and was about to hang up when she added, "Oh, and Norman, you will call me tomorrow, won't you? Just to tell that everything went okay?"

"I will. I'll call after six your time."

"Thank you darling. I'll see you next week. Bye!"

*

Inside a minivan parked in the lane behind the Pembury Hotel, the two Security Service technicians checked the data from the bug on Holt's room phone. The tape, which started as soon as Holt began dialing, was electronically transformed and analyzed by their computer.

"Great! We got it all," enthused the younger tech, as the printer spit out the word-by-word copy of the conversation between Holt and the woman.

"Good work, Jimmy. I'll radio it into headquarters," said Charlie Wilkins, the second man in the van, reaching for his two-way radio.

*

7:18 A.M., NEW SCOTLAND YARD

"Sandbox from Marconi One."

"Go ahead, One, you're loud and clear."

"Roger that. We've got a number for you that Skipper just called. Ready to copy?"

"Affirmative, One"

"'The number is 073662825. It's a mobile number, and it's ex-directory, of course."

"Roger, I copy. I'll read the number back."

Sandbox was the call sign for Rousseau's team running the Interpol operation from the conference room at New Scotland Yard. Their communications operator read back the number and Wilkins verified it. He told Sandbox about Holt's first call to Stansted, and advised them that the transcripts of both calls should be available on their computers by now.

"Check. They are coming off the printer just now. Thanks, Marconi One."

*

Rousseau strode into the room just as Harold Watson finished giving orders to Alan Broadhurst, his second-in-command. Broadhurst gave Rousseau a quick nod as he hurried out of the room.

Watson rose to greet the Frenchman and offered his hand. "Bonjour, Jean-Marc. We've just got our first break of the day."

Rousseau shook hands and returned the greeting. "Eh bien, what has happened?" He settled into the padded swivel chair at the head of the table and Watson sat down next to him.

"Skipper just called Tempest. Here's a copy of their conversation," Watson said, handing the printout to Rousseau. "It is a mobile phone number. So far all we know is that the phone would have been let by one of two companies, both with large numbers of subscribers in the Metropolitan area. Broadhurst will have men at both firms within the next thirty minutes. Shouldn't take long after that to come up with a name and address."

Rousseau was about to comment when the radio on the table in front of Watson squawked... "Marconi Two to Sandbox."

Watson reached for the walkie-talkie. "Go ahead, Two," he replied.

"Skipper is on the move. Just left the hotel on foot, heading west.

One other chap with him."

"Okay Two, keep a loose tail. He won't be going too far, they're due to be picked up at 9:15. Advise when he returns to hotel."

"Roger, Sandbox. Will do."

*

Holt spotted his flight engineer Ozzie Novak as he entered the lobby. Novak and three others were gathered around the front desk, talking quietly with Mary, one of the daytime receptionists. As Norman approached he saw the woman dab at her eyes with a crumpled white handkerchief.

Ozzie didn't notice Norman until he stepped up beside him.

"Oh, mornin' Norm," he said, his voice uncharacteristically muted. "Did you hear about Alf?"

"No, what about him?"

Ozzie took his captain's arm and turned him away from the desk before he answered. "He's dead. The poor old bugger was murdered, according to Mary."

"Murdered? Bloody hell! When did this happen?" Norman tried to remember if he'd seen Alf last night. But then he remembered he'd come in well before ten and one of the young women was still manning the reception desk.

"Yesterday morning. They found his body in his apartment. The morning papers are full of it, apparently. I was gonna pick one up on my way to the greasy spoon. Are you headin'out for breakfast?" Norman said he was, and the two of them started out, turning right as they reached the street. Neither of them paid any attention to the small panel van parked a few doors away from the hotel entrance. The 'greasy spoon' Ozzie had referred to was Bargain Ben's, best described as a working man's café. It was a ten-minute walk west of the Pembury, on a side street off Maida Vale. They stopped at the newsagent's shop next to the café and bought newspapers.

The café's early morning clientele consisted mainly of tradesmen looking for a quick and substantial breakfast before starting work at the numerous 'reno's' in the area. It wouldn't have been Norman's first choice - too noisy and too smoky for his liking - but the food was good and the prices inexpensive. The strong tea was always hot and refills were free.

'*An airline pilot's dream,*' was how he'd heard it described by more than one crew member.

This morning, to Norman's surprise, the place was relatively uncrowded. They placed their orders at the counter, paid Ben, who was manning the cash register, and found an empty table near the front window. A young waitress delivered a pot of tea and two cups and told them their breakfasts would be along soon.

Both men turned to their newspapers while they waited. In the *Daily Mail* the short account of Alf Heard's death was on page five.

NEIGHBOURS SHOCKED BY
MURDER ON THEIR QUIET STREET

The body of Alfred Heard, aged 68, was found Tuesday morning in his basement flat at 142 Heather St, NW 12. Police would only say that he had been a victim of foul play and that a motive had not yet been established. Nor would they say who had found his body. Heard, a bachelor, had lived in the house for more than fifteen years, according to his landlady Mrs Norah Queen, who lived above the victim's flat. Mr Heard worked as a night porter at a residential hotel for airline crews near St John's Wood. A spokeswoman for the hotel declined comment, other than to say 'Mr Heard was a reliable, long-time employee and the news of his murder has shocked our staff members.'

"Doesn't tell us much, does it?' said Ozzie, as he finished reading the same article.

"No, no it doesn't," replied Norman. "Did Mary have any other details?"

"No, not really. Apparently the police came around to the hotel yesterday afternoon and gave the manager the news. Said they would be back today to question the staff. See if any of them had any insight that might help them, that sort of thing. Did you ever talk to him, Norm?"

"No, at least not at any length. Just a few words when I was coming in late," Holt replied. "How about you?"

"Oh, had a chat with him once in a while, that's about all. He'd be hanging about when we were sittin' in the lounge. Never really had much to say, just sort've listened in."

Their breakfast arrived and conversation ceased as they tucked into their eggs, bacon, beans and chips.

"Want my fried tomato, Norm? Too darned mushy for my liking," said Ozzie. Holt declined, but enjoyed his own.

It wasn't until they were walking back to the hotel that Ozzie brought up the night porter's murder once again.

"I wonder if there's any connection between Alf's murder and the Atlantic Best captain?" When Norman gave him a quizzical look, he said. "It wasn't that long ago, you know, sometime last month when he was killed."

"Ah yes. That was rather unfortunate. So he was definitely murdered, too? I thought there was some possibility that it was an accident."

"Oh shit no! I was here four or five days after he was killed. We ended up at the pub that night with an AB crew and they had the straight gen. He'd been attacked and beaten and then thrown over a bridge. That's what the police report said."

"Really? I hadn't heard that."

"Yeah, well that's what we were told. And some of our guys even suggested that maybe Len Newson's fall into the Rhine wasn't all it seemed to be, either," Ozzie said. "Mind you this was late in the evening and it could've been the beer talking."

They were approaching the hotel now, and Norman offered no further comment. As they entered the lobby, Ozzie said, "See you at 9:15, Norm."

Norman sat down to watch the nine o'clock news after he finished packing his suitcase. A black and white photograph of Alfred Heard was displayed as the anchor woman read the latest report about his death. The photo was an old one, taken a good fifteen or twenty years ago, he thought. The younger Heard had a fuller face and a thicker head of hair than the night man Norman was used to seeing.

The report was a short one, and made no mention of the death of Captain Bert Rosen, or the Pembury Hotel. It ended with a phone number scrolling across the bottom of the screen for the public to call if they had any information.

41

0805 HOURS

Ten minutes after arriving at the cylindrical-shaped office building near the Hammersmith flyover, the MI5 team had a name and address for the number Holt had called. The building housed the offices of FoneFast, a newcomer in the highly competitive mobile phone market. The customer had paid cash for a three-month lease.

As soon as this information was radioed back to Commander Watson, he issued new orders to his deputy.

"Alan, did you hear that?" he asked, when Broadhurst answered. His radio was tuned to the same frequency the team in Hammersmith was using.

"Roger sir, I copied it all," confirmed Broadhurst. "We've located the address on our map. ETA fifteen minutes."

"Good. When you get there just set up a watch for now. I'll advise further once you're on station. I'll be sending a team from the Yard to make the first contact with the subject."

Broadhurst acknowledged his superior's directive and confirmed he would check in again when they were in place.

*

Rousseau had been leafing through the file on Neumann while Watson was busy on the radio.

"So, our lady has a new name, it seems," he said, when the latter signed off.

"Yes, but that's not surprising, is it? I would think she knew she was being sought as Renate Neumann, hence the change," said Watson. "But it's intriguing that this chap Holt apparently isn't aware of it."

"Hmm. We'll run 'Katrina Mueller' through our data bank on the off chance that she's known to us. Both identities she uses appear to be German."

Watson knew that the group Interpol was stalking was thought to be run by Russian nationals. "Agreed, but not so unusual when one considers the history of the Soviets and their spy rings in the former East Bloc territories, I shouldn't think," offered the Englishman.

"No, you're quite right. There are still hundreds of former KGB types out of work, and many of them were once agents of the East German Stasi. It's quite possible we'll find that's where her roots are," said Rousseau.

"Well, let's hope she hasn't flown the coop again. We should be able to pick her up within the hour, Jean-Marc, and bring her in for questioning."

Watson excused himself, saying he had to make a few calls to cover the legalities before moving in on the flat of one Renate Neumann, a.k.a. Katrina Mueller.

"Get me the duty officer at the Home Office, would you please, Gladdings," said Watson, addressing one of the comm operators, "and then track down DCI Upton. If you get him before I'm through with the Home Office, please have him hold, there's a good lad."

*

The duty officer at the Home Office listened to Watson's request, making notes of the details as he related them. When he was finished, she read back,

'Request for warrant to detain one Katrina Mueller, a.k.a. Renate Neumann, resident at flat six, twelve Simcoe Gate, London W15, and search said abode. Reason for warrant, classified Interpol operation directed by Assistant Director J-M Rousseau, Interpol Headquarters, Lyon, France.

Request initiated by Commander H. R. Watson, MI5.'

Watson confirmed the information and gave her his number in the event the magistrate handling the request had any questions. "We need this warrant ASAP, and thank you." He hung up before she could reply 'What else is new?'

*

Watson had time for a few quick sips of tea before Gladdings signaled that Upton was on the line.

"Good Morning, Inspector. I've got some good news for you."

He summed up the latest development and laid out for Upton how he wanted her arrest handled.

"That's where you come in, Inspector. You can question her about her involvement with Rosen. Don't even mention Holt. See how that pans out, for starters. We'll go from there once we see how she reacts," explained Watson. "Once we have the warrant, Broadhurst will have you detain her in regard to our investigation."

"Got it. You can advise Broadhurst I'll rendezvous with him in approximately thirty minutes," replied Upton.

"Thanks, Inspector. And remember - refer to her only as Renate Neumann. Let her think it's just her connection to Rosen you interested in."

*

0840 HOURS

DCI Upton and Sergeant Ross pulled in behind the MI5 vehicle parked on the north side of Simcoe Terrace Gardens. They were met by Alan Broadhurst, who had been leaning against the wrought iron fence surrounding the green space. After introductions, the agent indicated the building where the woman lived, directly opposite their vantage point.

"No one fitting her description has come out yet," he told Upton, "mind you we haven't been here that long. Let's hope she's not an early riser. Anyway, there's no name on the card for flat six. It's probably on the first floor," he added.

"I see," said Upton as he studied the surroundings. "We'll soon find out if she's in or not." He explained to Broadhurst how they were going to conduct the initial interview with her, and, when the warrant arrived, have the MI5 team take over.

*

There was no answer to his first rings. Upton waited fifteen seconds, then gave the buzzer two longer rings. He was about to select a button at random, identify himself as a police officer, and ask to be let into the building when the occupant of flat six answered.

"Yes? Who is it please?" The voice betrayed both surprise and anxiety.

"Miss Renate Neumann? I'm Detective Chief Inspector Upton, Metropolitan Police. I'd like a word with you, ma'am."

There was a pregnant pause before she answered. "Police? What is it about, please?" Both Upton and Ross noted her use of 'please' at the end of each question, a phrasing commonly used by some European nationalities when speaking English.

"I'd rather come in and tell you, ma'am. Won't take much of your time, just a few questions that might help us with an inquiry." Upton was speaking in a friendly manner, and waited patiently while she considered his request. Finally there was an audible click from the entrance door lock.

"Yes, you may come up," replied the woman, her voice now slightly stronger.

The lift was located at the rear of the wide, carpeted hallway that separated the four flats on the ground floor, but Upton and Ross took the stairs opposite instead. Number six was the first flat on their left as they reached the landing. There was no bell or knocker on the closed door so Upton knocked softly to announce their arrival.

Inside, Renate had used the short interval to compose herself and get over the initial shock of being tracked down by the police. How did they find her? Norman was the only one who knew where she lived. She couldn't think why he would have told the police. She thought back to yesterday: now she knew for certain that they must have been following him.

But the thought that buoyed her was the name the policeman used. As Renate Neumann she should have a chance to bluff her way through. As Katrina Mueller they would have the upper hand.

"Just a moment please, I am not quite dressed." She kept them waiting for another two minutes while she got straight in her mind how she would handle their questions. Finally she opened her door.

"Come in, please," she said, offering them a slight smile.

Upton showed her his badge and introduced his sergeant. They followed her into the flat's tidy living room and took the two chairs she offered them. Renate sat across the oval-shaped, glass-topped coffee table from them. To Upton's experienced eye, the attractive woman had not just thrown her clothes on in the last few minutes.

She was wearing a floral print off-the-shoulder top and a pair of black slacks that fitted nicely around her shapely bottom. Her toenails - painted a bright red - accentuated her stylish white sandals. And there was no way her perfectly made up face was a rush job, he noted.

There was no trace of apprehension when she spoke.

"You haven't come about me leaving the cat behind when I moved, have you?" she asked, almost teasingly.

Her opening parry caught Upton off guard. Ross came to his boss's rescue after a few seconds. "No, ma'am, we 're not here about the cat," he said, "Your neighbor, uhh, Mrs. Whitt, took care of it."

"Oh, that makes me feel better! I had to return to Germany without notice, you see, a death in the family and I couldn't find it."

Upton had finally twigged to what she was on about. *'Very clever, by admitting that she had previously lived in Highgate she's trumped one of my cards.'*

He and Ross exchanged quick glances. They both knew she was lying, but Upton wasn't ready to call her out yet. He changed the subject before she could say anything more.

"We're not concerned about that, Miss Neumann. It is 'miss', isn't it?" Upton asked, looking her straight in the eyes. When she nodded a guarded 'yes', he continued. "We are investigating the death of a man named Albert Rosen, an American whose body was found on the morning of Saturday, June twenty-first. We have reason to believe he was an acquaintance of yours. Can you confirm that?"

She didn't answer immediately. Instead she reached for the pack of cigarettes lying next to a huge crystal ashtray. She shook one out and lighted it. She didn't offer them to the policemen. She took a long, deep drag and exhaled slowly.

"Yes, I knew him," she admitted. "He took me out a few times, that's all."

"Did you see him on the night he was killed? That would've been a Friday."

"Yes, we did have a drink together earlier."

"By earlier, what do you mean?"

"Oh, I don't remember exactly. It was probably about seven, seven-thirty..."

"Did you have dinner together afterwards?"

"No, in fact he told me he wouldn't be calling me again."

"Really? Did he say why?"

Renate gave them a sultry laugh. "Why do middle-aged men like him do anything?" she asked rhetorically. "He was going to get back together with his wife, he said. The old story..."

"So, after this ah, 'farewell' drink together, he just left. Is that right?"

"Yes, that's how I remember it, Inspector."

"And what time would this have been?" When she gave him an exasperated look instead of an answer, he said quietly, "We need to account for his whereabouts in the hours before he was killed. That's why I need you to be as accurate as you can, Miss Neumann."

"Yes, I know, I'm sorry. If only I hadn't had to leave London so suddenly I might have been more of a help," she lied. "I guess it would have been around nine. Yes, no later than nine o'clock. I'm sorry, that's all I remember."

"Thank you. That's the information we need," Upton said.

Renate appeared to relax, thinking she had successfully dodged a bullet. Upton gave his sergeant a slight nod, and Ross picked up on the unspoken signal to shake her up.

"So Miss Neumann, you say that Rosen left after a few drinks. Are you positive he didn't spend the next few hours with you at your flat? And took his leave from there between eleven and midnight?"

A dark scowl came over her face. She jabbed at the ashtray with her half-smoked cigarette.

"Why don't you say what you're thinking, Sergeant? she said bitterly. "Did we say goodbye in the bedroom? No, we didn't! And that's all the questions I'm going to answer. Please leave now!"

Neither policeman made to move. They knew she was lying: the post mortem on Rosen indicated that he had engaged in sexual intercourse only hours before he died...

When Renate started to rise, Upton told her to sit down.

"Take it easy, Miss Neumann. My sergeant did not mean to be insulting," he told her.

Renate reached for another cigarette before she sank back onto the sofa. "Just a few more questions, if you don't mind. Tell me, when did you find out about Mr. Rosen's death?"

She'd been waiting for the question ever since Upton had told her why they were here, and launched into her rehearsed spiel.

"Well, it's crazy I know, but it wasn't until I was on my way to Germany. I bought a paper at the airport to read on the flight, you see, and that's the first I knew about it. I didn't take a newspaper at the flat, and I don't have the television on much, so I didn't know before." She paused for their reaction, and when neither of them spoke, continued with her lie. "I was shocked, of course, but there was nothing I could do."

And there was nothing Upton could come up at the moment to refute her story. It might even be true, but he doubted it.

"What day was this, ma'am?" asked the inspector.

"Oh, that was on the Saturday," she lied. "Yes, the day after we said goodbye."

"And how long were you in Germany, may I ask?"

"Oh, I think about a week," she replied slowly, trying to figure out where he was heading. She leaned over and stubbed out her cigarette. She had only taken three puffs on it, Ross noticed.

Upton changed the subject. "Can you think of any reason why he might have been killed? Had he made any enemies in London, perhaps?"

She gave him an incredulous look. "Enemies? I already told you I didn't know him that well. And married men like him don't volunteer much about their personal lives, you can be sure." She stood up, and looked at her watch. "Now I really must ask you to leave. I have an appointment soon and I must get ready."

Upton had hoped to keep her a little longer, but it appeared Broadhurst wasn't ready yet to take over. Reluctantly he stood up and offered her his hand. "Thank you for your time, ma'am." As they reached the door he stopped and rather casually asked, "Just one more thing. Is there a number at your place of work that we can reach you at? I presume you are working here in London?"

"I don't see why what I do or don't do has any relevance to your investigation, Inspector," she replied curtly. "Unless you consider me a suspect, in which case I shall retain a lawyer before answering any more questions."

With that she held the door open and ushered them out.

*

"I'll say this for her, she's got balls!" Ross said as he and Upton reached the entranceway. "And quite a looker, too. I can see why these men would have been taken in by her."

"Yes, she's a cool one all right," agreed Upton.

If she left the flat now, the MI5 team would follow her. That was the plan he and Broadhurst had agreed on.

They discussed their interview with her as they made their way to the MI5 team's vehicle.

"I wonder why she never asked how we found her?" asked Ross.

"Yes, I was waiting for that too, especially after she started to get angry. That was good timing, by the way," complimented Upton. "Subtly put, as well. I'm sure he did spend the entire evening with her before he was killed. There's no evidence to show he wandered around Highgate until after eleven. As I recall, the autopsy put time of death no earlier than half-eleven."

"That's right, sir," said Ross, "half-eleven plus or minus an hour." They discussed a few of her other answers that seemed plausible enough but were probably untruths.

Ross added one last comment as they stepped through the gate on the north side of the garden. "And I got the impression she was rather relieved when you didn't ask her why she had changed flats."

"Yes, we've left her a number of loose ends to ponder. But we're not through with her yet, not by a long stretch..."

*

After closing the door behind the police officers, Renate leaned back against it and closed her eyes. She remained that way for a few minutes, wrestling with the many aspects of the steely-eyed inspector's probing. Once she'd relaxed enough, she moved back to the living room and slumped into a chair. What most concerned her was the questions they hadn't asked.

He let me off pretty easily - too easily. How did they find me if they didn't know I had leased this flat under another name? Something's not right there. At least they didn't challenge anything I said about Bert. And no mention of Norman at all, which was strange.

Having considered her options, she concluded they were very limited. For one, she would have to leave the flat soon just to back up her story. She was certain they would watch to see if she did. She went into the bedroom and changed her clothes.

42

Upton had just finished a recap of their interview with Renate for Broadhurst's benefit when the MI5 agent's radio crackled to life. The call was from the agent bringing the warrant. He was nearing the area and requested their position. Five minutes later he arrived with the official document.

As Broadhurst was looking it over, his partner signaled that the woman had just stepped out of her building. Upton trained his binoculars on her. She was carrying a briefcase and wearing sunglasses, and was dressed in a light grey outfit. Her dress shoes matched her jacket and skirt. Without so much as a glance around, she turned left and started walking towards the corner of the square.

"Let's move! Time to reel her in," Broadhurst exclaimed. Upton and Ross hurried back to their unmarked car. Ross pulled out behind the MI5 vehicle and followed it around the gardens and past number 12. Their quarry was just turning up the west side of the square, striding purposely along when the vehicles braked to a stop beside her.

Olga stopped in her tracks. A premonition of doom engulfed her as two strangers stepped in front of her. Seconds later the policemen who had been to her flat came up behind her.

"Katrina Mueller? I have a warrant for your detention. Come with us, please," said Broadhurst. It was an order, not an invitation. He held his identity card in front of her just long enough for her to catch the words Military Intelligence.

*

0927 HOURS

"Sandbox from Marconi Two, over"
"Go ahead, Two."
"Skipper leaving the hotel, we're on him."
"Check. Hand off to Marconi Four once you reach Stansted."

*

At the very moment the crew transport left the Pembury, Captain Rod Weathers and Don Carling were buckling up in Rod's station wagon parked in front of the Beech Tree Inn. They were also headed for Stansted Airport, but fifteen minutes later than planned. During breakfast they had drawn up a draft of the bulletin Rod was going to circulate to members of the International Pilots Federation. A bulletin that would be released before the week was out if today didn't bring them any closer to resolving the four murders Carling had been investigating. The bulletin would identify Renate Neumann by name, and request any pilots who might have any knowledge of her to contact Captain Weathers. General release would come right after Don had time to fly back to Toronto and confront Norman Holt in person with their findings.

Rod had phoned his secretary and dictated the draft, leaving it to her to touch up and have ready for his signature tomorrow.

"We'll still reach Stansted well before the flight departs, mate," he assured Don, as he started the vehicle and put on his turn indicator. They were waiting for a break in the traffic streaming past them when Don's mobile rang.

The unexpected call came from New Scotland Yard. Don quickly drew his free hand across his throat, the pilots' signal to abort. Rod shifted into reverse, eased the vehicle snugly back against the curb, and turned off the engine. He waited patiently while Don listened to the caller.

Eventually Don said, "That's great news, sir, and I'll wait to hear from Inspector Upton." He had a large smile on his face when he turned to Rod. "That was Jean-Marc Rousseau, my friend. They've just taken our mystery woman into custody. He's asked me to be available when they start to interrogate her. Feed them questions about the victims, that sort of thing."

"Super! That's the break we've being looking for," agreed Rod. "So what's the next move?"

"Well, I'll have to wait here until I find out where they're taking her. Rousseau didn't have that information yet. He said either Upton or one of his men would contact me. But I'd still prefer that you to head up to Stansted as planned. Do you mind?"

"No, not a problem at all, Don. We can stay in touch by phone."

*

0938 HOURS

The call Don was anxiously waiting for came not from Upton but from Derek Houghton. He'd been contacted by Upton, who wanted to use Paddington Green Police Station for the woman's interrogation. There were two reasons for this: one, Paddington had a much larger interview room, complete with a one-way mirror, and two, the location was closer to Interpol's temporary Ops Center at New Scotland Yard. A patrol car was on the way to pick him up, Derek told him, and would reach him in ten minutes or less.

"Thanks Derek, I'll be ready."

*

0945 HOURS

During the short drive from Simcoe Terrace Gardens to Paddington there was very little talk, none of it directed at Renate. Outwardly, the Circle 17 agent tried to put on a confident air, staring emotionlessly out the window as they sped along. Inwardly though, she was fighting to overcome the feeling of hopelessness that was weighing on her. She needed to come up with some plausible answers to the incriminating questions that she knew were coming. Their knowledge of her double identity put her at a precarious disadvantage: one that might prove impossible to overcome.

After arriving at the station Renate was handed over to WPC Norah Oakley, who her escorted into the large and windowless interview room. The two were left alone for ten minutes until Broadhurst and his partner Trevor Kitchen appeared. Once again Renate demanded to be told why she was being detained. Broadhurst slapped a copy of the warrant down in front of her.

"Search her belongings please, constable," he instructed the WPC.

Renate insisted she needed to make a call to cancel her appointment, but Broadhurst turned her down with a curt, 'later'. The men watched as Oakley emptied the handbag onto the table. The contents of her briefcase received the same treatment. Broadhurst picked up her passport and a few other items and left the room, followed by his partner.

The document Broadhurst had produced quoted numerous sections and sub-sections of a surprisingly long list of acts pertaining to national security. The part dealing with offences she was being detained *'on suspicion of'* was clear enough to understand, though. Her spirits sank even further when she realized she was guilty on all counts. But whether they could prove them or not remained to be seen.

*

The phone call that led to the disastrous chain of events later that day was placed by Trevor Kitchen. It was a logical move on his part: a call to the number found on a business card in the suspect's handbag in order to check the veracity of her identity. The card identified Katrina Mueller as a consultant for a company named Modern Miss Creations, with offices in Paris, Brussels, and Dusseldorf, Germany.

The number rang four times before an answering machine picked up, told the caller he had reached Modern Miss Creations, and asked the caller to leave a message that would be returned as soon as possible.

Kitchen left a non-committal message, mentioning only an inquiry concerning a Miss Katrina Mueller, and gave his personal mobile number.

*

1010 HOURS [1110 BRUSSELS TIME]

Pavel Nadrony, code name Vlad, rewound the tape and listened to the message a second time. Other than his name, the caller from London hadn't identified himself. Vlad knew, though, that Trevor Kitchen was either a police officer or an agent of the British Security Services. He knew because the number found on the bogus business card Olga carried with her at all times was a poison pill of sorts. Its use warned him that Olga was in custody and could not communicate with him herself.

He wondered how she had been traced. The night porter was dead, but he couldn't have given up her location anyway. When Heard had identified a prospect, he passed the information to another member of the cell in London, code named Nord, who in turn relayed the pilot's name and description to Olga. If Olga needed further information, she initiated any contact between herself and Heard. The weak link could be her latest lover, but she had assured Vlad that Norman had no inkling of her covert role with Circle 17. It didn't really matter now how she'd been caught, he realized.

And there was nothing he could do for her. She was on her own...

He hoped she remembered her training: specifically, techniques on how to prolong interrogations. Time that was needed to ensure that the last and most lucrative consignment Circle 17 had contracted for would leave England today.

All he needed was a few hours to wrap up his end of things here in Brussels. First, he placed a call to Moscow. The General answered immediately. Without preamble, Vlad told him the bad news about his niece's arrest. There was no immediate reaction from the veteran Soviet spy. When he did reply, Vlad listened with astonishment to his terse orders. He respectfully asked his leader to confirm that he had heard him correctly. There was another heavy pause, before the older man spoke again.

"Da, that is my decision. We cannot take any chances this late in the game."

Not for the first time, Nadrony was reminded of the ingrained ruthlessness the old guard lived by. He reached for his phone and placed the first of two fateful calls to other members of the London cell.

Once he was satisfied the general's directives would be acted on as soon as possible, he went to work cleaning out the rented one-room office. He wasn't planning to return.

He filled two attache cases with papers and other supplies. That done, he unplugged the telephone and the answering machine and stowed them both into another small case. As a final precaution, he spent thirty minutes meticulously wiping down the sparse furnishings to remove any fingerprints he might have left during his occupancy.

He exited, locking the door behind him, confident there was little chance that he could be traced - even if Olga inadvertently gave away any pertinent information. He loaded the cases into the boot of his Peugeot 407 and headed out for his comfortable bungalow south of the city.

While he slowly made his way along the ring road towards the suburbs, he reflected on his now-finished assignment in the capital. He felt he had acquitted himself well. The general's praise, voiced during his last visit, seemed to confirm his feeling. As the youngest Circle 17 agent to be entrusted with heading a cell in a major western city, he knew a lot had been riding on his performance. The general had even hinted at bigger things to come.

Perhaps, mused Vlad, that might now be sooner than later. The only loose end to be dealt with was the cow of a Belgian woman he lived with. She would no doubt be pleasantly surprised when he told her they would be leaving early tomorrow morning for a long weekend in the Ardennes. And he'd need to call in sick for his evening shift at the air freight company he worked for at Brussels International Airport. That's the last contact he would have with them, too.

43

1020 HOURS

The night porter's murder was the only topic of conversation on the van ride to the airport. Gord Chalmers hadn't heard about it until this morning either, and was full of questions. Norman had other things on his mind though, and left it to Ozzie, who loved to hear himself talk, to fill in the younger crew member. After elaborating on what he'd heard and read, Oz continued to speculate until they were approaching the airport.

"Well, I haven't had too many London layovers yet, and I've never spoken to him," offered Gord. "But why did guys refer to him as 'Nosy Alf'?"

Holt perked up at this, and waited for Ozzie's explanation. "Because the old fella had a habit of eavesdropping when the troops were sittin' around having a nightcap or two, that's why," Ozzie chuckled. "He was always interested when they were talkin' about their divorces and alimony payments..."

*

Norman had never sat in on any of the late night sessions at the

Pembury, and he'd never discussed his private life at length with the crews he'd flown with since joining the Canadian charter airline. As he listened to Ozzie ramble on, he did recall one conversation he'd had with the night man a few years ago. Heard had recognized Norman's Lancashire accent, and, in their ensuing chat, they discovered that Heard and Holt's father had served in the same regiment, the Lancashire Fusiliers, during the Second World War. This was not surprising given that Holt's father grew up in Preston and Heard was from nearby Blackpool. Heard had been curious as to why Holt had moved to Canada, and Norman had mentioned his need for a change of scenery after his divorce. What he didn't remember discussing was his desire to move back to the UK.

But he had brought it up, and it was this disclosure that Alf passed on to his contact. And later, it became the key to Renate's exploitation of Norman after they became lovers.

As their transport approached the security check point at the entrance to the airport's cargo complex, Norman put thoughts of Alf Heard out of his mind, focusing instead on today's flight and the passenger who had the pull to secure passage in the jump seat on such short notice.

It never crossed his mind that there could be any possible connection between the woman he was in love with, the late Alfred Heard, and the passenger he would soon meet.

And only hours from now, when he finally realized he shouldn't have ignored the warning signals his subconscious had been waving in front of him, it would be too late...

*

The van driver unloaded their bags, and Ozzie slipped him three pounds, the unofficial pound per man tip. The uniformed threesome headed into the large and recently refurbished hangar that housed the Fleet Services cargo operation. Outgoing crews picked up their flight plan and weather package in a small office that served as a briefing room. The room was directly across the corridor from the company's operations office. Access to the tarmac area was via the operations office. Depending on where their aircraft was parked, crews could either walk to it or make use of a shuttle van.

The stranger Captain Holt was curious to meet was sitting in the briefing room. He stood up immediately and extended his hand when the crew entered.

"I'm Brian Roberts, Captain. Sorry we couldn't give you a bit more notice about using your flight deck seat today. Hope it's not too much of an intrusion," he said, a friendly smile on his face.

Holt shook his hand. "No, as long as the authorization is here I don't have any objections," he answered. The complete lack of enthusiasm in his statement told Roberts the opposite, though.

"Are you in the aviation business, Brian?" he asked.

"No, not directly. I'm with a small British company you probably never heard of that makes and sells mini-transponders for shippers. Mainly for transport vehicles and container ships up until now. They're looking to expand into the air cargo market. I'll be setting up an office in Canada, probably in Toronto. I've been over here on a training course for the past few weeks. Only been with them for six months. Your airline has expressed an interest in our product and offered me this free ride to come over and brief them on it. But listen, I know you've got lots to do before we go, so don't let me interrupt. If, you're interested, I'll be glad to tell you more about us once we're airborne."

Holt shrugged. "Sure, we'll have plenty of time for that," he said. "Anyway, say hello to Gord and Ozzie."

Holt's crew members shook hands with Roberts. Then Ozzie said to him, "Hey, maybe you can stick one of your gizmos up Gord's butt - then I'll be able to track him down when he gets lost in London!" Everybody laughed, including Chalmers. The two had failed to meet last night when the younger man ended up at the wrong pub.

"Yeah, I'm waiting patiently in the Red Lion near the Hilton - surrounded by more friendly broads then a squadron could handle, I might add - and this twit is listening to a guy playin' a piccolo in another Red Lion pub two fuckin' miles away!"

"It was your stupid damned directions, old timer," retorted Gord. "Besides, your lady friends were probably on an outing from an old folks home." This brought more laughter from Norman and their jump seat rider. A few more barbs were exchanged before the crew got down to business.

The captain did a quick scan of the flight plan, including a rough check of the fuel total. Satisfied, he handed a copy of the plan to the flight engineer.

"Looks okay, Ozzie. If I want more, I'll get Ops to call with a revised fuel figure. You can head out and get started with the refueling."

"Okay chief," Ozzie replied. "Our bird is parked fairly close, so we won't need the shuttle. Should I take Brian with me? I can check him out while you finish your flight planning."

"Yes, good idea," said Norm. He turned to Roberts and asked to see his passport. "Don't mean to be nosy, Brian, but I see on the authorization that I'm to check that you have a valid one. Big fine for the airline if you showed up without one, I'm told."

"Oh sure, Captain, no problem." Roberts extracted the document from the inside pocket of his suit coat. "Here you go - still got a few years before it expires."

Holt, with his reading glasses perched on his nose, checked the passport and handed it back. "Thanks, Brian, all in order. We'll be along shortly."

Moments after the two left the briefing room Holt saw Terry McDuff motioning to him from the doorway. "Excuse me a moment, Gord. Going to get rid of some coffee."

He stepped out into the hall and followed the ramp supervisor into the W.C., which was back towards the main entrance. McDuff looked under the door of the only stall in the smelly room's corner to make sure they were alone.

"What's the problem, Terry?"

"That chap 'yer takin with you," he said, just loud enough for Norman to hear. "He's got copper written all over him." McDuff lit a cigarette and drew a long, deep puff.

"...You don't say," answered Holt thoughtfully.

He couldn't prove it, he told the captain, but he'd seen enough of the police in his time and that's what raised his suspicions.

Holt rubbed his hand over his chin, thinking. "So, what about the ah-h, shipment. Perhaps we should wait until next week?"

"Too late I'm afraid. I've already stashed it onboard," replied McDuff with a frown. "It's in the usual spot."

"Bugger," exclaimed Holt. "You should have waited until I arrived."

"Hey, I only learned about him a few minutes ago," shot back McDuff, louder than he meant to. He paused, waiting until footsteps in the corridor had receded. "Anyway, we might be jumping the gun here. I could be wrong about him, and even if he is a copper, there's no way to connect you with the shipment. Just leave it where it is when you get to Toronto if you're not happy."

Holt closed his eyes and pinched his nose. "Okay, I'll just have to play it by ear," he said, and went back to the briefing room without further comment.

44

1025 HOURS, PADDINGTON

Renate was restless, waiting for the questioning to start. Her second demand to use a phone had also been ignored.

She really had no idea of her status. Would she be allowed a lawyer? Probably, but was it time to demand one? No, it would be better to wait and see how much they knew. She had to get word of her arrest to Vlad, but how? Calling him direct would be a big mistake - they could probably trace it. She had one other number memorized in case of emergency, and she'd have to use it. Yes, she would refuse to answer any questions until they allowed her a call.

*When DCI Upton entered the room - another surprise as she was expecting the MI5 officer - she refused to cooperate until she was allowed a call. "No, I don't wish to call a lawyer, why would I? I haven't been charged with anything, have I?"

"Not yet, ma'am." There was no point in denying her request again, he and Broadhurst had agreed. "And yes, you can make one call. You can use your own phone, if you wish." Her mobile was still lying on the table with her other belongings.

She wasn't going to take that bait. "Well, I would like a bit of privacy if you don't mind, Inspector," she said, speaking in a more courteous tone. Upton asked the WPC if there was a payphone in the station.

"Yes sir," she replied. "There are two just inside the back entrance. She'll need coins."

"Right then, please escort her to the phones and straight back when she's finished," Upton directed. "Give her two minutes," he added.

Renate picked up two 50p pieces from her handbag contents and followed the female constable out of the room. The phones were the partially-enclosed type, and she chose the one furthest from the door. After she dialed, she turned her back to the WPC, feeling a bit foolish as she did. It was answered on the third ring. 'What is your message?' a male voice asked.

She recognized the accent, but not the speaker. "This is Olga calling to cancel my appointment for today. I am at the Paddington Police Station. I'm here to help them with an inquiry. I don't know how long it will take. I will call again as soon as possible." She waited to see if the other party was going to speak. When there was only silence, she said goodbye and hung up. She was positive the policewoman hadn't heard her use her code name.

*

"First, why don't you tell us your true identity," began Upton, after Renate and her escort returned to the interview room.

She was prepared for this obvious question, and patiently began her cover story. She had no objection when Upton advised her that the proceedings would be recorded and Ross started the tape recorder. Renate had no doubt others were watching from behind the mirrored wall. But she didn't know that one of those observing her was the private investigator who had been tenaciously pursuing her for the past three weeks, Don Carling.

Her dubious account would take time to disprove, they soon realized, but initially they let her tell her story without interruption.

She told them Renate Neumann had been her married name, a marriage that ended in divorce in 1995. She was born in 1959 in Heidleberg, and Renate Katrina Mueller was her birth name. This matched the full name on the passport they had taken from her handbag. Her divorce hadn't come through until after she had started a new job, one that required her to travel to Britain. It was only after her trip home a few weeks ago that she was able to obtain a new passport in her maiden name.

When she finished her explanation, Upton decided to forego any further questions about her prior life and the identity issue. He'd leave that to MI5. He pressed on with his own agenda.

Q. Who did she work for when she lived in the Highgate flat?

She quoted the name of a fictitious company in the fashion industry.

Q. What was her connection to Flanders Holdings?

That was the parent company of the firm she worked for. They arranged for and paid the lease on the flat.

Q. Why did she vacate the flat so suddenly? There was a few months remaining on the lease, wasn't there?

Yes, that was true, but the sudden death of her uncle hastened her departure. She was planning to leave anyway, she told them, because the company wanted her to relocate back to Europe and she didn't want to leave London. It was while she was home for the funeral that she quit her job and took the new position that would let her remain in London.

Q. So you returned to London with a new job and a new passport. When was this?

Here she hesitated before replying. It would seem suspicious, she knew, if she gave the impression she was prepared for any and all questions. Eventually she said she had flown back on the twenty-ninth of June, but thought it might have a day or so either way.

Q. So you didn't return to the Highgate flat because you no longer worked for the company that leased it?

Yes, she had to find a new flat. And, anticipating what he would ask next, told Upton that she used an agency to find her a flat, and her new employer paid the lease. She had an answer ready if he asked her about the short-term lease, but the question didn't come up. Instead, Upton brought up 'the men'...

Q. When and how did she first meet Norman Holt? Did Alfred Heard introduce them?

The first crack in her composure didn't go unnoticed by those watching. The bead of perspiration that materialized on her brow was fine enough to be invisible, though. She had never met anyone named Alfred Heard, she told them, and turning the tables, asked Upton who was he and why did they think she would know him? Upton ignored her questions.

Q. Then tell me how you met Holt. Wasn't it at the Pembury Hotel?

She had never been to the hotel, but did acknowledge that she knew it was where he stayed when he was in London. They had met strictly by chance at the National Gallery. Probably in March or April, she couldn't be sure.

Q. So you were still living in Highgate when you met. I presume he stayed there overnight on occasion. Do you recall when he last stayed with you there? Would it have been just days before you moved out? Or weeks?

Yes, Norman had stayed overnight a few times. The last time would have been in early June, she thought. When he then asked if Holt had been to her new flat, she admitted truthfully that he had recently spent the night, two nights in fact, when his flight had been delayed. Again, Upton switched the subject.

Q. Did you ever go out with another airline pilot named Len Newson?

No, she answered without hesitation.

Q. Have you ever met a chap named Ramon Flores? An American, maybe you knew him as Ray?

She just shook her head.

Q. What about Daniel Krantz, also an airline captain?

Another unemotional 'no'.

Q. Did you ever live and work in Paris?

She had been there on business occasionally, but no, she had never lived there.

Q. Miss Mueller, have you ever had blonde hair?

The question took her by surprise, although almost immediately she realized she should have expected it. Rather than give a yes or no answer, she told them brusquely that blonde wouldn't suit her.

Upton thanked her and said they would be taking a short break. "Constable Oakley will escort you to the ladie's, if you wish.

*

"Well done, Inspector," Broadhurst said, when he joined them in the room behind the mirror. "We'll let her stew for a bit and then I'll have at her. Thanks to Mr. Carling here, we can prove most of her answers are a pack of lies."

During the wait, Broadhurst had his team get started on checking out some of the claims she'd made concerning her background. He knew the queries would take time, but the response they generated might be needed if they couldn't break her with the information they already had. He was also waiting to see if the German authorities could help: her passport details had been faxed to Bonn for verification.

*

1105 HOURS, STANSTED

McDuff's mobile rang as he was giving his crew instructions for the sequencing of the last four pallets to be loaded onto Flight 213. He excused himself and stepped behind a parked fuel truck to answer it. "I have a package that has to go on the Northern flight," the familiar voice told him. "It's a small one."

"It's too late - we're just about finished with the loading," he told the caller.

"Find a way. You don't have an option. It has to go in the rear of the aircraft."

"Not bloody likely, we're just loading that section now!"

"You can manage it. And you'll get a bonus for your trouble."

"How much?" He asked guardedly, glancing around to make sure there was no one within hearing distance.

"An extra hundred."

McDuff quickly replied, "Not enough."

There was twenty seconds of silence before the caller spoke again. "Two hundred, then. I'll bring the package to the aircraft in five minutes." The line went dead before McDuff could reply.

45

As they walked towards Northern Flyer 747, Ozzie said to Roberts. "So a new job, eh? What did you do before?"

"RCMP. Did my twenty years and took an early pension. I was stationed out west, mostly on highway patrol in Saskatchewan and Manitoba," answered Roberts.

"Holy shit! Twenty years on the prairies. You must really like wide open spaces!"

Brian laughed. "Ah, it wasn't so bad, but I was ready for a change. This job came along and gave me the motivation to get out before I became a 'lifer'."

"You married?"

"Nope. Came close a few times, though. How about you?"

Ozzie grunted. "Too fuckin' close! I've got two ex's still gouging me every month. Makes me glad I'm not a millionaire."

They had reached the 747. The flight engineer set his bags down at the foot of the mobile stairs leading up to the front entrance door. "Just wait here for a few minutes while I do my walkaround check, Brian."

Roberts watched as Ozzie began his inspection of the giant aircraft's external workings, starting with the nose wheel tires. He checked to see if there were any signs of tread separation, foreign object damage, such as pieces of metal that might have been picked up from a runway or taxi way, or obvious soft spots. Then he craned his neck to check for any visible damage to the radome and the all-important pitot tubes on either side of the nose.

Satisfied, he moved along the front of the left wing, glancing into the intakes of the two massive engines mounted beneath it. The walkaround route continued to the wingtip and along the trailing edge of the wing. He was checking for fuel leaks - either from the tanks located in the wing or from an engine - or oil or hydraulic fluid leaks from the many actuators fitted to operate wing flaps and the landing gears. Checking the tail assembly was another neck-craning but necessary exercise. The horizontal stabilizer, elevators and upper and lower rudders were all carefully scrutinized. He continued up the right side of the aircraft, and around the starboard wing and engines. The sixteen main wheels that supported the 747 on the ground were checked in the same careful manner as that afforded the nose wheel area.

Roberts had never been this close to the flight line at a major airport before and was amazed at the activity level. He counted seven aircraft either being loaded or unloaded, and another six closed up. He plugged his ears as a four-engined jet in DHL livery taxied by the Northern 747 and was marshaled into an empty parking stand further along the ramp. He recognized a few of the other names on planes parked nearby. Federal Express, UPS and Lufthansa Cargo were all airlines he had heard of. He couldn't figure out where the aircraft on the next stand was from, though, and said as much to Ozzie when he returned from his inspection.

"That piece of shit?" replied Ozzie, eyeing the plane in question. "That's an old Russian aircraft. One of the early Tupolov models. Probably belongs to one of the new countries that were once part of the Soviet Union. They all acquired a bunch of junk from Aeroflot when the national airline down-sized. See the glass nose? That thing was built as a bomber for the Red Air Force. Wouldn't risk my ass on one of those clunkers even if they offered me a free ticket!"

The flight engineer picked up his bags and led the way up the stairs to the forward cabin door. Once inside, he set them down and explained to Brian how this particular 747 had been converted for all-cargo use by the airline. The aircraft had come off the Boeing assembly line in the 1970's as a 'combi', meaning it was designed to carry a mix of passengers and cargo. Approximately the front two thirds of the main deck had been fitted with seats for about 300 passengers. The cargo section was aft, separated from the passenger area by a bulkhead.

A large, hinged door fitted in the fuselage behind the left wing gave access to the aircraft interior. More than a hundred thousand pounds of freight, secured on pallets, could be carried on any given flight. When Northern acquired their 747s from a bankrupt American airline, the passenger seats, galleys, toilets and the bulkhead were all removed allowing the full length of the main deck to carry cargo. However, it all had to be handled through the one main cargo door.

Brian marveled at the vastness of the interior without the seats, and couldn't believe how easily the loaded pallets were being pushed around on the steel rollers embedded in the floor. In the short time it took Ozzie to give his explanation, the ground crew had maneuvered two heavy-looking pallets into place and locked them down.

"Amazing, simply amazing!" was all he could say as they climbed the stairs to the upper deck. Most of the fittings that had been part of the upper deck lounge had also been removed for the cargo operation. There were still six passenger-type seats behind the flight deck, though, and Roberts remarked on this.

"So you can still carry a few passengers up here, can you?"

"Nah, not really. Officially we're only allowed to carry two extra bodies."

"Why is that?"

"Because we no longer have an operating PA system on these birds. You gotta be sitting in one of the jump seats in the cockpit for take-off and landing." When the puzzled look on Robert's face remained, he explained. "The captain has to be able to give you verbal instructions in case of an emergency, so says Transport Canada, or its aviation branch to be more specific."

"Safety first, right?" said Brian.

"You got it!" smiled Ozzie. "But once we're airborne you're welcome to come back and sit here. No movie, but a good place to read or take a nap"

*

Before Ozzie turned his attention to rest of his pre-flight preparations, he checked Brian out on the jump seat and how to access the oxygen mask stowed in a bin beside the seat. "You can move around until we're ready to start up, then Norm will want you seated up here," he told the passenger.

"Okay, thanks Ozzie. I think I'll watch some more of the loading operation. It's really quite impressive how they move those pallets around."

*

1123 HOURS

Rod Weathers watched from the control tower as the ground crew readied the Northern Flyer B-747 for departure. He hadn't noticed anything out of the ordinary since his arrival, and it looked as if there were only a few more pallets to be boarded before the flight would be ready to go.

Although the skies above Stansted were cloudless, the morning fog hadn't dissipated, and visibility from the tower was less than a mile.

A member of the MI5 team was also keeping watch on the activity around the 747. A few minutes after he'd made his way up to the tower, Rod had heard him talking on his radio, using the call sign Marconi Four. When Rod approached him, the man identified himself by surname only.

"I'm Knowlton. I was told you were coming, but not why." He didn't come across as impolite, but rather seemed to be saying, 'Tell me why you're here, then I'll decide if I have time to talk to you.'

Rod gave it to him straight. "I'm here because we're concerned for the safety of the captain of Flight 213. 'We' being the International Pilots Federation, of which I am the Safety and Security chairman. Four of our captains have been killed in the past two years and we have reason to believe there is a connection between the victims and this smuggling ring you have under surveillance. Fair enough?" he challenged.

Knowlton put up his hands as if to say 'truce'. "I wasn't aware of all that, Captain, didn't mean to sound impertinent."

"No offence taken," Rod smiled.

Knowlton had his binoculars trained on the ramp area around the 747.

"See the man with the clipboard? He's the one we're most interested in," he told Rod. "His name is Terrence McDuff."

He handed Rod his binoculars. "Got him," Rod said after he picked McDuff out.

"McDuff is thought to be actively involved with the smuggling ring operating here at Stansted. He has no criminal record, but is known to the security service because of his long-time membership in the British Communist Party. In its heyday the party recruited actively from leftist labour unions," explained Knowlton.

"Is he still a member?" Rod asked.

Knowlton didn't know. The party's influence had waned considerably since 1991 and McDuff's name had not been flagged since the late 80's. He'd only recently come to their attention in connection with the present investigation.

It was obvious to the watchers that McDuff was in charge of the ground crew working around Flight 213. In addition to the clipboard, McDuff carried a hand radio which, Rod knew, was used to communicate with the operations office. McDuff was seen to enter the aircraft two or three times during the loading, but returned to the ramp after a few minutes each time.

Shortly after the captain and first officer boarded the aircraft, Holt reappeared at the top of the stairs. McDuff mounted the stairs and held a brief conversation with him. Rod figured it might be just a routine chat between the captain and the ramp supervisor about how the loading was coming along and whether or not they would make an on time departure.

"Is he going to be arrested today?" Rod asked. The last few lower cargo doors were being closed as he handed the binoculars back to Knowlton.

Knowlton nodded. "The last word I had was that he and a few others we're watching will be detained later this afternoon."

*

1132 HOURS

The first indication that something was wrong came shortly after Northern 213 called Ground Control for start-up clearance. The clearance had been issued, and the flight advised to call again when ready to taxi. But a few seconds later, the flight made another call to the tower.

"Ground Control, Northern 213, cancel our start-up request. We're showing that one of our doors is still open. We'll get back to you shortly."

"Roger 213, start clearance canceled," replied the controller calmly. "Call again when ready. There are no departure delays at present."

*

On the 747, Ozzie swore in disgust. They had been running through the Before Start checklist when he noticed the offending light for the first time.

"The goddamn light for L5 is on Norm. Why in hell's name would that door have been opened?" L5 was the furthest aft of the five doors on the aircraft's left side. It was an emergency exit on passenger versions of the 747, but normally wasn't used on the cargo version. On the freighters, however, ground crews occasionally opened it for ventilation while working in the extreme rear of the airplane.

"Might be just the microswitch," suggested the captain, "But it will have to be checked. Can you get back there from the inside?"

"Shit no," replied the engineer. "Only an anorexic midget could squeeze past the pallets at the rear," he fumed.

Norman picked up his microphone. "Flight deck to ground. We've got a warning light indicating that L5 is not completely closed. Was it opened during the loading?"

Terry McDuff was standing beside the nose wheel, directly under the aircraft's nose, wearing a headset that allowed him direct communication with the flight deck.

"Not that I know of, Captain," he lied. "It looks to be closed from here, but I'll check it out 'meself. But it's gonna take a few minutes to get stairs back there so I can get up to the door," he explained.

While his crew was busy securing pallets at the front of the cargo area, McDuff had surreptitiously made his way to the rear and moved the inside handle of the L5 door just far enough from the closed and locked position to activate the 'door open' light on the flight engineer's panel. He'd made his move just after he'd got the call about the additional package.

"How long do you estimate?" asked Holt.

"At least ten minutes."

"I see. Well, get right on it. You won't able to open it all the way, though, but there will be enough space to check it. And leave a man on the headset. I'll advise him when the light is out."

McDuff acknowledged Norman's instructions, signaled for one of the crew to take his place and handed him the headset.

Rod Weathers had heard the exchange between the ground controller and flight 213 on the tower's speaker system. He watched as McDuff moved to the back of the aircraft and stared up at the door in question. The lingering mist meant Rod couldn't see the door clearly enough to tell if it was fully closed. But even if appeared to be, a visual inspection wouldn't suffice. Given the same circumstances, he would want it checked exactly the way Captain Holt had requested. The easiest way to check for a faulty switch was to open and close the door again.

*

Knowlton had returned to Rod's side. "What's the problem?"

"Apparently they have a door that isn't properly closed. The captain has asked the ground crew to open and close it again from the outside. Could be just a faulty switch or the door is actually slightly ajar," Rod told him.

Climbing and descending the mobile stairs after they were moved into position took McDuff just over a minute. Rod heard Northern 213 call ground control for start up clearance again seconds after McDuff reached the ground..

"Looks like they're okay now. Sometimes a microswitch will stick, causing the relay to the light on the flight engineer's panel to remain open," Rod explained.

"I see," said Knowlton. The MI5 agent's walkie-talkie crackled to life.

*

"Marconi Four from six, over."

"Go ahead, six." The agent calling was seated in a borrowed

maintenance panel van parked near Flight 213's stand.

"Were you watching the suspect on the stairs?"

"Uhh, Roger Six, apparently there was a problem with the door, and it had to be checked before the flight could depart," answered Knowlton.

"Copy, Four. But he also placed something inside the door before he closed it again. Did you see that? Over."

"Negative, Six. Visibility is still poor from the tower."

"It looked like a small box to me." said Marconi Six.

Knowlton glanced at Weathers. "Any guesses?"

"Beats me," Rod frowned. "More contraband, perhaps?"

"I doubt it. We think he's already boarded the shipment we're interested in."

It wasn't a normal action then, Rod knew. But what could they do about it now? A worried look covered his face and Knowlton picked up on it.

"Any way the crew can check it?"

An idea struck Rod. "No, but we might be able to get a better look at what he did." He turned away from the window, looking for Douglas Loudon, the tower duty supervisor. He'd met Loudon when he first arrived. The supervisor was leaning over the shoulder of one of the controllers, pointing out something on the man's radar screen. He looked up when he noticed Weathers standing beside him.

Rod agitation showed in his voice. "Sorry to interrupt you Douglas, but I need your assistance."

"That's okay. What's wrong?"

"The ramp area is monitored by video cameras, isn't it?"

"Uhh, yes. There are a number of surveillance cameras covering it from different vantage points. Why?"

"Well, something unusual just happened on the Northern 747 on Alpha Six. Who monitors the cameras?"

"They're monitored from a room here in the tower building. Is there a problem with the flight? 213 is the line up for take-off now."

"It may be nothing, but I'd sure like to see what the cameras might show just before they started up. He told Loudon what the agent watching the flight had reported.

"Well, that should be possible," said Loudon. "The monitoring room is two levels below us. I'll ring down and tell them you're coming. You can explain what it is you're after."

"Great, that should do the trick. Thanks, Douglas."

"I suggest you take the stairs, it will be quicker than the elevator," said the supervisor, pointing to the corner of the room. The lads refer to it as the 'black hole'," he smiled. You'll see why."

Before he left the tower level, Rod told Knowlton where he was going.

"Call me as soon as you're ready down there." he said.

46

1128 HOURS, PADDINGTON

The passport was the first thing Broadhurst brought up when he re-entered the interview room. He slapped it down on the table in front of her.

"Miss Mueller, did you apply for this passport in person?"

"Uhh, no. I had a travel agency handle it for me."

"Why? Is that the normal procedure in Germany?"

"It is not illegal, if that is what you're asking. One must have the proper forms filled out and witnessed. And the photograph, of course. It is quicker to have an agency handle it once you have all the documents. You must pay a fee for their service, but I was busy with family matters, as I told the other policeman, and it was the only way I could get it issued in the time I had available."

Broadhurst made a point of studying his notes before he continued.

"Let's get back to your ah, boyfriends." She bridled at his flippancy but kept her tongue. "Did you ever ask Captain Rosen or Captain Holt to carry anything for you on their flights? You know, as a favor, perhaps?"

"No!" she replied sharply. "Why would I do that? I don't know anyone in America."

"Well, did you put them in touch with anyone who was looking for a fast way to ship a parcel to Chicago, perhaps, or maybe Toronto? Something they didn't want to ship via normal channels. An acquaintance perhaps, who would pay your lovers to carry it?"

Her scowl deepened. *'If looks could kill,'* Broadhurst thought, *'I'd be a dead man.'* He stared her down, waiting for an answer. When she spoke, she bit off the words.

"I have never used my friendship with these men in any of the ways you are suggesting. They were men - lonely men - who I went out with a few times. That's all."

For fifteen minutes Broadhurst hammered away at the suspect, trying to find holes in her account of her relationships with Rosen and Holt. He asked questions that he knew she could easily provide plausible answers to: lies, for the most part, but lies that he had no immediate way of refuting. His line of questioning was designed to give her renewed hope that the authorities couldn't prove their allegations against her. And he achieved his goal...

When he told her they were going to take another break, Renate visibly relaxed for the first time since she'd been taken into custody.

*

Her self-control crumbled when Broadhurst returned less than five minutes later and slapped a folder down on the table.

"Miss Mueller, it's time to 'stop spreading the manure', to paraphrase one of your old German expressions," he told her.

"I...I don't know what you mean," she stammered.

"Four men - all airline pilots - have been killed in the past two years. All of them stayed at the Pembury Hotel at one time or another. And you knew them all. Just a coincidence? Or a conspiracy you have masterminded. *That's* what I think."

"I don't know what you're talking about."

Trevor Kitchen, sitting next to the senior MI5 agent, passed him a folder. Broadhurst opened it and extracted a photograph. It was the original Polaroid photo that Don Carling had found on the wall in the Greek restaurant. The picture the Canadian private detective had used so effectively to tie all four victims to Renate Neumann.

Broadhurst held the photo directly in front of her.

"I don't think you look so bad as a blonde, Miss Mueller. And Ray Flores - who you have denied knowing - seems to be quite fond of his happy blonde fraulein." He held the photo inches from her face until she turned away. "Oh, and by the way, the staff at the Italian restaurant in Highgate Village remember you dining there with both Flores and Bert Rosen.

Olga said nothing, just sat perfectly still, her eyes on the table.

"And Daniel Krantz. Are you sure you didn't know him?" When there was no response, he pressed on. "You had blonde hair when he dated you in Paris. It wasn't that long ago. Your memory isn't that bad now, is it?"

Renate's confidence was fading fast. It was non-existent after Broadhurst stated that a phone number found in the possession of both the Canadian Len Newson and Ray Flores had been traced to her. A number that had been discontinued shortly after Flores was killed, but a number that DCI Houghton's staff had recently been able to put a name to. Her resigned expression confirmed that Don's assumption was right, even if unproved.

There was a knock on the interview room's door. "Come," said Broadhurst.

A uniformed constable entered and approached the table, a sheet of fax paper in his outstretched hand. Without a word he set it in front of Broadhurst, who waved a cursory thanks. The fax had been transmitted from the Bonn headquarters of the German Security Service. He took his time reading it, then handed it to Trevor Kitchen.

"This is quite interesting, Trevor. Our German colleagues have just made our job a little easier, it would appear." His partner quickly digested the information, and slid the fax back to Broadhurst.

"Miss ah-h, whatever your real name is, it certainly isn't Katrina Mueller, is it?" Broadhurst placed his elbows on the table and leaned towards the woman who, with her head down, was now staring at her hands clasped together in her lap. "It seems whoever supplied you with this passport was a bit sloppy. Must have cut a few corners. Big mistake. You should ask for your money back, fraulein."

The information on her passport application had all been correct, he told her. Name, date and place of birth, parents' names, it all fit. But the real Katrina Mueller had never applied for a passport. And she probably never would. Katrina Mueller had entered a convent at the age of eighteen. Sister Dominica, the name given to her on the day she took her vows, has been cloistered in a convent attached to a Benedictine monastery in the Moselle valley ever since.

"So, Miss ahh, I don't suppose Renate Neumann is your real name either, is it? What should I call you?" Olga didn't move. "Well Miss, now we've established that you've been lying through your teeth to us, maybe you'd like to recant your past sins, so to speak, and tell us what you and these pilots were up to. We know others must be involved, in fact before the day is out most, if not all, of your co-conspirators will be in custody," he said.

He didn't know that for a fact, but neither did the disheartened Olga, who seemed to be aging with each passing minute. Broadhurst drummed his fingers on the table top, waiting for her to speak.

Eventually she looked up. "So what is it I'm to be charged with?" She sounded extremely tired.

"Good for you, Miss. I think you've finally realized how much shit you're in." Broadhurst made a production of gathering up his notes before continuing. "That will be for the prosecutor to decide. But I should think you know damned well that offences committed under the Home Security Act usually draw long prison terms. Even *very* long terms." The two MI5 men rose in unison. "It might be a few days before you come before a magistrate. In my experience the legal types always take longer to draft charges in security cases. You'll be made comfortable at one of Her Majesty's prisons in the mean time."

WPC Oakley made to put her arm on the prisoner, but stopped when Broadhurst waved her off. "No hurry, Constable. I think we'll just let her sit here a while longer. Give her some time for a bit of soul-searching, eh? She just might decide cooperation would be her best option now..."

*

1155 HOURS

Dan Blaisdell, the lone monitor on duty, welcomed the chance to tackle something other than his mostly monotonous duties. His work space really was a black hole, thought Rod, as his eyes adjusted to the low level illumination in the windowless room.

"What stand is the flight on?" he asked, after Rod told him what wanted to see.

"It was on Alpha Six, but it taxied away a few minutes before I came down here," said Rod. "The activity I'm interested in occurred about thirty minutes ago."

"Hmm, okay, we have two cameras covering that area of the ramp. That one would probably give us the best view." Blaisdell pointed to a screen on the top row of monitors in front of him. "Screen number three shows stand Alpha Six and you're right, the flight has departed."

Rod moved in for a closer look. "Yes, that's the view I need," he said. "How long will it take to retrieve the footage? I'm presuming you have the capability to do it remotely from here?"

Blaisdell chuckled. "Yes, of course." He indicated another console behind him. "It's just a matter of punching the right buttons in the right order. Do you need to go back any further?"

"No, no, thirty minutes will be sufficient."

"Right then, give me about ten minutes to set it up. Shouldn't take any longer than that."

1205 HOURS

Rod hadn't been in touch with Don Carling since they'd parted outside his hotel earlier.

He'd planned to wait until after he'd seen the video before calling him, but the Canadian contacted him first. Rod stepped out of the darkened room into the stairwell before he answered.

"What's happening out there?" Don asked.

"Holt's flight just took off. I'm waiting to check a surveillance tape to clear up something that happened before they left the ramp."

"Oh yeah? What was that?"

Rod told him.

"Cripes, I don't like the sound of that. When do you get to see this tape?"

"In five minutes or so. There are two closed circuit cameras that should help. Hopefully we'll get at least one good shot of his actions."

"Yeah, well, let's hope so," Don said. "What about the police? Have they made any moves yet?"

"No, but I think they plan to round up some suspects later this afternoon. At the moment the agent in charge is still here in the tower. I want him to see the tapes as well. Are you still at Paddington?"

"Yes, and so is Derek. It's been quite a show watching this woman's interrogation, Rod. She's definitely involved up to her very attractive eyeballs in this thing. Derek thinks they've got a real live undercover agent in custody. But they still aren't sure of her true identity, or who's behind her."

"Bloody amazing," uttered Rod. "What the devil is happening, Don?"

There was an audible sigh from Don. "Wish I knew, but we should have some answers soon. Anyway, Broadhurst has just returned to the interview room, so I'll have to turn my phone off. I'll check it every few minutes. Let me know what the tape shows as soon as you can."

*

1220 HOURS

The first VCR Blaisdell hooked up to a monitor didn't work, so the ten minutes had stretched to twenty before they got their first look at the tape. Knowlton and Douglas Loudon had joined Rod in the monitor room.

"Dammit!" blurted Rod, when the tape reached the sequence showing McDuff at the door. McDuff seemed to be aware of the cameras. It looked as if he'd purposely made sure he had his back towards the nearest one when he opened the door. Rod slammed the table in frustration.

"I can't see his hands from this angle! What about the other camera? Will it give us a better view? " he asked.

"No problem, sir. I rewound it just in case." He quickly ejected the first tape and inserted the second. The distance to the 747 was much greater and the persistent fog was more evident in this image, but one could see still McDuff's hand actions. The men huddled over the monitor. They watched McDuff pull the external handle from its recessed position and turn it ninety degrees. He pushed with his left hand and pulled with his right to open the door, but only a short distance before it contacted the pallet inside. Then he ran his hand over the door's locking mechanism.

"Probably making sure there wasn't something preventing the microswitch from making proper contact," explained Rod in response to the questioning looks from the others. The tape rolled for a few more seconds before it showed the movement Knowlton's agent had alerted them to.

"Yes, see, he's taken something out of his coveralls." exclaimed Rod. "Stop it there!"

After the others had taken a close look, Rod said, "Looks like a small box of some sort, doesn't it?"

"Yes, I suppose that's what it could be. Hard to say for sure, though." offered Knowlton.

They had Blaisdell rerun the sequence that showed McDuff kneeling and pushing the object inside the aircraft. Then he straightened up, closed the door, and stowed the locking handle. A few seconds later he acknowledged a 'thumbs up' from the ground man on the headset at the front of the 747, and descended the stairs.

They watched the sequence three more times in slow motion.

"Any ideas?" Rod asked them.

Both Knowlton and the tower supervisor shook their heads. "It's unfortunate the closer camera was blocked," Knowlton said. "It would have given us a better shot of what he was handling. But, I suppose--"

"Maybe I can help there," suggested Blaisdell. "I can make a print off the tape and then enlarge it. It'll be grainy, but it might give you a better image."

"Do it," ordered Knowlton. Blaisdell ran the tape again and stopped at the point they all agreed gave the best view.

Knowlton was on his phone continuously while they waited for Blaisdell to get the print ready. Rod could only stand silently by, his mind a turmoil of 'what if's'.

*

1241 HOURS

'Here you go, sir. That's the best I can do with the equipment we have," said Blaisdell.

Knowlton studied the enlarged image for a few moments, then passed it to Rod, shaking his head. "I still can't tell anything definite from that," he said. "Could be a box, but it looks like it's covered in something, doesn't it?"

Rod agreed. The object appeared to be about eight or nine inches long. From the grainy print it was impossible to say what it was wrapped in.

"We'll leave it to the experts, Captain. I'm going to have a helicopter fly it down to the Ops centre. They'll have the hi-tech equipment to enhance the image further."

"Yes, we've got to find out exactly what it is. If it isn't more contraband, what else could it be? I hope I'm wrong, but I'm worried that it might be explosives of some sort," Rod said, rubbing his forehead.

"Well, let's not get ahead of ourselves, but yes, that can't be ruled out. Commander Watson is calling in one of our top explosive chaps to take a look at it. We'll have a better idea after he sees it."

*

1245 HOURS

The Special Branch helicopter had been on standby at a small airfield twenty miles south of Stansted. It was positioned there in case Marconi Four decided to call for aerial surveillance during the operation. As soon as the pilot got the call, he fired up the engine and made the short hop to the larger airport. Rod had accompanied Knowlton down from the tower and onto the ramp to await its arrival. Minutes later the copter set down smartly twenty yards in front of them.

"I'd like to catch a ride on this bird too, Knowlton. If it is a bomb, the flight will have to be contacted immediately. I'm not trying to tell you chaps how to run things, but I could help as a go-between to the flight," said Rod, leaning close to the MI5 agent's ear. He was almost shouting to be heard over the noise of the helicopter's idling engine and a Fed Ex DC-10 taxiing behind it.

Knowlton handed him the envelope containing the print. "Go for it! I'll let Sandbox know you coming," he shouted.

47

1302 HOURS, PADDINGTON

It had taken Olga less than an hour to reach her decision. It was no use trying to figure out where she had gone wrong: it was too late for that. Her false identities had been discredited, and she knew it was only a matter of time before the investigators determined that her claim to be a customer representative for Modern Miss Creations was a sham, too.

And there would be no help from Uncle Georgiy, either. Gone were the days of the Cold War era when captured spies were eventually exchanged between the Soviet Union and the West. Even if the present leaders of Russia were aware of Circle 17's existence, she was certain they would never acknowledge it.

No, she was definitely on her own. She would have to make the best deal possible for herself. This would mean admitting that she had contrived to meet the pilots, but that alone wouldn't mean the police could find her guilty of any serious offences. And even if they could tie her to Vlad, proving she had any part in the smuggling activities that he arranged with the pilots from Brussels might also be a problem for them. A good lawyer should be able cast doubt on any charges that she was a key player in the conspiracy. Especially if Vlad disappeared before they made the connection between them...

And then there was Norman, the only one of her lovers still alive. Even if confronted with her deceptions, he wouldn't be able to provide the police with any damning evidence against her. Who knows? If his feelings for her were as sincere they seemed, he might even be able to help her.

*

"What time is it please, miss?" she asked WPC Oakley, the first words spoken in the room since Broadhurst and the others had left them alone.

"A few minutes past one, ma'am."

'Norman should be well on his way at least,' she thought. She rotated her head and neck a few times to relieve the tension soreness that had set in while she was thinking. "Would you please tell your superior that I wish to speak to him?" Her request was made in a quiet, untroubled tone. She would be damned if she would show any outward signs of weakness to those watching and listening from behind the mirror.

When the WPC left the room, she immediately reached for her cigarettes, only the third time she'd lit up since her interrogation began. It had been an effort to refrain, but she knew her nervousness would be obvious to them if she chain-smoked. After a few satisfying drags, she picked up her compact mirror, carefully touched up her lipstick and checked her hair.

The only observer on the other side of the wall for most of the past hour had been Don Carling. The MI5 team and DCI Upton were busy elsewhere in the station checking on the woman's story.

As he studied her, he realized why a middle-aged man looking for female companionship would fall for her. In fact a couple of them, not particularly good-looking themselves, probably couldn't believe their good fortune hooking up with her.

She was definitely an attractive woman, striking even, he would say. She either exercised often or had good genes, he thought. Maybe both. Her firm bust, snug hips and shapely legs were those of a woman years younger. And yet this dark-haired beauty had been living an evil agenda, one that should lead to a lengthy prison sentence.

A growing sense of satisfaction had crept over him as he'd watched her interrogation, in part because his leads had led the authorities to her. In addition, the evidence coming out gave credence to his belief that the pilots had been killed because they had fallen prey to a deadly conspiracy. A conspiracy that this attractive woman was unquestionably a key player in...

He still hadn't been told how she fit into the Interpol investigation, or even if she did. But he was beginning to draw his own conclusions. From what he'd learned, today's operation was apparently directed at a well-coordinated international smuggling ring. This woman and the pilots' deaths hadn't even been a part of that investigation until a few days ago, it seemed. At least that's the impression he got from his conversations with the RCMP officer, Brian Roberts. And the theory he'd put forward at Monday's meeting that the woman and the pilots must have had a contact at Brussels Airport was also looking like a good call.

*

1308 HOURS, NEW SCOTLAND YARD

The Bell 206 JetRanger was cleared by London Center to fly directly to New Scotland Yard at 2,500 feet. Rod had flown in helicopters before, but only at sightseeing speeds. The pilot had this one at max speed all the way, and Rod couldn't help but notice a few of its engine gauges were red-lined. Approaching the city, they scooted under commercial airliners being vectored for runways 27L and 27R at Heathrow. Rod admired the skill with which the pilot banked steeply over the Thames just west of the cavernous rooftop of Charing Cross Station, winged past the RAF monument, and sideslipped neatly onto the pad atop the Yard's imposing headquarters building on Victoria Embankment.

Rod gave the pilot a friendly 'thank you' pat on the shoulder as he slid the door open and jumped out. A hatless uniformed officer waved to him from the top of a stairway leading down into the building. Rod clutched the envelope to his chest and hurried over to meet him.

*

1310 HOURS, PADDINGTON

"Yes, that is my request," she replied, "I wish to speak to a lawyer, please."

"And then you'll give us some straight answers, is that what I'm hearing?" Broadhurst asked her. He and Kitchen were once again seated across from her in the interview room.

The suspect nodded her head resignedly.

"Is that a 'yes'?" challenged Broadhurst.

She raised her head and gave him a cold stare. "Yes," she exclaimed bitterly.

"Good then. I'll see if I can find a solicitor to represent you. It may take some time."

As he made ready to go, he added, in a more placatory manner, "If you need something to eat or drink Constable Oakley will see to it."

She spoke quickly before he could reach the door. "Could she take me outside for some air? It is very stuffy in here. Just for a few minutes? I'm feeling a bit faint."

Broadhurst smiled inwardly as he turned back towards her. It *was* stuffy - and that was by design. He ordered the air conditioning switched off when they left her to ponder her options over an hour ago.

"Well, that might be possible," he allowed, "but first I'll need an example of your willingness to cooperate. You could start by telling us your real name."

In a firm voice she replied, " I was born Tatiana Leonidovna Kravitchkevna."

"Write it out, please," he ordered, and slid a pen and notepad over to her.

Satisfied, he nodded to the WPC. "Take her out the back way, Oakley. Ten minutes, no more. And use cuffs."

48

1313 HOURS, PADDINGTON

"That's her," exclaimed Rainer. The helmeted man next to him looked up to see where he was pointing. "Here's our chance!"

Rainer Braun, 'Nord' to his Circle 17 comrades, couldn't believe it was going to be this easy. The coded call to the emergency number from Olga had only come a few hours ago, not that long after Vlad had called him from Brussels. If she hadn't mentioned she was being held at Paddington, if might have taken him hours - or days - to trace her. Time that meant danger for everyone she had connections with.

Nord picked up the uncommunicative passenger with the unpronounceable Slavic name from the cheap B & B near Victoria at 12 P.M. They'd driven to their present location behind Paddington Green police station and waited. This was the second time in two days that he'd been the driver for the assassin. They were sitting in a small car park at the west side of a boarded-up, six storey building on the opposite side of Newcastle Place from the police station. The short street ran behind the station between Edgware Road and Paddington Green. Newcastle Place was a one way street from east to west. Nord's plan was to wait to see if, as he suspected, a police vehicle would eventually exit the station with Olga inside, probably to transport her to Holloway

Prison for Women. He planned to follow and, at an opportune moment, carry out Vlad's order.

And now her unexpected appearance on what looked to be a loading dock at the rear of station presented them with a golden opportunity. He hopped onto the seat of the powerful Yamaha motorcycle and gunned the engine to life. The silent Slav slid onto the seat behind him and opened the pannier by his right knee.

Nord roared onto the street and turned east towards the station. The speeding bike quickly covered the short distance to a point directly opposite the target.

*

The fresh air had revived her, and even with her left hand shackled to the railing outside the rear entrance, Olga was feeling a bit better about her chances of playing the gullible yet innocent pawn.

"GET DOWN!" yelled the female officer, standing off to her side, and a few steps behind. Before Olga realized the warning was for her, the rapid and lethal stream of bullets from the machine pistol tore through her chest and throat. She sagged against the railings, her bloodied head catching grotesquely on the lower rung.

WPC Oakley was also down, blood running down the right side of her face. She had been in mid-tackle when the hail of gunfire erupted.

Stunned and shocked, her first reaction was to try and unlock the handcuff around the woman's left wrist. But her shaking hands made it impossible. Not that it mattered. Less than a minute after the bullets struck her, the Circle 17 agent died in Oakley's arms.

Her last two words, barely loud enough for Oakley to hear, were *'Why Uncle?'*

*

1330 HOURS

The wounded constable was lying on a stretcher in the police ambulance, one of three that had responded to frantic calls in the confusion that followed the shooting. Her wound was not serious, the emergency attendant assured her, but the one bullet that grazed her had taken a snip of skin off the top of her right ear. If she hadn't been in the act of tackling the dead woman, she would have taken more - and possibly deadly - hits herself.

More than thirty shell casings were recovered at the spot the shooter fired from, she learned later.

"We've got the bleeding stopped, young lady," smiled the attendant as he finished wrapping her head in gauze. "And once we get you to the hospital I'm sure a doctor will do a fine job patching you up," he assured her.

He nodded to DCI Houghton, who was crouched near the foot of her stretcher.

"Don't be too long, Inspector. She's still in shock, you know."

Derek nodded, and said he would only be a few minutes. WPC Oakley had already told him that she was up to answering his questions.

"There was just so much blood! I couldn't do anything to stop it." She sobbed quietly.

Derek's experience in questioning people in shock made it easy for Oakley to relive the fateful moments without breaking down. It took him only three minutes to get a clear picture of what she had seen. When he finished, he patted her hands and praised her efforts.

"Trying to save her was a very brave thing to do, Oakley. Most commendable," he said. "Now try and relax a bit and let these lads get you over to St Mary's. I'll send one of your colleagues along shortly to see how you're making out. Okay?"

Oakley nodded, and managed a weak smile. She closed her eyes as the DCI hopped out of the ambulance.

*

1330 HOURS, NEW SCOTLAND YARD

"Jocko! About time you showed up," admonished his boss.

"Aye sir, And if you'll be so kind and see to the traffic officer who's down at the gate and mad as 'ell cuz I didna' stop when he waved me down, I'll get on with the job."

John 'Jocko' Munro, 44 years of age and bald as a snooker ball, was the most experienced bomb man in MI5's London office. His knowledge of explosives had been honed during his fifteen years with the SAS regiment of the British Forces. The stainless steel prosthesis that served as his left hand attested to the only mistake he'd made during two stressful tours in Belfast.

Watson and Rod Weathers hovered anxiously while Jocko studied the grainy print through various magnifying lenses. To Rod it seemed like an hour passed before he leaned back and motioned to his boss. In fact it had been less than five minutes.

"Well Jocko, what do you make of it?" asked the MI5 chief.

Jocko shoved his chair back and handed his boss one of the magnifying glasses.

"Look at the right end of it," he instructed, after removing the unlit pipe he'd been chewing on from his mouth. "There appears to be some wiring visible, I'd say."

Harold Watson took the print and moved the magnifier in and out a number of times before he got his right eye focused.

"Well, if you hadn't told me what to look for I'd never have picked it out," he said. "But yes, I suppose that's what it could be..."

"And that means?" Rod asked cautiously, afraid he already knew the answer.

"As I say, this image isn't that conclusive, but in my opinion we're looking at an explosive device. The wires probably connect a timer to a detonator," replied Jocko. He flicked his lighter to begin the task of getting his pipe going again.

＊

Watson and Weathers peppered Jocko with questions, none of which he could answer with any certainty.

"I would think it is a plastic explosive. Anything that small precludes dynamite or a liquid," he told them. "The way the man handled it, that is, not treating it like a bowl of eggs, suggests the same."

"You're talking C-4, or something similar then," said Watson.

"Aye, most likely," agreed Jocko.

"Well then there's only one way to confirm it," We'll have to wring the truth out of the bastard who put it there," Watson said.

He reached for the radio and called Marconi Four.

*

1332 HOURS

"Marconi Four from Sandbox."

"Roger Sandbox, go ahead."

"Take McDuff into custody immediately. Once you've got him, sweat the bastard hard," ordered Watson. "I want to know exactly what he put on that aircraft."

That was all Knowlton needed to hear. "Understood chief. Do I have authority to use the vet if necessary?"

"Bloody right you can! In fact take him there directly, it's not that far from Stansted. Don't say a word to him until he's strapped down on the table. This is no time to fuck about with niceties. I'll let them know you coming."

Knowlton gave his radio a startled look. In the six years he had worked under Watson he'd never heard him use the 'f' word.

Knowlton wasn't there to hear him, of course, but Watson uttered the same profanity a few minutes later when word reached him that the Russian woman had been shot to death at Paddington.

*

Rod Weathers did some quick calculations while Watson, Jean-Marc Rousseau and their team digested the news of the assassination. It was an intense discussion, and one he was loath to interrupt. But the threat posed to the flight needed immediate consideration, too. When there was a short pause in their exchange he signaled to Watson.

"Yes?"

"Commander, we've got to contact the flight. And *now* rather than later," he stressed. "They have to be warned about this threat. I'd even go so far as to suggest they consider landing as soon as possible."

Watson sighed. "Any idea where the aircraft would be at this time, Captain?" he asked, glancing at the large wall clock.

"Yes, they've been airborne for almost two hours, and that would put them well out over the ocean, probably somewhere around twenty degrees west."

"And in laymen's terms, how far is that from land?"

"Roughly an hour's flying time. I don't know what his exact flight plan routing is, though," answered Rod. "But if I could get in touch with the air traffic control they could provide me with a radio link to the flight, even a relay if a direct link isn't possible."

"I see. Well then, the lads at the comm desk should be able to help you with that." He called a sergeant over and introduced him to Captain Weathers. "Just tell Sergeant Davis what you need, I'm sure he'll be able to make it work."

*

1340 HOURS, PADDINGTON

Broadhurst was on the phone to his boss when Derek got back to his office. Not surprisingly, the news of the female suspect's assassination was not well received, and if Broadhurst's facial expressions were any indication he was getting his ass chewed out.

"Right sir...yes, of course." he said, and hung up.

"Watson's bark is always worse than his bite," he said to Derek by way of explanation.

"But it was my call that exposed her to the gunman."

"Yes, well, there's no sense dwelling on it, is there?" commiserated Derek.

"Quite right. Were you able to get anything worthwhile out of Oakley?"

"Oh yes, she was quite lucid, considering she was almost blown away herself."

Referring to notes he'd made of his short interview in the ambulance, Derek reconstructed what she had seen. Her first hint of trouble was the sight of the motorcycle speeding towards them from her left - the wrong way on the one-way lane. The motorcycle stopped directly in front of the dock and the passenger aimed what she described as a large pistol-like weapon at them. That's when she reacted, shouted at the suspect to get down, and dove for her waist just as she heard a burst of gunfire. She remembers getting her arms around the suspect's waist at the instant she felt a searing pain in her head. Her next recollection was trying to free the woman's wrist, and pull her upright.

Derek looked up from his notes and said, "I think she must have blacked out momentarily when she was hit."

Two PCs about to enter the station heard the shots and turned to see what was happening. Their backs were to the street, so they didn't see the bike pull up. One of them was at Oakley's side within seconds, and used his handkerchief to cover her wound. Oakley doesn't remember that happening. When she looked up, the motorcycle had already disappeared. The second officer gave chase on foot hoping to get a glimpse of the licence number, but it was northbound on Edgware Road and too far away by the time he reached the corner. He could only say that it was a dark- colored touring bike with two riders onboard. Both constables thought by the sound that the weapon used was indeed an automatic of some sort, and shell casings found on the roadway will be turned over to forensics for identification.

"Christ! This is definitely major crime we're dealing with Derek. Nothing can convince me otherwise. Anything else?"

"Yes. Oakley heard the woman say something just before she died." Houghton closed his notepad. "If she heard correctly, her last words were, "Why Uncle?'

"Why Uncle?" repeated Broadhurst, a puzzled look on his face. "What the hell does that mean?"

"No idea. But both Oakley and the constable who came to her aid are positive that's what they heard."

"Doesn't make sense, does it? Would she have recognized the shooter?"

"Seems unlikely. Both were wearing helmets and had their visors down, according to Oakley and the other lads."

*

The scant description of the motorcycle was on the police net soon after the shooting. A constable on foot patrol near Paddington Rail station found it two hours later. He'd spotted it amongst a bunch of luggage trolleys parked along the west side of the station, and radioed the details, including the registration number, to his precinct. The bike had been reported stolen from a dealer's lot in Hemel Hempstead, northwest of London, ten days previously. The killers would have had numerous options for leaving the busy station once they had dumped the bike. A search of likely hiding spots in the area failed to turn up the weapon used in the shooting.

*

1348 HOURS, NEW SCOTLAND YARD

"What's happening?" Rod turned to find Don Carling standing behind him.

"Don! Glad you're here. I thought you were still at Paddington."

"Well, there was nothing further I could do there after she was shot. Derek is heading the investigation and the search for the killers. Thought I might be of more use here."

"For sure. We've got a real problem on our hands, mate. He pulled his friend aside and brought him up to date on the threat to Holt's flight.

The Canadian let out a frustrated sigh when Rod finished. "Shouldn't we advise him to get his plane on the ground ASAP?"

"Well, at least give him the info we have so far. Then he can decide what to do about it, right?

"Yeah, yeah, of course. Obviously it'll be up to him. But the sooner we can give provide him with more definite info the better."

*

Before Don arrived, Rod had spoken with a supervisor at the West Drayton Air Traffic Control Center, explained the situation, and told him why he needed a phone patch to the oceanic controller working Flight 213, or even better, directly to the flight. Initially the supervisor balked at his request, telling Rod they had procedures in place regarding bomb threats and he thought they should follow them.

Rod had to go over his head, which took two more frustrating calls and ate up another twenty minutes before his request to communicate directly to Flight 213 was approved.

While he was waiting for the green light, Rod called Northern Flyer's dispatch office in Toronto and advised them of the possible threat to the flight. It was well past two o'clock when Sergeant Davis finally signaled that all was ready.

"Okay, sir, use the phone at the end of the table, and use line four. You should be able to speak to both the Shanwick controller and Flight 213," he told Rod.

49

Rod paused for a few moments before he picked up the handset. He wanted to be sure he knew exactly what he was going to say...

"Northern Flyer 213 do you read this transmission, over?"

Seconds later Norman Holt answered. "Station calling 213, go ahead."

"213, this is Captain Rod Weathers in London..."

As quickly as he could, Rod explained who he was, why he was calling, and what the situation was as of that moment. Once Holt had heard him out, he agreed that Weathers should act as the direct link between the security team on the ground and Flight 213. Norman didn't need to be convinced that it would be better than having crucial information relayed to him via Shanwick Control or the airline's dispatch office in Toronto.

Holt told Rod he agreed with the suggestion that they start planning for a diversion, but for the time being they would continue on course until more details about the threat became available.

Shanwick Control concurred with the set up, with the proviso that any requests for routing or altitude changes would still have to be made through them.

"What is your present position, Captain?" asked Rod.

Holt was about to reply when Ozzie returned to the flight deck. As soon as he'd heard Weathers explaining about the suspicious object they had onboard, the flight engineer had hurried back to the cargo compartment for a 'look see'.

"Standby by a minute, London," he said. He turned towards the flight engineer and asked, "Can you see anything, Oz?"

"Nope. Can't get close enough to see much of the L5 door. The asshole that put it there probably knew that," he said, breathing heavily from both exertion and anxiety.

'Of course - the door light!' The thought hit Norman like a hammer blow. *'McDuff! It had to be his doing. He was the one who said he would check the door himself. So the door had probably been tinkered with on purpose. But a bomb? Why? Could it have something to do with their passenger? McDuff's warning that he might be a police officer jogged his memory. But who put Terry up to it?'*

"Norm? You okay?" The worried question from his first officer snapped the captain out of his preoccupation with the ominous thoughts his mind was wrestling with.

"Uhh, sure, just thinking, that's all," he replied. "Pass me the flight plan, Gord." He studied it for a moment before he called Weathers back.

"We're just coming up on Twenty-eight West, and estimating Five Niner North, Three Zero West at 1335." Holt's estimate was in Greenwich Mean Time, or GMT, an hour earlier than British Summer Time. "And we're unable to get near enough to L5 to see what you're talking about."

"Okay sir, copy your position and remarks. The police have the ramp worker who planted the package in custody and he's being interrogated as we speak. We should have more details for you very soon."

Rod wished he had more definite information to give the captain, but that wasn't possible just yet. He sighed and shook his head. Don Carling knew precisely what his friend was thinking: his own stomach was churning as he listened to the flight's position report. At 30 West, Flight 213 would be a long way from an airport - maybe too far.

*

"Land as soon as possible. Easy for them to say," offered Holt, more to himself then the others. "Okay chaps, I'm open to suggestions. Do we turn back now just in case it is a bomb, or press on until we know more about it?"

Gord Chalmers answered first. "Could it be a hoax? Most bomb threats usually are, aren't they?"

"True enough, Gord," said Holt, "but it wasn't a phone call that triggered the alarm. You heard what Weathers said. They have video tape of his actions when he checked the door."

"Yeah, I thought there was something fishy about the damned door light. There was no friggin' reason for anyone to open L5 while they were loading the cargo," chimed in Ozzie. "But why put it there? Why not just throw it in one of the lower cargo compartments?"

None of them had an answer for that.

After further discussion - mostly 'what ifs' - the consensus was to continue on track for the time being.

Holt studied the navigation chart for the area between Scotland and the Labrador coast. At a quick glance he determined that Keflavik, Iceland, was the closest airport to their present position. And on their route it would remain the closest for roughly the next hour. If they didn't hear anything positive from London in the next thirty minutes, he would then decide whether to divert to Iceland or press on to Goose Bay, Labrador.

"Talk about being up the proverbial shit creek without a paddle," said Ozzie, expressing aloud the thought that was weighing on the captain's mind. "Right in the middle of the fuckin' ocean with a bomb on board."

"Yes, and nothing is going to change that chaps, so let's not dwell on it. We'll start planning for a diversion," said the captain. "Ozzie, calculate what our fuel consumption will be at ten thousand feet. If we descend and depressurize the aircraft it should lessen the effect of an explosion - maybe it will just blow the door off."

"Couldn't agree more, Norm," replied Ozzie. "We've still got more than a hundred thousand pounds of fuel. You're thinking two hours or so at a lower altitude will get us somewhere we can land, right?"

"Yes. It wouldn't take that long to divert to Kef, but it will probably be a good two hours or more to Goose Bay."

"I'll have a number for you in a few minutes, skipper."

Now that the three men were over their initial shock, they focused on how to make the best of their dilemma. Norman called Shanwick for the latest weather reports for Keflavik, Goose Bay and Gander airports. Ozzie busied himself with the fuel calculations. Gord was left to monitor the flight profile. Coping with an emergency situation was an integral part of their training. There was no cut and dried way to handle a bomb threat, though - not after the flight was airborne. Until the plane was on the ground, any course of action would be up to the captain.

50

MI5 SAFE HOUSE

Terrence McDuff had been collared in the employees' locker room. Although his shift didn't end until three o'clock, he'd been planning an early exit. He didn't want to be around if something disastrous happened to the Northern Flyer flight. In fact, he thought of leaving for Spain as soon as he collected his extra two hundred pounds.

Shocked and surprised when the MI5 officers surrounded him, he vehemently denied their accusation that he had put anything on board the aircraft just before it departed.

Knowlton didn't waste time. He had McDuff handcuffed and manhandled into the unmarked Toyota van that had been backed up to door to the ramp area. McDuff continued to protest and demanded to speak with a solicitor as he was driven away. As soon as the van cleared the airport perimeter, a black hood was pulled over his head.

"Where are you taking me?" he kept asking. His pleas fell on deaf ears. He soon realized his protests were futile. The more he ranted, the more uncomfortable it became under the hood. His face was now covered in sweat, salt stinging his eyes. All he had was a sensation of speed. A few times his captors - one on each side - grabbed his arms to keep him from falling over as the vehicle careened around a sharp corner.

When the driver slammed on the brakes at the safe house, they weren't so helpful. He tumbled awkwardly into the seat in front, sending a sharp pain through his shoulder. With the hood still in place he was roughly half-walked, half-dragged into a cool building.

*

Despite the seriousness of the situation, Knowlton had to stifle his urge to laugh. The prone form of their prisoner was now stretched out on a stainless steel table, securely immobilized by straps across his torso, arms and legs. Only his covered head was free. He was naked from the waist down. The table was in the middle of a small room in the secluded safe house used by the security services. The inconspicuous country house was tucked away on a country lane a few miles west and north of the A25. The building sat in the midst of a stand of stately oaks and neatly-trimmed hedges. The nearest inhabited dwellings were more than a half mile away.

The 'vet'- actually a retired Army medical officer who did contract work for MI5 - stood beside the table. When he was ready, he nodded and Knowlton pulled the hood off McDuff's head.

An involuntary gasp caught in the startled man's dry throat. He scrunched up his eyes against the sudden brightness from the large lamp suspended over his exposed midsection. He couldn't comprehend the masked and gowned apparition standing beside the table.

"What...what the fuck is goin' on here?" he groaned. "You can't treat me like this! Who is this?" he cried, staring at the vet.

"All in due time, McDuff. First you're going to answer my questions," intoned Knowlton, standing unseen behind the head of the table. The room was darkened, the lone lamp providing the only illumination.

"What is he going to do? And why have you taken my trousers off?"

"Because if I don't get the answers I need the vet here is going to remove your knackers, boyo. Mind you he's used to working on four-legged creatures, but the procedure is much the same, he's assured me."

"No! You can't be serious! This is inhumane!"

"Perhaps, but so is placing a bomb on an airplane."

"Bomb? What bomb? I never-- You'll never get away with this!"

Knowlton slammed the table a few inches from McDuff's head.

"THE BOMB WE HAVE FILM OF YOU SHOVING IN THE AIRCRAFT DOOR! THAT BOMB!" he shouted into the prisoner's ear.

McDuff thrashed his head sharply away from the voice, his ears ringing. "It wasn't a bomb," he offered, his bravado gone. The vet had moved a tray of instruments onto the table. "It was, it was only..." he stammered, wild-eyed.

'Only what, McDuff?" Knowlton asked, almost whispering.

"Please, I don't know!" he pleaded.

"Start the freezing Doc. I don't have anymore time for this cowardly bastard's stalling."

The vet pinched McDuff's upper thigh and pricked it with a syringe.

"OUCH!" cried McDuff, straining against the straps. "You sadistic bastards! You can't do this to me!" He could only lift his head a few inches off the table, but it was enough to see the vet's hands. And what he saw now terrified him even more. The vet was brandishing a long and sharp-looking knife.

"The freezing takes about five minutes, McDuff. Then you won't feel a thing while the Doctor neuters you. So we're not as inhumane as you think. And once all the messy business is over and done with and you're doing time at Dartmoor, you might even thank us. The only other ahh...'patient' the doc actually turned into a eunuch is enjoying his - or should I say 'her' - stay as a guest of Her Majesty's Prison Service. A big favorite with the lifers, I'm told. They like to finger the scars while they have at him. Reminds them of a woman, they say. He's even taken to wearing knickers and a skirt."

Sweat was pouring off the terrified man's face once again. His eyes were a turmoil of hatred, fear and helplessness. When he could get words out he continued to insist that he wasn't told what the package contained. He gave up the name of the contact who had delivered the package and insisted it probably contained drugs.

"Anyway," continued Knowlton, checking his watch, "this chap I was telling you about, the one who gave up his manhood, did it for ideological reasons. An Islamic radical, he was, been nabbed for terrorist activity. Blew up a synagogue, killed two elderly people. Are you willing to sacrifice your balls for a cause, McDuff? I don't think so..."

*

McDuff knew he was in deep even before he'd been arrested: ever since he got a glimpse of the package Nick delivered to the aircraft minutes before departure. Terry had wavered, almost to the point of refusing to cooperate, but once it was in his hands it was too late.

"Just do it," Nick ordered, as he drove away.

Nick was a driver for a commissary firm that provided crew meals and other supplies for the smaller airlines, and the appearance of his refrigerated vehicle at Flight 213's stand hadn't triggered any alarm for those watching. Nor did they notice the driver and McDuff together during his short stop.

McDuff had figured out some time ago that Nick was probably the man in charge of the smuggling ring operating at the airport. He'd heard rumors about its existence long before Nick had recruited him. His connection with Captain Holt was a separate arrangement though, and as far as he could tell Nick wasn't aware of it. None of the smuggling activity he'd had a hand in seemed to pose much risk of discovery, either. At least not before today...

*

"Well, I see your five minutes are up. And you still haven't told me what I need to know," said Knowlton.

"How many bloody times do I have to tell you? I just shoved it in the door like I was told to!"

"Absolute bullshit!" retorted Knowlton. "How's the freezing coming, doc?"

The white-clad figure grabbed one of McDuff's testicles with his gloved hand and squeezed."OW-W-W!" came the anguished cry.

"Obviously it hasn't taken effect yet," said Knowlton. "How unfortunate. Can't wait any longer, though. Get on with it, Doctor. Pardon me if I don't watch - blood makes me squeamish."

The vet raised the gleaming scalpel up to make sure McDuff could see it. With his other hand he grabbed the terrified man's shrunken penis and bent over the table.

"NO! NO! STOP! PLEASE STOP!" he hollered. "It was reading four twenty-five!" he sobbed. "I'm sorry...I didn't do..."

" What was reading four twenty-five, McDuff?" whispered Knowlton, his face only inches above the broken man. "Was it a dial? A clock? What the fuck are you talking about?"

McDuff continued to weep. "It was sort of like a small clock. I, I didn't know what...."

Knowlton jerked McDuff's head towards him. "Look at me!" he ordered. "Was it a clock face? And when did you see the reading? TELL ME OR YOUR BALLS ARE COMING OFF NOW!"

"Yes, yes! It was a small clock face. I saw the numbers just before I shoved it in!" I didn't do anythin' to it myself!"

*

1440 HOURS, NEW SCOTLAND YARD

"Yes, I copy that, Four," replied Commander Watson, "and the clock was already running when he put it onboard, is that correct?"

"That's affirmative," Knowlton replied. He was standing under the portico at the front of the safe house. "He says it was reading four twenty-five when he closed the door."

Watson turned to the explosives expert who had been listening in. "So Jocko, where does that leave us? Some sort of timing device, I should think?".

"Definitely. Can't see it being anything else, sir," agreed the Scotsman. "And a digital timer is much more accurate than one fitted with a dial. If it's rigged properly to the detonator, it'll explode the charge four hours and twenty-five minutes after that bugger last saw it, I fear."

"That accurate?" asked his chief.

Jocko shrugged. "Give or take a minute."

Watson stepped over to the communications console and gave Rod and Don the bad news.

"Ah damn it, this is not good," Carling muttered. "How long have they been airborne now?"

Rod clenched both his fists in anger. "That's not the important number, is it? McDuff closed the L5 door at 11:40 - I checked my watch then and the videotape confirmed it. Adding four twenty-five to that we come up with, ahh..."

Don was a step ahead of him. "1605."

"Yes, 1505 GMT," added Rod. He grabbed a notepad and worked a few short calculations. "If the timer is accurate, the bomb is set to explode in eighty minutes."

"Not that it matters considering where they are now, but I would add in a fudge factor, wouldn't you?" Don said. "Maybe ten minutes?"

"Absolutely. Wouldn't want to cut it too fine," answered Rod. "But I think he's going to have a devil of a time getting the aircraft on the ground in eighty minutes, let alone seventy."

"And where is the flight now?" This from Commander Watson.

"Too many miles from nowhere," replied the Canadian.

*

1447 HOURS [1347 GMT]

"Northern 213, London."

"Roger London," answered Holt. "What's the situation now?"

"Not good news, I'm afraid sir, and there's no way to sugarcoat it."

"I'm listening," Holt replied, fearing the worst.

"The authorities are almost certain the object inside your L5 door is a bomb. It is timed to go off at 1505 GMT. That's as definite as they can be. In other words," added Rod, checking his watch, "seventy-eight minutes from now."

*

1350 HOURS GMT

"Well then, that's made our decision for us," said the captain evenly. "Gord, switch the autopilot over to the number one inertial nav system.

I've made waypoint number one the Keflavik VOR. Punch in a direct routing to it. And start a descent to 10,000 feet."

When the younger pilot gave him a questioning look, he added, "Just do it. I'll clear it with Shanwick in a moment."

Norman watched as the first officer quickly and deftly carried out his instructions. After the 747 had settled on a northeasterly heading and was descending at 2,000 feet per minute, he made the radio call he had been hoping wouldn't be necessary.

"Shanwick, Shanwick, Northern 213. Mayday, Mayday, Mayday! We are diverting to Keflavik at this time and requesting descent to 10,000 feet. Our present position is 5830 North and 34 West."

"Roger Northern 213, Shanwick checks you are declaring an emergency. Standby for clearance," advised the controller. After a short pause he continued, "Break, break, Iceland are you on the frequency, over?"

In perfect English, with only a trace of a Nordic accent, a calm voice replied. "Roger Shanwick, Iceland is reading both you and Northern 213 loud and clear."

After passing 30 West longitude, Flight 213 had entered Gander's area of responsibility and normally would have been switched to one of their frequencies. However, with the bomb threat still unresolved, Gander had agreed that Shanwick should continue to handle the flight and keep the connection with Rod Weathers in London intact.

Now that Holt had made the decision to divert, the Icelandic sector came into play.

At times all three sectors were monitoring the same frequencies, hence it was not surprising that the communications between Flight 213 and Ireland had been overheard by the controller in Iceland. On its new course, the flight would enter Iceland's airspace in ten minutes time.

"Do you have the current Keflavik weather, 213?"

"Ahh, Roger Iceland, we have the 1300 GMT report. Has there been any change?" asked Holt. He was hoping it had improved.

"No sir, but I'll have the 1400 actual weather report shortly."

The Shanwick controller broke in, "Iceland, Shanwick, I have no problem with 213's request for a lower altitude in my airspace, but I'll leave it up to you to issue the clearance, over."

"Thank you, Shanwick. Break, break, Northern 213, I'll need you to change frequencies: call me now on 10073 HF for your clearance, over."

Holt made the switch on the high frequency radio and checked in. Once he confirmed that the flight was receiving him 'strength five' on the new frequency, Iceland issued the clearance.

"Iceland clears Northern 213 from present position direct to the Keflavik VOR. Descend to and maintain 10,000 feet. Altimeter setting 1002 millibars. Request your ETA for Keflavik, over."

Holt repeated the clearance verbatim and gave their ETA for the field.

The weather for the joint military and commercial airport on the small island's southwest coast was definitely iffy. A tight, moisture-laden low pressure system was tracking towards the island resulting in thick cloud cover and steady rain at Keflavik. The ceiling had been hovering between two and three hundred feet for the past four hours. Visibility was one to two miles in light to moderate rain. Adding to the challenge was a strong surface wind, which, Norman knew, meant they would encounter windshear on the approach to the runway.

But the veteran pilot had been faced with similar challenges during his career and, even with the added stress brought on by the bomb threat, he felt confident that he could handle the marginal weather conditions.

*

"What's going on?" asked Brian Roberts, "Don't tell me we're there already." He was crouched beside the flight engineer's seat. The passenger had been dozing in the seating area behind the flight deck for the past hour. It was the sudden change from level flight to the descent path that had stirred him awake.

"Some prick put a bomb on board before we left Stansted," Ozzie told him.

"What?" exclaimed Roberts. "Uhh, how do you..."

Ozzie held up his hand. "That's all we know. We just got the word. But we've just changed course, heading for Iceland. We want to land as soon as possible. Probably be there for fuckin' hours till they can get someone to defuse it or whatever."

His reappearance on the flight deck had not yet been noticed by the captain or the first officer, and the shaken police officer stood back against the flight deck door to digest what Ozzie had just told him. His first thought was whether or not he should reveal his true identity and why he was on the flight.

Was this bomb connected to the undercover operation? Maybe he was the intended target... But that would mean there had been a leak back in London. If he told the captain his real name, would it make any difference to the emergency the crew was faced with?

No, no it wouldn't, he decided, after a few minutes of heart-thumping reflection.

He took a deep breath, urging himself to make a rational assessment of the situation. London, he told himself, would be grappling with the same questions. So far, it seemed, they hadn't thought it necessary to divulge his identity to the captain. And probably for the same conclusion he'd come to.

Roberts slipped into the jump seat behind Holt. Once Norman noticed his presence, he briefed him on what they knew so far about the explosive device.

"I don't suppose there's anything I can do, is there?" Roberts asked, rather lamely.

"Probably not, it's in an awkward position. Not enough room between the pallets and the fuselage to get close to it," admitted the captain.

An idea came to Roberts. During the loading he'd noticed that not all the pallets were the same height, leaving some with a fair amount of space between their tops and the aircraft ceiling. Maybe, just maybe, he could get a better look at the object from above the L5 door. He quickly explained this to the captain and suggested it might just be possible to see the L5 door from above.

"Sure, go ahead. Just be careful back there," he cautioned.

*

Roberts made his way back along the left side of the cargo compartment until he could go no further. From this point on, the two rearmost pallets were too close to the tapered fuselage to allow access along the wall. He edged to his left until he was in the middle of the second last pallet. This wasn't a difficult manoeuver as the pallets were a good two feet apart. The pallet's load consisted of cardboard cartons, each of them approximately three feet square. Using openings in the netting that covered it as footholds, Roberts pulled himself up the front and onto the top. The clearance between the top layer of cartons and the fuselage ceiling was approximately three feet. Crawling on his belly and using his elbows for leverage, he pulled his way towards the last pallet. His clearance with the ceiling lessened as he progressed, and when he made it to the last pallet his prone body was only inches from the ceiling. A brief wave of claustrophobia hit him at the same moment the 747 encountered clear air turbulence.

'*What the hell am I trying to prove?*' he berated himself. He gripped the netting tighter and screwed his eyes closed until the aircraft reached smooth air once again, and his panic attack abated.

Once his breathing returned to normal, he slithered over to the edge of the pallet. There was just enough space to let him peer down to the top of the L5 door.

The overhead lighting system for the main deck cargo compartment didn't illuminate the area he was trying to see, but the flight engineer had provided him with a flashlight. With difficulty Roberts managed to get his right hand and the flashlight into a position where it shone down on the door.

The result was disappointing. The bulge on the door's interior which housed an escape slide blocked out whatever was under it. Try as he might, Roberts was unable to get his head into a position to see under it from either the front or back.

Sweating profusely, Roberts retraced his movements and regained the aircraft floor once again. He surveyed the narrow space along the side of the aircraft. He could see why a man of Ozzie's girth couldn't squeeze into it, but he thought he might be able to make some progress if he pulled himself along the floor on his side. He decided it was worth a try. If he could just get as far as the front of the last pallet, he thought there was a chance he could see - or even reach- what was under the door.

Starting with his right arm and the flashlight above his head, he inched his body along between the pallet and the aircraft's outer wall. Five painful minutes later he could go no further. His shoulders were jammed. His hand was almost touching the front left corner of the last pallet, and the distance from there to the door was about ten feet. Salty sweat was stinging his eyes, and he had to close them until his tear ducts ran enough to clear them. He had ten seconds before his vision blurred again. It was enough time for him to see that there definitely was something there. But his extremely limited sight line made it impossible to discern exactly what it was.

If I had a ten-foot pole with a hook on it, I might be able to snag the object and pull it forward far enough to reach it. But would he really want to try that? Disturbing it might just set it off...

He reversed his movements until he had room enough to stand up and returned to the flight deck. Three heads turned expectantly towards him when he entered. He shook his head and gave them a thumbs down.

51

Before Roberts had a chance to explain, the flight received another call.

"Northern 213 from Iceland, say your passing altitude."

"Iceland, 213 is through flight level 220, " answered Holt.

"Sir, I suggest you stop your descent. Keflavik tower has just issued an operational advisory."

"Now what?" Holt sighed. "Ahh, Roger Iceland, we will level off at flight level 200." Holt reset the altitude alert to 20,000 feet and nodded to Gord. The first officer adjusted the autopilot's descent rate to 500 feet per minute.

"What's the problem, Iceland?" Holt asked.

"Tower advises the ILS has just become unserviceable. And the weather report is now showing the ceiling at two hundred feet overcast and visibility three quarters to a mile in moderate rain," replied the controller, almost apologetically. "It will be at least two hours before they expect to have the ILS operational again."

"Jeezus! What else can go wrong," groaned Ozzie, shaking his head. "We've got roughly an hour to get this sucker on the ground before we get blown to kingdom-fucking-come!"

"Take it easy Oz, we've still got an option," said the captain. He quickly entered another set of numbers into the INS set coupled to the autopilot, and came up with a new distance and time.

"Roger Iceland, 213 checks, 'no go' for landing at Keflavik. Request the weather and field conditions for Narsarsuaq."

"Copy 213. I think that is your best bet. As of 1200 GMT the field was open. At that time the weather was scattered cloud at 3,500 feet, visibility three miles, wind light and variable. There is a fog bank over the fjord west of the field. I'll call Narsarsuaq on the land line for an update."

"Roger, Iceland, call me back as soon as you have the latest, please."

"Should have it for you in five minutes, sir. You can route from your present position direct the November Alpha beacon. Descent at your discretion."

*

"Narsarsuaq? Where the heck is that?" asked the first officer after Norm had confirmed the latest routing change.

"It's an airstrip near the southwest coast of Greenland that twins use as a technical alternate. The runway isn't that long as I recall, but we don't have a choice. Go direct to waypoint two - that's the NA radio beacon. It's located on the field," explained the captain.

'Twins' referred to two-engine airliners such as the Boeing 767 and the Airbus 310. The smaller jets need less runway distance to take-off or land than a 747, and trans-Atlantic flights occasionally filed the field as mid-flight alternate.

"Ozzie, check the airport's data in the supplementary manual, will you?"

"Sure thing, Norm. It'll just take me a sec."

"But you think the runway is long enough for us, skipper?" Gord asked, a trace of skepticism in his voice.

"I'll get her down and stopped, even if we blow all the tires," vowed Holt. "It's our only option now...unless we want to ditch in the ocean." In the back of his mind Norman had already considered that might become a reality if time ran out.

"Yeah, I got the info here, Norm," said Ozzie. He was referring to airport chart and data for Narsarsuaq. "Runway is 6,000 feet long. I'll calculate how much fuel we'll need to dump to land in that distance."

"Good. ETA is 1452. We'll plan to jettison the fuel thirty minutes before our ETA."

*

LONDON, 1500 HOURS, [1400 GMT]

After Flight 213 switched over to Iceland's frequency, Rod Weathers lost his direct connection to the aircraft. The last transmission he'd heard was Holt's Mayday call advising his intention to divert to Keflavik. The controller in Shannon assured Rod he would keep him updated regarding the flight's progress. The nervousness gripping both Rod and Don eased somewhat when it looked as if the aircraft would be on the ground well before the deadline.

But their jitters peaked again when Shannon relayed the news that the ILS was down at Keflavik. They exchanged exasperated glances, which did not go unnoticed by Commander Watson sitting nearby.

"Problem, gentlemen?" he asked.

"I'm afraid so. A ground equipment failure means they won't be able to land in Iceland."

Rod explained to the MI5 officer how an instrument landing system - ILS for short - made an approach and landing possible in poor weather conditions. Without the electronically-generated beams for lateral guidance and a glide path, it would be poor airmanship - if not utter folly - for the crew to try an approach in the hope that they would see the runway in time to land safely.

"If the ceiling at Keflavik was higher, at least four hundred feet or more, and the visibility at least a mile, Flight 213 could probably carry out what is called a non-precision approach to locate the runway and land. But time-wise I don't think he can take that risk," summed up the airline captain.

"And he's diverting to where? Nars..sa...?"

"Narsarsuaq. An airfield situated on a fjord on the southwest coast of Greenland. It was a staging stop for aircraft being ferried from Canada and the US to Britain during the war. The Yanks ran it for a few years after the war, I believe, and then turned it over to the Danish authorities," explained Rod. "I landed there once when I was in the RAF. You need fairly decent weather to get in there, though."

"Well for their sake, let's hope that's the case," said Don Carling, "There is nowhere else they can put her down now, is there? What's left in that region? Sondrestrom is the only other airport I remember being on the west coast."

"You're right," answered Rod, "but it's quite a bit further north."

After the pilot and former pilot ended their discussion, Watson asked, "Can he land at this place in time?"

Rod held up his crossed fingers. "Should be able to. He's given an ETA for overhead the field of 1452 GMT. That's thirteen minutes before the deadline."

*

1519 HOURS [1419 GMT]

Holt studied the airport information as they descended. The published instrument approach for runway 07 used a combination of bearing and distance: a bearing to the NA radio beacon and a distance readout from another transmitter on the field. It was referred to as an NDB-DME approach: NDB for non-directional beacon and DME for distance measuring equipment.

Norman would have to fly an inbound on a bearing of 073 degrees. For each mile along the bearing an altitude was given: the closer to the field, the lower the altitude. In effect, a pilot flew an imaginary glide path by using a calculated rate of descent, normally in the five to seven hundred feet per minute range.

The hairs on the back of the captain's neck tingled as he read through the precautionary notes included with the approach information.

The first note advised that pilots not familiar with the airport should use extreme caution if they planned to make a visual approach up the fjord leading to the runway. Mountain peaks dotted both sides of the inlet. If the ceiling was less than 4,000 feet, some of the tops would be obscured and a visual flight up the fjord was not recommended. The reported layer of scattered cloud at 3,500 feet should give him some leeway, he thought.

The other note that caught his attention advised that a much steeper than normal rate of descent was needed once an aircraft got to within four miles of the field, at which point it should have the runway in sight. That would mean descending at 1,000 feet per minute - perhaps more. It could be done, but in an aircraft the size of the 747 it bordered on dangerous.

If visibility was really poor, he might have to fly a circling pattern once he cleared the fog bank in order to lose sufficient height before they could land. And the recommended radius for such a manoeuver was two miles, the limiting factor being the high ground just a few miles north of the runway. Another challenge in an aircraft with a two hundred-foot wingspan.

*

"Jeez, the terrain sure looks rough from here," offered Gord, as they approached the east coast of the Greenland. The large island was thought to be comprised of a number of smaller mountainous islands, fused together by the vast icecap that covered all but its coastal fringes. The island's glaciers and peaks that stood out so well from high altitudes were dramatically more impressive now.

"Yes, it's no wonder so many aircraft were lost trying to get over it in cloud and icing conditions during the war. With that in mind we'll maintain 12,000 feet until we get the west coast in sight. That will ensure we don't become a statistic ourselves" said the captain. "How's the cabin coming, Oz?"

The flight engineer confirmed that the aircraft was completely depressurized. The air pressure both inside and outside were now the same. If it were possible to open the L5 door now, the vacuum effect might suck the offending device out of the aircraft. Roberts told the captain he thought he could get a rope or cord over the inside handle from above, but he was told that wouldn't work. In addition to moving the handle, one needed room to pull the front of the door inwards a few feet before it would swivel open. And that space just wasn't there...

"Okay Gord, bring the speed back to 280 knots. That's the optimum speed for fuel jettisoning." Holt directed.

Chalmers smoothly retarded the throttles and thirty seconds later reset them to maintain the new airspeed. The autopilot re-trimmed the flight controls in response to the slower speed.

"Ready with the fuel jettison checklist, Norm," advised Ozzie.

"Go ahead, then."

Once the captain and flight engineer had confirmed the applicable switches and valves were properly set, and all unnecessary electrical systems turned off, Norman gave the command to start venting fuel.

Flight 213 was forty miles from the coast, and 140 miles from their intended destination. With only 6,000 feet of runway available, they had to reduce the aircraft weight to a maximum of 500,000 pounds to ensure they would be able to stop safely after touching down. On a normal landing, reverse engine thrust was used to slow the aircraft to less than 100 knots before the brakes were applied. This technique saved expensive wear and tear on the wheel brakes, but was only viable when runway distance wasn't a limiting factor. Holt was confident he could stop in the shorter distance using a combination of maximum braking and reverse thrust, particularly if the runway surface was dry.

Ozzie's calculations called for a fuel jettison duration of twelve minutes. That would leave them with enough fuel to reach Narsarsuaq, and, if they didn't land and there wasn't an explosion at 1505 hours, fuel to reach Goose Bay.

*

1432 HOURS GMT

"Fuel jettison complete, Norm. We've still got a tad less than sixty grand. Your estimated landing weight is 499,500," said Ozzie, who swiveled his chair forward to a position between the pilots. "How's it lookin'out there?" He half stood to get a better view out the front windscreens. "Too bad there isn't a field on this coast, eh?"

Flight 213 was now over Greenland, and the southern tip off to their left was cloud free. July and August were the peak melting months for the icecap. Now that the 747 was only some 3,000 feet above ground, waterfalls were visible coursing down the rocky slopes along the rugged the coast.

Holt had been trying unsuccessfully to re-establish radio contact with a ground station. HF reception had been lost once they descended below 15,000 feet, and they were still too far away from Narsarsuaq to communicate on VHF. He still hadn't received the latest weather report for their intended destination. It was the mention of the fog bank that concerned him the most. He knew it wasn't an unusual occurrence in fjords in the warmer summer months, but nevertheless it was another unsettling factor as the clock ran down.

A fog bank that close to the runway probably meant they would have to carry out an instrument approach instead of a quicker visual pattern.

When Holt had first declared an emergency, a number of other flights in range of Flight 213 had offered to relay messages for them. He'd asked a Northwest Airlines flight to advise Iceland that they had leveled off at 12,000 feet and were still estimating Narsarsuaq at 1452 GMT.

1439 HOURS GMT

Holt was about to call for Northwest's assistance again when he heard another aircraft calling them on the international VHF distress frequency.

"Ahh, Northern Flyer 213, this is Hunter 24 on 121.5, do you read me?" The speaker's voice had an unmistakable southern drawl to it.

"This is Northern 213, I'm reading you strength three," answered Holt. "Repeat your call sign, over."

There was a short silence before the next call. "This is Hunter 24, sir. How do you read me on this transmitter, over?"

"Hunter 24, you're five by five now." The call sign was that of a military aircraft, Holt knew, and the naval flyer quickly confirmed it.

Hunter 24 was an Orion P3C, a long-range patrol plane crewed by United States Navy fliers. It was on a training flight from its base in Brunswick, Maine to Keflavik, commanded by Lieutenant Commander Josh Cline, a 36 year-old Georgia native. The P3C was sixty miles southwest of Greenland, flying at 16,000 feet. A quick-thinking controller at Gander Center had contacted hunter 24 via military channels soon after Flight 213 had changed course for Narsarsuaq.

The Orion carried search and rescue equipment: life rafts, flares, etc. The controller reasoned that because of Hunter 24's proximity to Narsarsuaq, it could possibly be of assistance to the Canadian 747, even it was just to relay radio messages. When first contacted, the aircraft commander advised Gander Control that he had plenty of fuel on board and would be able to remain in the vicinity of the remote airfield until Flight 213 landed.

The navy commander quickly told Holt he was heading for the Narsarsuaq area, and would orbit there until Flight 213 arrived.

"Thanks 24, we're estimating overhead at 1452," Holt said.

Hunter 24 advised that they would arrive over the field five minutes before Flight 213, and would remain at 16,000 feet until the flights made visual contact with each other.

Once again it was Ozzie who blurted out what the others were thinking.

"Well, at least they'll know where to look for us if the friggin' bomb goes off..."

*

LONDON, 1540 HOURS [1440 GMT]

Rod and Don were nervously watching the clock. There was nothing they could say or do now to help the beleaguered crew on Northern Flyer 213...absolutely nothing. There had been no update from Shannon for more than thirty minutes. Rod had called British Global's flight dispatch office to get the weather report for Narsarsuaq. It was the same 1500 hours sequence that 213 had received. Rod had the same nagging concern about the fog bank as Captain Holt.

The interrogation of Terrence McDuff had yielded no further information about the object he had stashed on the flight. The ringleader who had supplied him with the device had disappeared from Stansted before he could be apprehended, and the MI5 team and local forces were still searching for him. But prospects of finding him before the deadline were rapidly fading. Four other airport employees - suspected members of the ring - were now in custody, but their interrogations were just getting underway.

*

1443 HOURS GMT

"Descend to 8,000 feet now, Gord, and bring the speed back to 220 knots after you level off," instructed the captain.

Flight 213 was thirty-eight miles east of the airfield, and, according to the aeronautical chart, the height of the ice fields below them was 8,000 feet and decreasing as they neared the west coast. As long as they were in visual flight conditions, Holt was comfortable flying just a few thousand feet above the terrain. The only cloud they could see was well ahead and Norman wanted to get as low as possible before they overflew the airport. He'd finally made voice contact with the radio operator at Narsarsuaq, who confirmed that he was fully aware of their situation and would have emergency equipment - limited as it was - standing by for their arrival.

There had been no significant change in the weather, he advised, but suggested an instrument approach to runway 07 would be their best bet because the fog bank was still lingering just offshore. Visibility to the west was variable between two and three miles, but much greater to the east of the field.

"Roger, Narsarsuaq, that's exactly what we're planning to do," acknowledged the captain.

"Will call overhead, still estimating at 52."

*

1447 HOURS GMT

"Thanks Gord, I'll take control now."

To prevent any misunderstanding, his first officer confirmed verbally, "You have control, skipper. I've got the radio."

"This is what I'm planning," he said, as he slowed the plane further and extended the flaps for the initial approach. "I'll descend to 4,000 feet after we cross over the field. At eight miles out, I'll start a left turn to intercept the inbound track."

Gord and Ozzie listened carefully as he continued his briefing. After intercepting the inbound track, and passing the published the four-mile limit, he would keep going, he told them, even if they were in the fog. He would go as low as four hundred feet, but only if he was bang on the stipulated bearing of 073 degrees.

"From four miles out, I'll use a thousand feet per minute rate of descent until we break out. We'll use four hundred feet as the minimum: I won't go below that unless we can see the runway. Gord, keep a sharp eye on my descent rate. Call out if I exceed a thousand per minute. Understand?" The first officer nodded his agreement. "If I drift off to either side - even if it's just few degrees and we're still in the fog - call out 'GO AROUND' and I'll start an overshoot. If that's happens, as soon as we see the runway I'll try and a make a right-hand visual approach and land in the opposite direction. Any questions?" Holt asked. He really didn't want any questions, though, and none were forthcoming

"Nope, I'm with you all the way, captain," answered the first officer.

"Good luck, Norm, this ain't a check ride. It's a 'save our asses' approach as far as I'm concerned. Go for it!" urged Ozzie. "And if you can't land straight in, just keep it real fuckin' tight on the overshoot - those hills are too damned close for comfort," he added.

A landing on Runway 25 was the last thing Norman wanted to deal with. He'd be faced with two negative factors: the surface wind was out of the east at seven miles per hour, and the runway sloped slightly towards the water. A combination that would almost guarantee the heavy aircraft would overrun the short runway and end up in the bay.

The approach profile Norman had briefed them on broke the instrument flight rules in more ways than one. But if there was ever a time for breaking limits, it was now...

52

1450 HOURS GMT

Hunter 24 radioed to advise 213 he had them in sight and would orbit south of the field until the 747 landed safely.

"Looks like y'all got some fawg down there, Captain. Good luck, we'll be watchin'."

Holt took a quick glance up and to his left but couldn't spot the smaller aircraft.

"Thanks 24. We'll call once we're on the ground," he radioed back.

*

1452 HOURS GMT

As the 747 passed directly over the airport, Holt had an all-encompassing view of what faced him below. It was just as the station radio operator had reported. The runway and the terrain to the east towards the icecap were reasonably clear. From above, the fog bank resembled a thin cloud layer, and delineated the bay's outline to the west of the runway threshold. Most of the smaller peaks along the fjord were visible, too. To the north, a layer of scattered cloud between five and seven thousand feet above sea level obscured the higher mountain tops.

As long as the fog bank doesn't drift over the runway, landing shouldn't be a problem, Norman told himself, but forward visibility will be drastically reduced until we get through it. For that reason alone he would have to remain on instruments until they broke out, hopefully at least two miles from the runway. A non-precision approach, particularly one to an airport he was executing for the first time, called for the utmost skill on the pilot's part.

Norman leveled off at 4,000 feet and kept his speed at 200 knots. He'd have to slow up soon, he knew, but even seconds counted as the deadline neared. The speed would bleed off quickly once the landing gear was extended, leaving him just enough time to get the aircraft established at final approach speed before they entered the fog bank.

*

1455 HOURS GMT

"Okay Gord, here we go. Flaps twenty, speed 170. I'll call for the landing gear and full flap as soon as I start the left turn."

The 747 was on a heading of 270 degrees, flying away from the field. The DME counter read six miles. If he'd calculated correctly, they should be on the ground in seven minutes - which would leave them three minutes to evacuate the aircraft.

Just before they reached the eight-mile point, the radio operator advised that conditions at the field were unchanged, and the surface wind was now from the north at five knots. Gord acknowledged, gave their position, and told him they were about to start a procedure turn towards the field.

*

1456:30 HOURS GMT

Gord called, "Eight miles, Norm!"

"Roger, turning left. I'll roll on a heading of 120 initially. Let's have the gear down now. I'm descending to 3,000 feet."

There was an audible thump as the heavy undercarriage doors swung open and as the landing gear started to extend. The first officer watched anxiously for the gear indicator lights to turn from red to green.

"Gear down, three green!" he called the moment they changed. "Ready for thirty flap?"

The captain stole a quick glance at the landing gear indicator and confirmed, "Roger, three green. Flaps thirty."

Gord had his left hand on the flap lever and moved it to the last notch almost before Norman got the words out of his mouth. Seconds later the needle and the lever position agreed.

"Thirty flap selected and indicated. Speed bug set to 148."

"Roger, 148," acknowledged Holt. He eased the throttles back to bleed off airspeed to attain the computed reference speed. "Turning final now." Seconds later he rolled out smoothly on a heading of 073 degrees. He could still see the runway threshold before he switched to the instruments only.

Flight 213 was now established on the inbound bearing to the radio beacon located a few hundred yards to the right of the runway threshold. Once they had the runway visual, only a slight turn to the left should be necessary to align the aircraft with the runway heading of 070. At six miles out, Norman had the airspeed at exactly 148 knots, and was descending to 2,000 feet.

Seconds later the flight engineer advised, "Can't see the airport any longer, Norm." Just as expected, at the lower altitude the fog bank was now obscuring their forward vision.

"Check that, I'm on instruments. Oz, shout out if you see the runway before we get to minimums," Holt told him. "Here we go - four miles, starting final descent."

"Roger, four miles," confirmed Gord. "You're right on track, Norm."

*

The next eighty seconds passed in almost breathless silence. Norman knew he had no room for error - they would be dangerously low when they broke out and he'd only have seconds to transition to visual flight, make any necessary heading correction, and reduce his descent rate before he crossed the threshold. If he didn't have the aircraft in the exact window when they cleared the fog bank, he'd have to overshoot. He willed himself to concentrate like never before. His heart was beating so hard he thought he could hear it above the engine noise as he struggled to keep his airspeed, heading and rate of descent coordinated. Adding to his discomfort, his mouth had suddenly become desert-dry. He struggled to swallow as the altimeter dropped rapidly through 800 feet...

'*What's the matter with me? I losing it!*'

"You're drifting left, Norm!" warned his first officer, "and watch your rate! You're doing 1,200 feet a minute."

Holt eased back on the control column, trying to finesse the descent rate back a few hundred feet. The pounding in his chest was now almost painful, and he hesitated a few seconds too long before making the necessary heading correction.

"Five hundred feet! You've gotta bring it starboard at least ten degrees," Gord urged anxiously, although he knew it was too late.

"We're still not visual! The fuckin' fog bank must've drifted," interjected Ozzie.

"Four hundred Norm, no contact!" Gord called.

"GO AROUND!" croaked the captain. The 747 pitched up in response to the sudden surge of power as he slammed the throttles forward. Norman's vocal cords seized up and he had to use a hand signal to indicate he wanted the flaps brought up to 20 degrees.

"Shit! I see it. The runway's off to starboard!" cried Ozzie.

Norman banked slightly to the right and both pilots saw the runway threshold pass by the right wingtip, tantalizingly close but impossible to land on.

"Norm, you'll have to crank it around for a visual approach! We've only got three minutes!"

"I know, I ...ahh, leave...gear down, I'..." Only his every other word was audible, and came out a raspy whisper.

"What's wrong, skipper? You'd better--" The words were barely out of Gord's mouth when the explosion rocked the aircraft.

The wounded 747 took a terrifying lurch to the left, as if both engines on the port side had quit simultaneously.

Gord instinctively pushed full right rudder on his foot pedal, hoping to help the captain straighten out the aircraft.

But he was acting alone... The violent yaw caused by the explosion was followed a second later by the last beat of Norman Holt's heart.

*

"WE'RE LOSING 'A' SYSTEM!" shouted the engineer, referring to one of the plane's four hydraulic systems. "Better see if the gear will come up!"

Gord had already moved the handle to the 'up' position. "I have control Oz, Norm's collapsed!"

"Oh Jeezus!" Oz muttered. His shoulder straps were keeping Holt's lifeless body upright: but his head had slumped forward and his right arm dangled beside his seat.

"DON'T TOUCH THE FLAPS!" he yelled, as he saw Gord was about to move the flap lever. "We don't want to end up with split flaps!"

"Okay, but the controls are real sluggish! " Gord answered. "I can't seem to get the nose down." In spite of his efforts, the aircraft remained in a dangerously nose-high attitude.

"We've probably lost hydraulic power to the elevators. Try decreasing the RPM's! You've still got go-around power. And all four engines are still running."

Gord grabbed the throttles with his left hand and pulled them back. The nose lowered immediately. It took him a few tries to find a power setting that maintained the pitch at a slight nose-up attitude. He'd corrected the initial yaw caused by the explosion on the left side, but now he needed to turn further starboard to avoid the hills looming in front of them. Power to the ailerons was almost gone too, and five degrees of bank was all he could manage. It took two tension-filled minutes before the lone pilot managed to steer the plane to safety - at least momentarily - over the valley east of the airfield.

"Whew! That's better, Oz. But I--"

A warning horn stopped him in mid-sentence, and a red light on the center instrument panel began to flash. The master fire warning light had been triggered.

"Ah fuck! Now we've got a fire back there!" groaned Ozzie. "Cancel the fuckin' horn. I'm going to activate the fire extinguisher system for the cargo compartment."

"How about the checklist first?"

"Screw that Gord, there isn't time! I'll fire one shot of retardant now and the second in two minutes. "If we're still here," he muttered, almost to himself. " That's basically what the checklist calls for anyway."

The young pilot's mind was racing, trying to find a plan to up their chance of survival.

The plane was now heading away from the airport on a northeasterly heading; altitude 3,500 feet; rate of climb 1,200 feet per minute; airspeed 175 knots. There was no hope at all of turning back to the runway, he realized. He'd have to try and keep the stricken craft airborne until they reached the snowy expanse of the icecap. But there was a formidable obstacle confronting them: the jagged face of a glacier at the top of the valley. And they were headed right at it...

"Ah, Jeezus. We've lost three hydraulic systems now. And the fourth won't last much longer." The dejection evident in Ozzie's voice left little doubt he thought they were doomed. "How are the controls now?"

"Almost gone...the ailerons must be jammed. And there's almost no rudder movement."

*

Overhead the US Navy patrol plane's crew watched the unfolding drama below them. They'd spotted the 747 as it emerged from the fog bank and passed by the field without landing. Co-pilot Mike Costa was the first to spot the smoke trailing behind the plane as it tracked away from the airfield.

"213 from Hunter 24, we've got you in sight again. Check you have plenty of smoke coming from your rear port side," he advised, speaking as calmly as he could.

"Uhh, yeah, we know. We've had an explosion and..." was all Gord got out before Roberts interrupted him.

Brian Roberts had been sitting in the jump seat behind Captain Holt during the approach, and had tried to revive the stricken man as the first officer struggled to keep them airborne. Finally, he felt for a pulse on the side of the stricken pilot's neck. There wasn't one...

No point in telling the others though, he realized. When he heard Ozzie's reaction to the fire warning, he'd acted on his own initiative.

"I'll try and see how bad it is!" he said, as he undid his seat belt and rushed out the door.

Now he was back.

"There's a big hole back there. I could see daylight. And there's plenty of smoke... I'm not sure but I thought I could see flames, too!" he told them, trying to keep the panic he felt from his voice.

"Okay, I'm gonna fire the second charge, Gord." Ozzie said. "Not that it will do any good," he said under his breath. The fire suppression system was designed to smother a fire in a confined area.

"Oz, I'm gonna have to crash land," declared Gord calmly, as if it were a routine procedure. With the engines seemingly the only method of control still available, Gord had applied more power to increase his rate of climb. "I'm goin' try for the icecap! Its gotta be a better option than this crap below us."

Ozzie had been too busy at his panel to look outside. When he leaned forward to see what Gord was pointing at, the color quickly drained from his face. He could only shake his head as he took in the view. They were alarmingly close to the valley's rocky slopes as it narrowed ahead of them. It was just as bad below: white water was coursing over the valley floor and they were closing fast on the face of a glacier scored with jagged rifts.

"Jeezus Gord! You've gotta clear that son'ova bitch. There's no way we'd survive a landing on that!"

"I know! I know! I'm trying for the top. But I don't know if I can make it." He was still struggling hard with the control column, hoping to get some response. "I need to climb steeper but I don't want to stall out." He was grunting from exertion as he fought the controls, his face a mask of sweat.

The airspeed indicator was at 165 knots, and decreasing. The extended flaps were hindering his efforts to maintain speed and pitch control.

"You should be okay down to about 145, 150. Keep it above 160 and we won't stall, Gord," he encouraged. "And leave the gear up."

' TOO LOW TERRAIN, TOO LOW TERRAIN!'

The Ground Proximity Warning System - GPWS for short - had

activated. The system was designed to warn pilots that the aircraft was on a dangerous flight profile that, if uncorrected, would lead to unplanned contact with the ground.

' TOO LOW TERRAIN, TOO LOW TERRAIN!'

"Ah, fuck! We don't need that yelling at us. I'll get rid of it." Ozzie reached behind him and pulled a circuit breaker which silenced the warning system.

Gord didn't need the warning. He was already aware they were coming dangerously close to the uneven and rocky ground. He added more power, and the rate of climb jumped to 2,500 feet per minute.

"How far do think it is to the top?" Between fighting the controls and juggling the power the co-pilot hadn't had time to take more than quick glances at what lay ahead. The airspeed suddenly decreased to less than 150 knots.

"You bitch!" he exclaimed, pulling the throttles back sharply. The nose dropped, but the speed only increased by five knots.

"Hang on, man! It doesn't look that far now. Maybe just another minute or two!"

"Yeah, it's gonna be tight. But we've got to make it at least a few miles past the glacier... Handle the throttles for me, Oz. I need both hands on the stick to get any pressure at all."

"I've got 'em! Just call for more or less."

*

Hunter 24 was flying approximately three miles behind the 747 now, and a few thousand feet above it.

"Doesn't look like they're going to make it, Commander" Costa said. "I can see flames comin' from the tail area!"

"Ah, hell, they're burning up! And he's still not clear of the glacier," replied the Orion's commander. "If they hit that they're goners. The rocks and ice will tear that bird apart. Might survive if they can drop 'er onto the snow, though... C'mon baby! Just another minute or two and you've got a chance!" he urged.

*

The Narsarsuaq radio operator had been anxiously calling Flight

213, asking them to check in. After the third or fourth call, the Orion's commander realized the 747 crew was too busy fighting their emergency situation to reply and answered for them.

Flight 213 was definitely in trouble, he advised the operator, and told him to standby for further information.

*

"MORE!" yelled Gord.

They were almost level now with top of the glacier. The nose pitched up violently in spite of the pilot's efforts to force it down. The wall of ice disappeared beneath them, scant yards from the 747's belly.

"Okay, pull 'em back Oz!" The nose fell quickly, and once again ground impact threatened them. "Not that much! MORE!"

The flight engineer advanced all four throttles once again, trying to gauge the right amount. The radar altimeter needle resembled a seismograph charting an earthquake. It was bouncing around between 75 and 150 feet, their vertical distance from the uneven terrain beneath them. But the struggling pilot had no time to check the instruments.

For another thirty seconds the stricken craft skimmed over the still menacing surface.

Just as Gord was about to say he thought they would make it, they encountered white-out conditions. All forward visibility was lost in a split second.

"Just land straight ahead, Gord! It's our only chance! I'm bringin' the power off slowly now."

"Okay, okay," Gord gasped, "we're still showin' two hundred feet. I can't hold it up much longer!" The vertical speed indicator was showing 800 feet a minute down. "MORE!" he screamed. "We're way too steep! I can't get the nose up!"

Ozzie advanced the throttles again, stopping when the vertical speed indicator moved to less than 300 feet per minute.

"LOOK OUT! There's a big rock straight ahead!" This panicked call came from their passenger. Just as suddenly as they'd flown into the white-out, they broke into the clear, and Roberts was the first to see the rocky outcropping.

"JEEZUS!" Gord blurted as soon as spotted it. The outcropping was only a few degrees to starboard.

"ONE HUNDRED FEET!" Ozzie cried.

The surface beneath them had flattened out, but it still had a perilous uphill grade to it.

"CUT ONE AND TWO!"

With the rudders useless, it was the only way to make the aircraft veer to the left before impact. If they had been much higher, the resulting asymmetric thrust would have put the plane into an uncontrollable and fatal roll to left. Luckily the 747 was less than 50 feet above ground when the left wing dipped.

"HOLD ON! WE'RE GOIN' IN! BRACE YOURSELVES!" Was all the pilot could get out before impact.

"DUCK!" Ozzie hollered, just as the right wing crashed into the rock.

*

Terrifying seconds after the 747 hit the ground, the deafening scraping and tearing of metal on rock and ice suddenly ceased. Gord Chalmers was the first to look up from his scrunched position. The surface outside was a bright, white carpet of snow. He was amazed to find the flight deck still intact. Papers and loose equipment littered the front console and the area around and under his seat. The only sensation he felt was a sharp pain near the back of his right shoulder when he turned to see how the others had fared.

Ozzie was the next to move. He too was shocked to find they were still in one piece.

"Mr.Boeing you make strong airplanes," he said, almost prayerfully.

The only one with a visible injury was Brian Roberts. Their passenger had a nasty-looking gash on his forehead, and blood was streaming down the side of his face.

"You okay, Brian?" Gord asked the dazed man, who was staring at his blood-covered hand.

Before Roberts could reply a loud explosion rocked their shocked silence. A ball of flame shot by first officer's side window.

"Let's get the hell outta' here!" he urged, as he whipped off his shoulder harness and unbuckled his seat belt.

*

1513 HOURS GMT

"They're down! Looks like the starboard wing tore off on impact," relayed the navy co-pilot, who had the best view of the crash landing. The aircraft commander started a starboard orbit over the wreckage.

"Better make a Mayday call to Narsarsuaq, Mike, and tell them what happened. Advise him we can hang around a bit longer."

"November Alpha Radio from Hunter 24, MAYDAY! MAYDAY! MAYDAY!" called Lieutenant Costa, "The 747 is down - it has crashed on a snowfield about twenty five miles northeast of the airport. Status of crew unknown at this time. We are over the site now and will have further info in a few minutes, over."

"Roger, 24. Understand Flight 213 down. There is a search and rescue crew on standby. They should be airborne within thirty minutes, perhaps sooner," the radio operator replied.

53

The first word of Flight 213's demise didn't reach London until well after the 1605 deadline had passed, and when it came it left Rod and Don fearing the worst. It was a short call from Shanwick, a relay from the Iceland Control Center in Reykavik.

The first message from Narsarsuaq Radio about the crash was received by Iceland at 1620 hours London time. There was no mention of survivors. The operator in Greenland advised that the Navy P3C was still over the downed 747, and a helicopter crew was preparing to launch a rescue mission.

When informed by Weathers that Holt's aircraft had apparently crashed, Commander Watson peppered Rod with questions, most of which he couldn't answer yet.

Why didn't it land? Was it because of weather conditions? Did the bomb bring it down? How long ago did it happen? What about survivors?

Rod could only reiterate what little he knew. The flight was down: no word on the fate of the crew. All they could do was wait for further information from Greenland.

*

LONDON,1642 HOURS [1542 GMT]

The second report from from the Navy crew lifted their spirits, but not completely. Hunter 24 advised that the crew had escaped from the wreckage. Three men were observed moving about in the snow near the downed aircraft.

"Only three?" groaned Carling, "I guess they didn't know there was an extra man onboard."

Rod could only shrug his shoulders. "Maybe he's just injured, and they couldn't see him from the air," he suggested hopefully. He gave the new information to Watson.

"Hmmm, that's a bit disturbing," he commented.

"It is, but nothing's confirmed yet. That's only what the navy pilots saw from the air. We'll have a better idea of the situation once the helicopter reaches the scene."

*

Hunter 24 circled the wreckage until the rescue helicopter arrived twenty-five minutes after their Mayday call. Not wanting to chance a landing at Narsarsuaq - the fogbank was still hovering over the bay - the patrol aircraft set course for Keflavik. The front had passed through the naval air station and weather for their ETA at 1755 was now forecast to be well above limits.

*

LONDON, 1725 HOURS [1625 GMT]

The next information they received came from an unexpected source.

"Commander Watson, Sergeant Roberts is on line five for you." called one of the men working the communications console.

"Watson here. Go ahead, Brian." The MI5 chief motioned for Weathers and Carling to come closer to his table. He punched a button to put Robert's call onto a speaker.

"I'm calling from an airport in Greenland. We crashed. The bomb went off just as we were going to land," Robert's voice was a mix of shock and weariness.

"Are you okay?"

"Yeah, I'm fine, just a little sore," he replied. The cut on his head would require stitches but that wasn't worth mentioning now. " We were picked up a while ago by a helicopter."

"What about the others?"

"Uhh, Captain Holt is dead, I'm afraid, but the other pilots are just a bit banged up. I think Holt must have had some sort of attack before the crash. Chalmers did a heck of job after the explosion. He had his hands full trying to keep the plane from crashing into the mountains. The explosion must have damaged the controls somehow."

"Understood," answered Watson tersely. From his tone, Rod Weathers could tell he didn't want to hear any more details about the crash just now. His next questions dealt with the overall operation.

The RCMP officer's replies were guarded, implying that there were others nearby who could overhear him.

Yes, he told Watson, he had discovered a suspicious package. It had been secreted in the bottom of a galley unit used to store food supplies for the crew. The problem was whether or not it could be retrieved. As far as Roberts could tell before they were airlifted to safety, the front part of the plane, although badly damaged, had not caught fire. He was hoping to return to the wreckage tomorrow morning with the helicopter crew when they flew up to recover Holt's body.

They had to leave him behind today, he told them, because the helicopter hadn't been able to land near the plane. The terrain where the 747 had come down was covered with wet snow - up to three feet deep in some places, he estimated. In order to get the three men away from the downed aircraft quickly, the copter pilot had hovered just above the surface while they climbed on.

Tomorrow morning, weather permitting, the copter crew would return to the scene and land on more solid ground about two or three kilometers from the aircraft. The crew would then make their way to the aircraft using sleds and skis.

"Fine, Roberts," said Watson after Brian finished his report. "We really need that evidence. If you get any static about returning to the crash scene let me know, is that clear?"

Rod Weathers signaled that he wanted to speak to the caller before the connection was broken. When Watson handed him the phone, he asked Roberts if the first officer was nearby.

"He's not in this office, Captain. I think the local medic is looking at him. He's probably got a separated shoulder. Can I give him a message?" Roberts asked.

Rod gave him two phone numbers. "Please tell him to call me as soon as he gets a chance. Thanks, Brian."

54

The next two weeks brought a flurry of activity to Narsarsuaq. Accident investigators flew in from Canada, the United Kingdom, and Denmark. The American FAA sent observers as well. A Newfoundland firm was contracted to meet their transportation needs and had two choppers and crews on the scene within 48 hours of the crash. A week later, there were as many as twenty-five people involved in the crash investigation, including representatives from Boeing.

Rod Weathers, in his role as IPF's safety chairman, was one of the first to arrive. He'd caught a flight to Reykjavik the next morning, arriving in time to connect with the only daily scheduled flight to Narsarsuaq. He was anxious to interview the survivors of Flight 213 before they returned to Canada. He checked into small community's only hotel shortly after 4 P.M. on Thursday - almost twenty-four hours to the minute after the crash the previous afternoon.

He found Gord Chalmers, Ozzie Novak and Brian Roberts huddled over Tuborg beers in the hotel bar. Chalmers had his right arm in a sling. After introducing himself, he urged them to continue with the discussion he'd unintentionally interrupted. The trio had been debating how much time had elapsed between the explosion and their crash landing.

The range of their recollections didn't surprise Rod. Racing adrenalin levels seem to skewer one's memory cells, as hundreds of aircraft accident investigations had shown. The passenger thought it was about five minutes. Ozzie figured seven or eight. Gord was sure it had been at least ten. Ozzie was trying to talk Gord into a bet: a case of beer on whose guess was the closest. It was an argument that wouldn't be settled until the flight data recorder - the so-called black box - had been recovered and analyzed. And that, Rod told them, would probably take a few weeks, perhaps longer.

After Rod sat in, he realized that Roberts must have revealed his true identity, and told them why he'd been on board. Not surprisingly, this revelation had come as a shock to the dead man's crew members. After Rod admitted that he was also aware of Holt's suspected involvement with smugglers, they turned their questions to him. His explanation concerning the similarities between Holt's activities and the other victims left them shaking their heads in disbelief.

Ozzie gave him an incredulous look. "You mean to tell us that Norm was a marked man, and the fuckin' bomb was meant to shut him up?"

"No, but that's one possibility. I don't want to give the impression that we have all the answers yet," cautioned Rod.

"Well, if we hadn't received your warning, we would've still been over the ocean when it exploded, right?" Gord said. "But I still can't believe Norm was mixed up with smugglers."

But the proof, it seemed, had been recovered from the wreckage of the 747 by the RCMP officer. An aluminum storage box from one of the onboard galley units was sitting at his feet.

The first helicopter flight that morning had radioed back word that the flight deck was was still intact and relatively undamaged by the fire that had destroyed the rest of the aircraft. They had set down on solid ground three kilometers away and used a sled to reach the site. The return trip to the copter with Holt's body took fifty minutes, mainly due to the wet snow conditions and the rugged terrain. His corpse was now resting in the local clinic where a refrigerated room served as a temporary morgue. Where and when an autopsy would be conducted hadn't been determined yet.

After word reached Narsarsuaq that the flight deck was accessible, Roberts had contacted London. It took a few calls between British and Greenland authorities before permission was granted for Roberts to return to crash site. The chopper crew flew him up and they were able to use a snowmobile and sled to retrieve the contraband and the crew's personal luggage. The return flight had landed an hour before Rod's arrival.

*

By Friday afternoon Captain Weathers had three hours of taped conversation with the still-shaken men. Both Ozzie Novak and the younger co-pilot were very open with their accounts of the last hours of the ill-fated flight. Their relief bordering on giddiness that Rod couldn't help but notice when he arrived yesterday - which he attributed in part to their brush with a fiery death - had given way to quiet reflection on Captain Holt's demise.

The only levity captured on the tapes was in Ozzie's telling of their ungraceful exit from the flight deck. It probably hadn't seemed very humorous at the time, though.

The fuselage had broken apart just ahead of the wings on first impact, it seemed, and the front section and flight deck had come to rest some distance away. The flight deck was listing some twenty or thirty degrees with the port side closest to the ground. The men had used the overhead escape hatch to get out. This involved each of them grabbing an inertia reel - secured to the aircraft just inside the opening - and sliding down the side of the fuselage while firmly holding on to the reel's handle.

'A one-way bungee jumping cord', was how Weathers had heard the escape mechanism described at a safety equipment seminar some years ago. In theory, the inertia feature would slow a man's descent as he reached the end of the thirty-foot drop from the hatch to the ground. In this instance, however, the distance was probably closer to twenty feet because of the tilt. All three survivors had tumbled awkwardly after hitting the surface. Chalmers, the last man out, landed unceremoniously on top Ozzie. Fortunately the wet snow acted as a cushion and prevented them from breaking any bones.

"Yeah, I was trying to scramble uphill in the fuckin' snow when he flattens me!" said Ozzie, shaking his head in mock disgust.

Rod couldn't help chuckling along with the rest of them. "How far from the icecap itself were you at impact?" he asked them once the mirth had subsided.

"The copter pilot told me we were about five miles short of it," answered Chalmers. "If I could've kept it airborne for another few minutes or so we would have probably been over a relatively smooth and flatter surface and maybe landed intact," he shrugged.

Ozzie reached over and squeezed Gord's shoulder. "You couldn't have done any better if your name was Chuck Yeager, young fella. All kidding aside, you did a great job up there," praised the flight engineer.

Rod asked if they'd been cold while they waited to be picked up. The three exchanged puzzled looks. It was obvious they hadn't given it a thought until now. The temperature at the airfield had been 17C, but Rod knew that it would have been relatively cooler at the crash site some seven thousand feet higher.

Gord was the first to answer. "Well, the snow where we came down was fairly wet, and I don't remember being particularly cold while we were waiting for the chopper, do you Oz?"

"Nope, but now that you mention it, my legs were getting cold," he said, "But that was probably because my pants were soaking wet from the knees down. I'm guessin' two or three degrees above freezing and we worked up a sweat slogging our way uphill. I know I was puffin' like a race horse by the time we stopped."

They both looked to their passenger for his recollection. "Yeah, I'd agree with that. It was quite sunny up there, definitely above freezing," offered Roberts. "I think the deepest snow was right where we hit. It was fairly crusty where we waited for the helicopter, wasn't it?" Gord and Ozzie both agreed with him.

According to the rescue crew's report, the survivors were spotted approximately two hundred meters from the aircraft, and it took approximately ten minutes to hoist them aboard one by one. The report also mentioned that the wreckage was still burning fiercely when they took off for the return trip to the airfield.

The retelling of their hasty escape from the aircraft was the only light-hearted moment on the tape. When they had answered all his questions, Rod was convinced that neither Chalmers nor Novak had any inkling of Holt's smuggling activities, or who his contact or contacts were. Not just on his last flight, but on any previous occasions.

Brian Roberts had been tight-lipped when Rod tried to draw him out about the contents of the box. He'd only managed a brief one-on-

one conversation with the undercover police officer. Roberts apologized for his reticence, explaining that any information about it would have to come from London. He did give Rod a general description of what he'd seen at the crash site that afternoon, though. The exterior of the flight deck area was noticeably charred from the heat of the fire but still intact, as was the upper galley area directly behind it. The burning fuel had melted most of the snow around the wreckage, he told Rod, exposing the rocky surface they had crashed on.

*

A chartered aircraft was due in Saturday morning to return Roberts and the evidence to London. Commander Watson had no objections to Rod catching a ride on it. They were the only passengers on the Gulfstream IV executive jet, and it gave them an opportunity to discuss freely the events of the past week. Rod's telling of the arrest, interrogation and bold assassination of the woman that had been the focus of Don Carling's investigation was the first Roberts had heard of it.

"You know Rod, she wasn't even on our radar screens before Carling told us about her - and her involvement with the victims. And we weren't looking at Norman Holt before, either."

The smuggling ring that the Interpol operation was tracking went well beyond Flight 213, he explained candidly, and it was just coincidence that Holt's flight gave them the chance to kill two birds with one stone.

"You mean to tell me that Holt wasn't the reason you were on the flight?"

"Not exactly. It was only after Don came up with Holt's identity that he became an issue. The drug shipment I found *was* delivered to the UK by a member of the ring we have been watching, that's for sure, but we weren't aware that a pilot was to be the courier," stated Roberts.

"Well, Don hadn't found any evidence connecting Holt or the others to a major smuggling organization."

"No, he probably wasn't," Roberts agreed. He felt it more likely that using the pilots was a 'one off' arrangement orchestrated by a smaller, more ruthless organization. Blowing up an aircraft was not how the larger ring would handle a problem, he explained. The smugglers they were after handled much more than drugs: stolen art works, luxury automobiles, and designer clothing were only some of the items moved around the world. And it was all accomplished without the knowledge or cooperation of the flight crews.

*

LONDON, SUNDAY, JULY 20

Don Carling, James Coates, Rod Weathers and his brother-in-law were gathered around a patio table in the Houghton's back garden. The venue had been chosen for its privacy. The weekend editions of the major London newspapers were rife with sensational accounts of Northern Flyer Flight 213. Most contained more questions and half-truths than facts.

Somehow the local press had been tipped off about the IPF's security chairman's quick trip to Greenland. Rod had risen early this morning to find reporters and photographers on his doorstep. Before he was fully awake, they were bombarding him with questions about the crash. When he was asked if there was any truth to the rumor that there was a link between Flight 213 and the death of the American Captain Bert Rosen last month, he realized someone had also got wind of Don Carling's investigation.

He turned most questions aside with a 'no comment', saying only that there would be an official statement from IPF headquarters in a few days. Shutting the door, he hurried to the phone and called his friend. When Don told him he hadn't been bothered yet, Rod advised him to change hotels before it was too late, and check in under an assumed name.

Luckily Don wasted no time following his advice. As his taxi pulled away from his hotel forty-five minutes later, a van braked to a stop behind it. Four men jumped out and rushed into the lobby. Two of them were carrying bulky camera cases. The newsmen knew better than to bother a senior police officer at home, though, hence their gathering in Little Venice had gone unnoticed.

Getting together had been Don's idea, a chance for them to conduct their own informal post mortem on all that had taken place over the past week.

Rod started the ball rolling with his account of what he'd learned about the last hours of Flight 213 from the survivors, plus what little Roberts had revealed to him about the contraband shipment that he'd retrieved from the wreckage.

When he finished, Don said, "So he believes that Holt was the target. The fact that others would perish along with him was just incidental. Bad luck on their part, in other words."

"Yes, basically that was his gut feeling, as he put it," replied Rod. "He didn't think the ringleaders of the group Interpol was after would resort to such tactics, or indeed have cause to do so."

"The ringleaders being?" asked James.

Rod shrugged. "He didn't name names."

Derek was next to comment. "Are we to believe then, that it was only happenstance that Holt's flight - and the contraband he was supposedly to deliver - coincided with the overall investigation?"

"Yes, that was the impression I was left with," agreed Rod.

"Well, I think any chance to get the real story disappeared when the woman was killed and Holt died," said Don. "Unless the authorities eventually arrest someone behind it all. But I wouldn't bet on it." When his opinion went unchallenged by the others, he changed the subject.

"So my Canadian friend wouldn't let on what was in this galley container, eh?" he asked Rod.

"No, but I don't think he knew himself. He had taken a look inside, but that's all. He described it as a package, weighing about five pounds, wrapped and taped in plain brown paper.

"Did he tell you where he found it?"

"Yes. Once they were airborne, he'd poked around likely areas on the upper deck. It was the only container not labeled, and it was sort of shoved into a corner behind the main galley equipment."

"What do you mean, 'not labeled'," asked James Coates.

"Ah well, when galley units are made up in flight kitchens, a card is usually attached describing the contents. For instance, hot meals, salad trays or beverage supplies, that sort of thing," explained Rod. "Most of them are approximately two cubic feet in size. Roberts thought at first it was just an empty spare."

"And it wasn't locked in any way?" asked Don.

"Didn't appear to be," replied Rod.

"So it was easily accessible to Holt if he was planning to take it with him once they arrived in Toronto. Would that seem logical?" wondered Coates.

"Yes, or perhaps it was supposed to be retrieved by someone other than Holt. Someone on the ramp with access to the aircraft after it landed," suggested Carling.

Rod agreed. "Both are possibilities, as are a few others we could speculate on."

"Well, if nothing else it's the ultimate proof that Don was right about the victims carrying contraband on their planes, is it not?" Coates asked.

"Yes, I don't think there's any doubt about that now," said Derek. "But what I find most amazing is that the aircraft wasn't completely destroyed."

"Or that it didn't explode over the ocean," said Rod. "Then we would really have been left in the dark. I didn't get to see the wreckage personally, but apparently they landed on a snow-covered slope which cushioned the impact. The snow was approximately three feet deep. And the 747's shape was no doubt a factor in their favor. The bulbous underside would've taken the brunt of the impact."

"That's right," Don chimed in, "if they'd been flying an older or smaller plane, a DC-8 for instance, they probably wouldn't have fared so well."

*

Their discussion moved on to the brazen assassination of the female suspect who, only minutes before she was gunned down, had revealed her real name.

How did the killers find out that she was being held at Paddington? was one question that baffled them. Although DCI Houghton hadn't been the one who gave the WPC permission to take the suspect outside, it still bothered him that the shooting had occurred on his turf.

"Only two possibilities - someone at Paddington tipped them off - or the call she made alerted someone to her whereabouts," said Derek, a tinge of bitterness evident in his voice. "I'd bet on the latter."

Coates nodded his agreement. "A call that effectively signed her own death warrant," he said, raising his eyebrows.

"Yes, that's how I see it," replied Derek. "Anyway, there have been no substantive leads in our hunt for the bike driver and the shooter. But we're not giving up. They must have been in London already by the quickness of their reaction, probably other members of her cell."

"Maybe so. But there's no way they would've known she would appear outside, is there?" Don asked.

"I wouldn't think so. Perhaps that was just pure luck on their part. But having the weapon with them suggests they were prepared to make an attempt to gun her down at the first opportunity," answered Derek. "On the bright side, though, I've been told unofficially that learning her true identity may be the key to finding out who was behind the conspiracy your victims were involved with, Don."

"How so?" asked Don.

"I'm just reading between the lines here, but it seems she was probably an agent for an organization whose leaders are former KGB hardliners. Men that lost status and power after the Cold War ended. They're suspected of being main suppliers of arms to terrorist groups around the world. Not directly, but through levels of 'cut outs', middlemen in other words," explained Derek.

"So using these captains as couriers was just one...uhh...contract, if you will, they were probably masterminding?"

"...Yes," Derek replied, "something along those lines."

"...Kravitski? Was that her name?" asked Rod, after there were no further comments to Derek's explanation.

"Kravitchkevna, Tatiana Kravitchkevna," responded Derek.

"Russian, if I'm not mistaken," offered Coates. "Her father's surname would be Kravitchkev."

*

They took a short break while their host refreshed their drinks. Gin and tonic for James, beers for Don and Rod. Derek was sticking with coffee. When they were settled again Don spoke first.

"I don't think Monsieur Rousseau will be any more open with their discoveries than they were before we came on the scene, but I don't suppose it matters now." He waited to see if anyone would refute his statement. Derek's shrug told him he was probably right. "Anyway Rod, I think the death of this femme fatale should put an end to the killings of your pilot fraternity. And that's a good thing."

"Let's hope so, and I think you're right. You've done a great job for us, and I'm sure IPF's board will agree." Rod raised his glass in thanks, and the other two Londoners joined in.

"What happens next?" Don asked Derek.

The policeman explained that each of the latest deaths would be subject to a coroner's inquest. The Rosen inquest would probably take place first, followed by Alfred Heard's later this year. He suggested both inquests would be open to the public.

"And the Russian woman?" Rod asked.

Derek took his time answering. When he did, he chose his words carefully.

"...Hard to say," he began, "it depends on the outcome of Interpol's investigation. I wouldn't be surprised if they invoke some clause pertaining to the Official Secrets Act to keep the inquest closed."

Inquests would be held whether or not the killers were apprehended, he told them. In spite of round-the-clock efforts by Scotland Yard teams, no solid leads had turned up in any of the London killings.

The four were just wrapping up their discussions when Carling's mobile rang.

"Brian, good to hear from you. What's up?"

The Canadian listened intently, only injecting a few 'I see's and 'uh-huhs' from time to time. When Roberts finished, Don said, "Yeah, no kidding, so Holt must have been in on it, even if he didn't know what he was carrying. Thanks, Brian, I really appreciate your letting me know. Cheerio!"

"Okay Sherlock, let's have it," urged Rod. Don took a few large swallows of his beer before he spoke. The Interpol-MI5 team had just received the lab report on the contents of the package Roberts had brought back from the crash site.

The stash contained approximately three kilos of Ecstasy pills, one of the so-called designer drugs fast becoming a favorite among the younger patrons of the club scenes in Europe and North America..

The chemical name was a real mouthful, and Don gave up after his third try at pronouncing it. "It's known as MDMA for short," he finally said.

Even the printed word was hard to comprehend methylenedioxy-methamphetamine. The drug was most commonly distributed in pill form. Sold singly, they brought the seller the equivalent of fifteen to twenty US dollars. Roberts hadn't said how many pills were in the shipment, and could only estimate the street value in North America. The best guess was three million dollars, and the pills were probably manufactured at a drug lab somewhere in Holland.

"And that's why Holt would have been well paid for his cooperation, one assumes."

"No doubt, Rod. I'm sure of that. But why bring down the plane? Doesn't make sense that whoever owned the drugs would want to destroy their investment," reasoned Don. "I mean they would have paid a good buck for the stuff to begin with, probably not in the millions but at least ten or twenty per cent of the street value."

"Yes, that doesn't quite fit," offered Derek.

They tossed around a number of theories about why they thought the flight was marked for destruction, but that's all they were. An insight offered by the retired intelligence officer ended the discussion.

"Unless those behind the bomb had gotten wind that the authorities were closing in on them. And just maybe their heinous reaction was sanctioned to protect other schemes, either underway or planned for the future," he suggested.

*

James's somber appraisal was still on Don's mind late that night as he sat alone in his hotel room, reflecting on the tragic happenings of the week past.

Three more people connected to his investigation were dead. First, the elderly night porter, murdered in his own humble surroundings, probably to prevent him from talking about his role in the conspiracy. Second, the key figure, the woman boldly gunned down in full view of police officers, and apparently on the orders of someone she trusted. And finally the last man who had yielded his integrity to her charms, Captain Norman Holt, dead at the controls of his aircraft. Not exactly as the perpetrators had planned, but dead nevertheless.

And not for the first time he wrestled with the question that was still the largest unknown puzzling him... *Why?*

Why would five supposedly responsible and law-abiding airline captains get involved with international criminals? Was it just to solve their financial problems? On the surface, that appeared to be the only valid reason he had come up with. Did they actually know who was behind the monies paid to them? Or know exactly what they were carrying? He just couldn't believe they did. Or maybe at some point they did twig to what they were being used for and wanted out. Perhaps because they were being asked to transport something - or someone - that would put them at even greater risk...

He struggled into bed, still none the wiser.

*

Before he flew home Don met with the International Pilots Federation board to give his report. At the meeting the board approved a carefully worded letter - drafted by Don and Rod Weathers - to be circulated to the Federation's members.

Neither of them was completely satisfied with the letter's wording. It was short on details and long on generalities. But it was the best they could come up with, given that no arrests had been made in any of the killings. Basically, it reiterated IPF's stance that individual pilots should always be wary if anyone asked them to convey items or goods on their aircraft. The letter, therefore, did not mention names or specific incidents. It didn't need to...

It was only a matter of days before articles began appearing in London newspapers linking the deaths of Rosen and Heard with the demise of Northern Flyer Flight 213. Adding fuel to the speculative reports was the 'no comment' stance taken by the police concerning the woman killed at Paddington Green Police Station. The airline rumor mills quickly picked up the scent. For many months it was the hot topic among pilots in the Pembury Hotel lounge as they speculated about others from their ranks who might have come in contact with the mystery woman.

EPILOGUE

TORONTO, JULY 25, 1999

Looking back on those last months of 1997, Don Carling recalled the sleepless hours he spent pondering the same question. It stood to reason, he felt, that others might have known her intimately and been offered the same deal as the victims - sizable amounts of money for their seemingly risk-free cooperation. The letter did draw a few responses, according to Rod Weathers, but not from anyone admitting that they had known the woman personally. The information provided in confidence by other colleagues of the dead men only confirmed what Don had already determined - each of them had known the Russian agent intimately.

As the months passed, Don was eventually able to put the thought out of his mind. By late October he was once again fully occupied in Canada with his expanding investigative business. KayRoy had all the work it could handle and Don's staff had grown to include four full-time operatives plus as many part time employees. Increased air traffic, both passenger and cargo, meant more opportunities for the criminal element that targeted the aviation industry. As soon as one case was wrapped up, Don's teams were on the move to another location. And the work wasn't always connected to one of the country's major airports. KayRoy had conducted undercover work at sites in the Canadian northwest for the country's burgeoning diamond mining industry. Most investigations involved theft or fraud.

But on this summer day, the hottest in Southern Ontario in recent memory, Don was spending the afternoon in the air-conditioned comfort of his office. He had turned down an invitation from Ralph Woods to golf with a group of Northern Flyer pilots. The mercury had climbed to 34C at 1 P.M., and the humidity was off the clock. The humidex reading was an even more obscene number, even though he didn't know exactly what it meant.

He'd decided to tackle a job he had been putting off for months: sorting through files and notes from his investigation on behalf of the International Pilots Federation. Updates had continued to come his way even though his personal involvement had essentially ended in July two years ago. True to his word, Derek Houghton had kept him abreast as information and reports became available in the final months of that year.

There had been no suspicious deaths of airline captains on layovers abroad since 1997, which came as no surprise to Don. He'd been quite sure the woman's death meant an end to the seduction strategy her masters had devised, and she had carried out so successfully.

There had been no surprises from the inquests into the killings of Captain Albert 'Bert' Rosen or Alfred Heard. In both cases, a coroner's jury returned a verdict that confirmed what the initial police investigations had determined. Both men had been fatally assaulted by a person or persons unknown. Heard had bled to death as a result of having had his throat slashed. Severe trauma injuries to the head and body of the American captain had been the cause of his death.

No evidence had come to light to suggest that the same person or persons were responsible for both killings. Nor could authorities say with any certainty they were same men identified as suspects in two of the other deaths: Flores's in Glasgow and Rosen's in London. Both these men had learned their deadly craft as mercenaries for the Bosnian Serb forces during the bloody civil wars in the former Yugoslavia in the early 90's. They were believed to be hiding somewhere in Europe, probably with new identities.

Circumstantial evidence also put the same men on the Rhine cruise ship the night the first victim died, the Canadian Len Newson. Interpol warrants for their arrests were still outstanding.

Very little from the inquest into the woman's death was made public, other than the fact that she had died of bullet wounds. DCI Houghton had been right: national security provisos had been invoked to keep other details about her covert life in London from public scrutiny.

Don had asked Derek if anyone had claimed her body. 'Not initially', he'd answered. The Russian government was advised via diplomatic channels of her death, but declined to take any action because the British authorities had no passport or other proof to confirm her citizenship. Three months later, the Home Office issued authorization for the woman's body to be cremated. Her ashes were buried in a south London cemetery, two representatives from the crematorium and a local minister the only attendees. The Russian Embassy was notified that burial had taken place, and provided with the grave's location.

Two weeks later, a letter signed by the Russian Ambassador was hand delivered to the Home Office. In it, he thanked the British government for providing a proper burial for the 'unknown Russian citizen'.

*

There had been no public disclosures by authorities as to who might have been behind the bombing of Flight 213. No group or organization had claimed responsibility. But snippets of information had come Don's way, either from Derek Houghton in the UK or Inspector Brian Roberts of the RCMP. Now based in Ottawa, Roberts had been promoted a year ago to head up the force's Anti-Terrorism division. Don had given both men his word that he would treat information they gave him in strictest confidence, ergo a lot of what he had been told was not recorded. But it did go a long way to filling in some of the blanks surrounding the flight's demise.

Terrence McDuff had confessed all he knew about the plot, but the professionals who had recruited and paid him had covered their tracks well. None of the others arrested at Stansted airport that day provided any usable leads as to the origin of the device planted on the 747.

McDuff was serving a twelve-year sentence at Dartmoor Prison for his crimes. His trial was held in secret. His protestations of his mistreatment during his traumatic interrogation on the day he planted the bomb fell on deaf ears. After all, he could provide no witnesses to back up his claims.

The man who delivered the bomb to him just before Flight 213 departed had eluded capture. His successful disappearance on that fateful day had probably been planned for well in advance - an escape plan to be used when and if necessary.

Next Don turned to the file on the accident report for Norman Holt's last flight. Rod Weathers had e-mailed him details as they were made known in the latter part of 1997, and eventually sent him a bulky package containing the final report.

The first item in the report was a copy of the autopsy carried out on Norman Holt's body in Reykjavik three days after he died. There was no indication that his death was other than from natural causes, and not, as the UK tabloids had speculated, as a result of foul play. No, Holt had died of a massive heart attack. A review of his medical examinations for the past five years showed no indication of impending trouble. His blood pressure had always been in the normal range, and his ECGs showed no indication of damage. Don remembered thinking that his untimely death had been a lucky break for the plotters.

*

Don took a short break to stretch and refill his coffee cup. Seated again, he opened the accident investigation report and quickly flipped through the first section dealing with the aircraft's maintenance history. There was nothing out of the ordinary about the aircraft. It had been deemed completely airworthy before take-off and no anomalies were recorded by the plane's black boxes before the onboard explosion.

Reading through the next part sent chills up his spine, even though he had already perused it a number of times

The L5 door had been recovered from stony ground a mile north of the airport. Accident investigators had determined that it been blown off by a plastic explosive, probably the Czech-made Semtex. This could not be confirmed, though, due to the time lag between the explosion and arrival of experts to Greenland. Traces necessary to positively the explosive used would have dissipated within hours. The amount used was thought to have been approximately two pounds - more than enough to blow off the entire tail section of a pressurized aircraft.

That is exactly what the conspirators had planned on. Had McDuff's suspicious actions not been observed before the flight departed from

Stansted, a catastrophic break up at altitude would have plunged the craft and crew to a watery grave in the North Atlantic Ocean.

The overwhelming difficulty the first officer was faced with after the bomb exploded was attributed to complete loss of hydraulic pressure to the flight control systems. The explosion had severed the hydraulic lines which passed under the aircraft floor near the L5 door. It was also suggested the door may have struck the left horizontal stabilizer mounted on the tail, causing severe damage to the elevators and complicating the pilot's efforts to control the aircraft's pitch attitude.

The fire that destroyed all but the aircraft's flight deck section made it impossible for the investigators to come up with more definitive conclusions.

As to what was to have been the disposition of the contraband cache of amphetamines stashed on the aircraft, there were only educated guesses. Four employees of the aircraft service firm that were to have handled Flight 213 once it arrived in Toronto were arrested, according to Roberts. Their arrests were connected to the larger investigation that day, not specifically to Holt's flight. They were charged with being members of the well-coordinated smuggling ring that used flights from cargo airlines operating in and out of Pearson International Airport.

The authorities were never able to connect any of them with Captain Holt, either directly or indirectly.

A search of Holt's personal luggage and his apartment in Brampton confirmed Don's suspicions about the captain. Holt had been involved with the female Russian agent for some time, and had been paid for handling previous shipments. The most irrefutable evidence was a bank statement mailed to his Canadian address. The numbered account was with a bank on the Isle of Man, a popular tax haven for overseas residents. Five wire deposits totaling seventeen thousand pounds had been processed to it in the four months prior to his death. The transactions had all originated from Brussels, investigators determined.

*

Don turned to the files on the three American pilots. Very little information had been added to them since July, 1997. Before leaving London, he had provided Interpol with copies of his files. Watson told him the information would be passed on to the appropriate American authorities. He assumed this meant the FBI. He had also included his business card with each file in case anyone delving into the financial and smuggling activities of Krantz, Flores or Rosen wanted to speak to him. So far, he had not been contacted, nor had he received any feedback from the Americans.

On his own, Don had tied up loose ends with two people he'd had personal contact with: Juan Flores in Miami and Lori Wilson.

His call to Ray Flores' father in late 1997 was warmly welcomed by the Florida businessman. Don gave him a complete accounting of events leading up to the Flight 213 accident, and his reasons why he felt the same group that had murdered his son was behind it. He laid out the evidence he'd uncovered connecting Ramon to the female agent. The liaison that had been the source of cash Flores had apparently come up with to repay his gambling debts. There had been no way to gloss over his son's illicit activity and he knew the elder Flores wouldn't have wanted it any other way.

*

Don had been pleasantly surprised when Lori Wilson called his office in October, 1997. It was his first contact with her since July. He had phoned her from London twelve hours after she had called to tell him that Wilson Halpern was dead. She was still upset then, and he'd spent almost an hour calming her down and reassuring her that she wasn't in any danger from whomever had killed the private detective. Still, he was relieved when she told him she was leaving Atlantic City for good the next day.

This time it was all good news from her end. Lori and a friend were partners in a busy pet grooming business, she told him, and she'd put her past behind her. No drugs, no turning tricks. She also had a new identity. 'No', she told him, politely but firmly, she wasn't interested in hearing anything more about how his investigation had ended. And guardedly, but politely, she declined to give him her new name. She'd just called to thank him for his understanding and assurances after Halpern's slaying, she told him. In return he thanked her for calling and wished her luck.

He could have traced her. Her number was right in front of him thanks to Call Display. He recognized the area code for Atlanta,

Georgia. If the US authorities were ever looking into Daniel Krantz's past and wanted to talk to her, he knew they would have no trouble tracking her down. Apparently this hadn't happened, and for her sake he hoped it never would.

*

His last contact with the New Jersey detective in charge of Halpern's murder had also been in the fall of 1997. There had been no developments, no arrests. The FBI had interviewed him about the case, though, which he thought a bit unusual, he told Don. Krantz's name was mentioned during the meeting, he recalled, but he wasn't sure if he or the federal agents had brought it up.

By three o'clock, Don had cut the accumulated paperwork in half. The basket below the paper shredder was overflowing.

There was only one file left - the largest one. It dealt with the major player - Renate Neumann/Katrina Meuller/Tatiana Kravitchevna... code name Olga. The closest he'd ever come to the woman was during her interrogation, when he'd observed her from behind the one-way mirror at Paddington Green Police Station, on the day she was gunned down. Later that same afternoon, the man whose love had caused her to question her previously unwavering commitment to her uncle and Circle 17, also died unexpectedly.

It seemed such an improbable story even now. Had the events taken place during the height of the Cold War it would have been much more believable. But Interpol's subsequent investigation left no doubt as to her role: she had really been an undercover agent for a Russian criminal organization, one that had operated relatively unnoticed until Don stumbled on it.

Olga herself had provided the keys to unlocking the mystery just before she died. Her admission that her real name was Tatianta Kravitchevna gave authorities their first clue.

The Kravitchkev name had first come to the attention of Western intelligence agencies during the Cold War era. The file on the death of Major Leonid Kravitchkev - Georgiy's older brother and Tatiana's father - still carried the highest security classification. Only the CIA director, his top-level managers, and their allied counterparts could access the file. The classified document contained the details of a skirmish involving the CIA, West German agents, and the East German Stasi near Berlin in 1975: a wild exchange of gunfire in the middle of the night that resulted in the Russian's death.

Interpol was aware that terrorist organizations and rebel groups from the Mideast region and Africa had been purchasing arms and munitions, including thousands of automatic weapons, that had been secreted away from military bases during the Soviet Union's last days. The buyers included factions of radical Islamists who were attracting ever-increasing numbers of young and gullible volunteers to their training camps. Interpol knew, because arms shipments had been intercepted by police forces in the Pan-Mediterranean region, and a number of middlemen had been arrested. By routing the shipments through layers of agents, however, the leaders of Circle 17 were able to remain anonymous.

. But dealing in stolen arms wasn't Circle 17's only business, and self-contained cells - like the one in Brussels - were set up to handle contracts for clients with specific needs. It was this cell that had come to Interpol's attention before the bombing of Flight 213.

Olga's dying utterance, *'Why Uncle?'* was the key that linked General Georgiy Kravitchkev, the former KGB officer, to the cell running Olga and ultimately exposed him as the leader of Circle 17.

*

It took Interpol until late 1997 to piece together an accurate picture of Karl Stasny, the name used by Circle 17's man in Brussels.

A few weeks before Christmas, boar hunters found the decomposed remains of a woman in a secluded area of the Ardennes forest near Arlon. The body was that of Margret Heuvel, 33 years old, a Belgian of Flemish descent. Co-workers had reported her missing in late July. The shy, plain-looking woman, orphaned at age four, had been on her own since leaving a foster home on her seventeenth birthday. She'd found employment as a clerk in a low budget department store and lived a quiet, humdrum life until the handsome Karl, - seemingly a loner like herself - picked her as the perfect partner for his undercover life in the Belgian capital. After a short courtship, she was more than happy to accept his unexpected invitation to move in with him, a proposal he made in early 1995, just three months after they met. Marriage was never mentioned.

She had been dead for five months - killed in cold blood by the first man she had ever truly trusted...

That man was eventually identified by Interpol as Pavel Nadrony, a former low-level KGB agent. It was only after the discovery of Margret's body that authorities were able to make sense of his sudden disappearance. He had been working for the aircraft handling company at Brussels International for four years. On his employment application he listed Aeroflot, the Soviet airline, as his previous employer and supplied the name of his supposed superior in Moscow as a reference. His background was never checked. His fluency in four or five languages spoken by former Soviet bloc airline crews was enough to get him hired. He was a reliable employee, investigators were told, and none of his co-workers had suspected him of leading a double life. As operations foreman, he came in direct contact with the airline crews on a daily basis. Once Olga had accomplished her part, the rest was up to Karl, known as Vlad to his other cell members. He arranged for the targeted captains to carry consignments on their flights departing from Brussels and became their paymaster.

Two shell companies used to make lease payments for Olga's flats in London - one being Flanders Holdings - were eventually traced to Nadrony as well. Funds from the same accounts were no doubt made available to Olga for her day-to-day expenses.

Karl Stasny had simply vanished. Whether he fled by car via the open borders of EU member countries, or flew using a different identity, his exit was never traced. Authorities assumed he would have made his way back to Russia. An international warrant for his arrest on suspicion of murder was forwarded to Moscow after Interpol had identified him, but was never acknowledged.

*

Don fingered the only one item left from his files. It was a faded, index card with a handwritten address on it: 714 rue Ricaille, Montreal, Quebec. There was no name to go with it.

Fred Newson had sent it to Don in October, 1997. The son of the first victim had found the card while cleaning out his father's '91 Ford Taurus. The card had been stuck to the underside of a floor mat. After receiving the card, Don thought back to his initial investigation into Len Newson's background in February of 1997. Nothing he learned at the time had provided any clues as to what Newson did with whatever he'd been paid to carry once he landed back in Toronto.

The address had given him an idea. On the chance that Newson might have used Canada Post to forward the contraband, Don canvassed a few of the local post offices hoping to find a clerk who might remember him. A long shot, given that almost two years had passed since Newson's death, but worth a try, he'd decided.

On the second day - and at the sixth outlet he checked out - his idea paid off. The sub-post office was located in a strip mall just north of Bramalea, five kilometers from where Newson had lived. A woman named Janice Humphreys recognized Newson from the photograph Carling showed her.

"Yes, I remember him. But he's dead, isn't he?" she'd asked, a puzzled look on her face.

Don nodded. "Did you know him?"

"No, not exactly," she'd answered. The Humphreys woman and Len's ex-wife had once belonged to the same bridge club. She had seen Len a few times when he picked up his wife or dropped her off for their weekly sessions. No, he hadn't recognized her when he came into the post office, and she'd never mentioned that she knew his wife.

She wasn't sure how many times he had used the post office, but personally she recalled serving him twice.

Did she remember what he had mailed? Was it a letter or a parcel?

No, other than that he used priority post both times. She remembered, because he'd complained about the high cost for the service. Yes, they were both mailed to Canadian destinations, but she couldn't remember which city.

The last question he'd put to her concerned the timing. "Any idea when Newson made these visits?"

"Not really," she'd replied. She remembered seeing his obituary in the local paper, though, and thought the last time she had served him would have been two or three months prior. Newson died in May,1995. If her memory was accurate, Len was still handling deliveries in February or March.

*

Don had immediately contacted Brian Roberts, given him the Montreal address and explained how he thought it might be connected to Len Newson. The RCMP officer agreed it was worth looking into, thanked him, and assured Don he would let him know what turned up.

A few days before Christmas 1997, Inspector Roberts called.

714 rue Ricaille was a nondescript, low rent apartment building on a residential street close to downtown Montreal. The location was handy to the city's universities and catered to short term occupants, mainly students, and mostly from foreign, French-speaking countries. The building contained twelve two-room apartments. Obtaining a list of occupants for the time period in question - the winter months of 1995 - had been a frustrating and time-consuming task, mainly because of sloppy bookkeeping on the leasing firm's part. Or more likely, Brian suggested, accounting practices designed to evade taxes.

The list of tenants eventually provided to the security service was incomplete, and forwarding addresses almost non-existent. Without a specific name to work with, trying to track down the person Newson *might* have mailed something to would be a fruitless task, Don recalled thinking at the time. And he didn't have a name to give them...

*

Tired now, Don leaned back in his chair, hands behind his head and eyes closed. He took a few minutes to reflect back on those first seven months of 1997. The challenge his friend Rod Weathers had insisted Don was the best man to tackle: find out the truth about the suspicious deaths of the pilots who had died on layovers.

It wasn't exactly the kind of work he'd envisioned when he gave up his flying career to become a private investigator, and he'd probably never get another case even closely resembling it. But that's okay, he mused, no doubt other intriguing cases will come my way. Unfortunately terrorism would always be a threat to the aviation business, he knew, no matter how much money and manpower were expended to try and thwart it. He wished it weren't so, but in his heart he knew he was right.

It wasn't a matter of *if*, but *when*...

*

TORONTO, DECEMBER, 1999

The first shoe dropped on December fourteenth, 1999.

A thirty-four-year-old Algerian national was arrested trying to enter the United States via ferry from Canada. US Customs agents in Port Angeles, Washington found more than a hundred pounds of explosives hidden inside the rental car he was driving.

He was soon dubbed the *Millennium Bomber*. He confessed to authorities that he had planned to explode a bomb on New Year's Eve at Los Angeles International Airport, and insisted he was operating on his own initiative. Before long it came out that he was a member of a cell of the *Armed Islamic Group*, and had trained in an Afghan camp run by the terrorist organization named al-Qaeda. As more details of his past were made public, Don Carling's sense of foreboding increased. When it was revealed that the would-be bomber had lived in Montreal for an extended period in the mid-nineties, he feared the worst. His suspicions were confirmed when he reached Inspector Brian Roberts in Ottawa a week after the man's arrest.

Yes, he was told reluctantly, the Algerian had once shared an apartment at 714 rue Ricaille, from September, 1994 until the summer of 1995. Two of his acquaintances, who had also lived in the city, were now in custody for their suspected roles in the plot, Brian added.

"These guys are terrorists, right?" Don said. When there was no reply from the inspector he continued, "It's not going too far then to suggest that both Len Newson and Norman Holt were being used as unwitting couriers to carry packages destined for members of their cell, is it? Or one like it. We both know these people need money, travel documents, false passports and other ID's to sustain their cover for extended periods, even years. That was the case with the Islamic militants living in the New Jersey area before they bombed the World Trade Center in 1993, as I recall. This is just theory, I know, but you've got to admit that it might've gone down this way..."

Roberts didn't answer, and Don sensed from his silence that there was probably a great deal more known about the Montreal connection, but such information was off limits, even to a trusted friend.

Don broke the silence, hoping it didn't sound like he was preaching.

"Well Brian, don't forget the three American pilots that were killed were also suspected of the same type of smuggling. And uhh, well, I only hope the federal authorities down there have made a genuine effort to find out who was on the receiving end of their deliveries...."

*

On September eleventh, 2001, the other shoe dropped.

ABOUT THE AUTHOR

Russ Graham is the pen name for Graham R. McLeod, a native of London, Ontario.

After ten years in the RCAF, he joined Air Canada and spent the last eight years of his career flying 747s on the company's global routes. Graham and his wife Patricia live in Orangeville, Ontario and winter in Tucson, Arizona.

CPSIA information can be obtained at www.ICGtesting.com
Printed in the USA
BVOW042346310112

281862BV00002B/75/P